WITCH
OF THE
WILD
WOODS

AUTUMN G. HUGHES

INDIEOWL
PRESS

Seattle, WA 98121
info@indieowlpress.com
IndieOwlPress.com

WITCH OF THE WILD WOODS

Cover art © AlterDimensionDesign.com
Cover design & Interior layout/design by Vanessa Anderson
at NightOwlFreelance.com

Paperback ISBN-13: 978-1-949193-35-0
Hardcover ISBN-13: 978 1 949193 36 7

With all my love to you, Bush Dragon.

"Do not ask me, love, to linger

For you know not what to say

For duty calls your sweetheart's name again

And your heart need not be sighing

If I be among the dying

I'll be with you when the roses bloom again"

— *Will D. Cobb*

CONTENTS

PROLOGUE

SILVER & GOLD

Apollena left the window open again, inviting an obnoxiously frigid breeze into their shared guest room. Lane couldn't sleep. An earlier attempt to bring himself to orgasm and exhaustion failed. There were a myriad of other ways to get himself to sleep: get up, close the window, maybe even find a way to turn on Uncle Dan's ancient heater. It wasn't like the house was an original colonial or anything. Nevertheless, when they'd first arrived in Washington nearly a month ago, it felt like their uncle had gone out of his way to make everything in his home older than it had to be. "Retro-style," is what he called it.

So for the last few days, when Apollena would sneak out of their guest room around midnight, the "Retro-style" window panes wouldn't close all the way after they'd been opened. Owls hooted. Late summer breezes whispered through the dense trees. Branches scraped against one another in an eerie nocturnal symphony. Lane was torn by doing what little he had to in order to get some rest and breaking his comfy position under a thick down comforter in the old twin bed.

That's when Lane heard the scream.

He immediately sprang out of bed, reached for his navy-blue vest, ball cap, and black aluminium Maglite. He slid his bare feet into scuffed Timberland Boots and bounded toward the window. Lane waited. His hands gripped the pale oak windowsill. Cool summer air blew across his knuckles. The night symphony had resumed. Leaves danced upon the wind. Branches scratched together and forest creatures moved unseen through the brush.

That scream wasn't Luna's.

His sister did not scream.

He and his adopted sister had only been siblings for three years. That time had flown with all the grace of a peregrine falcon in a nosedive pursuing prey. They'd gotten into more than their fair share of mischief for barely being thirteen: pub fights, conspiracies, and a dozen absurd supernatural situations. As harrowing as the predicaments they found themselves in, Apollena, or Luna if she dropped her faux air of formality, never screamed. A squeal of delight, perhaps? To scream in fear was something Lane had yet to hear escape his sister's lips.

Having scanned the woods behind their uncle's obtusely rustic shack, Lane eventually saw a single light on in the second-story bedroom a few houses up the road. They weren't too deep in the woods, barely at the base of mountains. Uncle Dan had managed to purchase what started out as a modern ranch home across the street from Mount St. Helens' National Volcanic Monument. At first read that sounds like a busy tourist spot. It was not. At least it wasn't from the perspective of Lane, who'd spent most of his life in Santa Fe, New Mexico, with a modest civic centre and downtown. In this town, if you could even call it that, the silence weighed heavy.

Screams echoed for miles.

After a few minutes of staring at the light up the road, Lane awkwardly manoeuvred his gangly limbs and body out the window and onto the grass outside. That not-too-distant light was still on. It flickered and strobed. It called to him. Thoughts of phoning the sheriffs were immediately dismissed. Lane had learned time and again that law enforcement, while not entirely unhelpful, were usually more of a hindrance. Whatever danger may lie in wait, Lane and Luna worked more efficiently when they dealt with a mystery directly rather than waiting for questionably useful officials to arrive.

Lane had walked nearly a quarter mile up the empty road when he realized Apollena was not by his side. Three years may not be a long time, but in the spring of his youth, Lane considered himself radically fortunate to have a sister like Luna. She simply had no fear—at least none that they'd encountered so far. Her confidence was contagious, and Luna, in turn, admired Lane's ingenuity. Being reliant on Lane wouldn't be giving her the credit she was due. Individually, they could manage just fine. Together? They were an unstoppable force and immovable object that worked in tandem to overcome obstacles no ordinary pair of siblings could. But, when the frightened scream broke the still of the night once more, Lane felt the absence of Apollena's fearlessness and the courage it fostered.

Lane stood there, frozen in the middle of the street across from the house with the second story light blinking in odd sequences. His eyes had adjusted enough to the dark. No streetlamps lit his path. Only the bright, waxing crescent moon and trillions of stars shone down from above. It was a young girl who'd screamed, judging by the pitch and timbre. There was terror laced in the scream that made Lane's skin crawl. Someone needed help and by the looks of things, only a thirteen-year-old armed with a flashlight was going to answer that call.

Taking a deep breath, Lane sprinted around the side of the house. Luna's methods were usually more direct. She would have burst through the front door without knocking. Lane, however, solved a puzzle by finding the edges first. Making a complete lap around the house, panting for breath, there was no immediate evidence of forced entry. No clear and present danger from the outside.

Now came the moment of truth.

Stepping up to the front patio, wooden floorboards creaked, bending under boot, Lane balled up his fist and knocked on the door. "Miss, it sounds like you're in distress. Is everything okay?" Still waiting for his final bout with puberty to deepen his voice, Lane's attempt to come across as authoritative and masculine was comical at best. He probably would die from embarrassment if whatever was waiting inside didn't kill him first.

Suddenly, there was a motion in the house. Footsteps pounded down the stairs. A *crash* of something porcelain shattering and muffled sobbing. Lane stepped back; flashlight held like a club above his head, ready to strike.

The door flew open.

Lane held his impulse to close his eyes and start swinging. Instead, he was captivated by a girl of unspeakable beauty. She was the kind of lovely that caused Lane's jaw to lock in place and words to lose all meaning and vanish from his lips. Pale bare feet under powerful legs ran past him. Bare pearl-white arms dotted with freckles pumped up and down while she propelled herself forward off the deck. Ample breasts were loosely concealed under an oversized black shirt with Chris Jericho's face on it. Her flowing, curly auburn hair bounced in thick ringlets under the dim porch light. Those eyes: sapphire oceans to drown in, stared back at Lane when she stopped and spun around to face him.

Her rose petal lips parted in a gasp, "IT'S IN THERE!"

Lane blinked away his instant infatuation and came back to reality. There was a girl. She was in trouble. He had a job to do. Jogging after her to the grass covered empty lot across the street, Lane asked in the manliest voice he could conjure. "What's in there, miss?"

The girl finally came to a stop. Her shimmering blue eyes locked onto the second-story window. She breathed heavily. With the back of her left hand, she wiped away tears streaming down her cheeks. Once she caught her breath, she quickly looked Lane up and down. "Who are you? What are you doing out here?"

Lane cleared his throat and dropped the macho act: It ended up just hurting his throat and sounding objectively silly. "I'm Lane. Lane Woods," He stated calmly, without any stoicism or false bravado. "I heard a scream from my uncle's house, just down the road there. Are you okay?"

"Why aren't you wearing pants?" The girl asked, pointing.

Slightly more self-conscious, Lane tried to gloss over his choice of wardrobe or lack thereof. "It sounded like an emergency. They're bike shorts. It's sometimes hard to regulate my temperature at night because the… never mind. Not important." Her perfect rose lips flashed a small smile. Lane blustered, "My apologies for not coming to your aid in the proper attire. You screamed, so I ran over. Are you hurt? Is someone hurting you?"

The girl shook her head. Red locks swayed. "There's…" she trailed off, biting her lower lip, "I'm fine. It's nothing."

Lane raised an eyebrow, "No one screams like that over nothing." She glanced away, embarrassed. Lane offered a sincere smile, "I know you don't know me from Adam, but helping people is what I do. It's okay. Is it your parent's? Or a relative?" Glancing up to the house, Lane watched as the light in the upstairs room suddenly flickered and shorted out with a loud *pop*!

The girl gasped and shivered.

"It's a ghost," came a familiar, jovial voice with a Parisian accent from behind Lane.

Turning on his heels, Lane let out a sigh of relief. Apollena casually strolled up to the two teenagers standing in the grass with a satisfied smile. Her dark, cropped pixie cut made her look about a year older than she was. Those sea-foam green eyes searched over the girl who had run screaming out of the house at the end of the lane.

"It is a ghost, is it not?" Luna asked delicately.

There was a pregnant pause that hung in the air over the girl. So many questions in Lane's mind waited to spill out into the frosty early morning air. Reluctantly, the wild red-headed girl replied, wrapping her arms around herself like a cocoon while nodding her head.

"Yes," she whispered.

When confronted with the supernatural, scepticism was usually the default position for most individuals. For Lane and Luna, it was more a matter of narrowing down exactly what category of supernatural the situation fell under in comparison to all the other weird shit they'd encountered over the years. Digging into his pocket, Lane withdrew the palm-sized spiral notebook he kept for recording such instances. Thumbing over the tabs, Lane flipped open the section labelled, 'Spooks and Spectral Phenomenon.'

"Ghost," Lane said mostly to himself while uncapping his pen, "If you don't mind, can we ask you a few questions to narrow down exactly what kind of ghost we're dealing with?"

"Have you recently had a close relative pass away?" Luna began while pacing back and forth behind Lane. Her delicate fingers plucked imaginary violin strings in the air while her brain was busy turning over the possibilities.

"I'm sorry, who are you two, exactly?" The red-headed girl asked, bordering on breaking down into angry tears again. Couldn't blame her. This time of night, alone, a possible ghost. Lane should have developed a better bedside manner for this sort of work, but he was thirteen. He shouldn't even be doing this kind of work at all.

"I'm sorry, I know this must be difficult, terrifying for you. Everything is going to be okay. I promise. My name is Lane, and this is my sister Apollena. We literally deal with stuff like this all the time," Lane said, taking a cautious step forward.

"All the damn time," Luna added impatiently, "So are we talking multiple voices, one voice, no voice and just knocking on stuff? What?" She smacked her lips for emphasis.

Lane shot his sister a stern look. She held up both her hands in temporary surrender.

"What's your name?" Lane asked the gorgeous girl. Her red hair was a shade darker than his own. He tried to keep his eyes on hers, but the rise and fall of her chest was distracting even for the most well-meaning thirteen-year-old.

"Jordan," she sniffed, "Jordan Breathnach."

"Breathnach," Lane repeated, mulling the origin over in his mind, "Celtic for those who have Welsh ancestry, right?"

"I guess?" Jordan answered, still a little breathless and bewildered.

Less angry now.

"It probably is," Luna added, "My brother's nothing if not a wealth of obscure information." She rolled her eyes at Lane and whispered, "May we continue, please?"

"You two are siblings?" Jordan asked.

Apollena beamed, "Yup. We are twins. Obviously."

Jordan looked back and forth between the two, who couldn't look more unalike. For one, the girl was black. Specifically, she was of Nigerian and Iranian descent, a uncommon combination of parentage, but one that created an unparalleled beauty. Her sharp facial features and athletic build created what some would consider a radiant, androgynous fashion model physique exceptional for a budding teenager. Lane, on the other hand, was a typical awkward American ginger: unkempt hair, gangly limbs, and the makings of a square jaw that still lacked definition. He wasn't unhandsome, but if puberty hit some people like an eighteen-wheeler speeding down a highway, this boy was a VW Bug politely waiting to change lanes.

"Twins in that we share a birthday, but Luna is adopted," Lane admitted gently, more so for Luna's sake than Jordan's curiosity. Her journey through foster care still held bitter memories, even after their three years of living under the same roof.

"We also have the same eyes," Apollena added, batting her long dark lashes, "But enough about us. You're hosting a ghost, oui? Up there, where were you screaming from?" Luna gestured demurely with a finger to the second-floor bedroom.

Jordan nodded, drew a deep breath and recalled the events of the last month. "You were right about the knocking. For the last few weeks, almost every night, I woke up to hear something pounding on my window. The first night, I was… I couldn't bring myself to get out from under the covers. Every night since, the knocking got worse. Louder, more violent. It shook my dresser. Nearly knocked it over…"

Lane placed a gentle hand on Jordan's shoulder. She didn't recoil, but looked up, startled. With a reassuring smile, he asked, "If you don't mind, we'd like to investigate. May we have a look inside?" Jordan glanced up to the bedroom window once more and shivered. Lane added, "We'll be right there with you, okay?"

With a fair amount of reservation inviting two strangers into her home, Jordan allowed Luna and Lane inside. Luna bounded up the stairs, seemingly without a care. Lane remained by Jordan's side. The wooden steps were carpeted. No stereotypical creeks as they journeyed up to the haunting on the second floor. Even so, silently creeping through a possibly haunted house in the dark after midnight was plenty unnerving.

Lane whispered, "Your parents aren't home?"

"They drove down to Portland to visit my grandma. She's in hospice. Hasn't been doing well since my grandpa passed," Jordan answered in a low whisper. Lane wrote down the facts in his journal, only occasionally glancing up to catch a glimpse of Jordan's lips.

There was something about those rose petal lips that overwhelmed his thought process: *what would it be like to kiss a girl like that?* Kissing was not an activity Lane was tangibly familiar with. That was Luna's department. Boys, girls, non-binary people of every flavour were always on his sister's radar, and she'd often kiss and tell him all about the experience ad nauseum. It sounded like something he'd want to try but had next to no idea how to go about it. *Just as well,* he thought, *I've got a job to do. Someone needs help, not a kiss.*

Luna stopped outside the bedroom, waiting for her brother and Jordan to catch up. "This the room?" she asked, gesturing with her head.

Jordan nodded.

Cautiously, Luna tapped a foot on the royal blue carpet on the other side of the door. Nothing. She stuck her hand into the room as if testing the waters. Lane noticed all the hair on Luna's arm suddenly stood up on end, like she'd grabbed hold of a Van de Graff generator, creating a high concentration of static electricity or an unusual magnetic field. That wasn't uncommon. There was definitely some kind of... presence in the room.

Lane flipped on his Maglite and swept the room. Jordan gasped at the sight. It looked as though a small tornado had ravaged everything from the bed, the contents of the closet, and the dresser that had been pushed up against the window. In addition to the disaster spread out over the floor, several smaller objects hung in the air, orbiting nothing in particular. Shirts, a small porcelain figurine, and a hairbrush were all suspended, rotating at different speeds.

Instead of screaming, Jordan reached out and grabbed hold of Lane's hand. If he weren't so fixated on studying the room, he would have noticed an impossibly beautiful girl had impulsively woven her fingers between his. Instead, he took a step forward after Luna. He was compelled to solve this mystery, but Jordan held him back.

"Don't go in," Jordan pleaded in a hushed voice.

Lane suddenly became aware of his recent attachment to Jordan and touching her soft, snow-white skin. "Oh, I'm..." Lane stammered. He forgot how to... um, word? SPEAK. He forgot how to do that thing with his mouth. Staring into Jordan's brilliant blue eyes, he also failed to notice her expression change from frightened to weirded out.

Then came a flick on the back of his head.

Luna.

His sister's sing-song French lilt chided. "Come now, loverboy, we've got a job to do."

Lane squeezed Jordan's hand gently and slipped out of her grasp. Luna was right: stay focused on the task ahead of them. There was a haunted room an arm's length away that needed to be dealt with.

Apollena strode forward into the bedroom. Her eyes scanned the floating objects and searched the mess that had been piled up in the centre of the room. "Strange: I'm not seeing any significant build-up of ectoplasm. Activity like this usually takes a lot of effort, or maybe they weren't being manipulated for a long enough period of time. Kind of placed here… haphazardly…?"

Luna bent down and pushed through the pile gingerly with a pencil.

Lane started on the edges. He moved slowly, counterclockwise around the room. The open closet, the bed that was stripped of its sheets, and finally the wall and window that overlooked the street. Lane stooped down to pick up the lamp that had been knocked on the floor. There was a little slime running off the side of the lampshade. Ectoplasm: a sort of coagulant or mucus side effect produced by some spirits pushing through their plane of reality into ours. It was and will be forever gross to touch.

Fortunately, Lane had stumbled upon a clue.

"Perhaps whatever *it* is, is searching for something?" Luna suggested.

Lane stepped back from the dresser. "I'd say that's a fair hypothesis. Jordan, you mentioned your grandfather passed away recently?"

Jordan remained outside her bedroom door. "Yeah. Almost a year ago."

"Is there any other special occasion coming up for him? A birthday or anniversary?" Lane probed, tracing a finger along the silver frame of the mirror attached to the dresser. He considered the scene of the crime. The series of events leading up to this night. The Knocking. Someone or something trying to get Jordan's attention to find something. There was something missing to bring the borders of this puzzle together.

"Yeah," Jordan said, a finger pressed against her temple while she recalled, "My grandfolks anniversary is tomorrow. It would have been seventy years together since—"

Furious *knocking* rattled the room.

Luna stepped back as the pile of random objects suddenly leapt up and fell back down into the pile.

Lane smiled, "Jordan, what's your grandfather's name?"

Luna had already backed out of the room to stand beside Jordan.

Hesitantly, Jordan whispered, "Patrick."

Again, there was a violent *knocking* that shook the bedroom. Jordan nearly fell over. Apollena held her steady. The banging didn't cease as the temperature in the room dropped nearly twenty degrees. Lane could easily see his breath. Reaching into his pocket, he pulled out an ancient black ink pen and thumbed through his notebook.

"Lane, get out of there!" Jordan screamed over the deafening *thuds*.

"It's okay," Lane shouted back, "What you thought was someone banging on the outside of your window is actually coming from the other side of your dresser mirror."

"What the hell are you talking about?" The girl with the wild red hair cried.

Luna gave Jordan a reassuring pat on the shoulder and leaned in. "Watch this..."

Lane began scribbling something onto the surface of the mirror—runes, glyphs, some kind of language Jordan had never seen before. As he wrote the inscription, he used one hand to write and the other hand to steady himself as the room continued to quake. Flipping to another page in his notebook, Lane recited something Jordan couldn't quite hear. No. She heard voices. Not just Lane's, but other voices, languages she didn't recognize.

When he'd finished, Lane turned to Jordan, "Patrick, your granddaughter is here and wants to help you find what was lost. Can you help us, show us what you're looking for?"

As the surface of the mirror continued to frost over, gradually something began to take shape. It was as if an invisible finger were writing inside the glass. Jordan was horrified and morbidly curious. She couldn't look away as the shape of a watch was drawn into the frost covered mirror.

Lane turned from the mirror to Jordan, "Did your grandfather leave a watch or bracelet, maybe?" Jordan reflexively glanced down at her left hand. Lane noticed Jordan was covering the small golden watch on her wrist with her right hand. He smiled. The missing piece had been found.

Now for the tricky part.

As if nothing paranormal at all were happening, Lane beamed as he paced and explained. "For whatever reason, silver mirrors are notoriously tricky for spirits. If a vengeful spirit were haunting you, using one in a pinch could trap 'em. On the other hand, if a lost soul were simply finishing things up here on earth and accidentally caught their reflection, well…" Lane gestured to the mirror that continued to vibrate and beat itself against the wall.

"Seems like your grandfather was trying to find his old watch: a gift given to him by your grandma on an anniversary, I reckon? He'd spent a lot of energy trying to get your attention, but clear communication ain't a ghost's strong suit." Lane turned back to the mirror and withdrew a tiny orange BIC lighter from his pocket. He flicked on the flame and held it close to the mirror.

"This next part could get a little intense. Would you mind taking off the watch?" Lane asked politely, "We're gonna help your grandpa pass over."

Before Jordan could protest, Lane touched the flame to the mirror's surface. The writing on the glass suddenly burst into neon orange, bright, blinding light that flooded the room. Then, in a flash, everything was covered in pure daylight.

"Hello, pumpkin. Sorry to rattle you," spoke a raspy, gentle voice from the bedroom.

Everything was so bright, Jordan had to shield her eyes. "Grandpa?"

"Please tell your gran that I miss her. I'll be waiting for her, counting the days," The voice was so close, practically in front of Jordan's face. She breathed in his scent of cigar smoke and butterscotch. Now she could barely see through the tears pouring down her face. The outline of the face she'd grown up with was just starting to come into focus, and the tears fell even harder.

Without any further prompting, Jordan held out the watch. "I miss you so much, Pop-pop," she choked out, heaving into a sob.

An impossibly warm, suede smooth hand brushed against hers. "I miss you too. Be good. I'm always here for you. Always."

As quickly as the daylight had burst into Jordan's bedroom, the creeping darkness and chill of the early morning returned. The generations-old gold watch had vanished. Buried under an emotional avalanche, Jordan collapsed beneath the crippling emotional weight. *His voice. His hand.* She'd been so numb when her grandfather passed almost a year ago, to see him now…

Luna knelt beside Jordan. "You're going to be okay now, Jordan. The first time's always the hardest."

"Did you…" Jordan started but was still terrified to admit what had actually happened. But it couldn't have? Could it?

Lane gingerly stepped over the clutter of Jordan's room to kneel beside her. "It was real. I know, my first time encountering the other side, it was a little traumatic."

Jordan tried to shake off the tears with a laugh as she shook her head. It was all so much, and these two weirdos were here with her like it was just an everyday occurrence.

Lane gave Jordan some space, a moment to breathe. Turning to his sister, he asked, "Hey, how did you know about the…" Lane gestured vaguely to the room where the ghost of Jordan's Grandpa had just ascended.

"I listen," Luna whispered back with a smile. Lane waited eagerly for elaboration. Luna complied. "So, you know that cute blonde who lives on the other side of the 503 by Prairie General Store? No? Of course, you don't. Anyway, she told me like two weeks ago about mysterious sounds, knocking, etcetera. All scary, like there was some kind of haunting. So, we've been going on midnight walks for… research."

Lane raised a half smile. "To research the ghost or the girl?"

Luna shrugged, "I can multitask."

With a wink, Apollena stood up and stretched, "Well, our work is done here."

Jordan sniffed, "Wait, what? That's it? You're just going to leave?!"

Luna looked back into the room. "Yup. That's it. Ghost is gone. We won't even charge you for this one. First exorcism is on us. Although..." Giving Lane a sly look, she added, "I suppose it's only courteous if someone helps you clean all this up. Lane, you mind giving Jordan a hand? I got a busy day tomorrow or else I'd stay—"

"Wait a minute," Lane protested, but Luna gave him a swift sisterly punch in the arm. "Help. Her. Clean. Up. Get me?" He didn't, but Lane nevertheless stood up and began to tidy up the disaster pile in the bedroom. Apollena shook her head and chuckled at Jordan, "That there is the most compassionate, dumbest, smart person you'll ever meet. You two have a goodnight."

Wiping her eyes, Jordan looked up at Luna, but she'd already skipped halfway down the stairs. Soon, the energetic girl was gone. Lane, however, was still organising the mess her room had become. This strange boy was actually making her bed without any complaint after having encountered a ghost—her grandfather, from beyond the grave. Or maybe this was all some kind of fever dream?

"Lane," Jordan whispered, "You don't have to do that."

"Oh," Lane said, turning on his heels. "I'm sorry. I know people have a certain way of doing things: sheets, making the bed, and I'm just—shouldn't have invited myself in your room and touched your—" he glanced down at her chest again, winced, and shot his eyes back up at the ceiling, "I'll just, see myself out. Thank you for—you have a goodnight, miss."

Lane made it to the doorframe, eyes still locked on the ceiling. Then the left wall. Then the front door down the stairs. He'd failed to notice Jordan hadn't moved. They both stood there in the doorframe in each other's way.

"Do you wanna stay?" she finally asked. "I'd like it if... somebody stayed. Just in case?"

"I—I don't wanna intrude, but I'm happy to help clean up," Lane stammered.

Hesitantly, Jordan reached out, touching Lane's hand. Not holding, simply touching her fingertips to the boy's. "Would you stay?"

Lane finally managed to glance in her direction. Eyes on hers.

"Please?" she said.

Lane nodded.

WITCH
OF THE
WILD
WOODS

MISUNDERSTOOD

They'd finally made it to summer. Spring semester was nothing less than a slog to get through. No electives. No extracurriculars. No sleep. Only seventeen units worth of core classes and a part-time job that often became more than part time. Still, Lane was thankful both he and Luna had survived long enough to settle into a mostly ordinary life. University courses, a customer service job, and a quiet studio apartment to come home to at the end of a long day. It didn't hurt either that the University of Irvine in sunny Southern California was a stone's throw away from the beach, mountains, and a fist full of national and state parks. There were ample places outside to relax, if only Lane ever got the time to do so.

"You need to get out," Lane pleaded as he knocked on the shower door once again. The faucet was going full blast, but that didn't muffle the soft squeals and occasional moan from making their way audibly into the kitchen. "Luna, please. Becca is gonna be here in ten minutes. We talked about this two days ago!"

The rushing water cut off abruptly.

The door flew open, and a wall of steam hit Lane in the face. Stepping out wrapped in a purple linen towel, Apollena licked her fingers and smiled. "Finished. Okay? I'm going. I wouldn't want to intrude on you and your... girlfriend? This is the volleyball one, right?"

Lane stepped aside to allow Luna room to saunter over to the dresser. She unwrapped the towel and tossed it over her shoulder at Lane. He caught it in his off hand and threw it onto the towel rack before addressing his naked sister, taking her sweet time getting dressed.

"She's a friend. Possibly girlfriend material. Could you hurry up?" Lane replied, exasperated. Not necessarily because his sister was deliberately stalling, but he honestly didn't know where things stood with Becca. It was unlike him to leave things so ambiguous in any kind of relationship. For the last two semesters, Lane hadn't been on any supernatural quests or dangerous missions overseas. He had been a simple college undergrad slinging coffee on the side. Becca was a nice classmate, coworker, friend? Life was simple for once, but that surprising lack of otherworldly tension or impending doom left Lane on edge.

"Here, how's this one?" Luna had stepped into a cowl neck, thigh length, satin slip. At first glance, Lane thought the cowled neckline made it appear as if she were wearing the dress backward, but there was no back. Wearing it the other way around would have only been slightly more revealing than Luna's typical garb. The marbled green satin hugged her slim, athletic frame. Luna gave a quick twirl and threw a mischievous smile at her brother.

"Looks great. Where are you going, exactly?" he asked while stepping from the bedroom through the living space, and back into the kitchen—a whole fifteen feet.

"Bowling," Luna shouted.

"Don't think that's the sort of dress that goes well with socks, or bowling shoes... or, Bowling," Lane considered while dicing mushrooms.

"I appreciate your concern for my wardrobe. I've got it handled."

Luna had returned to Lane in their kitchenette holding a pair of black Spanish Heels. She lifted her right leg up and set it gently on the kitchen countertop like a barre, "See? Stockings. Perfectly acceptable bowling attire. Oui?"

"If you say so. Leave now. Begone," Lane pointed his spatula toward the door.

Luna remained, smiling, raising her leg off the kitchen counter and bringing it around perfectly at a ninety-degree angle before bending the knee and sliding it back to the floor. She'd only trained as a dancer for a year, mostly as cover for one of their adventures. Years later, she still had that same ballet grace. *Good for her*, Lane thought and kept his focus on adding the finishing touches on the toasted ravioli he'd been preparing.

"So," Luna said, leaning over the counter, "You're gonna ask her out then? In the afternoon? In the apartment? Super romantic." She rolled her eyes and leaned back on the countertop. "You'll both have plenty of time to sleep before the late hour of seven, like the elderly folks in the apartments across the street."

"I'm cooking an early dinner and we're going to the beach. That's all we have on the agenda today," Lane replied, adding the diced mushrooms to the sauce simmering in the pan.

"No sex then?" Luna asked with a pout.

"Out," Lane said again, a little more forcefully directing his sister once more with the spatula, unwittingly sending a few flecks of the marinara sauce arcing across the room.

"Oh, no," Luna exclaimed in a mock whine.

Lane's patience was running thin. "What now?"

Luna pointed to nothing in particular on her chest. "You got sauce on my dress. Going to have to change now and it's all your fault. Thanks."

Lane was a hair-trigger away from throwing his sister in the garbage, "Fine, go change! If you want to meet Becca so bad, then you can stick around when she shows up. But you gotta—" Luna had already stripped down in the living room and wandered into the bedroom. Keeping his eyes on slicing green peppers, he shouted, "Get dressed, Ursa Minor!"

"Fine," she huffed.

Lane could practically hear Apollena's eyes rolling to the back of her head. She was in a mood. Unfortunately, Lane was not in a state of mind to do anything about it.

Tapping her brother's shoulder, Luna asked, "I don't know which one goes better with the heels, now that you've ruined my dress. You pick."

Lane spun around and nearly knocked the saucepan over. "Apollena Arkto Woods, what part of 'Get dressed,' don't you understand?"

His twin stood in the buff, mirthfully defiant. Luna's honey-brown skin glowed softly in the afternoon sun that shone through the cracked blinds. She feigned innocence to the entire scene. "Just pick one."

Lane growled, "Black dress, white waist belt, switch to the white heels and put some underwear on for once in your life, please!"

Lane's phone rang on the countertop, nearly vibrating off the edge and onto the floor. He reached out to answer, but Luna was quicker. She answered and stepped back just before Lane could tackle her. "Good Afternoon, Lane's phone, how may I direct your call? Oh, of course, glad you called! One moment, please." Luna pressed the mute button while practically vibrating with excitement. "You have to take this call."

Ordinarily, Lane would find a way to calm himself and centre his mind. Instead, he tackled Luna into the couch. She barely resisted, flailing her legs and arms wildly all while happily squealing, "Take the call, take the call, take the call!"

Sitting on his sister's stomach, pinning her on the couch, Lane swiped the phone out of her hand. He took a breath, and calmly answered, "Good afternoon?"

Half expecting a crank call or telemarketer, an overly enthusiastic voice answered, "Lane Guster Woods, how are you, bud?"

Lane checked the number. It wasn't logged, but was pinged as coming from Seattle, Washington. "Fine. How can I help you?"

"Jude Abidalli, Trillion Pines Youth Camp director. I was looking over your resume and wanted to reach out to you. Do you have a minute?" spoke the giddy voice over the phone.

Lane pressed the mute button. "Luna, what in the seven hells is Trillion Pines Youth Camp?"

Luna squeaked, "Keep talking!"

"No, no. Explain. Trillion Pines Youth Camp?" Lane interrogated his sister as he tickled Luna under her armpit.

"Just keep talking, I'll explain after, I swear!" she yelped.

The man on the other end continued to hold. "Um, hello? Lane, bud, still there?"

"Sorry," Lane said as he unmuted himself, "Bad connection. How can I help you, Jude?"

"As I was saying, we received your resume and wanted to offer you the position." There was silence for a moment while Lane waited for Jude to further explain. "The Youth Camp Counselor gig?" Jude chuckled, trying to fill the silence. "You're more than qualified. Perhaps overqualified? Four years in the Coast Guard, overseas humanitarian trips—says here you also helped Interpol with dismantling a sex trafficking ring in Thailand?"

Lane stared daggers into Luna, but the topless girl simply grinned back at him from ear to ear. "Jude, let me put you on hold for just one more moment, okay?"

"Sure thing, bud. Standing by!" he replied with another nervous chuckle.

"Luna," Lane said calmly, shifting his weight on top of Luna, "Explain. Now."

"So, you were whining about how you didn't have time all year to go to the mountains, or Joshua Tree, or the beach, "*Bitch, bitch, bitch, whoa is me*," That's you, by the way. That's what you sound like." Lane pinched the muscle underneath Luna's armpit. She yelped, but continued, "I was thinking about how we never really got to do normal kid stuff growing up, like go to a summer camp or whatever—"

"We've been to camps," Lane interrupted.

"We toured Auschwitz when we were fourteen," Apollena corrected, "I mean a fun, relaxing, drama and genocide-free camp. You and me, up in the mountains. AND, we get paid a little on the side for watching other normal kids have fun too." She looked up into her brother's eyes, trying to stop the gears in his head from over thinking, "Please, Lane. I think we could both use a vacation. For once?"

Without a second thought, Lane caved. "Jude Abidalli?"

The man on the other end of the phone answered gleefully, "Right here, bud. So, whatcha say? Wanna join us up here for some fun in the sun, under the stars, and a stone's throw from the shore of beautiful Spirit Lake?"

"Sure," Lane shrugged, "Count me in. What are the details of the job?"

Jude proceeded to rapidly dump an encyclopaedia's worth of legal details and minutiae that Lane only vaguely paid attention to. Instead, he looked down at his sister and recalled the last sixteen years they'd spent together. The victories. The heavy losses. It was rather incredible that they'd lived so long. He'd always been taught, trained to keep pushing forward and growing. Perhaps it would be healthy to take a moment to breathe?

"So we'll see you up here on Monday, then. Don't forget those passports and sign those medical release forms. Take care of yourself, Camp Counselor Woods," Jude chuckled again, and the line went dead.

Lane continued to sit on top of his sister. "You drafted me into a youth camp?"

Crossing her ankles, Luna held her cheshire grin, "I did, yes. I drafted us for fun."

"What. The. Fuck?" A distressed voice from the front door.

Becca.

Standing about an inch taller than Lane, the Olympic level volleyball player was the picture of disgust and wrath. The buzzed blonde crew cut presented an edge of intimidation meant for the court but resonated in this particular situation too. Becca crossed her strong, tanned arms across her washboard chest and rapidly tapped her foot. Her fiery blue eyes shot daggers into Lane.

"Rebecca, hey!" Lane shot up from the couch. He reached out to greet her, but Becca recoiled. He continued to explain rationally, obliviously, "Sorry, I lost track of time, but dinner should be ready—"

"Dinner? You have the nerve to invite me over when you're fooling around with some side-chick? Are you serious right now about dinner?" Becca spat out, livid.

Lane had grown up with Luna. Modesty was not something regularly practised in their home, even less so after their parents disappeared. So having Luna in any state of undress near or around him was more annoying than shocking by this point. Of course, Becca hadn't met Apollena yet and admittedly this was the worst possible introduction.

Unabashed in her nudity and not at all concerned about social norms, Luna sprang off the couch and waved, "Hi, I'm Lane's sister, Apollena. I was just leaving, but it's nice to finally meet you. My brother says you're a middle blocker for UCI with their eye on the Olympics? Magnifique."

Becca's open jaw shut, and her face contorted from rage to revulsion, "You're fooling around with your Sister?!"

"What? Of God no! No, no she's... she's French. Clothing isn't really a thing she does well." Lane stammered. "The girl hates clothes. That's just her malfunction."

"And, hold up, you expect me to believe you two are related," Becca added with a bitter laugh. "You think I'm just some stupid jock? Is that right, Lane Guster Woods?"

"We're twins, actually," Luna said, leaning up against the wall.

Lane was a blur of embarrassment and frustration as he shouted, "Apollena, get changed, and get out, please!" Luna shrugged and sauntered toward the bedroom. Turning to Becca, Lane pleaded, "I know, I know, it's weird, she's weird, *I'm* weird, but—"

"No, you a freak, Lane," Becca snapped.

Luna shouted back from the bedroom, "Clothes are the real 'freak', actually. Goes against nature, we're the only animals that wear them. If we weren't a shame-based society, everything would be easier naked."

"Seriously, not the time, Luna!" Lane shouted back, exasperated. Again, he turned back to Becca, "I am seriously so sorry, she takes forever to get ready—"

"You live with her?!" Becca shouted, "Oh, and you thought you could just slide her out the backdoor before I got here. Unreal."

"We don't have a backdoor and I'm not trying to hide anything," Lane tried to take a step forward to console Becca. She took one more step backward out the door.

With a hand raised up in aggressive defence, Becca scowled, "Give me a reason, Lane, one reason why I shouldn't tell everyone on campus about how sick you are? *Insta*, *Twitter*, fucking *Linkdin*: you are unacceptable."

"If you slander Lane for something that isn't true," Luna said calmly, fixing an earring into her lobe, "Then, you'd force my hand to expose your extracurricular activities."

Becca snapped and waved a finger at Luna. "I don't wanna hear a word from you. So shut your ho-ass-mouth and keep steppin."

"You're right," Luna agreed, nodding her head. She straightened out the black cocktail dress she'd chosen and stepped into her white heels. "You don't want anyone to hear a word from me, because I'll tell everyone everything I know about The Library."

"You think I care about books?" Becca snorted with a nervous laugh.

"No. Not books. The Library gentlemen's club you moonlight at," Luna replied, pulling out her phone. She opened her photo app and began scrolling through a handful of shots. "A friend of mine dances there regularly. You know, Ruby? She's pretty talented. And I've got nothing against showing off your body, obviously." Luna gestured to herself and smiled, "But, if you even think about spreading false rumours about my brother: the faculty, your coach, your family, everyone will know the truth you chose to hide."

Becca was mortified.

Lane was bewildered, "Becca, how come you never told—"

"'Cause it's none of your damn business! That's why," the athlete screamed. She turned to Apollena stern, but pleading, "If any of those photos get out, do you have any idea how much trouble that'll be for me?"

"Tons," Apollena nodded, "So wouldn't it be easier to simply hear my brother out, have some dinner, and go to the beach instead?" Lane's sister gave a small smile. "Look, I'm overprotective of my dumb twin. He's caring, loyal, and his cooking is out of this world. Give him a chance. I'm genuinely sorry for interrupting. You two have a fun date night."

Becca was still fuming and recovering from the whiplash of being exposed.

Lane was equally pissed, but once again attempted damage control, "Becca, I've got food on the stove, my sister's heading out. Can we just talk? Please?"

Taking a deep breath, Becca threw up her hands. "Okay, so I wasn't expecting to get blackmailed into a date tonight. I'm trying to hustle an education, sports career, and future, just like everybody else. A relationship is probably just gonna over complicate things. Maybe you are a nice guy, Lane? But I don't need 'complicated' right now." Before she turned to leave, the athlete made one last appeal to Apollena, "Please, don't post those photos."

"Don't spread rumours and you have my word: your secret is safe," Luna spoke gently.

Becca turned on her heels and walked away.

Both twins stood in the entryway. Silent.

"That was uncalled for," Lane sighed, trying to control his anger.

"It was. I'm sorry," Luna admitted, "But, I know your heart and I have a responsibility as your sister to help it remain unbroken, if I can. It was an impulse."

"That's how you justify stalking someone, taking pictures of someone?" Lane started, but again drew a breath, counted backward from ten and strode across the room to the kitchen. The sauce boiled over onto the stovetop.

"I wasn't stalking. I was already at the club with Ruby. When I was scrolling through the photos we took, one of the background dancers looked familiar. That's when I did my homework," Luna lingered in the doorframe, "Again, I'm sorry, Ursa Major."

Lane was trying to salvage the sauce while taking the ravioli out of the oven. He set the tray with a meal made for two on the stove top. He'd burnt the ravioli and a bridge to an uncomplicated relationship all in one night.

"Do you..." Luna stammered, "What do you need, Lane?"

He slid the overcooked meal into the trash can and shut off the oven and range.

Lane needed a vacation.

COMPANY IN MY BACK

Their two-day journey began before the sun peered up over the Santiago Mountain Range. At five in the morning, Lane and Apollena left their apartment nestled beside UCI's main campus and headed north toward Washington. The first leg of their journey would end up taking just under thirteen hours with a break in downtown San Jose. They enjoyed a light lunch at a little poke bowl place Luna wouldn't shut up about, and it was absolutely worth it.

Detours weren't Lane's forte. He enjoyed the simplicity of the straight shot up Highway Five without interruptions. The novelty of a straight path from 'A' to 'B' was the complete opposite of their life. At least it used to be. It should have been. He tried not to think about the absurd amount of paranormal encounters they endured and enjoyed the amber waves of grain and browning farmland beside them until the scene transitioned to redwoods and junipers.

In addition to swinging through San Jose, they planned their first night's rest at a beachside campground near RedWood National Park.

For those long hours in between rest stops, their 2011 Jeep Compass Limited Apollena coveted since high school ran smoothly across the uncongested farmland highway that blanketed Central and Northern California.

Lane wasn't a stereotypical car guy. He knew how to drive. He knew how to fly. And with the exception of one crashed catamaran, he could pilot a handful of seafaring vessels competently. Luna, on the other hand, loved cars. Their middle sister, Katarina, was a gear head and responsible for most of the maintenance and *unique* upgrades on the Compass. But Luna? That girl was a completely different animal behind the wheel of a car. There was something about the rush from the driver's seat, the leather wheel clutched within her grasp, and her foot anchored on the accelerator that gave Luna a spiritual experience. Suffice to say no amount of sex satisfied Luna compared to the thrill of driving. (With the noted exception of having sex *while* driving.)

"Last call, Ursa Minor. We save two hours if we keep going into Oregon. You're sure you won't change your mind?" Lane asked for the third time as their exit came into view.

Lane was the navigator. Apollena was the pilot.

That was their typical rhythm. However, this mission to capture a missing piece of their childhood, or whatever, was Luna's conception. Lane had agreed to make an attempt at being flexible. This wasn't a mission. This was a vacation; the journey was supposedly greater than the destination. Even so, Lane found it difficult to push past his tendency to enjoy an efficient journey.

"Two hours out of our way is more than worth the price of camping at this spot, I guarantee it," Luna said emphatically, tapping her bare feet on the dashboard. An open copy of 'Things Fall Apart' rested face down on her chest. Astonishingly, she'd kept most of her clothes on for the whole journey. A welcome surprise for Lane. Luna paired light blue denim cutoffs with a loose kiwi spaghetti strap midriff. Somebody was feeling their early 2000s pop era.

A few hours later and the burnt umber Jeep Compass pulled onto the beachhead of Redwood State Park. Looking over the pure blue waters of the West Coast, the afternoon sun irradiated their surroundings in a beautiful golden glow. Salt air, fresh pine, and gentle waves lapping up the shore were enough to ease anyone's deepest anxiety. Pulling into their reserved spot, Lane opened the door and stepped out onto the sand with a satisfied smile. He breathed in a lung full of ocean air and sighed. "Luna, you were a hundred percent correct. I promise not to question you for another twenty-four hours."

"Oh? That's a dangerous promise," his sister admitted with a feral grin.

They had their fill of barbecue. The fire pit had been snuffed out safely and the sun had set over Golden Bluff. With the last light fading into the ocean, the twins pitched their six person tent with time to spare. It was the same tent the six of them had grown up with. Before their parents disappeared, before Katrina went into the air-force, before Robyn graduated and moved out to attend New York University, they camped as a family. An odd family, but one that met every adventure and danger head on. Sure, like the tent, their family could be cumbersome and difficult to handle. But, whatever insurmountable obstacle veered into their path, they always overcame the challenge, great or small.

For years, they'd been a team of six unique warriors.

Now, only the twins remained together.

"Your move," Luna spoke calmly without giving herself away.

Lane gritted his teeth and looked down at his hand. It was abysmal. He'd played *Unstable Unicorns* with his sisters before and had never once managed to win a single hand. Now, with the stakes raised, he wasn't looking forward to losing. The game was tied six to six. It was match-point, but there wasn't anything in his hand to secure a victory this round. All Lane could do was try to hold back the inevitable.

"I play *Tiny Stable*, that takes off three points from your..." Lane glanced up to see Luna's poker face crack. He quickly back pedaled,

"No, I mean, ah shit!"

Apollena slapped the top of her brother's hand. "Nope. No take backs."

Readjusting herself on their air mattress in the centre of the tent, Luna leaned forward and laid down her card, "First, I'll play my *Neigh, Bitch!* Card. I'll go ahead and remove that trash *Downgrade* card from my stable. Thanks. Next, I'll play *Queen Bee Unicorn.*" She threw off the sleeping bag that had been draped around her shoulders and stood up with arms raised. "The game is mine, along with your clothes. Hand 'em over." She gestured impatiently.

Lane was a man of honor.

He'd made a bet, a promise, and he'd keep it. That didn't mean he would enjoy it. "Fine. Could you, ya know? Step outside maybe?"

Luna shook her head. "How do you still get embarrassed so easily?"

"I'm not... Okay, I am embarrassed and it's cold, and you're my sister, and everything else. Could you get out or toss me a towel?" Lane tried to keep a stern face, but he could feel his cheeks burning. Apollena's gaze as she impatiently waited for him to disrobe was sweltering.

Luna huffed, "You'll get your towel after you get wet and naked. Honestly, you were in the Coast Guard for how long? Don't be a coward; it's bad for our reputation."

"I'm not walking outside in the buff all the way to the ocean. It's freezing out!" Lane protested, but he knew Luna wouldn't relent.

"It's only sixty degrees out, you wimp. And you won't be walking. You'll run your bare ass to the ocean. Now, you get naked or I'm taking those clothes off myself, Ursa Major," Luna thrust her hands on her hips and stomped her foot. Her face dipped from mock scorn to compassion, but only for a moment as she whispered, "I'll be right behind you. Promise."

Lane could feel Apollena's eyes on him as he ran from the tent. She'd grown up alongside him during most of his formative years: witnessed his attempts to become a capable man, a partner, a detective, but never a lover. Girls would come and go, sure. Sadly, none seemed to have any lasting impact. It obviously had nothing to do with the lack of toned muscle definition or obvious erogenous parts currently exposed in the moonlight. He wasn't vain, but there was a reasonable amount of pride in taking care of his body. That wasn't the problem.

The problem wasn't on the outside, but somewhere in Lane's heart and mind. At some point, he'd set the bar far too high for any significant other to clear to his satisfaction. Sooner or later, he'd have to accept reality and the flaws of others. It would take longer still to accept his own flaws. *Why am I waiting for perfection when I know it doesn't exist?* Lane lamented while he ran across the sand. *Why can't I just be happy with normal?*

Lane ran faster than he'd ever run before in his life. Sixty degrees beside the ocean at night felt a hell of a lot colder than it should have been. It had only been two years since he'd been discharged, but jumping into icy waters wasn't something he had fond memories of. There were plenty of mistakes that weighed on Lane and being in the ocean had always reminded him of every single one of them. Those mistakes seemed more cumbersome to bear, especially while running naked in public.

A waxing crescent moon hung in the night sky above him. Trillions of shining stars blanketed the sky. As his bare feet smacked against the wet sand, he heard the rhythmic roar of the ocean grow louder and louder. The smell and spray of surf bit at his nostrils. Soon he couldn't feel the goosebumps, or even the cold any longer. Adrenaline and muscle memory overwhelmed his senses.

Lane took one long, deep breath.

His toes, his ankles, his thighs pushed through the wet sand and frigid water, but Lane was no longer deterred. He pushed forward. Harder. Faster. As another chest-high wave rapidly approached, he took one last breath, steeled his nerves, arms outstretched, and dove forward.

Lane plunged headfirst into the darkness and felt an unexpected sense of liberation. Surprisingly, he'd never been skinny dipping before. There was a surreal sensation of freedom that came from being stripped not only of his clothes or a wetsuit but the daily anxieties that had accumulated in his life. The monotony, the routine, the regrets; everything simply fell off his naked body and sank into the depths below. While he held his breath, swimming just below the turbulent surface, in this weightless moment, Lane unburdened.

Perhaps this vacation really was what he needed?

Lane's lungs gently reminded him of a pressing need for fresh oxygen. Letting out the last of his air, he sank down. His feet quickly found the seafloor and kicked up off the bottom. Rocketing to the surface, Lane gasped for breath. He must have been under longer than he thought. His chest burned, but he lingered in the ocean a little longer, moving his feet like eggbeaters to stay afloat. Looking up at the stars and moon, something familiar ignited an old memory. A spark or recognition; a freckled face and wild red hair.

"Okay, your contract is complete. Now get out before you catch your death of cold," Apollena shouted over the waves. Lane's concentration broke. That small spark faded away. Standing on the shore, Luna held her arms open wide with a giant purple beach towel outstretched between them, waiting for him.

Sprinting out from the frosty surf, Lane ran into his sister's arms and towel. A jolt of hesitation caught Lane as he noticed Apollena had also stripped down to nothing. It only took a single sharp breeze of ocean air for him to acquiesce to Luna's open invitation. He wrapped himself up in the terry cloth and kept on trudging forward to their tent. The cold had caught up with him. Lane continued to shiver and shake as his sister plodded along beside him, smirking.

"Satisfied with yourself?" Lane asked, teeth clattering.

"Always, and never," Luna spoke with her delicate French lilt and signature grin.

Lane tilted his head and glanced over at his bare sister for clarification, but she was gazing off into the middle distance. Her gait slowed. Fear had washed over her face. Suddenly, she froze in the sand and gasped. Quickly turning his attention to his sister's line of sight, Lane immediately came upon the terrible vision.

Sitting beside their tent, an adult Leopard stared back at the Mystery Twins with golden, glowing, unblinking eyes. Its black fur seemed to be perpetually moulting, falling out in oily, steam-covered clumps. Its paws were as wide as catcher's mitts, covered in the pool of dark ink and fur. Lane could feel the low bass growl of the animal reverberate in his chest. Instinctively, Lane stepped in front of his sister.

"Stay behind me," Lane whispered. "I'll distract—"

Luna whispered, "You see it too?"

Lane glanced back at his sister skeptically, incredulous. Of course, he could see the hundred and sixty-pound jungle cat. It was only twenty feet away. Pouncing distance. There would be no escape, no surviving if the creature decided to attack.

Lane shifted his weight, ready to go out fighting when…

Nothing.

The leopard had vanished.

3

COMMENT

Uncle Dan looked as if David Bowie had actually fallen back to Earth. Not any less handsome than the original, just a little more grizzled and unshaven, but retained that radiant otherworldly charisma. Appollena remembered only seeing their uncle outside of his pressed tan suit, indigo tie, and polished hiking boots once when they last visited Spirit Lake ten years ago. His style hadn't changed. Their uncle sat across from the twins, wearing the same outfit at their table against the bay window of Portland's *Royal House of Noodles*. They'd ordered only moments ago when three bowls of piping hot pork ramen, steak, and tofu were delivered by one of the undergrad wait staff.

"Where's the beef?" Luna asked Uncle Dan with mock concern.

"Trying to save a few extra years. Ain't got your Aunt Sally 'round to look after me any longer so, it's on me to stay ahead of the curve. Eat healthy, exercise, all that rot. It's exhausting," Uncle Dan chuckled as he picked up a square of tofu with his chopsticks and tossed it up into his mouth. He caught it, chewed, and with a disappointed frown, swallowed.

"Admirable," said Lane dryly, flipping through his notebook. *The Notebook.*

In the years following their first shared paranormal encounter, Lane's college-ruled palm pad had evolved into a hardback, nearly four-hundred-page brick of a book. Lane continued to thumb through some of the sections, subsections, footnotes. There was nothing about disappearing animals that matched what he'd seen last night.

"Thanks for lunch, by the way," Luna said at their uncle while jabbing a finger into her brother's ribs under the table.

"Yeah, thank you. I've missed *RHN*," Lane glanced up at Dan, smiled, and dove back into his notes. Somewhere, at some point in all their adventures, they'd had to have encountered something similar. Something about ghosts? Ghost animals? Anything?!

"So," Luna began, swallowing a bite of steak, "What brings you down from the 'Ole Shack down to Portland? Needed a break from the tourist trap business?"

Uncle Dan smiled and sipped his tea. His attention was on something that'd caught his eye out the window. "Oh, it's probably nothing. Got a call from an old colleague at the city precinct that wanted me to look into a robbery yesterday."

Lane's ears perked up. "What kind of robbery?"

Uncle Dan kept his eyes out the window, "Something about a handful of books being stolen from *Powells*. Expensive. Old. Occult. Apparently, the manager was in hysterics—"

The boy's full attention came about like an excited child, Lane blurted out, "Occult? What branch? Witchcraft? Do you think the Azure Coven has come back to Portland—"

Apollena poked Lane again, hard.

"Ouch!" Lane yelped, "A fork, Luna, really?"

"I know what you're thinking. Please, don't," Apollena asked, her voice low and earnest.

"You're not at all curious if one of the most dangerous covens is back and—" Lane was brought to silence by Luna's hand pressed against his mouth. Her seafoam green eyes shone brighter, begging Lane to slow his mind down.

Holding up his hands in surrender, Lane wrestled his curiosity into submission; a lone cowboy trying to restrain a bucking bronco. There were literally millions of questions he wanted to ask, arguably the foremost expert in the occult sitting directly across from them. Uncle Dan had spent his whole life studying, exploring, and fighting the supernatural. Even more than the questions, there was a slim chance the robbery was linked to the shadow leopard the twins had encountered last night.

"I know you're curious, brother," Luna said gently, with a hand on his thigh. "Please, promise me we're going on a vacation. Six weeks. Wilderness and relaxation, that's all."

There was a sadness in Luna's bright eyes that immediately took priority over the mystery at hand. That curiosity-horse was instantly tranquilised. Sure, before they left, Luna had heavily implied the vacation was for him. Believing that would have been selfish on Lane's part. Luna worked just as many cases, experienced the same horrors and tragedy he had, if not more so. It wasn't just Lane; they *both* needed a break. Together.

With a solemn nod, Lane wrapped a hand around his sister's shoulders. "I promise. We're going on a vacation. Together. No mysteries."

"It's just as well," Uncle Dan finally added, "Probably nothing. That's what us oldies are reduced to in our twilight years: transitioned on from the badge to a librarian, entertaining tourists with stories of old." His attention remained fixated on whatever was out the window.

As the bell above the entryway to the *Royal House of Noodles* chimed, the Twins' attention shifted from their conversation to the young woman who stepped into the foyer. Leaning against the wall while the rest of her group entered, her hair was a mess of long neon blue ringlets flowing down to her pert chest. She'd pulled out her phone and started texting. Luna especially took notice of her long, elegant fingers as they danced across the screen: not painted, no acrylics, just neatly manicured. Lane was a sucker for nose piercing, of which the girl had two: a small, jeweled stud and a silver horseshoe high nostril. Rustic black sandals, black jean skirt, and a loose white cotton tank top: just the twins' type.

They glanced at one another, suppressing a dumb grin. Both twins noticed the bohemian girl had foregone a bra. This wasn't the first time they'd been in this particular situation, and Lane had kept track of who had previously attempted to court a stranger.

With a polite and subtle gesture toward the young woman with the neon blue hair, Lane informed his sister, "I believe it's your turn."

Apollena was practically salivating. She nodded but stopped herself short of sprinting toward the door. "I appreciate it. However, if someone could help take your mind off another weird mystery, present a happy distraction...?" Luna gestured with her head in the girl's direction.

Lane chuckled softly, "I'm fine. Really. Go ahead."

Luna gave her brother a pat on the back and ejected herself from the seat. Lane watched. His sister certainly knew how to turn it on: charm, seduction, every trick of the trade to capture someone's attention. Everything from the sway of her hips to the well-timed push of her long fingers through her undercut. Luna had it all down to a science. It was odd to see his sister in a baggy pair of dark blue jeans instead of her typical style: barely there. The jeans hung lower on her waist, exposing the warm brown skin of her midriff. That's when it struck Lane with a spurt of laughter that Luna was actually wearing *his* jeans.

"So, what've the remaining Woods Clan been doing lately?" Uncle Dan asked casually after another long sip of tea. "Besides chasing girls, apparently."

Lane considered, keeping his eyes on Luna flirting with the girl in the foyer. With a shrug, he admitted, "School, work, grinding to get that degree. It's been busy, but quiet."

"Keeping out of trouble?" Lane's Uncle asked with a slight edge to his voice.

"Yeah," replied Lane, distracted. There was a touch of melancholy truth to his words. University work and pushing coffee wasn't any trouble at all really. Lane did indeed miss the kind of trouble he and his siblings regularly found themselves in. But Lane promised that he wouldn't dwell on it. He'd keep his word. They were on vacation.

"Are you certain, Lane? Nothing of note in, say, the last twenty-four hours you'd consider out of the ordinary?" Uncle Dan said. His hand shook slightly, rattling the teacup as he set the porcelain face down on the wooden table.

Lane remained distracted, watching his sister and the neon blue bohemian girl. With a soft melodic laugh and subtle brush of her fingers against the girl's arm, Luna moved in for the kill. All it took was a whisper, lips centimeters away from the stranger's ear. The bohemian girl melted into Luna's arms. It wasn't until the clatter of the porcelain cup on the table that Lane was brought back to his senses. He glanced over at his Uncle. Perplexingly mesmerized, the man's eyes narrowed, still locked onto whatever was across the street.

"Not really, why do you—?" Lane stopped himself, finally following his Uncle's gaze.

Sitting across the street on its haunches, a lone timber wolf stared back at them. The same black mottled skin rotted away from this animal just as it had the leopard. The same golden glowing eyes. Bared black teeth dripped foam and deadly paws were only meters away from them, ready to strike. That same sickly black cloud of soot also pooled at this creature's feet.

Lane moved for his phone, but his uncle's hand caught him.

"No," Uncle Dan hushed, "No sudden movements. Just watch."

Lane waited.

The creature continued to stare back. Silent. Watching.

As people passed beside and around the creature, no one else seemed to mind or care for the massive gray wolf with inky liquid flowing out its mouth and onto the sidewalk. Just another stray dog, apparently. The animal didn't mind either. It only seemed to be interested in Lane.

"Last night," Lane whispered, "There was a leopard. Same black aura, skin, gold eyes. It was only there for a second or two. Then it vanished."

Uncle Dan turned away from the window for the first time and addressed Lane, "It's an omen." His facial expression wasn't any more grim than usual, but the way his voice wavered at the end shook Lane.

He'd only glanced over at his uncle for less than a moment before looking back at the creature, but in that split second of dropping his guard, the creature was gone. Balling his fist, Lane struck the table. "I could have gotten a shot of it, done a spectral analysis: I could have found out if—" Lane turned back to the spot where the wolf had been, but still, nothing. Gone.

"But you made a promise, didn't you, boy?" Uncle Dan asked as he steepled his fingers.

Lane sighed. Yeah.

Frustrated, Lane's eyes drifted back to his sister. Apollena just happened to walk by their table, arm in arm with the neon-blue-haired girl. Luna's seductive smile broke just once as she glanced over her shoulder at Lane to wink with a goofy grin. Lane watched his sister mouth, '*Her ass is perfection*,' and rolled her eyes back in euphoria. He smirked and watched the two girls continue to stride lockstep toward the bathroom.

"Lane," Uncle Dan spoke low, hushed, "Omens are signs of things to come. Usually, not great things. I know your mind fairly well, so don't dwell on the possible terrible future heading around the bend." The younger man was about to interrupt, but Dan held his spoon in the air, "Instead, trust in yourselves. You've come across many strange tidings before and have survived so far. The future will take care of itself. You are more prepared than most in many ways to meet that future. Let that be enough. Enjoy the time you have. Understood?"

"You make it sound like we're about to die," Lane said, a little shaken.

Uncle Dan scoffed and reached over for Luna's unattended bowl of steak ramen. He fished out a piece of steak with his chopsticks. Placing the steak in his mouth, Uncle Dan's face lit up with joy. Flavor. Honest to God, actual savory, seasoned to perfection, wagyu steak. As he swallowed, Uncle Dan smiled widely. "My boy, that's the trick of it; we're not promised a second more of life on this earth. It's on you to live in the moment to the best of your ability."

The man had a point. Even as well trained as they were, neither Lane nor Luna were consistently perfect. They'd made plenty of mistakes in the midst of battles, saved only by dumb luck at times. Many of Lane's carefully crafted plans were unravelled by the smallest, unforeseen detail. Sometimes all they could do was fight moment to moment. On the other hand, Lane's father had taught him, "A man plans for his future without guarantee or promise that any future shall come to pass." If these omens of unforeseen terror turned out to be true, Lane wanted to have at least some semblance of a plan ready.

That, of course, would mean he'd have to break his promise.

Luna fell into the seat beside her brother with a frustrated huff.

"You're back early," Lane scoffed. He was about to throw in a dig about, 'Under performing', but Luna's mortified and frustrated face tempered his jest. "Not the one for you?"

Luna groaned, dropping her forehead on the table. "No. Mother Nature came early this month. The Bitch."

ASHES OF AMERICAN FLAGS

They were deep in the trees now. Two hours into the wilderness that ran alongside the river, Highway 503 turned into an evermore lonesome road on that last stretch toward Spirit Lake. Nearly a hundred miles of dense, scenic woods toward one of the most active volcanoes along the ring of fire. At least on the mainland United States. Sure, it had been decades since tons of ash had been thrown up into the air. That didn't make it any less dangerous.

Apollena had the window down in the passenger seat. Her monthly 'gift' didn't lend itself to comfortable travel. She'd loosened Lane's pair of blue jeans she'd continued to wear and reclined in the passenger seat. Her swollen eyes watched the rays of noonlight sift through the trees, strobing across the empty highway.

"Did you ever read about the guy who died here during the eruption?" Luna asked, massaging herself. Her face scrunched up, fighting back the latest bout of cramps.

Lane kept his eyes on the road, "Yeah, I think a few dozen people died when it erupted back in 1980. Did you mean someone specifically?"

Luna nodded and groaned, "There was this one man, Harry something, in his late eighties. He refused to evacuate as the lava came down the mountainside. Kinda makes you wonder, huh?" There was a palpable pain in her words, not just from the cramps, the motion-sickness, or bloating. A deeper sorrow hung in the air that neither of the twins would fully understand until much later.

"I suppose if there wasn't anything left..." Lane considered. He watched the lonesome road while the end of that sentence rolled around in his mind. He had a mental picture of the man staying behind with his meager earthly belongings as twelve-hundred-degree molten lava gradually made its way toward him. It wasn't a quick way to die. Lane's parents had impressed upon him that material goods were never more valuable than any one person's life. Even the memories attached to trinkets weren't really a part of the items themselves, but locked away in the individual's mind. If the mind was lost, that was where the true tragedy lay. Lane grimaced. He pitied the man who died for stuff and chose not to save himself. It was a despairing reality.

Luna groaned, "There's always something left to discover. The man had no hope. He'd forgotten that tomorrow always comes."

Lane scoffed, "That's funny."

Still massaging her stomach, Luna countered, "No. That's the truth."

"Sorry, I meant, 'Tomorrow always comes,' is almost the exact opposite of what Uncle Dan told me this morning while you were... busy." Lane caught himself. They'd lived with each other long enough that there was a quiet, respectable dance around openly talking about sexual partners. More often than not, however, Luna was the one who danced right on the line. Lane was always the one to keep more of a healthy distance from that subject.

"You two were talking behind my back?" She tried to force a wink but ended up scowling through another bout of cramps. "Shock."

"No, not directly. When we saw the black wolf—" Again, Lane bit his tongue.

"Wolf? What wolf?" Luna asked in a near growl. Lane drummed on the steering wheel, hesitant to answer. Luna insisted, "Ursa Major?"

"I don't wanna break my promise," Lane spat out. He kept his eyes on the road, the pines, the blue sky obscured behind the branches reaching over the road. He couldn't look at his sister. He felt her disappointment and the guilt that came rolling behind it.

A moment of silence passed between them.

"You saw another creature, like the one on the shore, didn't you?" Luna whispered.

More silence filled the jeep.

With both their windows down, the wind rushed through their hair. Birds cawed in the distance. Forest creatures chittered somewhere in the woods. The mix of unseen sound and visible stillness all around them was unsettling, lonely, foreboding.

Luna's judgement continued to hang as a knife in the air.

"Uncle Dan speculated that wolf and the leopard, or whatever they really were, might be an omen," Lane started. He waited for his sister to chime in, but the unsettling silence remained. "He suggested it's on us to live in the moment, not worry about the future. I made a promise. I'm keeping it. We're on vacation. No mysteries. No missions. Just us taking our time—"

Luna reached over and grabbed Lane's hand. She gave it a soft squeeze. That was all he needed to feel reassured that whatever doom was headed their way, The Twins would tackle it together just as they always had.

"Looks like we're here," Luna said quietly.

A weathered oak sign pointed toward a nearly invisible driveway in the thick line of pine trees off the main road. Turning left off the two-lane highway, the orange Jeep tumbled over well-worn asphalt. Being conscious not to jostle the Jeep too much because of Luna's state, Lane

WITCH OF THE WILD WOODS

carefully maneuvered forward between the pines.

They made their way up a modest incline and found themselves at a fork in the road. To their left a gravel road wound deeper into the thick woods, seemingly to nowhere. A line of mailboxes on a wooden hitching post suggested private residences beyond the twisting driveway. In the center of the fork was a small pond with a model lighthouse floating on a pontoon. Their destination was to the right. On either side of the road stood two massive black oak totem pools with a carved sign that arched high over the road:

WELCOME TO TRILLION PINES YOUTH CAMP

Lane studied the carvings, and a chill ran up his spine. From the base to the top, intricate and surreal depictions of a leopard, a wolf, and a lion all stood intertwined together. At the top of either pole, the animals held up a stoic woman that appeared half-deer, half-human. Each Deer Woman held their arms outstretched to hold up the carved welcome sign.

"She's got a nice rack," Luna said.

Lane raised an eyebrow.

With a pained chuckle, she pointed, "Of antlers?"

"Sure," Lane winced and rolled the jeep forward under the sign, into the camp. The asphalt road snaked upward at a steady incline. It was a few minutes before they saw any visible clearing in the dense mess of trees and brush. Off to their left was an empty football-field-sized stretch of open lawn with a steep downward slope. There were chalk marks along the edges at random intervals. Probably an actual football field, albeit one that heavily favored one side over the other. On the opposite side of the road, directly across from the sloped field, Luna pointed to an asphalt clearing with a row of portable bathrooms.

"That better not be the only lavatory up here. I'd rather shit in the woods," Apollena spat in indignant ire.

They drove a few minutes more and finally came to a less dense space in the woods. Another fork, another sign, and a welcomed absence of creepy animal totems. If they continued forward, the road took a sharp upward incline into thicker woods. To the left, however, was the first semblance of civilization. The left path dipped down into a horseshoe-like cul-de-sac; most likely a drop-off for buses full of campers. At the base of the horseshoe was a large log cabin. It held a distinct blend of modern and western-heritage styles in the design; large stained-glass windows, stone brickwork along the base, and thick cedar support pillars lined the forward deck. Uncle Dan would certainly have opinions on the architecture.

To the left of the main cabin was a combination infirmary and post office. Maybe a gift shop? The building was one-fourth the size of the main cabin, but of similar design. On the right, sat an odd, tilted two-story building that resembled two original *McDonald's* drive-thrus stacked on top of one another. Or, perhaps more locally, two *Dutch Brothers Coffee* shacks mounting one another. An unlit neon sign hung above a metal garage door: SNACK SHACK, and another sign posted above was labelled: STAFF LOUNGE.

The twins parked the Jeep Compass in front of the main cabin and let it idle. Lane checked his watch. They were exactly an hour early. Other than the occasional crow or breeze flowing through the massive pines that towered above them, there was not a soul to be seen or heard. Reluctantly, Lane cut the engine and opened the door. His feet stepped onto the gravel driveway and crunched toward a circular flower garden across from the Main Lodge. A bronze bell with a large crack running down its side sat in the center among several lilies waiting to bloom. A bronze plaque and inscription were posted at the base of the bell:

> *"Arise, arise, arise, arise, and lift your spirits to the skies*
> *Gift me your flesh to the earth*
> *Upon your climax shall I pull you into my depths*
> *Ring, ring, ring, ring, together we shall sing and conclude our*
> *dance around the stars."*
> — *Xwa'ni Creed (Cowlitz Tribe, 1806)*

Apollena clicked her tongue and cocked her head, "Don't think I've heard that one before." Lane tapped his temple. An old habit, taking a mental snapshot of the inscription.

Before adding another wry remark, Luna doubled over and groaned.

Rushing to her side, Lane's concern was waved off by his sister. "I'm fine." She groaned again. "I'll just die here. Maybe find a shovel?"

"Luna, the infirmary is twenty paces to our left. Let's at least get some *Benadryl* or *Midol* in you," Lane urged, trying to help his sister to her feet.

Again, she declined, instead suggesting, "How about you find the meds and I rest here by the Jeep? Not moving around sounds like a good idea."

Lane nodded and sprinted over to the infirmary. The place seemed vacant. There were no lights on inside, and a thick layer of soot and dust caked the exterior windows. He brushed through a spider web while trying to peer through one of the windows.

Nobody home.

Pivoting on his heels, Lane called back to Luna, "I'm gonna try the staff lounge."

Luna offered a pitiful thumbs up and climbed back into the passenger seat of the Jeep.

Much the same as the infirmary, everything was dark, locked, and appeared abandoned. He'd also made a quick circle around the Main Lodge, to no avail. In the back of his mind, Lane knew his sister would be fine. This wasn't her first period, after all. He'd been there for that. In perspective, she was mildly inconvenienced at best. Whether it was being this far out in the wilderness, the eerie stillness, or lack of humanity, panic had begun to flirt at the edges of Lane's nerves.

He came around to the front of the main lodge once more, Lane remembered his standard operating procedure. *Start at the edges, dummy.* He stopped and scanned his surroundings. Sure enough, there was a signpost to the side of the staff lounge he'd overlooked. Several wooden boards cut into arrows, pointed to their respective dirt trails:

BOYS' BARRACKS - SOUTHWEST TRAIL

POTTER'S FIELD (Formerly Potter's Lake) – EAST TRAIL

GIRLS' BARRACKS – SOUTHEAST TRAIL

STAFF CABINS – WESTERN TRAIL

UPPER FIELD/LOW ROPES/HIGH ROPES – NORTHWEST TRAIL

Staff Cabins. *Surely somebody had arrived before them.* At the very least, there would be evidence of where the rest of the staff might be meeting. Lane jogged along the white sand trail lined with rocks and small solar-powered foot lanterns intermittently jutting out of the soil on either side. A quarter mile later, he'd arrived at a complex of five gray, rustic cabins.

Five old wooden steps led up to a raised deck that connected the small, three-man cabins and a sixth building directly across from him. In stark comparison to the five neglected bunkhouses, the sixth building appeared brand new: warm cedar siding, fresh paint, stone accent around the base. Steam wafted out from a cracked window in the back as Lane approached the new cabin marked: BATHHOUSE.

Crossing the length of the gray deck, Lane heard running water. He reached his hand out and tapped on the door. Unlocked. The heavy cedar door opened without a creek and a wall of steam enveloped Lane's face.

As the steam cleared, there was a clear stylistic shift from neglected Western American architecture to culturally appropriated Japanese. This bathhouse was an elaborately decorated and furnished onsen complete with personal bathing stations, an 'L' shaped hot pool in the upper right corner, and a bank of private toilets in the opposite corner. Along the walls was a beautiful, elaborate black and white wrap-around tile mural of tree branches that reached out like arms toward the same Deer Woman as seen at the Trillion Pines Gates.

"Are you here to help me?" asked a silvery, pained voice that floated up from the bath.

Lane's scattered thoughts shifted focus to rescue mode. *Someone was in trouble and needed help.*

"Yes. I can help. Can you describe what's wrong? Are you injured?" Lane spoke calmly, scripted. The first aid and water rescue training that was beaten into him played back with perfect synchronicity. It wasn't until Lane caught sight of the young woman reclining in the bath that his well-played record skipped a beat.

Flawless alabaster skin, silvery hair that went down past firm, honeydew breasts. A petite frame that was neither too athletic nor unfit. Natural, unshaven, silver hair between her legs matched the long locks that floated around her head like a neutron star.

Lane cleared his throat. *Stick to the script.* "Are you in any pain?"

"Yes," she gasped. "I've been marked."

Lane kicked off his boots and waded into the hot tub. The water was scolding, but he approached the girl cautiously, checking for wounds, gashes, slits... *Stop staring, you idiot, and get to work!* Lane kept to the script, "Miss, my name is Lane Woods, I'm certified in water rescue and first aid, I'm going to help you out of the tub. Do you understand?"

"Lane," she repeated, reaching up for him with both arms.

Lane paused, "Before I move you, does it hurt to move your neck, arms, legs?"

"I've been marked. I need your help," she repeated, making more of an effort to reach out to Lane. He leaned back just outside of her fingertips.

Okay, Lane thought, *She's bending at the waist,* able to move her head and neck. No visible surface lacerations. Lane made the call: a spinal injury seemed unlikely. Her speech was slowed, dazed. Her sapphire eyes were heavily dilated. Drugs? Maybe a concussion?

Lane positioned himself to carefully lift the girl. She barely weighed anything at all. Cradling the back of her neck as steady as he could, Lane lifted the young girl out of the shallow pool and gently set her back on the cedar deck. "I'm going to find some towels to get you dry. Try and remain still." Lane was about to climb out of the pool himself. Instead, the girl's long arms and feet wrapped around his neck and waist.

Lane was ensnared.

"Please, you have to help me. I've been marked," The girl whispered as she brought her wet, wanting lips to meet Lane's.

5

SPIDERS

She tasted like desperation and electricity. There was a feral urgency to her kisses and searching hands as the lithe girl continued to grasp Lane tighter. For someone who appeared inches away from death a moment ago, the girl had suddenly sprung strength to spare. Her soaking wet, nude body grasped onto an aroused and disoriented Lane. He was far from his long lost virginity. But, in this particular moment, his higher brain still functioned faster than the one between his legs.

With a gentle hand, Lane attempted to push himself back far enough to gasp for air. "It's not that I don't appreciate the gesture, but maybe dinner first? Or, your name?"

"There isn't time," she pleaded and wrapped her arms ever tighter around Lane's neck. He could feel the girl's whole body shudder as she entered once more into their kiss, tongues colliding. Although there was physical reciprocity, the exchange was mentally one-sided. Lane knew the motions. His lips knew how deep or gentle to push against his partners'. He knew the basics. However, Lane's mind continued to

distance himself from the moment. He was still looking for signs of trauma, injury, running through the script of how to best aid this girl: heatstroke, delirium, overdose? What did he need to do to make sure she survived?

What did she mean by, 'Marked?'

Lane broke off from the kiss and started searching the girl for marks, wounds, scratches. Her pearl white body appeared physically undamaged. Her modest chest heaved as she panted for breath. His hands attempted to pry the woman off himself to better examine his patient, but she was stronger. Far stronger than she appeared. Her grip tightened. While Lane's mind was distracted in the academic, literal physical care of this stranger, the woman proceeded to pull Lane's leather belt from its loops.

She savagely rolled Lane onto his back with a growl and a moan. The sheer strength and animalistic want in her eyes were intimidating. Lane's attempt to lean forward was easily and quickly thwarted by the woman pinning his shoulders down onto the cedar spa deck, hard. The force nearly knocked the wind out of him. Her shaking hands tore apart the buttons holding Lane's fly together before peeling his jeans down to his hips.

"You know," Lane said breathlessly, "You may not be as helpless as you've claimed."

Her eyes were heavily dilated, black saucers fixed upon Lane's. With trembling lips, the stranger spoke, "I'm marked. You have to help me. Help me. Please. Please, Lane—" She planted another deep kiss onto his lips, then several rapid, passionless kisses greedily inhaling his taste.

Lane clamped the sides of her head in both his hands, trying to hold the girl at bay. "I'm Lane. Yes. And your name?"

"Alice," She spat out, "There's not much time left. He's coming for me."

Alice shook free from Lane's hands. Her long silvery hair, like tinsel, slipped through his fingers and shone in the refracted light, dancing off the churning bathwater. Her hands kept Lane pinned down at the waist and chest. Her head swiftly dove down equal to his hips. Her teeth grabbed hold of and wrenching down the seam of his boxers.

What would Luna do in this situation? Lane thought as he felt himself pass through the girl's lips. Her head bobbed feverishly. He hadn't even been fully conscious of becoming erect until Alice had taken in his entire length in her mouth. Perhaps he should take Uncle Dan's advice, 'Live in the moment?' After all, this was a rather unique moment. Obviously, an exciting moment, to say the least. On average, it took time for any of his relationships to bloom into something physical. Sure, Lane and Luna had often each pursued partners for casual and continued relationships. Never could he recall either of them simply pouncing on someone in the heat of the moment without so much as an introduction. At least, Lane couldn't remember.

She didn't wait for consent, Lane gasped as a jolt of discomfort struck his brain, still moving faster than his hips, subtly thrusting up off the cedar deck into Alice's hungry mouth.

"Alice, wait!" Lane yowled. She opened her mouth wide, grinning, delirious, as she readjusted her hips and positioned her sex directly over his. Lane watched as Alice's silvery trail rubbed uncomfortably close to his exposed shaft.

Before she could guide his hardened cock into herself, Lane kicked himself out from under Alice. His body slid across the slick floor for about two feet back until skidding to a sudden stop. He reached down and swiftly pulled his boxers and pants back up to his waist. His fingers had just managed to deftly button his fly back up, uncomfortably maneuvering his erection back into his pants, only for Alice to reach out and grab hold of Lane's hands, prying them apart.

"Lane, please!" Alice begged. "You don't know what he'll do to me."

Lane regained some semblance of self-control. He remembered his training, like an automatic light flipping on, and easily slipped from

Alice's grip. He braced both her hands together. Not too tight, but with enough force to keep her still. She may have been unnaturally strong, but the careful application of leverage and basic physics had halted Alice's ravenous advance... for now.

"Alice, I don't know what kind of trouble you're in, but I'd feel more comfortable if we resolved whatever it was before we get any further... involved." Lane was nearly hyperventilating, soaked, and still uncomfortably aroused. He couldn't think of a more compromised position to be in. He could barely think at all. Another deep breath, and he managed to force out a polite proposition. "How about we get dressed and talk about how exactly you're marked, deal?"

Lane desperately attempted to regain his composure. It wasn't working. It didn't help that Alice's change in countenance was so abrupt that it stung worse than her open palm as it collided against his face. She slipped from his grasp and struck him again so hard, Lane nearly doubled over. He held a hand to his burning cheek and heard Alice's bare feet slap against the wet wooden floor. One of the bathroom stall doors opened and slammed shut. Then, the soft howl of tears broke the silence.

Daylight, strong pine scent, and a sharp breeze that shook the trees gradually brought Lane out of his state of panic. He'd caught his breath, breaking from a jog to a sudden stop at the gray steps across from the bathhouse, Lane propped himself up on the wooden railing. He cracked his knuckles and counted backward from ten. He needed to get centered, but anxiety coursed through his body like a downed power line in a storm: wild, dangerous, and disconnected.

"Howdy, Lane!" Came a familiar, ecstatic voice approaching the cabins from the white sand path. Lane nearly jumped out of his skin. He forced his heart rate to drop to a steady beat, but Lane could still only manage a weak wave as Jude Abidalli continued forward. The man practically had a spring in his step. "Glad you could finally make it," he beamed.

"Finally?" Lane panted out, "I'm... We got here an hour early?" Lane checked his watch. His heart skipped a beat as he swallowed hard. An hour late? No. That was impossible. He couldn't have been in the bathhouse for a full hour. Why he'd only just left Luna—

Luna! He'd left to go get her pain medication a whole hour ago? Lane dropped further from feeling anxious to horrendous. How could he have spent an hour with some stranger while his sister was counting on him?

"Whoa, somebody just had sex!" Came Apollena's way too boisterous voice behind Jude.

Both men now watched as Lane's sister waddled her way up the path toward them, leaning on the gray wooden railing.

Lane scrambled to turn the conversation around, "Jude, my apologies, we'd arrived here early. My sister needed some pain meds. I must have got turned around, or lost track of time. Where is everybody meeting?"

There was a moment of weighted silence as Jude's grinning face examined Lane. With a click of his tongue and chortle, the camp director stated, "The infirmary is to the left of the Great Lodge. That's where you left your Jeep out front, right? In the camper drop-off section?"

"Yeah, that's us," Lane admitted. *Good*, he sighed internally. *We're moving past whatever just happened in the bathhouse. Which was nothing. Nothing happened*, he lied.

Apollena had strolled up the steps to stand beside Lane. She ruffled her brother's damp hair and looked Jude over. Cocking her head to one side, she asked, "What's up with your shirt there, Jude?"

Lane blinked back the last of his panicked stricken nerves and inspected the camp director's outfit for the first time. Tan hiking boots. New. Unscuffed. Tattered, soot-covered blue jean shorts. Nothing out of the ordinary except for the black soil and ink-covered graphic t-shirt of a lion. It was one of those creepy, photo-realistic screen prints of a male lion, mid roar, smeared in thick black liquid.

Jude smiled and halfheartedly attempted to wipe away some of the grime. "Well, good news and bad news. The good news is, our newly built patio deck on the great lodge is finished. We'll have meals outside under the sun and stars. Bad news: a family of raccoons found themselves trapped in the vents inside the lodge. They died. A whole family, dead, mucking up the air filters. So, Doc and I—that's our groundskeeper here—we had to crawl in and fish 'em out."

Luna looked to Lane and raised an eyebrow. Convenient.

"Dead raccoons?" Lane repeated, skeptically.

Jude shrugged, "Happens. Possums, raccoons, little critters just love getting into places they don't belong and making a mess of things. What can you do?"

Luna threw up her arms in mock bewilderment, "Fish 'em out of the vents, I guess?"

"Exactly," Jude boomed enthusiastically and snapped his fingers in agreement.

"So, about that shirt then?" Lane queried once more. Those eyes of the lion, albeit a photo shopped facsimile covered in mysterious ink, continued to burn into Lane's mind. There was something unnatural about that shirt, something sinister.

"You're right—we can't kick off the summer orientation looking like this. Gross, right? But now that you're all officially here, we can start our camp counselor meeting. Why don't you two go park your car in the staff lot, then meet everyone down at the LakeView Amphitheater? Let's bring that Trillion Pines magic to life!" Jude took several bounding steps away before halting, pivoting, and making an awkward dash back to Lane.

"And by the way, bud," Jude spoke in a whisper with unnerving giddiness, "This is a family camp. Best to keep those 'urges' under control, if you catch my drift?"

Lane was about to protest, but Jude had already given him a firm pat on the back and sprinted back down the dirt trail toward the Main Lodge. The twins waited a moment to confer after the camp director turned the corner out of sight through the trees.

Luna smirked, "So, who was she?"

"Who was she?" Lane repeated, still shocked, fighting against the current of his mind to process the two abnormal interactions he'd just experienced.

"Don't play dumb," Luna scoffed, poking her brother in the side. "The girl? The one who gave you the crazy hickey and the dazzling ABF Hair. Or..." Luna gasped with excitement, "Have you finally popped your man cherry? Has our Lane found a young man worthy of his love? If so, Katarina owes me money. I should call our little gear head." Luna patted herself down but realized she'd left her phone in the car.

Lane looked behind him, hesitant to even acknowledge the bathhouse. His fingers traced the bite mark Luna had poked. The girl, Alice, barely noticed she bit him. He wasn't terribly concerned, but certainly rattled at what he'd just ran away from. He kept his eyes fixed on the heavy cedar door. "First off, no. There's no boy. When there is, you'll be the first to know. Second, yeah, I did catch her name—"

Luna gasped and fanned her face with her hand like an old southern belle, laying the French accent on thick, "My word, Lane, what has become of my dear brother? Barely an introduction before you just mount up and give it to 'em raw!'"

"That's not what went down, Luna," Lane spoke in a hushed and heavy tone. He clenched his fist as if at any minute, the girl with the silver hair would reemerge and resume her attack. That's what it felt like, after all. That wasn't a random romantic encounter. What Lane had heard was a cry for help and he'd failed to provide any meaningful aid.

Omens. Marks. The panther, the wolf, and now the lion? There was something going on behind the scenes and the roots of madness were beginning to take hold. What weighed on him most was that Lane had made a promise that he would have to break. It was that, or let this madness take hold and have its way with him.

Mysteries were fated to follow the twins till the ends of the earth.

Luna took hold of Lane's shoulder. Her playful tone vanished, replaced with a protective almost animalistic growl, "She's still in there, yes?"

Lane nodded.

They both watched the door intently for a moment more, then Apollena took off like a shot. Before Lane could protest, his sister had already reached the door and shoved it open with her shoulder. Luna stood in the entryway like a hound off its chain: scanning, sniffing, waiting to sink her teeth into her prey. But there was no one to be found.

"Nothing," Apollena whispered, disappointed.

Lane had gathered enough courage to approach the door frame of the bathhouse and stood behind his sister. "She *was* here. In the stall." Lane pointed.

Without turning to acknowledge his presence, Apollena agreed. "I believe you." She pointed at the slim, open window above the bank of toilets. One was opened slightly wider than the others. Lane desperately wanted to reach for a fresh page on one of his palm-sized notebooks and outline the facts, suspect description, motives... but he couldn't. He wouldn't even ask permission. He wouldn't know how to. His mind desperately needed to be reorganized and focus on some kind of task, but all Lane could think of was the electric shock from the girl's tongue making its way down his swollen head and surging through him still.

"We should get going," Luna whispered. She turned to her brother and placed a hand on his cheek. "Are you going to be okay?"

He nodded. A lie.

Together, The Twins jogged back to the cul-de-sac in front of the Great Lodge. Back to their Jeep. Lane could tell Apollena was livid, but her anger wasn't directed toward her brother. If anything, she'd laugh it off and say he needed a good lay to unwind his perpetually uptight mind. What had Luna fuming was the inevitable truth: there was no escaping their fate. Another dark mystery had once again settled over them like a thunderstorm, ready to release its fury.

6

THE LATE GRATES

The hike back from the staff parking lot took nearly fifteen minutes running at a full sprint. Turns out that the left fork in the road at the driveway to Trillion Pines Camp did lead to private residences: the guest speakers' cabins and the on-site Abidalli Family residence. Off to the right of those three single-family cabins was an open gravel lot surrounded and shaded by thick pines. Most of the other staff cars were collecting a thin layer of pine needles and dust over their hoods and roofs.

Lane and Luna backed their Jeep into an empty space at the end of the lot closest to the exit. Once they locked up, they slowly made their way across the lot. Lane glanced over to Abidalli Residence. It was quaint and peaceful. The longer Lane stared, quiet was the word that felt more appropriate. It may have been midday, but there wasn't anything to suggest anyone else was home.

"I'd feel a little stupid if I hadn't done my research ahead of time. Jude has a wife and daughter, does he not?" Lane said, mostly to himself.

Luna was busy looking up at the trees and listening to the bird songs drifting through the air. "Yup. That's what his Linkedin page said at least."

"You don't find it odd that he doesn't have any other social media?" Lane said, jogging forward after Luna.

"Only as odd as how it's socially acceptable to post all of one's personal information across the internet for anyone to take advantage of. Lane, let's just get through this day, okay?"

With a sigh of conceit, Lane agreed, "Yeah. One day at a time."

There was no signposted, but they eventually found the small dirt path that wound its way through dense overgrowth back to the main camp. Luna caught her second wind as the pain meds kicked in and off they went.

After a quarter-mile or so, the thin tree-lined path opened to a dried-up lake bed. It was easily a half-mile in circumference, but if it had once been a beautiful man-made lake before, it was a red clay pit now. A cracked asphalt jogging track still outlined the perimeter. That path and a series of wood-carved signs led the Twins through another grove of trees that created an arched tunnel of branches. They found themselves running along the base of the sloped football field, past the girls' camp two-story bunkhouses, and at last up an inclined hill to the Main Lodge.

"There's a set of stairs down to the amphitheatre behind the Great Lodge," Lane panted out breathlessly.

Their boots kicked up the gravel as they turned sharply toward the lodge and stood at the top of the stairs. Three flights down, the thin staircase led to a concrete amphitheatre built into the grass-covered hillside that looked out over the beautiful Spirit Lake. There were five rings of stone benches that encircled a rectangular stone stage about half the size of an average basketball court. Above the bench seats, several tan canvas sails were stretched out from the trees by cables, angled to provide shade from the setting sun. The dozen or so counselors were reclining on the stone seats facing the stage, facing Jude.

"Everyone, give a round of applause to the Woods' Siblings for finally joining us here at orientation," shouted Jude as he clapped his hands together with an overabundance of glee.

The other counselors clapped along at various degrees of disinterest.

Lane and Luna descended the wooden steps in silence as the other counselors watched on. *So much for first impressions*, Lane rued.

"Why don't you come on up here for introductions," Jude said, not particularly as a request. The Twins obliged and once at the base of the stairs, walked up the five stone steps to join Jude on Stage. "Now, it's kind of a tradition, that... Wait, we've got one more newbie with us here. Where's Nina Montgomery?"

"Don't we wanna wait for our resident space case?" One of the male counselors shouted. "What happened to Alice?"

"I'm present," Alice's voice floated down from the opposite staircase. She was dressed far more modest than Lane had seen a few minutes earlier. Considering how he first met her, anything at all would have counted for modesty. Alice, however, had completely transformed into an outfit one might expect to see an extra from *Little House on the Prairie* wearing: burgundy colonial dress, straw hat, and her silver hair intricately braided. "Sorry. Just making my way from the lavatory—not that it's any of your business."

Lane caught the look Alice shot him from across the aisle: devastating, sinister, and lustful all in one sideways glance.

"Please, let's remember our PROPER names," Jude encouraged the counselors. "Sitka, please take your seat. With the others. Our traditional baptism is about to begin."

Lane scanned the faces of the other counselors: bored, disinterested, and listless. One face, in particular, sent a bolt of lightning down his spine. That ferocious gaze, fiery red hair, and freckled porcelain skin. *It couldn't be her. Could it?*

"Ah, there she is," Jude continued. He pointed out a shy girl cowering behind the woman Lane hadn't forgotten about since that day more than a decade ago. She'd grown some, or perhaps shrunk some, but it was definitely her.

Jordan Breathnach.

Lane felt the trauma of what had happened in the bathhouse covered by a sudden wave of rose-colored memories. A smile turned up at the corner of his lips. That girl, the ghost of her grandfather, and the aftermath of that whole encounter flooded his mind. Like any wave, however, the cool waters of treasured memories quickly receded. The look in those eyes that met Lane's did not hold the same amount of coveted nostalgia.

She looked pissed.

"There you go, come on up, Nina. Excellent. We're all here now," Jude proclaimed, clapping his hands together, "I'm aware most of you know each other already, but this is all part of the process. This year is extra special. As my final year as director..."

There were some groans and cries of protest.

Jordan remained silent.

Her fiery eyes locked onto Lane's and narrowed.

"During my final year here, I want to make it memorable. In keeping to the traditions most of you grew up with here at Trillion Pines, we shall all see that this summer goes out with a bang. So, without further adieu, let's meet our new counselors and prepare for their baptism." Jude turned to the three on stage with that toothy smile, "New people: kindly step up to the microphone, state your name, where you're from, one thing you hate, and one thing you love."

Lane, Luna, and the petite girl with the dark brown pixie cut all shrugged.

"Ladies first," Lane suggested, waving Nina up to the microphone.

The pixie grimaced, "Gee, thanks."

Stepping up to the center stage, Nina gingerly grabbed hold of the microphone. She spoke so quietly, even the amplifiers that flanked the stage had trouble reproducing her voice.

"We can't hear you!" Someone shouted from the bleacher seats.

"I'm Nina, from Salem, Oregon. Love being alone. Hate public speaking," Her voice cracked slightly on the last point and she took one giant step back from the microphone.

The same beefy heckler spoke up again, "You must hate being up there then, huh?"

Nina took one giant step back up to the microphone again. Her tiny fingers wrapped around the neck of the mic stand while staring daggers at the boisterous counselor. "Yes."

The boy kept laughing until he caught sight of Nina choking out the microphone.

His forced laughter came to a sudden stop.

With a delicate chuckle, Jude broke the silence, "What do we say, counselors?" he asked expectantly with a wide grin.

The other counselors rose to their feet in unison and in one voice they sang back, "Thank you for your words, Nina."

"Nina you are now a new person at this camp, remade, and during your new summer adventure with us, you shall now be known as... Providence."

The crowd gave their refrain, "We thank you for your words, Providence." With smiles spread wide, the other counselors reached down for the water balloons floating in coolers at their feet and pummeled Nina. She attempted to keep composure, but her graceful walk off stage turned into a jog. Humiliated, the young girl sprinted up the slim steps to the Great Lodge.

"I guess I'm up then," Luna announced without a care.

Lane reached out for his sister, but with a wink to her brother, she took hold of the mic.

Laying on her natural French accent on thick, Luna curtsied and began, "My name is Apolloene Woods, born in Nigeria, trafficked through Uganda, Sudan, Egypt, Tunisia and eventually liberated in France. After a year or two in Normandy's foster care system, I was adopted by my darling brother's family and traveled here to America, settling in sunny New Mexico. I may have been born into bondage, but my home is the good old US of A." The crowd was intrigued, and more than a little shocked. She continued, "Now lemme see, a nickname based on a US Capitol City? I suppose the Land of Enchantment would suit me, I am rather enchanting. But, Santa Fe seems too cliched, no? Has anyone taken Cloudcroft?"

Jude shook his head, "Um, no? Typically, I dub the nicknames, but... I suppose..."

"Magnifique. Cloudcroft it is. You may proceed," Luna smiled and stuck her arms out to her side. An open invitation. Judging by the audience's reaction, no one was itching to lob a water balloon at the former orphan who'd been abducted and dragged through Africa.

At least, all but one.

The same blonde buzz cut heckler stood up, balloon in hand, "Thanks for your words, Cloudcroft," He halfheartedly tossed his balloon high and outside.

Apollena quickly snatched the stray missile out of the air with one hand and held it above her head. The crowd of counselors drew a collective breath. "Wouldn't want this to go to waste, would we?" She crushed the balloon in her palm. Water burst out and ran down her arm and soaked her thin cotton teal tank top. Before sauntering away, Luna leaned back to grab hold of the microphone, "Oh, almost forgot, I love bears, and I hate not being bare."

With a subtle bow, she let the loose, damp top of hers show a healthy amount of cleavage. Luna slowly drew herself back up and skipped off the stage.

A stunned Jude attempted to recompose himself, "O-okay. Cloudcroft it is. Thank you for your words. Lane, you're up next, bud."

Lane couldn't take his eyes off Jordan; mostly because of a deep longing he'd forgotten, but also in fear that should he look away she'd attack. Her eyelids narrowed. Brow furrowed. Fists and teeth clenched.

There was no mistake that Jordan's scorn was aimed squarely at Lane.

He cleared his throat and feedback shot through the amplifiers. "Hi. I'm Lane." *What the hell was she mad about?* His mind desperately spinning for an answer. *I hadn't even seen or talked to her since that day we...* Oh. Yeah. That might be it.

"Hey space case, you wanna keep going? We got stuff to do today," The heckler called out. He gave his buddies high fives followed by sneers and muffled laughter. Typical.

"Brad," Jude shot out, "Let's keep the commentary to a minimum. Lane, you mind wrapping it up? Location, like, dislike..." There was an exaggerated hand motion given to help Lane move the introduction along and get to the embarrassing rite of passage.

"Right. I'm Lane, from Santa Fe, I like photography, not a huge fan of the ocean," He started to walk off before the water balloons could find their mark, but Jude held one hand in the air to halt the bombardment and another outstretched to hold Lane in place.

"Lane, bud, how about some more conviction? 'Like? Not a fan,' Where's the passion? The desire?" Jude insisted with a grin.

Lane glanced at the camp director then quickly back to Jordan. Yup. Still pissed. She looked ready to pull Lane's head off with her bare hands. He scrambled for something to say, "I really love photography, and I hate the ocean," he lied.

Fortunately, Lane's lie was convincing enough for Jude to drop his arm and let the balloons fly. "We thank you for your words... Roswell."

Most of the counselors' shots missed. As Lane turned to shuffle off stage-left like a good sport, one fastball caught him at the base of the neck. It had enough force that he almost fell forward. A few hoots and hollers from the crowd of counselors erupted.

Lane put on a smile, wiped his eyes, and kept walking, but he knew who threw the balloon. Her face wanted him to know. Jordan kept the same scowl aimed at the twin she probably hadn't forgotten since that early morning nightmare years ago.

"Alright everyone, with our baptism concluded, we are now one new body here at Trillion Pines Youth Camp. We are all one. Committed to the end. Ahmen?" There was a dramatic pause where Jude flared his nostrils and scanned the seats. "Let's give a round of applause for our transplanted organs in our administrative body: Roswell, Cloudcroft, and Providence."

More cheering and shouts as Lane joined his sister among the other counselors on the benches. It wasn't until one of the other counselors pointed it out that Lane had some concern about this little welcoming ritual of theirs.

A thick girl with gorgeous blonde locks and a demure Southern accent spoke out, "Jude, I don't think our lady Providence is back from the ladies' upstairs. You think she'll be alright? I'd be happy to check in on the poor girl; she looked awful hurt... and wet." She giggled.

Jude waved her off. "She'll be fine. Now, it's time to reveal this year's camp t-shirts!" Giving a hand signal to the blonde buzz cut kid, the counselor leaped from his seat and set a cardboard box at Jude's feet. "Thank's, Brad—"

"Brad is my dead name," the blond crew cut kid laughed, "I am Vegas." Brad turned and flexed to his fellow counselors who all screamed and repeated his new name.

"Vegas!" they cheered.

What a tool, Lane thought to himself. Although, it might be helpful to make himself useful in the meantime. Standing from his seat and making his way to the stairs, Lane turned to the camp director, "Jude, I don't mind checking on Nina, er, Providence, I mean. Make sure she's okay and everything."

Jude rolled his eyes and shrugged. "Fine. Toss her a camp t-shirt while you're at it."

Brad, or Vegas rather, threw a T-shirt at Lane. Extra small. He snickered. "This should work unless she shrank again in the cold water. You don't have that problem too: shrinkage in cold water, do you,

Roswell?"

Not that Lane was devoid of wit. His mind was currently occupied on four fronts: the Omens, the Bathhouse Incident, encountering Jordan again, and lastly, making sure Nina wasn't traumatised post bombardment of water balloons.

"Hey, Roswell, are you gonna answer? Or are you in outer space again?" Brad demanded.

Lane continued up the narrow stairs when he heard his sister declare above the noise, "No use sitting in this soaked shirt," she cried out, peeling off her t-shirt to a chorus of gasps and howls from the counselors. "Heathered cotton-polyester mixes, and it's in my colors, too. How 'bout it, boys and girls? Does it look okay?" Lane smiled. Her new shirt was a size too small and hugged her body in all the right spots—of course, it looked okay.

But that wasn't what Luna was after.

With the majority of the counselors distracted and fawning over Luna, Lane slipped up the steps, undeterred at the Great Lodge in search of the lost counselor. He didn't look back, but as Lane ascended, he could feel the burning, watchful gaze of Jordan's eyes on his back.

7

KID SMOKE

Lane found Nina on the deck that overlooked the amphitheatre. Her back was pushed up against the floor-to-ceiling glass window that wrapped around the rear of the dining hall. Sure enough, inside the cafeteria that could have accommodated a hundred or more persons was a disaster area. Tables were covered in filthy sheets. Chairs were stacked and pushed into corners. Multiple ladders stood under opened and exposed vents, ventilation, and wires dangled precariously from lighting fixtures. It was a mess splattered in the same dark viscous residue that covered the phantom Panther, Wolf, and at least the facsimile of a Lion that appeared before the twins: the same omens that stood guard outside the very camp where they now worked.

Nina flinched as Lane approached.

"Are you alright?" Lane asked, keeping his distance from the petite girl.

Nina glared up at him. Black and neon green mascara stripes ran down her cheeks. Recognizing Lane didn't pose much of a threat, she

retreated back into the fetal position: knees pressed up to her chest, arms wrapped around her tan legs.

"Fine," Nina choked out. "Perfect. Love being miles away from home surrounded by jerks. It's my favorite."

"Okay, wait right here. There's like buckets of sarcasm dripping all over the deck right now. I'm gonna need to go get a mop," Lane chided. He waited for a response.

Nina tilted her head to the side, one eye peering up at Lane. Eventually, a small smile revealed itself. "So, you tell jokes then, huh? That's your thing?"

Lane already had enough on his plate as it was. Omens, sexually aggressive strangers, and someone he longed for had suddenly returned from his past. Nina wasn't a problem he needed to get involved with, but she was something he could easily solve. It didn't take any energy out of him to show kindness to someone. And that's what was needed in this particular moment: an easy win and some compassion shared with a stranger.

Lane knelt down beside Nina. "What brings you up here, then, if being trapped in social situations isn't your glass of whiskey?"

"Whiskey?" Nina chuckled, "What are you, like, forty?"

"I didn't want to assume tea and have you peg me for ninety," Lane added with a smile.

Nina scoffed, "I like tea."

"Who doesn't like tea?" Lane agreed. "But you're not a fan of being here?"

Nina sprang up and stomped her foot on the deck. "I just don't understand why she had to drag me all the way here? Like, 'You've been coming here on your own for the past ten years by yourself,' and now she pulls the Best Friend Card. Now I'm guilted into coming. Thanks, but that's ridiculous."

Lane's ears perked up at the pronoun game. "Someone dragged you here against your will, huh? That doesn't sound fair."

"Jordan," Nina spat out, "Love her to death, but sometimes I forget why we're friends. Like, we're polar opposites on almost everything. She didn't even tell me about the stupid water balloons!" With a frustrated huff, Nina peeled off her damp shirt and threw it over the balcony followed by a scream of relief. Her neon green binder covering a wonderfully flat chest was equally soaked but remained in her hands.

Lane's mind was rapidly compartmentalising the details at hand. Nina was best friends with Jordan. She wears loud neon binders. Nina's petite yet muscular frame is absurdly alluring. Blinking back to reality, Lane held out the dry camp shirt he'd received from Jude. "Maybe something less wet will help?"

Nina growled, then turned to Lane. Scruff of orange hair not unlike Jordan's, maybe a shade darker. His green eyes were wide, calming, friendly; just some dumb guy trying to be nice and not utterly failing at it, either. Nina took the soft, dry cotton shirt and slipped it over her head. "Thanks."

"Least I can do," Lane shrugged. "Look, if you need an escape from having to socialize with the masses, my sister and I are always more than happy to hang out and share a cup of tea at the end of the workday?"

Nina laughed, "Fat chance." Lane was taken aback, but Nina waved him off, "Sorry, I mean, thanks for the offer. Unfortunately, from how Jordan tells it, we don't really get an 'end of the workday'. Activities. SO many activities. Jude's not a fan of downtime."

Lane's suspicions perked up, but he played it cool, "Should you need an end of the day, I'm sure we could find a way for that to be arranged." Lane listened to the trees rustle in the wind and distant collective laughter from the amphitheater, "You need some more time, or are you feeling okay to rejoin the group?"

"No," Nina said, her voice slightly lifted from the growl it had been, "But I'll join you and your bangin' sister if that's alright?"

Holding out the crook of his elbow, Nina hooked her arm in Lane's and the two walked back down the steps together.

Nina wasn't lying. Jordan's insight had been correct. There wasn't much breathing room or downtime. After the lecture, the group was ordered to climb back up the stairs to the deck and were given a brisk walking tour of the camp. More of a jogging tour, actually. Jude had led the group in his golf cart driven by Brad—or Vegas—as he insisted.

They'd jogged the entirety of the campus counterclockwise, going down to the boy campers' bunkhouse, up to the staff cabins, both ropes courses, low and high. They sped past the soccer field where they'd played the night before, ran down the sloped football field, and around the cracked asphalt path of the man-made lake aptly renamed Potter's Field. By the time they'd circled back to the girls' bunkhouses, the thick blonde girl nearly collapsed.

Gracie, aka Athens, as she'd been christened, wasn't out of shape for her size. In fact, as a defender for the Ducks, her lacrosse team had nearly made it to the state finals. Despite her athletic prowess, at the end of the day, the dry heat was a punishing ninety degrees in the shade and was nearly enough to melt both Lane and Luna.

As the sun sank into the horizon, the other counselors and the twins ate on the deck facing Spirit Lake. An eerie mist had settled over the waters. Given the heat, it wouldn't be surprising if it were actually steam and the lake itself was boiling.

They sat in exhausted silence and watched from the relative safety of the Great Lodge's rear deck as night crept over the campground. Lane and Luna selected the table furthest from the other counselors against the railing. Without any prompting, Nina had joined them.

"What a bunch of elitist bullshit," Nina snorted, and dropped her plate onto the table.

Lane caught the direction of Nina's glare and followed it back to Jordan's table. Several of the other counselors were laughing, chatting, and eating at their leisure. Jordan must have felt Lane's gaze. Breaking from the conversation for a split second, she shot him back a scowl.

"We're always open here. Love your hair, by the way, has a real autumn vibe to it," Luna said, reaching out and gently stroking a strand of Nina's pixie cut.

"Same. I'm not really a fashion girl, but I loved that top of yours: simple but sexy," Nina gushed, taking the open seat between Lane and Luna.

"Nina was telling me that Jude is kind of a taskmaster," Lane said, still taking in the scene, noting the cliques, trying to get a better sense of the social hierarchy.

"I mean, I guess that's true. What Jordan had said was there's always something going on. We have the weekends to ourselves, sorta, but not much time alone in between," Nina lamented while nibbling on some steamed vegetables.

Apollena nodded along. "How long have you been friends with Jordan?"

Nina swallowed, thought it over. "Since high school. Start of freshman year. Why?"

"It's just surprising seeing her again here. We'd run into her first when we were... When was it, Lane? Middle school?" Luna looked expectantly at Lane, but his attention was on Jordan two tables over.

"Thirteen. Yeah, about that time I guess," Lane whispered.

"Wait!" Nina said, eyes wide. "You two met Jordan before?"

Apollena twisted some spaghetti onto her fork and took a bite. "She never mentioned what happened to her and her grandpa? Or, mentioned what happened after that night? I'd have thought that would be a big deal. Interesting." With a shrug, Luna took another bite.

Lane turned to his sister and shot her a stern look, "If she hadn't mentioned it, I don't think it's our place to bring it up, *Sis*."

"Hold on, you two legit have a history with Jordan? How? I thought you were both globe-trotting twins... or whatever? What happened when you two were thirteen?" Nina's eyes were wide, beaming with anticipation.

From behind Lane, a harsh voice spoke up, "Go ahead, Lane Guster Woods. Explain exactly what kind of con-artists you two are and what happened to my grandfather's watch." Jordan gripped the back of Lane's seat. Her muscular, porcelain arms could have snapped the bass wood with enough pressure. Her wild red hair was now contained in one long, thick, intricately braided ponytail, like a whip.

Lane's throat went dry. *Con-artists?*

"What do you mean, con-artists," Nina chuckled nervously.

"Go on. Tell her, Lane," Jordan insisted, pulling out a chair from the table and dropping onto the wooden seat, hard. She was close enough he could feel her breath against his cheek. Her eyes narrowed, locked on to a nervous Lane. "Try telling your side of the story and not sound insane. Explain what happened without being ridiculed, without having to change schools, or being laughed at by everyone you know. I've waited a long, long time to hear your lie again. Well? Come on. We're waiting."

Lane could feel sweat building up along his brow.

She thought what had happened was *fake?*

Or, by the sound of it, everyone else around her thought she was lying. The ridicule must have been unbearable. To know the truth of something and have everyone shame you into believing a lie was something Lane knew all too well. He'd experienced that loneliness. Now, face to face with the first person he'd fallen for filled with a decade worth of resentment? That was beyond heartbreaking. Lane couldn't construct the words fast enough to conjure an apology powerful enough to heal that many years of pain.

Apollena cleared her throat. "Jordan's grandfather was haunting her. We helped complete his unfinished business. That's about the end of it."

Nina almost choked, "The fuck?! Haunted? Like a ghost? A *real* ghost? JoJo, how come you never mentioned—"

"Because it wasn't real, Nina! That's why. Honestly, being this gullible might be the end of you one day." Jordan huffed out, then turned her attention back to Apollena, "The end, huh? I assume you already pawned the watch too, right? Won't bother shedding any more tears for that. It was only a priceless heirloom, anyway. Hope you bought something pretty with it."

"Jordan, that's not—" Lane started, but was silenced as Jordan lifted her hand.

"Please, do yourself a favor and don't waste your breath," Jordan interjected. She turned her attention to Nina. "I'm sorry I kicked you out of our table. It's a senior counselor thing, kind of a tradition. But, as your *actual best friend,* I'll do you a solid and warn you about these two colossal liars before they steal something valuable, like your virginity, from you, too."

Nina's jaw was still hanging open. "JoJo, but..."

Jordan offered a sour grin. "Y'all enjoy your dinner. And Lane, stay the hell away from me." Without another word, the girl that had captured Lane's heart spun on her heels and proceeded to stomp it into oblivion with every step back to her table.

Nina was still dumbstruck. "Was there really a ghost?"

Luna dabbed her napkin at the corner of her mouth. "Yup. It can be rather jarring the first time one experiences the paranormal. Especially so if there's no support system to help see you through the darkness. No one believing in your truth can be more terrifying than any ghost."

Nina nodded along and bit into her salad, eyes bulging with curiosity.

"I can't believe I was so stupid," Lane muttered, "I should have—" he stopped as a bread roll collided with his head, "What the hell, Luna?"

With a stern finger, Lane's sister warned, "No. No pity party at this table. If you want to go fix something," she gestured with her hand toward Jordan's table, "You have to fix it here, in the present. You can't go backward. Right?"

Lane was obligated to agree, "Right."

"Of course, I'm right," Luna winked, took the uneaten roll from Lane's plate, and sank her teeth in. She tried to give Lane a comforting smile, but she knew her brother. He would dwell on this until something more pressing came along to distract him.

"Attention Trillion Pines' Youth Counselors!" Vegas hollered. His voice echoed throughout the still forest of massive trees. An unnerving silence followed. The ambient buzz of the woods dimmed to near silence. As the rest of the counselors now fixed their attention onto the small stage against the bay window, the woods gradually settled back into their natural rhythm. Vegas continued, "Tonight is our inaugural night and at the stroke of midnight, our first official training day will commence. As per tradition, there is only one night-game to usher in this momentous occasion."

Vegas's voice was drowned out by the half dozen campers cheering.

Regaining the stage, the young man formerly known as Brad continued to explain, "Tonight, after we've cleared our plates and thanked the kitchen staff for our meal, we play the one, the only..."

The senior campers screamed out in unison along with Vegas, "Tiki Tiki Fire Drum!"

8

HEAVY METAL DRUMMER

They marched in the darkness up the gravel path. Senior counselors spoke in hushed, listless tones that blended into the dry winds sweeping through the pine trees. Leading the pack was the boisterous Brad (Vegas), the second in command under Jude. Jordan followed shortly behind. Moving down the line of the dozen or so camp counselors, a brick house of a young man carried a ninety-gallon metal trash can over his head. Furthest from the single torch held by Vegas, Nina and the twins followed at the end of the line.

"Let's hurry it up, Aiden. Sorry, I meant, hurry up, *Buffalo*," Vegas shouted back from the front. His voice carried through the sweltering summer night air. His torch bobbed up and down, illuminating just enough of him in the dark to highlight that impish smirk plastered on his revoltingly smug face.

"You're more than welcome to roll this thing up the hill yourself, asshole," Aiden shouted back, straining through a forced smile.

Lane strode up a couple of paces beside Aiden. "You wanna split the weight on that thing?" he offered.

Aiden glanced over as Lane gestured to help shoulder some of the burden. The linebacker-looking boy with a well-kept, shining blond mullet smiled and shook his head. "I appreciate it, but I've got this. It's the principle of the thing that irks me."

"I get that," Lane paced beside Aiden, waiting for a few steps before asking, "What is *Tiki Tiki Fire Drum,* by the way?"

Aiden chuckled, "It's the most violent version of *Ring Around the Rosey* you've never knew you needed to play. They'll explain it up there. The presentation is part of the fun. At least, that's the most fun for Brad."

Sure enough, as the gravel path opened up to a large clearing, Brad bellowed out, "Counselors, form a circle. Aiden, bring forth the Tiki Drum to the center."

"I know where it goes," Aiden grumbled to himself. He lugged the barrel to the middle of the ring of counselors and let it drop with a *thud.* Without so much as a thank you from Vegas, Aiden wandered over toward an open space in the circle between a slim soccer girl, Korri, and some boy still wearing his sunglasses. Korri had been renamed Reno, and everyone referred to the boy as Bozeman. Lane couldn't recall his actual name, and Bozeman hadn't said a word to anyone since his 'baptism' at the amphitheater. He was simply Bozeman.

"Most of you already know this, so new people listen up. I won't repeat myself," Vegas yelled. He was stalking around the circle, passing out pieces of rope about twelve inches in length or the average span from wrist to elbow. They were terribly frayed and coarse to the touch. Everybody got one piece while Brad continued shouting.

"Two rules: don't let go of the rope and don't touch the Tiki Drum. If you should find any one of your hands ain't holding a rope, you're out. If you touch any part of your body to the sacred Tiki Drum, you're out," Vegas continued, stalking around the circle. With the torch held under his chin, the dim glow cast Brad in an animalistic light: a creature contained only by a timorous human fence. All fangs. All maw. Lane saw Vegas as an all-consuming hunger for competition.

Or maybe he was just an overzealous jock who needed to be taken down a peg?

The idea crossed Lane's mind and was quickly chased away. Didn't he have enough on his plate already? Wasn't this supposed to be a vacation? Where was this 'fun' Luna had so enthusiastically promised them?

"When I blow the whistle, begin." Vegas dropped his torch into the drum. Whatever kindling had been in there instantly went up in flames. A five-foot-high pillar of fire illuminated the dark, dense forest that surrounded the upper soccer field. Vegas trotted back to the human fence and forced himself between two other co-counselors.

Whistle clenched between his toothy grin.

One sharp blow broke the chilling silence of the woods.

Nothing happened.

Not at first.

Suddenly, Lane was jerked to the left. Then, another collective jerk to the right. The circle was moving. Abruptly at first, erratic, but the pace rapidly increased until a loud *CLANG* followed by a *yelp* of pain prompted the spinning bodies to come to a staggering stop.

"Our first out goes to our least coordinated five-timer—way to go, Reno," Brad disingenuously applauded the lanky blonde, violet, and neon pink-haired girl till she was outside the circle. Korri was also from Nevada and a party girl with a rather boisterous, self-promoted reputation. But Brad outranked her by two years as a volunteer. So, he got Vegas and Korri was stuck with the second biggest-little city.

Throwing her middle finger up, Korri laughed, "Enjoy getting your rope tugged for the rest of the night, Brad."

"I always do. Thanks. Let's keep going," Brad shouted and blew his whistle.

Again, the circle spun and spun. Again, counselors collided into the metal drum or released their grip on the sandpaper rope. Lane panted for breath. His legs felt like they were on fire, but he held onto the ropes for his life. Despite his sore, splintered hands and burning muscles, this actually started to feel like a fun game.

After a handful of more outs, Luna eventually met her end. She'd just barely skated by until she was tugged laterally into the Tiki Drum.

"Cloudcroft, you're done. Go ahead and sit— W-what are you doing?" Brad stuttered.

Apollena had peeled off her shirt and tossed it at Nina who had been the second one out after Korri. "I'm buying back in. Fair?" She thrust her hip out and folded her arms, daring a stunned Brad to say, 'No.'

Vegas cocked his head to the side and let a sickening grin spread. "I'll allow it. For those of you still in, should you choose to try again, it'll cost you one article of clothing."

Lane sized up the competition: Luna was winded, but as always, a good sport, if not equally or more competitive than anyone he ever knew. Aiden held his own by sheer strength and size. Vegas was certainly strong, but more cunning when it came to manipulating the direction of the circle. Bozeman proved to be fairly nimble, dodging the trashcan with impressive acrobatics. Finally, there was Jordan.

Lane tensed up. A shorter blonde girl, Julia, had been at his side. Alice, with her long braided silver hair, had replaced her shortly after. It was an uncomfortable last round until she'd been swung into the trash can. Lane hadn't even realized Jordan had been right beside him for the last few rounds. She didn't glance in Lane's direction or say a word, but now he felt the heat radiating off her white-knuckle fist so close to his. She had something to prove.

"Alright, are we all ready for the next bout?" Brad didn't wait for an answer. The moment Apollena's hands regained their grip on the ropes, the whistle blew.

After what felt like half an hour of dancing around the burning metal drum, Luna finally got out. She elected not to strip down any further. Lane saw her clutching her stomach as she limped to the audience that had been seated in the damp grass.

Lane called out before reconnecting his ropes to Aiden. "Time out!"

"What?! Nope, no time outs. This ain't softball, Roswell," Brad shouted and blew the whistle, but Lane jerked the rope away before Aiden could grip it and reconnect the circle.

"Luna, are you okay?" Lane shouted over his shoulder.

She'd collapsed on the grass, her head in Nina's lap, but gave a weak thumbs up. "Just going to slip into a Midol coma. I'm fine. Go have fun. Avenge me," she added with a wink and a smile. Apollena used Nina's hands to gently massage her stomach. Nina was more than willing to comply.

"She's fine, Roswell. Get your head out of your sister's business and back in the game," Vegas scoffed. The second Lane rejoined his rope to Aiden, the whistle blew once more, and the circle continued its chaotic dance around the barrel of fire.

Another hour passed. Boseman had tripped over his own feet and Brad took advantage of the mistake. Tugging hard on the rope, the kid in the sunglasses nearly rammed his head into the metal drum. Bozeman barely managed to catch his bare shoulder at the last second. He didn't buy back in. He didn't have anything left to gamble with anyway.

Most of those who remained were down to their briefs and underwear. Aiden had ditched his shirt, but unrelenting jeers from his peers discouraged him from playing a final round. With a respectful nod to Lane, the linebacker limped to where the rest of the counselors watched and waited. One of the other boys, muscular and a head taller than Aiden, picked up the latters' shirt, only to toss it out of reach with a laugh. "A sail, a sail, Buffalo!"

"Wow," Aiden said breathlessly, lumbering to where his shirt had fallen, "Didn't know you bothered to read, Cole. Isn't Shakespeare a few grade levels above yours?"

"First, my new name is Olympia. Second, I went to Duke on an academic scholarship, big boy. Maybe up your insult game with a little bit of research first before you flap your fat lips at me again, yeah?"

"Expelled from Duke, I think you meant to say, *yeah*?" Aiden shot back over his shoulder as he strode away after his shirt.

Cole balled his fists, started to charge, but his peers held him back, laughing all the while. Pushing a hand through his shaggy bleach blond hair, Cole relented and sat back down in the grass. He pouted, arms crossed, and all at once, the muscular bravado deflated.

As Aiden bent over to pick up his shirt, Nina was waiting. Her small hands were outstretched, patiently offering up the folded fabric.

"Here," Nina said, "you dropped this."

"Thank you," Aiden said earnestly. With a polite pat on the grass beside her, Aiden took the seat beside Luna to watch as the final rounds were about to commence.

Only three remained: Jordan, Brad, and Lane. Brad was down to his boxer briefs, still smiling wide, a toxic confidence that could asphyxiate an elephant. Lane managed to keep his black jeans on minus his shirt, shoes, socks, hat, and vest.

Jordan was completely nude. This would be her final stand. The fury radiating off her came in nearly visible waves of steam. She still hadn't spoken a word to Lane or directly acknowledged his presence, but he felt each and every violent tug on his rope. The last round nearly ripped his whole arm right out of its socket. Part of Lane wanted to simply give her the win. With her build, strength, and sheer transparent tenacity to win, Jordan could have beaten Brad head-to-head.

Unfortunately, despite his exhaustion, Lane's primal sense of justice compelled him to be the one to take Vegas down. Or maybe it wasn't about justice, but pride? It was a thin line.

"Let's finish this already," Jordan growled.

"Just taking in the view, sweetheart," Licking his lips before biting down on the whistle, Vegas flashed an unsettling grin at Jordan.

Lane couldn't bring himself to glance in her direction to judge how she took the senior counselor's disgusting gaze. He didn't need to either. He could feel her thrust both ropes down toward her, forcing both Lane and Brad to stutter-step closer to the flaming metal drum.

The whistle blew. Lane nearly lost his footing as Brad threw all his weight forward at Jordan, sending her toppling backward onto the grass. Once downed, Brad planted his foot, switched directions, and sprinted back to the Tiki Drum. Jordan was dragged feet first into the barrel. She screamed in pain as her bare toes touched the metal that had been heating up for the better part of two and a half hours. Releasing her iron grip on the ropes, the wild redhead leaped to her burnt feet. She screamed again into the woods. The second time was louder than the first, dripping with rage and frustration.

Brad offered another round of mock applause. "Nice try, Wichita. Well fought."

Jordan simply threw up the bird as she bent down to gather her clothes. Her beautiful bare pearl white skin and freckles glowed in the firelight. That tight braid had come undone and once again that wild red hair flowed freely down to the small of her back. Lane was captivated. As she walked off the field, his discipline broke. His eyes were drawn to Jordan's perfectly shaped ass, like how Giotto drew circles: flawless.

Clicking his tongue, Brad ruined the moment. "Hate to see her go, but I love to watch her leave. Don't you agree, Roswell?"

With his eyes still fixated on his first crush, Lane nodded absentmindedly.

Then the whistle blew.

Lane was caught mercilessly off guard, pulled face-first into the steel drum.

He felt his lip split open.

"Fowl play!" Someone from the crowd cried out in a Parisian accent. It almost sounded like Luna, but the ringing in Lane's ears and buzzing in his brain hadn't subsided yet.

"Hey, don't blame me. Roswell nodded. A nod means ready, right, buddy?" Brad chuckled. "I guess that's the game, then?"

Reaching down to his fly, Lane peeled off his belt, unbuttoned his black jeans, and stepped out of his pants one leg at a time. He kicked his black jeans to the side and gripped the rope. Without another word or movement of his head, Lane let a bloody, bitter grin spread.

Brad, for a fraction of a second, dropped his facade of machismo and looked... Terrified. Before anyone else could notice, Vegas doubled down on the manufactured bravado.

"Alright, Roswell, that's the sportsman-like attitude we're known for at Trillion Pines. Are you ready now?"

Brad was stronger. Much stronger. The senior counselor had Lane beat in reach by at least a hand length, and an inch or two in height. So, it all came down to strategy and experience. Lane knew his opponent would fight dirty. Four out of the five direct knockouts Brad was responsible for came within the first few seconds of the game. If Lane could wear him down like Mike Tyson, his endurance after the first minute should decrease rapidly.

Lane nodded.

The whistle blew.

Taking a page from Brad's own book, Lane charged straight for Brad. Instead of body checking the larger opponent, however, Lane simply spun around, forcing Brad to keep his back to the Tiki Drum. The crackle of fire still raged inside the steel barrel remained the loudest sound echoing within the clearing. The counselors on the sidelines all held their collective breath as they watched a modern David battle Goliath.

Brad scoffed, unphased. He pulled hard, jerking Lane to the left. Fortunately, Lane didn't offer resistance. He watched Brad closely, studied the micro-movements of his body language for the last twenty rounds, the last few hours. He knew his subject well enough. When Brad jerked hard to the right, Lane had already anticipated the movement. He shifted his body weight *with* the flow of motion, not against. With Lane intentionally throwing his weight into each move, Brad had to waste more strength and effort to over correct and stay upright.

After a dozen failed attempts at tossing Lane to the ground, Vegas' footing became compromised. The larger opponent panted for breath. His arms trembled.

Lane kept himself on his toes and watched his opponent's slightest shift in body weight and muscle movement. A single twitch, a subtle flinch: Lane waited for the perfect opening.

Brad was getting desperate.

Jeers from the crowd began to crack the boy's eggshell ego. "What's taking you so long, Vegas?" and "Thought you were stronger than that," and "You're gonna lose to the new kid, *Bradley*!"

That last insult was like waving a red cape in front of a bull.

Lane found himself suddenly tossed about like a rag doll as Brad caught his second win.

Hard to the left.

Harder to the right.

Every other pull lifted Lane up off the ground. He used almost every ounce of strength to force his center of gravity down to the earth. His bare feet kicked around the cool matted grass, loose dirt, and bits of gravel. His bare legs burned as they fought against fatigue and Brad's overwhelming strength. His fingers gripped tight to the coarse rope, slick with sweat and blood. Splinters dug deeper into his shaking hands. Lane's lungs carried a rack of iron weights. Still, he endured. That's what divers did. They always endure.

"Roswell, your sister, she's open, right? Single? Available?" Jude panted out in an almost bark, a hyena with a sore throat. "Willing?"

That single, insulting breath of laughter was all Lane needed.

Brad had been so busy working Lane left and right, he hadn't paid attention to where they were in relation to the barrel.

Brad failed to notice the increasing amount of loose dirt and rock Lane had intentionally kicked up in just the right places behind his opponent. Precious minutes spent crafting a slippery path on previously solid ground.

Brad assumed that Lane's muscle mass wouldn't be a match for his own, and he'd be correct. As the senior counselor braced himself for a head-on blitz. Lane jumped up and kicked his feet out into the air. His heels landed directly on Vegas's bare chest. Proving to be a solid springboard, Lane held the ropes tight and kicked back off Brad, angled himself down toward the ground. Brad may have withstood a flying kick from Lane but wasn't braced for the sudden eighty-six-kilogram weight falling back to earth he'd attached himself to.

Lane's back hit the dirt hard. Brad was forced to lean forward, clutching his end of the ropes, slipping some as he bent over; his stance was now compromised and top heavy.

Having pulled his opponent down right where he wanted him, Lane focused the last of his strength into one last powerful kick into Brad's hips.

Nine years of swimming, diving, and Coast Guard training delivered the final blow to Brad. That force sent him stumbling a whole ten inches backward into the barrel. The steel drum toppled over. Charred embers spilled out onto the dirt with a *hiss*. Several counselors rushed over to douse water and dirt over the burning embers. A handful of others feigned concern over Brad.

Springing to his feet with embittered glee, Brad shouted, "WHOA, what a play by Roswell! Seriously, a surprising upset. Let's give him a hand, folks." Brad clapped and no one else followed suit.

The wind blew through the trees. The tension remained.

Lane was still sprawled out on the ground, the wind knocked out of him for the second time in one day. He half expected some random naked girl to run up and attack him again. He'd have zero energy left to put up a fight. Standing over him now, however, was Aiden.

With a concerned grin, the linebacker asked in a whisper, "How are you doing down there, Lane?"

"Fine. Think I might stay here a bit longer. Like, forever. Forever sounds nice," Lane wheezed out.

Aiden knelt down and, in a voice loud enough to reach across Spirit Lake, he hollered, "What's this? Our challenger is down for the count? He might not make it back in the ring, ladies and gents. Our reigning champ may yet pull off the win." Howard Kitell would have been proud.

"Bullshit!" Vegas called out. He immediately stripped himself of his boxers and stalked back up to the barrel. Setting the extinguished steel drum upright, he added, "You tell that faker to get on his feet. I want my final round. Right? It's not over till it's over folks. Let's go!" Brad's flaccid penis slapped against his thighs as the counselor paced relentlessly, waiting for Lane to recover. It was a laughable tantrum if Lane had the energy left to laugh.

Aiden ignored Brad as he slapped his massive hand down in the dirt beside Lane. "Three. Two. One! Roswell is down. Roswell's down! Ladies and gentleman, your reigning champion, Brad, VEGAS, Aleman!" Still using his mock announcer voice, Aiden gave a half-hearted attempt to start a round of applause. Surprisingly, the others lazily joined in, knowing that this meant they'd finally get to turn in for the night.

"Hooray, the cockfight is finally over. Can we all go to bed now?" Korri asked with a yawn. She was already half asleep on the grass anyway, but awake enough to whine about it.

Luna knelt down beside her brother and kissed him on the forehead. "Okay, time to get up. Time for sleep, Ursa Major."

"Sleep, good," Lane groaned and allowed his sister to help him to his feet. Luna shoved the pile of clothes she had collected into her brother's gut. Together, Lane, Luna, Nina, and Aiden followed the rest of the exhausted counselors back down the trail to their cabins.

Only Vegas and another remained. The former shouted, still naked in the darkness, "Hey, that wasn't official. This isn't over, Roswell. We have unfinished business!"

Meanwhile, the girl with long braided silvery hair watched Lane with covetous intent, and unrequited lust in her shining blue eyes.

9

SHOT IN THE ARM

Exhaustion claimed them all like a boa constrictor. After hours of playing Brad's insane night game and a quarter-mile hike downhill, the last of their energy had been squeezed out of their souls. They ignored cabin assignments. Lane, Apollena, Nina, and Aiden collectively entered the first available bunkhouse together and locked the door behind them. The prefab cabins were simple, outdated, but furnished with the essentials: desk, chair, and bunks comfortable enough to catch a few hours of rest before the sun came up again.

The interior was separated into two spaces. The front door opened into a narrow foyer with the desk and chair pushed up against the far-right wall under the window. Walking the handful of paces toward the writing desk, the thin wall dividing the cabin opened up to the bedroom. A queen-sized bed was pushed against the left wall, a double-decker bunk bed occupied the right.

Aiden called the lower bunk. Lane climbed up onto the top. Nina and Luna shared the queen-sized bed. Within moments, they'd all drifted

off into a slumber that was anything but peaceful.

Barking, growling, clawing; no matter what position Lane turned in his bunk, a persistent restlessness hounded him. It felt impossible to tell whether the animal noises were coming from outside in the surrounding woods or within his imagination. Maybe this whole trip was a bad dream? If Lane ever did manage to sleep, he may as well wake back up at their apartment across from UCI. He could conjure a sufficient apology to Becca. They might end up going to that lake house she'd mentioned for the summer. No mysteries there. Becca was simple enough, easy to get along with. There would be no panthers, wolves, or lions prowling outside, ushering in a dark omen. Why were they all so hungry, so loud, so… ravenous?

Lane's eyes shot open. He was still in the tiny cabin at Trillion Pines Youth Camp, face-up on the top bunk above a snoring Aiden. He adjusted to the darkness, making out the shadow of his sister that sat on the edge of the queen mattress, feet swaying over the side of the bed, while she stared at the wall.

"Luna?" Lane whispered.

She scoffed and turned to look up at him. "Can't sleep either, eh?"

Lane shook his head.

"Come," Luna yawned, stretching her arms above her head, "Maybe some tea and fresh air might help before the sun comes back up?" She bent over the side of her bed and reached into the duffle bag they'd brought up earlier from their Jeep. Inside one of the pouches were her standard emergency rations: granola pouches, dried fruit, a jar of hazelnut spread, and an unopened box of rose petal tea.

Lane climbed down the creaking bunk ladder. Fortunately, Aiden was a deep sleeper. Nina was curled up into a ball pressed against the wall, sleeping a little less soundly. Slipping on his boots and vest, Lane grabbed the travel mug in the side pocket of his backpack. Both brother and sister felt their way out of the dark cabin and onto the patio deck.

"Seems we're not the only restless ones this morning," Luna pointed to the bathhouse. All the lights were on. Steam poured out from the cracked windows in thick white sheets along with a soft choir of moans.

"Restless is one way of putting it," Lane said under his breath. "How about we try the kitchen in the Great Lodge or the Snack Shack?"

"Do you have keys for either of those buildings?" Luna asked.

Lane rubbed his eyes. Did the moans from the bathhouse grow in volume and intensity, or was it his imagination again? He shook his head. "They shouldn't be locked, right? Even if they were, not particularly a problem for us."

Apollena clicked her tongue, taking a few steps toward the bathhouse. Like a waltz, she danced across the aged gray planks of the deck, "Breaking and entering doesn't warrant a great first impression, Ursa Major. Come on, we're just popping in for some hot water. Fair bet says whoever is in there won't particularly notice."

"That's not a gamble I'm in the mood for, Ursa Minor," Lane nevertheless followed his sister as they both approached the bathhouse door. It became clear that more than one pair of voices sang from inside. Even if it were only one other person in there, Lane was hesitant to enter after what happened to him hours earlier. Between walking in on someone having an intimate moment and breaking into a building for hot water, he'd have preferred to take his chances with the Snack Shack.

Luna, on the other hand, had gradually pushed in the door. Steam flowed out into the early summer morning. Lane tried to reach out for his sister, but she'd already stepped inside.

Lane groaned in frustration, annoyance, and exhaustion. All he wanted was sleep. Luna's insatiable desire for adventure had grown into a formidable barrier to that goal. She just *had* to go inside. Maybe if he better explained what happened to him, but Lane had yet to come to terms with that himself.

There were screams of pleasure, cries of lust, and intermingling moans that could wake the dead. Why hadn't Lane simply walked back to his cabin, buried his head under the pillow, and forced himself back to sleep? It felt as if the dozens of regulators on his body were slowly being picked. Those particular barriers were not easy locks to pick either. Years of mental conditioning and barriers had been erected like a series of mental dams.

Still that unfamiliar presence was persistent. There was something crawling up along his skin. Lane felt some recognition in the unwanted mental touch; the same sensation from when he'd first been inside the bathhouse. Only, it was much stronger now. Like trillions of tiny spiders running up over his body, spinning invisible webs and drawing him in, pulling him forward into their woven trap.

"Luna," Lane called out in a stage whisper.

No reply.

His hand was already pressed on the warm, heavy cedar door, pushing inward into steam and the deafening sounds of sex that echoed off the tiled walls. At first, Lane could only make out shadows, outlines of people concealed by walls of steam. Then the group of counselors became graphically visible.

On the far left, Grace faced the wall, bracing both hands above her head. She'd been partially stripped down, jean shorts still around her ankles, and her plaid t-shirt halfway off her shoulders. Pulling on her long mane of curly blonde hair was another girl, Zoe. They'd been baptised Athens and Tallahassee, respectively. Athens continued to grunt and whimper while she was mercilessly and skillfully pegged by Zoe from behind with a strap-on.

On the long wooden table in the center of the room, Cole lay on his bareback with his face buried deep between Korri's thighs while she straddled him. She reached one hand behind herself, and gripped Cole's solid cock, working it in her palm. "Faster," she screamed and encouraged him by stroking with equal intensity. "Harder," she cried and pulled upon Cole with giddy enthusiasm.

The boy's tongue complied.

Leaning against the far-right wall, with his hands behind his head and sunglasses inexplicably still on his face, was Bozeman. He wore a Mona Lisa Smile that made it impossible to tell whether he was bored, or truly satisfied by what was going on below his waist. Curiously, both Brad and a fiercely built Japanese boy knelt down in front of Bozeman, playing Russian Roulette with the mute kid's cock. Lane recalled that Brad's current rival, Brandon, rechristened Topeka, was the twenty-something speech and debate champion from Kansas. He shared a playful rivalry with Brad during Tiki Tiki Fire Drum. Apparently, that sense of competition extended off the field.

"And, time!" Brad exclaimed, exchanging places with Brandon.

Topeka wiped his mouth and took the stopwatch from Brad. "Thirty seconds back on the clock. Come on, baby, you gonna make this kid come or what?"

"Well, look who else showed up," came a suggestive voice dangerously close to Lane.

Lane gasped. He actually audibly gasped and nearly tripped backward over his own feet.

Jordan stood a little more than an arm's length away from him, wearing barely enough to cover her stunning figure. Her open black silk robe revealed a nearly invisible one-piece teddy. The sheer, intricately designed, black singlet was mostly see-through. The combined heat, condensation, and sweat rolling down her porcelain skin made it more so. Her long, damp red ringlets were thick enough to cover her breasts, and Lane followed her sunset hair up to those piercing eyes staring back at him.

"If it isn't Lane Guster Woods, once again wandering into somewhere he wasn't invited. Unexpected, but not unsurprising," Jordan spoke with an unrelenting edge. The verbal lacerations were palpable to Lane.

"Jordan," Lane started, willing his tired mind and body to focus on her face and not her ample chest, rocking hips—*Stop. Focus. Maintain eye contact,* he pleaded with himself. Those spiders playing with his senses kept working their limbs, unravelling his self restraint.

"So are you here spectating then, or are you coming in...?" Jordan asked, and took the smallest step toward Lane.

"Oh, shit!" Floated Brad's voice up from the other side of the room. "Look who it is. Has Roswell awoken from his beauty rest for a rematch? Let's go then!"

Before Brad could stand up, Brandon slapped his bare ass hard. "Yo, one match at a time. You still haven't lost to me yet. You wanna lose again to Roswell?"

"Hey, that was a draw at worst!" Brad relented. "Fine. I'll play nice. Lane, you want in on some of this cock? I don't know what Bozeman does to it, but this thing tastes amazing!" With that, Brandon shoved Brad's head back down onto Bozeman's.

"What were you expecting here, Lane?" Jordan asked, inching closer still to where Lane could almost taste her watermelon lip gloss, "Did you really want to repeat that childish hero act, swinging to the rescue?"

Lane swallowed hard. "I was gonna get hot water. For tea. Couldn't sleep."

"Why don't you come over here, Lane? Relax a little. I've got an open seat for you," Korri suggested, pulling once more on Cole's stiff shaft.

Tilting his head back to catch a breath, Cole coughed out while looking up at Korri, "Hey, I don't roll that way, honey—"

Korri weaved her fingers through Cole's hair and brought his face back up into her pussy. She silenced her partner in a soothing voice, "No, no, sweetie, tongues are for licking, not for talking." Reno turned back to Lane and flashed him a wicked grin before grinding her hips harder into Cole's face.

Gracie laughed, "Maybe Tallahassee over here can help turn you out, if that's more your thing?" Athens suddenly let out a yelp and moaned in the same breath as Zoe slapped her ass.

"One pussy at a time, dear. You're more than a handful as it is," Zoe said, breathlessly.

"I'm two hands full and you love it!" Gracie let out another excited yelp as her partner pumped harder and faster from behind.

"So what's it gonna be, Lane?" Jordan asked, her hand reaching out ever closer to Lane's thigh, "Are you heading out, or coming in?" With the tips of her fingers barely making contact over Lane's skin, Jordan glided her hand toward his waist.

Lane followed the trajectory of her fingers, stunned, petrified. He glanced over again at Jordan's other hand lingering just over her bush: a tuft of fire engine red hair trimmed neatly into a triangle that pointed down.

"Are you going to run away again? Hm? Are you scared, Lane Guster Woods?" Jordan whispered his name and simultaneously stabbed him in the spine with icicles.

"There you are," Luna spoke up from behind Lane, "Glad to see you two are getting along after all," she continued, casual as can be. The thermos was gripped in her off hand, presumably full of hot water and tea.

Jordan retracted her hand and sneered, "I think 'getting along' may be a premature assessment of the situation."

"Oh, I'm not cutting in, promise," Luna rushed to apologise. "I just need to borrow my brother for a second or two, then he's all yours."

"Who says I want him to be all mine?" Jordan snapped.

With a polite smile, Apollena dismissed the wild redhead woman's rising anger. "I'll be just a moment. Merci." Luna tugged at Lane's shirt, pulling him out of earshot from Jordan. With a whisper, she proclaimed the obvious, "I think something may be a miss here, dear brother."

"Really?" Lane mocked, "Nothing wrong with a twilight orgy every now and again?"

Luna slapped Lane upside the head, "Not the sex. Obviously. Look at the eyes."

Lane subtly looked over his shoulder at Jordan. It was difficult to tell, but her pupils were slightly more dilated. That could have been from any number of factors: adrenaline, low light, pleasure... Then it hit him.

Alice.

That girl from earlier, the one that jumped his bones, displayed similar symptoms: slow and altered speech pattern, dilated pupils, exaggerated, um, desire for physical contact.

Apollena's hand redirected Lane's attention back to her. His sister's hand remained, "Look, as much as I hate to admit it, we're neck deep in another mystery," Apollena sighed, visibly bothered. No. Not simply bothered, but... aroused? "I'm sorry, Lane, but that's the situation. That's *always* how it is. You and me, in the middle of some fucked up puzzle we have to solve." She held Lane closer, pulling him into an embrace.

"Apollena, you don't have to apologize. This is—" Lane stopped as his sister pressed a finger to his lips. She wore a sombre smile, "And as excited as you might be, I'd appreciate it if you curbed your enthusiasm, please," Luna added sharply. "This is not how I wanted our summer to end up—yet again." Then, her lips connected with his. It was quick as lighting and produced the same effect if he'd just been struck by the same voltage.

All at once those legions of mental spiders froze as did Lane. He swallowed hard, "Are you saying..." Lane glanced over at Jordan, "You don't think it's a good idea for Jordan and me to..." Gesturing with his hands for Luna to fill in the blanks, she instead pulled him in closer. Her other hand was now busy caressing her fingers through his scalp.

"First, no, decidedly not a good idea at the moment," Luna whispered close to his ear, "Not until we figure out what's gotten into these people." Lane's blood began to boil as his sister planted kisses along his neck. "Second, with the exception of the first part, I'm excited you get a chance to pursue your first crush. Just..." Luna bit her lip, then pulled Lane in for another deep heart-stopping kiss. When they both resurfaced, a forlorn frown hung on Luna's face, "Don't set your expectations too high, okay?"

Lane tilted his head like a confused puppy.

Luna sighed. *Of course, he needed her to spell it out*, "People change. If you're going to do anything with her, take the time to get to know who she is *now* instead of expecting her to live up to someone your imagination has spent years creating." She cringed. That last bit may have landed a little harshly, but Luna must have felt she needed to make sure the advice stuck.

That's when Lane felt her hands working feverishly at his belt buckle. Lane was still paralysed. Or, perhaps he was permissive. Like an out of body experience, he watched while guiding his sister's hands. The buckle, the button, and the zipper were all undone in this odd repeating blur.

"Lane," Luna whispered, kissing her way down his chest. "I need you to really listen, okay?" She was on her knees now, her cheek rubbing against his cock.

Lane nodded, weaving his hands through Apollena's short hair. It almost looked as if he had four pairs of hands gently massaging her scalp. "I'm not fully in control here. Understand?"

There was a flicker of recognition in her brother's eyes. Lane nodded again, *Maybe he'll take a different approach this time, maybe he'll be happy?*

Luna's warm breath on Lane's steadily stiffening cock sent a shiver up and down his spine. *What did she just say? Something about... Control?* The atmosphere was dense with moans and the sound of dripping sweat.

"Okay, so, what's our play?" Lane shivered as he asked, watching Luna's tongue wrap itself around his head. Her eyes gazed up at him.

Another flicker of recognition. The fidelity of this whole scene was dangerously off.

Apollena's deft fingers continued to stroke her brothers hard on. Her lips were a breath away from swallowing him whole, "It's possible, but we've both been... Ah," Her sudden moan shook Lane from the inside out. "...We've both been compromised. Exposed to the air, or water, or something... I've got about a few more seconds till I completely lose it. How about you?" She put two fingers against her carotid artery and checked her pulse. Her other hand continued to pump Lane all the way up the shaft and down to his hilt.

"Hey, check out the two love birds over there by the door. Get you some, Roswell!" Brandon cheered, still on his knees, holding the stopwatch.

Brad took his lips off Boseman's cock long enough to mock Brandon. "Dude, that's his sister, you idiot." He paused. Thought about it, and gagged. "You got a thing for your sister there, Roswell? That ain't right, you sick fuck!"

There was laughter echoing off the walls that sent Lane into a vertigo inspired tailspin. Luna stood up to catch Lane before he collapsed. For the first time, Lane felt himself pressed up against his sister and a whirlwind of desire made that initial nose dive all the more dizzying. *Had they always felt this way?* His mind was a rave with contradicting thoughts. Those tiny spiders spun their mental webs, stealing away his ability to reason.

"Nina and Aiden were still asleep when we left. You keep an eye on them..." Apollena licked Lane's lips before pulling him into another kiss. She tasted different than he expected. Couldn't put his finger on it. Those fingers were busy pulling down her navy blue gym shorts. Like a flash flood in his brain, Lane thirsted only for what his sister's pussy would taste like. Luna broke off the kiss, eyes fluttering, "See if they exhibit similar behavior: a control group." Luna subtly gestured to encompass the room, but found herself drawn back to her brother's lips.

"Agreed," Lane half moaned into his sister's mouth.

"Good," Luna nodded and handed him the thermos, "You keep an eye on our two new besties in the cabin, I'll dive into this hot mess and see if anything else—"

"Whoa," Lane interrupted, "You think I'm gonna leave you alone in here with—"

"Ursa Major," Luna cooed, her fingers raked down his broad shoulders, down the back toned by years of swimming, diving, and God only knows what else. "Which one of us has more sexual experience?"

Lane sighed and reluctantly pointed at Luna and her perfect, humble breasts.

"AND which one of us gets stressed out and flustered in virtually any overtly sexual situation?" She held a pout while she continued to undress herself.

"That's not entirely fair..." Lane relented, turned his hand, and pointed to himself.

"Hey, we play to our strengths, right?" Luna gave Lane another kiss. There was so much more being spoken in the meeting of their lips than could have been conveyed with words. If only Lane spoke the same language as his Sister, he might have understood it all at that moment. She was using him as leverage while standing on one leg and wriggling out of her pink boy shorts. "Now, you open up a fresh page in the field journal, make sure we write up a full report, and compare notes tomorrow over breakfast. Deal?"

Luna handed over her navy blue shorts, panties, and removed her size too big Ice Wolves' jersey. Lane was too busy reeling from having been blown by his sister to bother questioning why she'd just handed him all her clothes.

Luna gave her brother one final kiss on the forehead. "You're sweet. If anything happens out of the ordinary, I'll scream."

"You never scream," Lane shot back, reaching out for her.

With a grin, Luna took his wrists in her hands, "And why is that?"

Lane sighed and smiled, "Because you're capable and know how to handle yourself," he remembered, mostly reminding himself, competing with all the noise inside his mind. Luna was, in fact, overqualified when it came to defending herself. She'd received the same training and was equally disciplined when meeting any objective or obstacle in her path without fail.

Ursa Major and Ursa Minor: equal partners.

"Go watch our control group. I'll see you at breakfast," Luna added, pushing Lane up against the wooden wall. She'd pinned his hands up above his head. Now only using one hand, Luna leaned in close. Lane drew in a sharp breath in anticipation. Then he felt her tongue paint its way back up his neck, little circles, painting a target. Almost about to break his limit, Luna's teeth sunk into her brother: hard.

"Ouch!" Lane cried. That wasn't the sexy, passion filled bite he'd been expecting. It was the same bite she'd used over the last decade while they were siblings. It sent a different shock through his brain now. Like a fan that suddenly cleared away a dense fog.

That's when Lane felt his sister shove him through the spa door she'd opened. He came tumbling out, dropping the thermos, the clothes, and finally tripping over his own boxers to land face up on the hardwood deck.

All that passion began to melt off Lane in waves. Left on the shore of his battered mind, besides the immediate physical pain: confusion, anger, regret, and a little jealousy for good measure. Balling his fists, the half naked boy sprang up and tried to push himself back through the door, sadly, to no avail. It had been locked from the inside.

Lane quickly rounded the building, ignoring the cold and the pine needles under his feet. Through the frosted glass of one of the side windows, he could see Luna's outline. Her posture changed. Shoulders back, hips swaying, and finger poised. Like a predator on the prowl, Luna stalked straight for Brad.

"Vegas," Luna boomed out, her voice echoing off the tile walls, "What are you doing down there on your knees?"

Brad whipped his mouth, licked his fingers and stood up. "We're playing a little game called—"

"Did I order you to stand?" Luna reached out and grabbed Brad's partially erect penis captive in her hand and gave it a firm squeeze. Brandon chuckled, only to be quickly silenced by Luna snapping her fingers, "Undisciplined boys. How disappointing. How long has it taken you to finish Boseman off?"

Luna poised arm shot down and with her free hand grabbed hold of the stopwatch around Brandon's neck. She tugged it upward, like a leash. She checked the time and clicked her tongue, "Unacceptable." Looking up into Brad's eyes, she asked in a soothing tone with a wave of malice behind it, "Now, do you want to learn how to properly suck a cock, like a good boy, or do you want to waste more of Boseman's time, like a bad little boy?"

Brad stammered, "I, um, do you wanna show us how to suck—"

"Silence. I will teach you how to properly please this poor, bored young man if you behave and listen. Now, on your knees!" Luna commanded and released Brad's now rock-hard junk. Vegas complied and knelt down, level with Boseman's waste. Before he could say anything, Luna gripped the bottom of Brad's chin in her palm. "Now, open wide..."

To the casual observer, Lane considered, it may have appeared that Luna had snapped and lost her mind. With his new found clarity rolling in, he knew better. Luna was at least in some respect in partial control, or about as much as one gliding a plane that had suddenly lost its engines. She may be going down, but she could guide the trajectory of the crash.

Still as the icy waves of cognizance washed over Lane with greater urgency that inescapable question lingered: had he forever destroyed his most treasured relationship?

Lane felt that body-blow to his heart, but shook it off. He had to. They both had a job to do now. With one last glance into the bathhouse to check in on his sister, he stooped down and collected her clothes.

10

HUMMINGBIRD

Alice sat cross-legged in the center of the weathered deck that connected the counsellor cabins together in a crude star. Her eyes locked onto Lane's, then drifted downward. At first, he didn't recognize her, but then it clicked. She'd been by his side for almost the first half of the night game, and he hadn't even noticed. Granted, her appearance was dramatically different from when they'd first met. For one, she was wearing clothes.

Unfortunately, Lane was not.

At the start of the night game, it had been Alice in that scarlet cotton prairie dress that swept down past her knees. Her long silver hair had been woven into two long braids that reached halfway down her back, wrapped in black satin ribbons. Now, seated only a few feet from where Lane stood, what appeared to be a large gray faux fur blanket was draped off her shoulders, concealing the rest of her body.

For a moment, Lane simply stood outside the bathhouse, still as the grave covering his modesty with his hands.

Alice stared back. Maybe it was Lane's imagination, but her stunning sapphire eyes appeared to flicker in the dark. "How was it?" she asked in a smoky voice.

Lane studied the girl and narrowed his eyes. "Not my scene."

"Not surprising," she scoffed. "How's your lip?"

"I'll live," He waited for a beat, and listened to the breeze snake through the tall pines swaying above them. "Are you still marked?"

Alice offered a bitter grin, nodding, "Yup." She paused, clicked her tongue, "You still not gonna help me with that, are you?"

This version of Alice was significantly more cognizant than when they'd first met. She wasn't an exaggerated mix of mania and melancholy, but a tempered spark of wit mixed with a reserved sorrow. It was rather alluring to Lane, but between his exhaustion and skin-crawling discomfort from the bathhouse orgy, and what he'd done with his sister, he kept his cards close to the vest. Now was not the time to solve the mystery that was Alice.

"I'm always happy to help someone in need, under a few reasonable conditions," Lane admitted. "How about you elaborate on your condition tomorrow, first thing in the morning?"

Alice raised an eyebrow. "You really have no idea how little time we all have, do you?" Slowly rising to her feet, Lane was relieved to see the cotton dress still underneath the faux fur blanket. But he was still just awake enough to have caught Alice's dire warning.

"You know, I'm usually in the mood for a good riddle," Lane scoffed.

"Oh, yeah?" Alice's face lit up in mock surprise.

"Yeah. Not tonight, though. So how about a straight answer. What do you need help with? How are you marked?" Lane shot back, direct, with less than a subtle edge as his voice shook from a sudden chilling breeze stabbing through his t-shirt and gripping his genitals like a vice.

Alice wrapped the blanket tighter around her chest. "No riddles?"

"That'd be nice, yeah," Lane nodded.

"Something more direct?" Alice suggested.

"A straight answer, direct, yes," Lane agreed, his patience about to snap.

Alice took an authoritative step forward, letting the fur blanket fall. "Do you wanna fuck? Right here, right now?" Another stiff breeze raced through the trees and the two counselors stood alone, facing one another on the old wooden deck.

Lane's mind tumbled over the implications, the consequences, the reality of what it would mean to lie with a girl he'd just met; someone he was certain he didn't truly love.

"Is that a, 'No,' then? Don't know if I can get any more direct than that," Alice snorted. "It's not a trick question either, Lane. It was Lane, right?" She paused, stretching her arms to the sky, arching back, and finally cracking her neck. "Yesterday morning feels a lot further away than it should be. It's all a bit blurry, really. I'm sorry if I came on a little strong, but again, I don't really have the time to flirt and pine for an answer."

Still no response. It looked like Lane was having a silent stroke. "See, I'm not really that complicated." Alice continued, "I've got a problem, and the easiest way to solve it is for us to have sex, like right now. If that's not something you're up for, I kinda need an answer sooner than later. Time is running out, Lane."

Lane swallowed. "You make it sound simple, but I'm willing to bet there's some context around the edges of why you think you need to fuck so urgently."

Alice laughed and spread that same bitter smile. "You're right, of course. And if I were capable of explaining the situation, I would. What I can tell you is that I have a problem and a solution. I'm inviting you to be a part of the solution. Simple as that. It's your choice if you want to make things more complicated than they have to be. So, what'll it be?"

Before Lane had a chance to answer, Aiden came bursting out of the cabin. He appeared distressed, hands flailing awkwardly, unable to hold them still or at his sides. He was missing a shirt, but the layers of muscle around his large chest negated the early morning chill that had settled over the woods. No sooner had Aiden stepped onto the deck than Nina appeared following after him, equally distressed.

"Aiden," Nina called out, only for Aiden to walk further away. She was on the verge of tears. "Please—I'm so sorry. I didn't think things would escalate so fast. Please, talk to me?" Nina had caught up to Aiden, leaning up against a rail facing Spirit Lake. She reached out her delicate hand. "Please, just talk?"

Aiden flinched, swatting away Nina's hand and taking a step back. "Oh, God. Sorry. I'm sorry. I need some—just, give me some space for a minute, okay?" His deep voice trembled. Perhaps he came off more forcefully than he'd like as Nina hid her face.

"I swear, I wasn't trying to hide anything," Nina started, but couldn't force anything else out over the sobbing. "I'm sorry—"

"The fuck did you do, Aiden!" Jordan shouted, bursting out onto the deck. "Answer me! If you laid a single hand on her—"

Aiden towered over Jordan, the young man literally twice her size—and everyone else at the camp, for that matter. Surprisingly, he bolted. Kind of like watching a mouse scare off a bull elephant, Aiden stumbled his way past Nina and darted over the sand trail.

Jordan didn't give chase, turning to Nina instead. "Did he hurt you? What in the hell happened? If he dared to do anything fresh—"

"Stop!" Nina screamed through flooded eyes. "Just stop. It was my fault. I made a move and he… he got scared, I guess?" She kept her face hidden in her hands and couldn't lift her head. The dam of tears broke and kept rolling off her face.

Jordan wrapped an arm around Nina's shoulder and pulled her into a comforting embrace. The smaller girl collapsed into Jordan's hug. "It's all my fault," Nina whispered.

"Whatever happened," Jordan assured her, "It was his fault, okay? I'll take care of it. I'll take care of you. I promise, Nina."

The pixie girl shook her head but couldn't argue through her tears. For the briefest of moments, Jordan glanced back over her shoulder and noticed Lane for the first time.

"What did he do to her?" Jordan growled.

"I don't know," Lane answered, "But I'll find out."

Aiden was still pacing along the rear deck of the Great Lodge when Lane arrived. It had been a simple matter of deduction to determine how far the agitated linebacker would have traveled without shoes under the dark canopy of trees. There were no lights on throughout the campground except those tiny solar-powered foot lamps that bordered the white sand trails. Among those few lamps, only two trails were lit: the one leading to the staff cabins, and the one leading to the Great Lodge.

Consequently, the rear deck of the Great Lodge also offered the most natural light, the widest possible clearing from the dense pine trees that towered overhead. Spirit Lake was serene, basking in the half moonlight setting on the horizon. The sky had begun to turn a lighter shade of gray as dawn rapidly approached.

"You okay, Aiden?" Lane spoke from across the deck, calm, even-tempered, concerned. It was a lot easier to be even tempered when he had a clear mission and pants on.

Aiden stopped in his tracks, facing away from Lane. The young man rolled his shoulders back and sighed, "I'm…" he started, searching for the words, "I'm a little shook, to be honest."

"Honesty is a good start. The beginning is also a good place to start," Lane offered. He took a few careful steps toward the large counselor. Aiden stayed put.

Drawing in a deep breath, Aiden finally turned toward Lane. The former's eyes were red, the rest of his facial muscles fought to control a trembling lip and keep it stiff. "Did you know?" That was all he managed to get out.

Lane cocked his head, "I find that as each hour goes by, there's more and more I don't know about this camp and it's less fun with every revelation. Odds are, no, I don't know. Can you be more specific?"

"You swear you didn't know about Nina?" Aiden asked again, a little more desperation in his voice. "Like, you didn't know she was—"

Lane didn't want to fill in the blanks based on where and how Aiden was gesturing. Instead, Lane kept a calm, neutral posture, giving Aiden the space he needed to open up.

"I mean, I don't have a problem with that, right? I'm not, you know, homophobic or whatever," Aiden began with a nervous laugh, "Transphobic? Whatever personal preference people make about their body is none of my business." He started pacing again, throwing up his hands. "I like girls. That's my truth. I am attracted to women and the female body."

Lane started to put the pieces together. "Are you attracted to Nina?"

"Hell yeah! I mean, she... They? Fuck, I don't know! I don't know what it says about me that I'm attracted to Nina." Aiden was visibly more distressed than he was a second ago. "I thought... I just thought, man, she's really cute. She is. She's objectively, really, truly cute."

Lane tried to jump in before Aiden broke down again. "Okay, how about we just take it from the top. When Luna and I left, both of you were asleep in your bunks. What happened when you two woke up?"

Aiden gradually halted his pacing, while his breathing remained a bit erratic, "Woke up a little after three, I think? Four? Whatever time it was, Nina was by my bedside, poking my shoulder. She thought there was some kind of animal noise." He paused, Lane offered a nod encouraging him to continue. "We scoped out the cabin, maybe thought it was a mouse or a raccoon, like the ones in the lodge. Weren't nothin' there we could find, so we ended up talking. We talked for about an hour about everything: family, school, the future. Everything." Aiden offered a smile. His mind slipped back into the memory of the moment,

"We were sitting on the edge of the bed, our knees kinda touching. I've never really been like a ladies' man or nothin'. It was nice, you know? Just talking with somebody pretty. I didn't wanna overthink it, so I took a risk and kinda leaned in. Then she smiled and leaned in." Aiden chuckled, "It was really nice. Like, I've kissed maybe two people before. It was—" He shook himself out of the memory, staring at Lane with wide-eyed, nervous energy, "It was amazing! Really. And now? Now I'm trying to figure out what the fuck that means!"

Lane offered a gentle suggestion, "Sounds like it means you had an amazing kiss?"

"Yeah! I mean, no?" Aiden shouted, then reeled back, "I mean, yes, obviously. It felt really good, but I'm nearly a hundred percent certain I'm straight. Like, I am straight-straight. I like women, always have—"

"Do you like talking with Nina?" Lane stepped in.

"Yeah!" Aiden replied with a clap of his hands.

Lane nodded. "Do you two have stuff in common?"

Aiden was tapping his foot so fast the whole deck shook subtly, "We both hate the Seahawks, she's into jazz *and* metal, we're both in marching band: you know how hard it is to find two band geeks that are attracted to one another?" Catching his breath, "Our family lives aren't great, but aren't terrible either. We just sorta—"

"Get along?" Lane finished. Aiden nodded, wiping the back of his hand across his face. There was a long pause. The gentle churning of the lake, the morning birds tuning their voices before the dawn gave way to a sliver of peace.

Lane risked another step closer to Aiden. "You don't strike me as the kinda guy who cares much about what other people think. Am I wrong?" Aiden shrugged, "Okay. Fair to say if someone did have a problem with you, they wouldn't have the guts to say it within swinging distance." Lane gave a subtle punch into the side of Aiden's intimidating bicep. "So maybe consider if it doesn't matter what other people think about who you're attracted to, and you've found a person you get along with, just take it one step at a time? Before I showed up here, my Uncle told me, 'The future will take care of itself.'"

Aiden shrugged. "This doesn't seem like something that will just magically go away, Lane. This is a big deal. Huge. I don't know if I can—"

"The future will take care of itself, not disappear. Did you ask her out?" Lane broke in again, trying to curb another panic attack.

Aiden took a breath, "No."

"So take it slow," Lane leaned up against the wooden railing. He watched the lake shimmer as the first rays of sunlight crept over the mountains. A light vapor trail, or perhaps steam rising off the top of Mount St. Helen across the way. For a split second, Lane considered taking his own advice. "If we stress out about the future, we miss the moment we're in. Sure, past behavior can give us a good indicator of where we're headed, but things change. We have the freedom to change, adapt if we need to. Or, if we *want* to."

"I don't know. It feels like a big change, Lane," Aiden glowered.

"Most things that are worth it require a big change," Lane agreed, "And the choice is yours. It shouldn't have to feel like life or death, or stressful to the point of weeping blood. Maybe just consider if the cost of changing something about yourself or your perspective is worth the outcome?"

There was a long pause before Aiden released a heavy sigh, "Lane," he started and shook his head like an elephant, "Do you know how hard it is to have deep philosophical discussions about sexual preferences BEFORE, coffee?"

"Aiden, it's nearly fucking impossible," Lane agreed. "Why don't we figure out how to break into the Snack Shack before we start talking about the Kinsey Scale, deal?"

The two men laughed and turned their backs on the rising sun as they shifted their mental gears to hunt for a much-needed cup of coffee.

11

MISUNDERSTOOD

After two lackluster cups of black coffee, Lane dressed out and wandered back to the rear deck of the Great Lodge. He'd worn what had recently become his standard adventuring outfit: black Timberlands, a pair of gray cargo pants, a faded red cotton shirt, navy blue vest, and his lucky ball cap with the lambda symbol accented by the Roman Numeral 'III' embroidered on the front. He needed a moment alone to gather his thoughts. He may have been mentally uncomfortable with his experiences in the last twelve hours, but at least he was physically comfortable in his attire.

With the start of a new dawn, Trillion Pines had officially become far more than another job. This was far from his warped definition of normal. Lane's brain churned over what average people considered 'normal' and struggled to find a baseline.

A mountain resort?

Watching the sunrise over a calm lake?

Spending time with a beloved sibling?

Sure. All of those elements were present. Unfortunately, those bits of objective calm and peace had been increasingly outweighed by a pile of bizarre happenstances. The omens were new, but not out of the twin's wheelhouse. Usually, the supernatural didn't telegraph its arrival. There was some thin silver lining in being able to anticipate something strange headed their way. Whatever they encountered, Lane and Luna would be more prepared than most.

On the other hand, he could have ruined best chance of surviving their latest nightmare. After what he'd failed to stop, the feeling that had been pulled up from the darkest corners of his mind: *had Lane really loved his sister this whole time? More than a sister?* He was too close to that particular problem at the moment. He'd force himself to look at the bigger picture. For now.

There was in fact a larger social drama at hand: a tangible and volatile web of interpersonal relationships that manifested in a twilight orgy in the bath house. Sex was fun. Or at least it was supposed to be. The tension in that sauna, however, was thick enough to cut with a hatchet. Even as hostile as their new social web would be to navigate, that wasn't even the most critical existential crisis that plagued Lane as the new sun cleared the horizon.

Alice wanted Lane. Desperately. Or so it seemed. Whether there were some invisible strings attached to that offer wasn't Lane's biggest concern. Instead, he grappled with the results of what happened when he tried to help someone with the best of intentions.

On top of that, Jordan resented Lane. Hate may not have been too far off the mark, either. Even when acting in good faith, helping Jordan's grandfather pass on, that encounter had left her scarred. What's more, Lane had failed to be there for her when that wound had been freshly opened again, and again, by her peers.

Now there was someone else who sought Lane's help. Would the result be the same? Would he only be patching a temporary problem while the resulting trauma would continue to plague the recipient of

Lane's so-called help? Doubt was a terrible thing to fester in Lane's mind, and yet, he could feel those roots burrowing deeper into his brain.

"Brother, goodness, I've found you. Finally," Apollena panted out. She let slip her sly smile with a thousand meanings behind it: impossible to decipher at a glance.

Lane leaned back against the railing and turned to his sister as she approached him from across the deck. She wore a tight, hunter green v-neck cotton shirt, and a pair of low-rise khaki shorts. She'd kept the well-worn pair of hiking boots Lane had gifted her last year, paired with a knee-high socks with bear prints on the kneecaps. She looked like a ray of sunshine skipping toward him.

Raising his third cup of coffee off the deck rail, Lane asked, "Did you get any sleep?"

Luna gently took the cup from Lane, downed the contents in a single gulp, and shook her head. "Nope." She wiped her mouth as her Cheshire grin reappeared. "Actually I'm hoping you could tell me what happened, help fill in the gaps?"

Lane felt his stomach twist itself into a pretzel, "You don't remember anything?"

She shut her eyes, furrowed her brow, forcing the memories to surface, "We both left the cabin, yes? Then we… Something affects our inhibitions. Effected is too mild a word I think. Especially for the likes of us. It's not like anything can go scratching away in our brains, right?"

Luna was right of course. Their collective decade and change of dealing with the supernatural and occult had forced them to develop a rather unique set of mental armor. Given his sister's experience, she'd focused her efforts on protecting her heart. Lane on the other hand valued his mind above all else. Through years of trial by fire, they'd each used their learned skill sets in alchemy and craft work to protect what they valued most.

Lane looked out over the lake, considering what it would take to break down all those protective barriers the twins had woven into themselves. "I haven't felt any signs of genuine witchcraft. Those omens, they don't radiate energy like ordinary familiars…"

"No," Luna agreed leaning against her brother, her head on his shoulder.

Her fingertips absentmindedly played with his hair. Ordinarily a welcomed, passive habit. But, those familiar fingers now sent a discomforting chill up his spine. Lane took a step back to pace, trying to remain calm and not think about his cock sliding into Luna's wonderfully experienced lips. "We're dealing with a user far more experienced than we've come across. Maybe something using an older magic—?"

"Let's not jump to conclusions before we have data," Luna jumped in. Implausibly, she grinned wider. "Whatever happened after you left the bathhouse, I at least vaguely recall placing myself in a position of authority over the top dog in this kennel."

Lane swallowed and wretched, "You don't mean… Oh, God. Brad?"

Rolling her eyes, "Prison rules apply to most standard social situations: find the biggest dog in the yard, shank 'em, and *you* become the biggest dog."

Lane tried to mentally vomit out the image of his sister fucking Brad. He knew in his heart that she considered it simply part of the job. He knew Luna had resigned to the inevitable last night; they were in the middle of some larger mystery. The game was on, and they would need to use any and all skills at their disposal to win.

Still, it was *Brad*.

"I'd almost prefer if you did literally shank Brad, as opposed to metaphorically," Lane offered, trying to distract himself with the dazzling vision of Spirit Lake.

Luna leaned up against her brother playfully. "Oh, no metaphor here. When I finally came to my senses, I was still wearing Zoe's borrowed strap-on. The way Bradley's legs were spread I'd apparently done some extensive, literal shanking. My initial hypothesis that his boisterous, obsessive competitive behavior may be a variant of

Borderline Personality Disorder may prove to be accurate. He acts out for attention because he feels empty. So, I must have offered to... fill 'em up. At least filling in so much that we may be able to successfully exploit a weakness and gain an information advantage. Namely, Brad being second in command to Jude. With some gentle coaxing, we'll know what Jude knows."

Lane nodded along, looking down into his empty cup of coffee. "At least whatever Jude tells Brad. We have an access point to information that might be otherwise kept from us. Smart. Gross, but smart." Once again, Luna's ability to analyze and exploit an asset's psychological strengths and weaknesses danced across a thin ethical line. It was difficult to argue with the results, considering they were in dire need of more information.

Apollena sighed, "Or, maybe we can just pack up? We could find a cozy little B&B in Portland and spend the summer as normal people do. Relax. Get fat. Read a paperback thriller by the side of the pool?" Luna's arm fell over Lane's shoulder as she looked into his eyes.

Lane exchanged a bitter, knowing smile with his sister.

Retreating from a challenge wasn't in their nature.

"Till the end, Ursa Minor?" Lane held up his pinky finger for Apollena.

Luna wrapped her little finger around Lane's, "Jusqu'à la fin, Ursa Major," she repeated.

"Woods siblings, a merry morning to both of you," Jude's voice boomed from the other end of the deck. Both the twins turned to face the energetic camp director, striding toward them at a breakneck pace. He wasn't moving nearly fast enough that Lane couldn't spot a few flecks of dark black soot on his boots, knees, shirt, and neck. "How'd you two do in the inaugural game last night? How'd we sleep?"

"Didn't do much sleeping," Apollena admitted dryly, stretching.

"Came in second," Lane added.

"Second place? Not too bad for a first-timer. I can certainly guarantee you'll sleep tonight, though. Like a rock at the bottom of the ocean." The camp director flashed another toothy smile and walked toward the other end of the deck, toward the staff cabins.

"Jude, one question, if you wouldn't mind?" Lane asked.

The camp director turned about face but kept walking backward. "Have to get the others ready for breakfast. Meet afterward? Glad you two are early risers. That's the Trillion Pines' Spirit!" Jude pumped his fist up, spun around, and jogged on.

"It would appear the Trillion Pines' Spirit would include acting elusive," Lane grumbled. He tapped his temple to review a mental picture of Jude for later. That last comment, it couldn't have been coincidence.

"I was going to say it must be a cocktail of cocaine and Adderall," Apollena scoffed.

The Twins enjoyed the peacefulness of the early morning view for themselves for another five minutes before the rest of the counselors ambled onto the deck, like a herd of recently resurrected corpses.

Doc, the facilities groundskeeper, temporary chef, and ropes course engineer, had set out breakfast buffet-style on several tables pressed up against the large bay windows of the Great Lodge. Those windows were now covered in white curtains. Eggs, sausage, waffles, and fresh fruit served as secondary distractions. Most of the counsellors, however, went straight to their respective seats and face-planted directly onto the tables. Groans and whining filled the air like an untuned symphony warming up before their concert. Lane and Luna sat at the far back table, and watched, taking note of the counselors daylight interactions.

Lane first caught sight of the most energetic pair from the bathhouse, Gracie and Zoe. They now sat inexplicably at opposite ends of the deck. Of the three tables closest to the buffet line, Grace was at the furthest to the left. Zoe kept walking and sat on the far right. Neither seemed to pay any attention to the other: no greetings, no snide remarks, not even so much as casual wandering eye contact. Regret perhaps?

Luna noted the exact opposite case with Korri and Cole. The pair sat at Zoe's table, Korri's arm wrapped tightly around Cole's waist. She made it obnoxiously apparent that they were joined at the hip. The subtle discomfort in Cole's expression, and exhaustive attempt to smile, let slip that such affections may not be equally reciprocated. Regardless of Cole's feelings, Korri made sure both their chairs were pulled as close together as possible.

Brad and Brandon's behavior seemed to show the least amount of change from last night. They sat at the center table with Jordan. One of them had produced a small bottle of ghost pepper sauce and began liberally applying it to one of the sausages. A contest to see who could eat the most meat coated in the nearly fatal flavored hot sauce was soon underway.

Absent from last night's festivities were two of the more reserved counselors, Julia and Franki. Both girls sat at opposite ends of Grace's table. Julia, shorter, stocky, with strawberry blonde hair, whispered a good morning to Gracie. Franki, a lithe London-born black woman, simply fell into her chair without saying a word. A visible edge of discomfort showed itself through rehearsed politeness on both girls' faces.

"Alright you animals, breakfast is served. Get up, grab a plate, you know the routine," Doc grumbled. Lane noted Doc's voice came across as a 'happy grumble', similar to how his uncle pretended to be upset to mask his pride in his niece and nephew. That happy grumble usually verbalised itself when it may have been socially unacceptable to be proud of two adolescent trouble-making children. For instance, when a particularly libidinous Nigerian-born, French step sister was caught making out with a neighbor girl on the roof of Uncle Dan's gift shop one eventful summer, long ago.

Unlike Uncle Dan, Doc didn't stick around to offer any sage words of advice on growing up. The man with the trimmed beard, torn plaid shirt, and ripped blue jean shorts simply wandered off into the kitchen without another word.

"Good morning Trillion Pines Youth staff!" Jude shouted loud enough to wake the dead.

The reply from the exhausted counselors was lackluster. Jude made another attempt to get the counselor's attention, and the results were only slightly better than the first. The director continued, regardless of the lack of enthusiasm. "We have a ton of fun to get through today. Before we get started, make sure you grab seconds, or thirds on the spread Doc laid out for us. Did anyone say, 'Thank you, Doc,' by the way?"

A thank you was exhaled on the back of a collective groan.

While Jude desperately tried to rally the counselors, Aiden finally arrived, shuffling onto the deck. Lane watched as he timidly approached Nina sitting at Grace's table. The larger boy's shoulders were slumped forward as he knelt beside Nina. She turned to him, a half-smile on her face. Both the boy and girl were subtly whispering when Jordan marched over to the table. A muted argument began to rise as Jordan, Aiden, and Nina's cross-talk gained the attention of Jude on stage.

"Oh, excuse me," Jude interrupted, "Perhaps we can solve our little drama at the appropriate time, not while your director is speaking. Fair?"

Jordan shot Aiden a stern look, kicked over the empty chair beside him, and stomped back over to the senior counselor's table. "Come on, Nina. You can sit with us this morning."

Nina refused.

Jordan offered again, but still, the smaller girl remained.

Aiden had already lumbered over to Lane and Luna's table, head lowered, and sat down with a heavy sigh. Luna stood up and offered to grab a plate for their new guest. She didn't wait for his reply and dashed toward the buffet line with a smile.

"Hey," Lane began, "You spoke your peace, right?"

Aiden nodded, "Told her how I felt, offered a sincere apology for acting like a goon."

"Then you did your part," Lane offered the larger boy a pat on the back like he'd seen in movies: an appropriate fraternal display of comfort. It didn't seem to have helped any, but Lane was compelled to show some kindness. He remembered having grappled with his own sexual identity. It was a difficult, painful, and largely embarrassing process. Ultimately, Lane formed his core identity as someone who would show affection toward others regardless of sex or gender, rather than pigeonhole himself into any particular leaning. He'd imagine the Kinsey scale hated people like him. Perhaps that utilitarian view wasn't entirely socially acceptable? *Fuck it.*

For Aiden, at least internally, the matter may not have been so cut and dry. Lane saw a man who was attracted to a woman. Simple. She may not have originally identified as such, but that was the past. What mattered going forward was how they identified in the here and now and the choices made in the present. Lane acknowledged that to draw up one's mental anchor of perception rooted in the past and sail into the future was harder for some than it is for others.

Luna returned with a plate loaded with food. "Didn't know what you wanted, so I got a lot of everything to share," she whispered, popping a piece of cantaloupe into her mouth.

"Thanks," Aiden replied, still forlorn, but less so than when he'd arrived.

"You wanna hear a secret?" Luna asked.

Aiden shrugged.

"Sometimes," Luna said softly, leaning in to brush her lips against Aiden's ear, "Women can forgive men for not knowing what they want."

Aiden blushed and gave Lane a befuddled look. Lane could only smile back.

"Now that you're all awake," Jude hollered, "I want to invite Vegas onto the stage to explain our team building exercise for this morning and maybe the afternoon? That, I suppose, will depend on you. Let's give our lead counselor some love!" Stepping back on the stage, Jude attempted to conjure hearty applause from the others with moderate success.

Apollena snickered, whispering to Lane, "Oh, I already gave him plenty last night."

He raised an eyebrow, "Of love? Really?"

Luna popped another melon ball into her mouth, juice running down her chin. "He's not the sort to know the difference. But, even at my lowest point, I still do."

Again, Lane wretched, but felt a little better as he watched Brad waddle up to the stage as if he'd ridden a bicycle race with no seat. He reached out to take the microphone from Jude, and the boy renamed Vegas tried to smile through the pounding he'd received from Luna only hours earlier that morning.

"Alright, Apple Scruffs," Brad began, clenching his jaw, "I'm not going to repeat myself. If you need to take notes on what we're doing, now is the time. Here's what we have for a team-building exercise you will all be participating in exactly ten minutes from now..." A lengthy explanation followed. Lane did not take notes.

What did catch Lane's attention was Alice, who'd seemingly just appeared out of nowhere. She sat at Korri's table. She wasn't paying Brad any attention, either. In fact, her gaze was squarely on Lane.

She wore another variant of her cotton prairie dress. This particular selection was violet with less embroidery than the previous dress. Her hair was re-braided into one long, silver ponytail that hung over her left shoulder. With a chilling neutral expression and her chair turned toward Lane, he watched as her fingers slowly pushed their way down from her hips, her thighs, and grasped the tops of her knees. Arduously, almost imperceptibly, Alice pried her slender legs apart, inch by inch. The base of her dress rose like a stage curtain, higher and higher, drawing out the revelation of what was concealed under her dress for as long as possible. She leaned back in her chair, face tilted up toward the sky.

Alice licked her lips.

Lane reverted his attention back to his own table.

"Aiden?" asked a soft voice from behind them.

Aiden looked up at Nina with big, hopeful eyes. He rose to his feet and offered the empty chair beside him, pulling it out for her. There was a moment of silence between the two. That brief, innocent moment was broken by Brad.

"You two wanna make out already, or are you content to keep interrupting everyone else's morning?" Vegas berated them over the microphone.

Apollena shot Brad a sharp look. Although he showed some initial confusion, he eventually got the message. With a slight change of tone, the lead counselor cleared his throat and continued. "As I was saying, this will be a timed event, so it's in everyone's best interest to work together quickly and efficiently to complete all your objectives…"

Nina took her seat beside Aiden. The linebacker sat beside her.

"I just wanted to say," Nina began in a whisper, "I feel the same way. Are you comfortable with that?" Not waiting for a reply, the pixie girl began to fidget with her many neon, black and studded arm bracelets.

"Yeah," Aiden timidly placed a hand on Nina's cheek, lifting her face to meet his, "I think I'm willing to make some changes… for the better." They exchanged smiles and grabbed a handful of fruit and toast off the shared plate Luna had brought over.

Nina swallowed a piece of toast before completely changing the tone of the table. "So," she began, eyeing Apollena, "We didn't get a chance to follow up with what you and your brother mentioned before. Ya know, that *thing* with you and Jordan?"

Lane almost choked. He'd forgotten about his close encounter in the bathhouse. He'd hoped everyone else didn't need or want to get involved with Lane's cringe worthy response to affection. What an absolute tool he'd proven to have been over the last twenty-four hours.

Virgins have more subtlety than he did last night.

Luna held her fork aloft, pointing demurely at Nina, "Remind me, which thing?"

"Oh sure," Nina replied, swallowing, "Ghosts are fucking real?!"

12

ANOTHER MAN'S DONE GONE

They'd gathered on the gravel-laden cul-de-sac in front of the Great Lodge and the old Iron Bell. Lane kept replaying the lyrics to the ominous song engraved on the plaque. He felt the itch to start his investigation and the irritation of having to waste time with team-building exercises. He'd mostly ignored Brad's introduction. The counselors likewise stood confused by what sat before them: a large pile of thick rope about an inch and a half thick, forty feet long, and a sealed manila envelope that lay on top of the pile.

"Well," Brad chided, "Get going. Y'all are on the clock, after all."

"Okay sure, but..." Julia asked, "What exactly are we supposed to do?"

"Did none of you pay any attention at breakfast?" Brad huffed out. Pacing along the gravel driveway, holding a stopwatch in one hand and a wooden placard sign in the other. Vegas shouted, "You all see this sign? You see the watch? You have two hours to solve this obstacle course. After the first two hours, every thirty minutes after that," he jabbed a

finger at the sign, "we take away a course of your dinner for tonight. So, if I were you, maybe find a clue before you lose it all."

Jordan stepped forward, snatched the tan envelope off the rope pile, and tore it open. Lane studied her face as she silently read the letter she'd pulled out. Her countenance swiftly contorted from sorrow to rage. The wild redhead girl discarded the envelope and marched up to Brad, fists cocked and ready to fly.

"You think what happened was funny? You think it's fair use for your stupid obstacle course? The fuck is wrong with you?" Jordan threw her first punch as unbridled hatred dripped off her every word and landed at Brad's feet.

Vegas was unmoved.

It wasn't until Jordan threw the second punch that Brad finally bothered to casually evade the assault. She hit nothing but air and Vegas kept smiling. "I don't know what you're talking about. That's a riddle. There's your team. You wanna lead 'em? Feed 'em? Keep 'em all happy? Then start leading and stop making other people responsible for your emotions."

Jordan threw a final punch.

It didn't land.

She gathered her breath, still staring Brad down, but the buzz-cut-blond stood out of reach without a care in the world. As the tension continued to rise, Brad simply held up his stopwatch and subtly swung it back and forth.

"Grab the rope," Jordan hollered. She spun around to address the stunned counselors. More forcefully than her first command, Jordan repeated, "Everyone grab hold of the rope, follow me up to the High..." She bit back a lump in her throat, "We're going to the Low Ropes course. Move out!"

Trying to get any number of twenty-something-year-olds to do anything in a coordinated fashion was no easy task. Having all fourteen sleep-deprived counselors march single file uphill in an eighty-degree dry heat before noon proved to be a monumental chore. They groaned. They muttered their dissent. Jordan, at the head of the line, ignored all of it. At least, it appeared that way. Whatever Brad had done to trigger her into such furor, motivated Jordan to single-handedly pull the thirteen counselors forward at a breakneck pace.

"So, like, what else have you two seen?" Nina asked Luna. For the last half hour, she'd been pelting Luna with questions about the twins' past adventures. Lane's sister was more than happy to recite their many tales with the same flair and enthusiasm as if she'd recalled and performed the memories for the first time. This, of course, was all old hat: a well-rehearsed but not wholly unwelcome show and dance.

"I mean, it'd be quicker to tell you what we haven't encountered," Luna claimed with a smirk. "Aliens... Don't think we've had aliens on the list, yet. Lane thinks he saw a Kraken—"

"I was wrong, okay? It was a giant squid. I *wanted* to see a Kraken. My apologies for the millionth time," Lane corrected sheepishly as he marched onward after Aiden. "If you don't mind, Nina, can I ask about what you may have seen last night?"

Nina drew in a sharp breath. "Oh, I'd almost forgotten."

Lane saw the girl visibly shrink within her own memory. Fear washed over her face as if someone had doused her with a bucket of ice water.

She replied softly, secretly, "I don't know what time it was. I remember the sound. It was sharp, deliberate, almost like..." Nina bit her lower lip, concentrating, "Like tap shoes?"

Luna raised an eyebrow. "Tap shoes? Like a *click-clack* type of sound?"

Nina nodded.

Lane ran through the likely animals that could have produced a similar sound that would be naturally occurring in the area. Cloven hooves on wood planks would've been a close contender to tap shoes on wood. Goat, small hog, or perhaps a deer? The latter seemed most likely, but how often do wild deer wander so close to populated areas, especially with the choir of moans from the spa this morning?

"Aiden," Lane asked, "There's plenty of wild deer up here, right? Did you see anything when you woke up?"

The larger young man hefted the thick rope higher up on his other shoulder. "I suppose a deer would have made more sense. Plenty of 'em up this far into the mountains. Except, Nina, you thought it had been *inside* the cabin, right?"

Nina shook her head. "I mean, I thought I saw something. Definitely heard something. I don't know. Maybe I just imagined it?"

Luna caressed the smaller girl's shoulder. "Hey, it's okay to keep an open mind, but until definitively proven, don't doubt your intuition."

With a bit more of a smile, Nina nodded. "Honestly, I've had some issues listening to my intuition before, ya know? Been burned before."

"We've all doubted that voice inside ourselves sometimes," Apollena assured her, "But remember when you did listen? You found the truth about yourself and became the woman you are today because of it. Right?"

Nina gasped and nearly teared up. Without another word, the pixie girl wrapped her arms around Apollena. Luna returned the embrace and added a sisterly kiss on the cheek.

Brad, not beholden to the rope line, ruined another moment of kindness. "Providence, I'm getting tired of reprimanding you for disruptive behavior. Keep marching."

From the front of the line, Jordan hollered back, "Lay off her, Vegas! I'm leading. You're supervising. If you keep disrupting my team, I'll come back there and kick your ass myself."

Vegas chuckled, "I mean, you do need a bit more practice, but be my guest."

Before he could walk on, Luna had stepped out of line and grabbed Brad by the waistband of his shorts to whisper. "And if you're intent on picking on my girl here, I'll do something more invasive than simply *kick* your ass. Understood?"

Brad swallowed hard and nodded. In a whisper, he replied, "Yes, mistress."

Luna gave the taller jock a loud slap on the ass. "Good boy."

A few more minutes of trudging up the hill, and they arrived at the Low Ropes Course. Jordan shoved off their group tether from her shoulders and turned to face the other counselors.

Cole dropped to his knees and nearly collapsed on his side. "Great, we've finally made it. How about our leader of the day clue us all in on what we're supposed to be doing here?"

Korri knelt down beside Cole, wrapping her fingers around the side of his neck until the tips of her nails scratched his stubble. With her tongue sliding down the side of his ear, she asked, "What did we agree on when it came to using our tongues?" Cole gulped and shot Korri an apologetic look. "That's better."

Jordan looked visibly distraught as she barked out her orders. "We're looking for another clue: an envelope, tan, about the same size as the first. Fan out. Search the trees or the supports... The clock is ticking. Get moving!"

Lane started at the edges. In a clearing roughly the size of two full basketball courts parallel to one another, there were a handful of rope and wood plank obstacles: balance beams, rope ladders, and a few variants of the uneven bars. The other counselors listlessly wandered through the various obstacles. Brad remained on the trailhead, not particularly paying any attention to the group. He glanced down at his watch, smirked, and gazed off into the forest. Either he'd suddenly established a killer poker face, or the team wasn't actually going to find anything at this location.

"Aiden," Lane called out to the linebacker. The tank of a man jogged to Lane from one of the steel poles that held up the wire rigging of a nearby obstacle.

Sweat dripped from Aiden's forehead as he panted for breath. "You find somethin'?"

"Could you offer a bit more context to why Jordan might wanna murder Brad?" Lane asked as he kept his attention on a nearly manic Jordan. "Specifically today, I mean."

"Yeah, this whole thing is a low blow to those in the know," Aiden admitted. "I don't know what was written on the clue exactly, but bringing up the *former* high ropes? I mean, this particular place is a sore subject with Jordan, to say the least."

"What happened?" Luna asked softly.

Swallowing hard, Aiden whispered, "Her second year up here, Jordan was monitoring the high ropes course. She'd looked away for a second when some dumb kid unhooked himself, tryin' to be a daredevil. He slipped. Fell. Ended up in a coma for a month or so."

Nina gasped and shook her head, "Oh my God. I remember that summer. She came home early. Jordan didn't tell me the whole story, only that there had been an accident."

"The guilt she must carry," Luna spoke in a whisper, "For someone to exploit that…"

Lane saw the look in his sister's eyes, those sea-foam green embers smoldered. She'd started to march on the warpath to Brad when Lane intervened. "Wait," he whispered, grabbing hold of her shoulder, "We don't wanna play that ace just yet."

Luna shook off Lane's hand but stood her ground, "I'm not going to play an ace; I'm going to punch that boy in his tiny dick is what I'm going to do. Enculé!" cursing in French, she attempted to shake out of Lane's hold.

Lane continued to hold Luna's gaze. "Or, we could go talk to Jordan and help her beat Brad at his own game?"

Calming some, Luna relented and took a breath. "I'm still going to punch him in the dick later tonight."

"Fine, but for now, let's try to ease someone's suffering rather than create more pain. Nespa?" Lane encouraged, tempering his sister's rage.

"*Agreed. Then* we band together to exact our revenge and serve justice for the people. All for one, and one for all," Nina spoke in near textbook French.

Luna replied, her mood making a full one hundred and eighty degree turn on the spot. Roughly translated, she said, *"Nina, darling, that was magnificent! Did you take French in high school, college? You made the correct choice in languages to learn, my dear."*

The Pixie girl blushed, "I've actually settled on majoring in foreign language and literature at PDX, finally."

Lane tried to interject when a natural lull in the conversation between Nina and Luna presented itself. But the speed and frequency at which the two girls discussed French was nearly imperceptible. The team was on the clock. By the look of his body language, Brad was content to have everyone search aimlessly to run that timer out. Jordan continued to frantically inspect the course. Lane would have to brave it alone. He gathered his strength and marched purposefully over to his first crush. With every step Lane took, however, it felt as if he moved closer toward his adolescence and further away from the man he'd grown into.

So much for hefting away that anchor of past experiences.

By the time Lane reached Jordan, his voice nearly cracked, "Um, Jordan, what was on the note? The first clue, I mean. May I see it?"

Jordan didn't bother addressing Lane directly. "Pretty sure I said to stay the hell away from me." She kept moving to nowhere in particular.

"Look, whatever Brad wrote was a dick move," No response from Jordan, "But, I think it's a misdirect. He's intentionally messing with you in order to—"

Jordan spun around and took an aggressive step toward Lane, "Oh, you think so, detective? You think the hyper masculine little boy Jude put in charge this year is messing with the more qualified woman? Wow. What do they call you back home, Dr. House? Fuckin' Batman? Why don't you be more useful: find a clue that actually applies to what we're all doing and stay out of my way."

"Let me see the first clue then," Lane said—more forcefully than he'd like.

Jordan scoffed, reached into her pocket, and threw the crumpled piece of paper back at him. "Be my guest, Detective." With another snort of discontentment, she marched over to inspect the next obstacle course.

Lane watched the woman who radiated rage and beauty wander closer toward the edge of the clearing. She nearly stepped into the woods and out of sight. Lane wished he hadn't frozen up earlier that morning in the bathhouse. Jordan's flawless body had been within arm's reach. He'd dreamed of seeing her again, the impossibility of meeting the first woman he'd fallen for. Now, it all seemed like those dreams had soured, darkened, and disintegrated back into the earth like rotted fruit.

Apollena's voice broke through the gloom that had settled over Lane.

In her French lilt, she asked, "Lane, won't you share with the rest of the group what you've discovered?"

"Notes will arise when you fill up what's inside, standing tall in what once reflected sky, across from where The Son died."

"I can see why she ignored the first stanza and fixated on the last part," Nina admitted, combing a nervous hand through her pixie cut.

"Wait a minute," Aiden spoke up, taking hold of the note, *"...Where The Son died?'* That kid didn't actually die. He may have slipped into a coma, but he survived. Brad is being uncharacteristically cruel if he's trying to gaslight Jordan into thinking she killed someone."

Luna mulled over the first stanza miming an invisible violin, *"Notes will arise...'* We are looking for some kind of cylinder, free-standing. Once reflected sky alludes to a lake, or what used to be a lake...? Aren't there a few dried-up lakes or ponds on the campus?"

Aiden nodded, "Three: Potter's Field, Red Marsh, and Xwa'ni Pond." He balled up his fist and further recollected. "They're all in opposite directions, too. It'd take at least an hour at our collective pace to check 'em all."

Lane considered the capitalization over 'The' and 'Son' and snapped his fingers, "It's a little on the nose, but do any of those ponds have a church or any kind of Christian iconography nearby?"

Aiden clapped his hands together and smiled. "Potter's Field! The old chapel sits on the furthest end. What a sneaky bastard."

Lane clasped a hand on his friend's back. "Nicely done, Aiden." He dashed back to the discarded rope and swung it over his shoulders. He gave a sharp whistle. "Everyone, we're moving on." The other counselors turned, but none seemed particularly eager to follow Lane. Thinking quickly, he added, "Jordan figured out the next clue. We're going to Potter's Field."

Luna, Aiden, and Nina had already grabbed hold of the rope. Still, the other counselors were weary to side with the outcasts over one of their own.

Jordan sprinted back from inspecting the far end of the course and now stood nose to nose with Lane. "I'm giving you one last warning, Woods: don't you fucking test me—"

"Hey," Lane interrupted, raising his hands in defence, "When I'm wrong, I'm wrong. I'm not afraid to admit it. You were right. The next clue, '*Once reflected sky.*' A dried-up lake across from the old chapel? I would have never guessed. I apologize."

Jordan studied Lane carefully, mulling over the words. He could see Jordan working out the riddle in her mind and deciding if she was gonna let a fist fly, regardless. A fresh perspective wasn't an easy arrow to find its mark in the midst of guilt and anger. It was a gamble, but Lane didn't have any social chips to bet with, and sometimes bluffing with a handful of nothing was a cool hand to play.

"You heard him," Jordan boomed. "Everyone grab hold. We're moving on."

The counselors hadn't seen the first clue. They'd never know Jordan had got it wrong. For all they knew, she'd been the first to find clue number two, and they all had to march along to find clue number three.

Jordan would save face, remain in command, and they might solve this ridiculous team-building challenge before their time expired.

Lane wasn't expecting any gratitude, but maybe this was at least a foot in the door to speak with Jordan again.

While the standoff with the veteran counselors continued, Bozeman silently wandered up to the rope and grabbed hold. He took a pack of cigarettes out of pocket, withdrew a single smoke, pressed it between his lips and grabbed hold of the rope. Once he'd hefted it over his shoulder, those mirrored shades looked up and patiently waited for the others. Eventually, the counselors lazily resigned and joined in. Together, Jordan led them all on the long trek down toward the opposite end of the campus.

After a quarter-mile of silence and rising tension hiking downhill, Nina asked the other question that had been itching at the back of Lane's mind: "So, what exactly do you think is going on here? With the other counselors, I mean? Ghosts? Some kind of creature?"

Luna tossed the question gently back at Nina. "What do you think is going on with all the counselors? You know them better than we do."

Nina thought for a moment. "I don't really know. Have you two ever experienced something to make a group of people suddenly want to break out into an orgy in the middle of the night? Or get super, *super* horny?"

"There's one thing I've learned from my adopted father," Luna rolled back her shoulders and deepened her voice. "'Data, data, data.' Always collect as much data before constructing a hypothesis. Unfortunately, you two were supposed to be our control group compared to the folks in the bathhouse. I guess we'll have to experiment a little more," she added with a wink.

Aiden lowered his head. "That was my fault. If I hadn't freaked out..."

Nina gently stroked Aiden's back. "Hey, you're forgiven. Don't need to keep flogging yourself about it. Okay? Let's keep going forward."

Aiden smiled and turned to the pixie. He took her free hand in his.

Lane replayed the scene of the counselors engaged in explicit acts: moaning, thrusting, roughly groping one another... It didn't feel like something natural. There wasn't any love. It was like a sport, or a ritual. How you'd imagine a computer explaining sex: all of the actions imaginable without any genuine emotion behind it. He tried to push past the theater of it all and come up with some variable he could test, or some unforeseen element he may have missed.

"Are you all talking about the bathhouse?" asked Julia quietly, fearfully.

Apollena nodded, "Indeed we are. Didn't see you in there. Were you still in your bunk?"

Julia shook her head, "No. Not exactly."

Lane moved down the line a little closer toward Luna and Julia, holding up the rear. Julia was bright red, and not from the sweltering summer heat. In a gentle voice, he asked, "Where were you exactly when the others were, um, otherwise engaged?"

Julia swallowed hard. "I was there, in one of the shower stalls, with Franki. I didn't want to…" she started to choke on her words, "I'm sorry, it's just, she asked me not to say anything. But, I'm scared. Scared I won't be able to control myself again." Visibly shaking now, she coughed out through tears, straining to hold a whisper, "I have to know why this is happening to me. If my parents find out what I've done, they'll disown me. Or, maybe worse?"

Lane, Luna, Nina, and Aiden, shared mortified looks.

"Please," Julia begged, "I need to understand why I did it. Why did I surrender to sin?"

13

Jesus, Etc.

Julia kept her head down. She walked the path directly in front of her with the heavy rope across her shoulder, too terrified to look up at Aiden, Nina, Luna, and Lane. Her shaking hands gripped the rope tighter as the counselors were all pulled forward across the slopped football field toward the clay pit that was Potter's Lake.

"I'd just gotten out of the shower when I heard them all enter," Julia started in a strained whisper. "I don't know why I got scared. Embarrassed? Whatever," The invisible burden on Julia's shoulders seemed to have doubled in weight, "I just reacted. I hid."

Nina tried to comfort her fellow counselor, "I understand not wanting to be around crowds, especially when changing—"

"No," Julia interjected quietly, "I mean, sure, I'm not used to communal bathing. I was afraid they could tell that I'd just..." She subconsciously glanced down at the space between her legs. She bit her lower lip almost hard enough to draw blood.

"Masturbated," Luna spoke delicately.

Julia nodded.

"I wouldn't have been able to tell," Aiden offered. The rest of the group immediately shot looks to silence the well-intentioned boy. "I mean, it wouldn't have occurred to me that girls even did that. At least, not as much as guys. You know what?" The others had the tact not to audibly groan at a poor man just trying his best. "I'm gonna go ahead and see myself out of this conversation—sorry for interrupting."

Lane tried to steer the conversation back on track. "Our apologies, please, continue. What happened next from your perspective?"

Julia swallowed and nodded quickly. "I hid, ducked into the closest place before anyone could see me. I hadn't realized the shower stall I'd walked into was already occupied." Shifting nervously. "I'd never really seen another girl naked before. Like, I've changed at the gym before, but this was different. It felt like, for the first time, I actually *saw* her."

It did not go unnoticed by both Lane and Luna that Julia's cheeks were glowing red hot.

Lane looked up the line of counselors at Franki a few paces behind Jordan. Athletic, shaved head, a loose tank top covering a tall, muscular frame. She was certainly beautiful to look at. It would be an entirely different thing to actually see someone as Julia had. Not merely physical beauty, but the type of connection that two souls make when bonded for the first time.

To clarify, Lane asked Julia, "You saw her differently?"

"I don't know if I can…" Julia stammered. "I shouldn't."

Appollena took the short blonde's hand in hers. "It's okay. We're here to help, not judge."

Reassured, but still mortified, Julia's free hand reached across her chest defensively as if to cover up with an invisible blanket, "She was... breathtaking." She waited for the others, but no one interjected. "She must have just finished showering. The way droplets slowly rolled off her shoulders, cascaded off her caramel skin, her hands, her lips: my mouth watered. She has eyes like pools of honey. I kept wanting to dive in closer. She was right there, naked, staring back at me, unblinking. Each step I took toward her, my heart pounded faster and faster." Julia shuttered. Her eyes were closed. She had fully sunken back into that sweet memory. "Then I reached out, my fingertips caught a stray bead of sweat that rolled off her cheek. My hand touched her cheek. Then I—I kept touching. I wanted to feel every square inch of her. How could I not?" Julia laughed a tiny, desperate laugh. "She didn't stop me either. She opened her arms up wider and invited me in. My heart was going to explode out of my chest."

"I couldn't stand it, like electricity that kept flowing through my arms, and legs, and..." Julia shuddered again at the memory. A bolt of pleasure shot through her like lightning. She tried to hide her smile as she adjusted her swim shorts. "I couldn't stand. I-I fell to my knees in front of this beautiful woman. The cold tile. The steam from the sauna. The open invitation from Francine, as she spread her legs open wider, and gripped my hair tighter. She drew me up toward h-her..." Julia stammered. Luna noticed the girl's free hand wandered dangerously down south under the waistband of her swim shorts.

Apollena pointed between her own legs and mouthed, '*Pussy?*'

Julia coughed, "Her... Yeah. She let me... I wanted... Oh, God." Shame slapped Julia's hand away from her crotch. She kept her eyes closed and continued in a different voice; the voice of embarrassment and repression. It was a voice someone else had taught her to use when discussing something so raw and beautiful. "I was told that I shouldn't have those feelings. It's not natural. It's wrong. *I* was wrong."

Lane caught Nina chomping at the bit to say something in protest, but Aiden encouraged her restraint with a gentle brush of his hand over the pixie's shoulder.

Suddenly, something visibly came over Julia. That conditioned repression suddenly melted away, and the girl almost burst out loud, "But I tasted her! And, and s-she tasted better than anything I'd ever had before." Catching herself, Julia opened her eyes. She wiped her mouth, salivating at the memory. "If I could only taste one thing ever again, it would be to savor Franki's pussy. And I know I shouldn't, but… I felt something. I don't… I don't want to forget what I felt and at the same time…" Julia swallowed a torrent of tears.

Luna draped her arm around Julia, fighting with everything that had been drilled into her and the experience she'd genuinely enjoyed. It was an uphill battle. Repression and guilt were heavily fortified in Julia's brain, but cracks had begun to develop. Luna was adamant that sororal love would endure. "Julia, what you felt was *not* wrong or right: it is simply real. I understand you're feeling everything all at once right now. Maybe that's too much? Clear your mind and ask yourself two things. First, can you change what happened?"

Julia sniffed and rubbed her red eyes with her free hand. "No? No, I can't change what happened." She gleaned up at the others for confirmation. Julia was confused by the genuine smiles returned to her.

Luna nodded, "No. You can't change what happened. The next question is harder: would you want to, if you could?"

Aiden and Nina exchanged knowing glances, layered with the same amount of confusion, fear, and excitement Julia was wading through in this present moment.

Lane rubbed his temple with his forefinger counterclockwise, rewinding the tape in his mind. A particular detail had caught his attention. "Julia, you were in a shower stall, one that was against the left wall, correct?"

Taken aback, the conflicted blonde cleared her throat. "Um, yeah. I think so. Why?"

"Did you happen to notice whether the thin window along the wall was open or closed? Even just a crack? Or was it closed?" Lane asked while replaying the memory of his own encounter in the shower. After Alice had slapped him, she'd sprinted not toward the main door, but toward one of the shower stalls. Each had a thin, frosted window above their respected stall. Each window was just large enough for someone to slip out of. Or thin enough for someone to slip inside. Perhaps something to enter the sauna while unsuspecting persons were otherwise distracted?

Julia shook herself free from the memory of her and Franki. "I-I'm sorry. I don't remember. Why?"

"Alright, drop the rope," Jordan shouted from the head of the line. The counselors had finally reached the jogging path that circled Potter's Field.

They didn't bother circling the cracked asphalt path. Collectively, the fourteen counselors marched through the dried-up, red clay lakebed toward the abandoned chapel at the furthest end. Between the group and the rundown church, a copper pipe had been planted in the ground and stood about two and a half meters in height.

"Topeka," Jordan commanded, pointing at the copper pipe.

With a snort, the young man broke into a modest jog and launched himself at the pipe. It must have been buried deep to withstand Brandon's full strength slammed against it. A few others joined in, trying to knock down the pole. Even with Aiden's combined strength, the pole remained upright.

"Must remind you of something from last night, eh, Topeka?" Gracie chortled.

With a forced laugh, Brandon pointed back at Gracie. "I wasn't the only one getting skewered last night, Athens." Then Lane caught Brandon shake his head—almost like a misremembered thought had suddenly jumped in front of the screen he was viewing.

"Yeah, but I think mine had a bit more skill behind it," the curly blonde countered with a cackle, and then an abrupt pause. As if forcing herself through a momentary lapse in confusion, she added, "Maybe if you rocked your hips a bit harder, you could bring this pipe down?"

"How about you wrap your fat lips around it and swallow?" Topeka shouted.

Jordan interrupted, "Enough!" The crowd simmered some, but

tensions were still on a razor's edge. "Topeka, climb up and see if the next clue is inside."

With sufficient dexterity, the former debate champion scaled the pipe. He peered inside, adjusting his head to see into the pipe without blocking the sunlight. "I see something at the bottom. Something metal, shiny... It's a lot farther down."

Lane cycled through his most recent mental photographs and recalled the page Jordan threw at him.

"Notes will arise if you fill up what's inside."

Lane then took in the puzzle in its entirety. As was custom, he started at the edges of the problem. Here they were in the middle of a dried-up lake bed. If the pole was eight feet high, it must be just as deep, if not more so, in the ground to withstand the collective force of the counselors trying to push it down. Some of the disturbed clay revealed that a layer of concrete bolstered the poll within the lakebed. Most likely, a concrete foundation was buried at the base too. Lane stepped back to get an even broader perspective when he heard something crunch beneath his feet.

Under his boot was a red solo cup. In fact, there were dozens of red solo cups littered about the copper pole. They hadn't been there when he and his sister ran around the lake yesterday.

"Somebody, everybody, give me your belts, shoelaces, or whatever; I can try to fish it out from the bottom," Brandon shouted.

Cole unbuckled his belt while Korri yelled at him, "We're not handing over our shit if you're just gonna drop it down that hole and lose it all!"

"I won't lose it, just hand it over," Brandon protested.

"The circumference is too small anyway," Korri pointed out, "You can't even fit your hand inside. How do you expect to maneuver a hook or…" She continued to argue her point while the others argued among themselves.

"Wouldn't be the first tight hole I've forced my way inside of,"

Brandon shot back with a cocky smile. A collective groan rose up from the crowd.

"Apollena," Julia asked softly, "What's your brother doing?"

Luna kept her eyes on Lane as he knelt down to pick up one of the solo cups. "Oh, he's just keeping a broader perspective on things. Say, is there a water fountain nearby?"

Julia thought some, "Yeah, we could use the church's—"

Brad suddenly spoke up, having been uncomfortably close to both Luna and Julia. He shouted loud enough for the others to hear. "By the way, minor detail that slipped my mind: the water on campus has been temporarily shut off. No water fountains, showers, or toilets are available until the team-building exercise is concluded. Sorry for the inconvenience."

Most of the other counselors were either arguing with Jordan, Brandon, or didn't bother to pay attention at all to Brad's seemingly unrelated announcement.

"That's kind of an extreme measure to take for a team building exercise, wouldn't you say, Bradley?" Apollena asked pointedly.

Brad shrugged, "First, camp names only, please. Second, The LA didn't want to make things too easy for y'all. I'm sure you'll think of something."

Luna remembered Jude had given himself the name Los Angles at some point. Brad insisted on the moniker 'The LA', pronounced 'Law.' A bit pretentious, but in character.

"I see. And where is our Camp Director this mid-morning, Bradley?" Apollena replied.

Brad began to wander away, avoiding eye contact with Apollena, "He's busy. Family stuff, I reckon. Back at his cabin. Maybe you should focus more on helping your co-counselors instead of worrying about The LA?"

"Roswell," Jordan called out. She'd diverted her attention to Lane a few yards away from the group. "Everyone participates in the exercise.

No excuses. Get back here."

Lane was mentally measuring how far a chain of fourteen counselors could extend out from the copper pipe. Cupping a hand over his mouth, he shouted, "Hey, Aiden, is there any other body of water or pond about twelve meters away...?"

"Last warning, Roswell—get over here and start pulling your own weight," Jordan demanded once more.

Luna smiled, "He is helping." Striding over to Jordan, she smiled and attempted an explanation, "If we use the red plastic cups, the counselors could form a chain..."

Jordan waved in front of Luna's face, silencing her. "Guess what? You're not in charge here. I am. Take off that belt, those laces, and help the rest of us. And don't you ever run your mouth at me again, understood?"

Luna bit her lower lip and sighed through her nostrils. She turned to Brad. His back was to the group, but his shoulders looked like they were heaving up and down from laughter.

Aiden also began to wander away from the group before Jordan took notice. "Buffalo! We're not following Roswell's example."

"I found something," Aiden shouted back at Lane from a few yards in the opposite direction. He jogged from a modest-sized puddle. It didn't appear naturally occurring. Faint tire treads leading from the hole suggested some kind of heavy machinery was used. Someone must have recently dug a hole in the red clay and filled it with water.

Nina excitedly put the pieces together and attempted to enlighten the others, "If we form a human chain, we can fill the solo cups and pass them up to Brandon to fill the pipe."

Bradon remained at the top of the pole. "What's the pixie saying from down there?"

Korri scoffed, "Just being smart is all. Not a common experience for you, I'd wager."

Jordan caved. She redirected the group to form a line from the puddle to the pole. After a few minutes, they'd nearly filled it to the brim. Occasionally, Brandon or someone else would spill some of the limited resource. Lane noted that it looked less like water and more like blood. Still, enough dirty water remained to get the job done. It was an admittedly clever exercise and a decent riddle, but it definitely didn't fit Brad's sensibilities. In all likelihood, Jude developed this odd scavenger hunt and Brad was simply supervising.

If that was true, it struck Lane as peculiar that the architect of this overly elaborate puzzle wouldn't want to at least observe its progress. Where was Jude?

Along with a fist full of other questions Lane intended to ask, he wanted to understand how and why Jude had developed this "team-building" exercise. For now, Lane was content to observe his co-counselors interactions and gather data. '*Data, Data Data*,' the voice of Lane's father echoed. Even with Brad dangling the stopwatch in front of their faces, it was Alice's comment earlier that struck a deeper nerve.

"Do you even realize how little time you have left?' That's what she'd said earlier that morning. Lane loved a riddle, but he was starting to feel the pressure that his mystery needed to be solved sooner rather than later.

"I've got it!" Brandon shouted as he jabbed his fingers down into the opening at the top of the pipe. Leaping down from the pole and landing in the red clay, he held a little capsule wrapped in foil.

"Well," Jordan snorted, "Give it here."

Brandon scoffed and tossed over the capsule.

"Maybe you could read it aloud this time," Apollena suggested loud enough for the group to hear. Jordan shot Luna a dirty glare, but it didn't seem to affect her cheery disposition. "You know what they say, 'Many minds make for light work'."

"Nobody says that," Jordan grumbled, opening up the capsule. She cleared her throat and read aloud:

"Follow the arrows, join your flesh together, let fall your coupled burden and it shall reveal the path ahead."

Topeka said, "Got to admit, I'm starting to dislike your attempt at poetry here, Vegas."

The buzz-cut blond shrugged. "It's not my poetry. Think you folks will be able to finish this course in the next half-hour? Hmm? I hope so. It would be a shame to waste all that food."

"Back to the rope," Jordan commanded.

The group complied. Everyone trudged back to where they'd dropped the rope, except for Julia. Luna looked over her shoulders at the short blonde, petrified, eyes locked on the church. Striding toward the girl who had frozen, Luna gently rubbed Julia's shoulder. "Hey, you okay in there?"

Julia didn't take her eyes off the condemned chapel, or the rotted wooden cross on top. "I don't know." She glanced quickly over at Luna, then back to the church. She shivered. This time, it wasn't the electric sensation of pleasure that shot through Julia's body, but the chilling touch of dread that gripped her spine. "I don't know if I would want to take that moment back."

Luna nodded. "Perhaps that would be a conversation to have with Franki? How does she feel about what happened?"

Julia shrugged, "Don't know. Too afraid to ask," A moment of silence, then Julia turned her back on the chapel and walked toward the others. "I know what they'd say if anyone found out," she jabbed a thumb over her shoulder at the abandoned church.

Luna tugged Julia forward with the others and paced beside her. "If their opinion matters to you, I understand your anxiety." Luna gently turned Julia about-face by the shoulder. The two young women faced the old chapel once more. "But consider that place is just a building full of regular people, with the same struggles as everyone else and perhaps the person who knows your heart best is you?"

14

HANDSHAKE DRUGS

"I'm forming a hypothesis," Apollena whispered to her brother. Lane continued marching along with the others. He tapped his ear, encouraging his sister to continue her explanation. They had another quarter mile or so to hike before reaching the archery range. Just following the arrows. Following the crowd.

"This isn't really a team-building exercise," Luna suggested in a hushed tone. Something about the fearful delivery of such an obvious observation mixed with her subtle French lilt sent a shiver up Lane's spine. That, and the vivid memories of their illicit, intimate affair–

"I would agree, but only because team-building exercises rarely accomplish what they're supposed to. Namely, building a team. At best, those subjected to such an exercise can rally behind the common enemy of whoever forced them into the exercise in the first place," Lane replied in a quiet, measured tone. As the counselors approached the two-hour time limit, tensions rose sharply. The afternoon sun seared their flesh and a lone pine needle falling from the trees the wrong way could cause

the lot of them to combust at any moment.

Luna leaned in closer to Lane. "Sure. But something feels more malicious here than a silly, albeit antagonistic, game." Her breath, a mix of coffee and watermelon hard candy.

Lane took a moment to observe the line of counselors in its entirety. At the head of the line, Jordan relentlessly pulled on the rope that connected them all like a stubborn sled driver whose huskies had fallen dead in the snow. Franki refused so much as glance over her shoulder back at Julia. Brandon, or Topeka now, kept poking fun at Cole for being on Korri's short leash. Zoe and Gracie had bickered over nothing before the exercise began and continued to do so now with greater intensity. So much so that it appeared Gracie would break into tears any second.

In the middle of the rope, Alice and Boozeman each gave off a chilling, unsettling sense of calm. Occasionally, the former sent an icy glare back at Lane, along with a wicked smirk.

Luna again spoke softly into Lane's ear. He could taste her breath now; the memory of their kiss was a tonic he couldn't keep from swallowing with greedy abandon. "I think this course is designed to elicit a much more nuanced emotional response. Not comradery, but..." she trailed off, still trying to place her finger on the right word, "I'm not sure." She frowned. It was right on the tip of her tongue.

The Tiki Drum strip show and now this scavenger hunt did feel less like a game and more like a ritual to Lane. It triggered a deeper memory of the cultists from his family's mission to Thailand years ago. He remembered the girl who'd escaped the compound and shared her experience. It wasn't simply that the cult had been watching, controlling, dictating her every move prior to her exodus. The cult leaders had deliberately broken the spirits of their members. Then, once those under their director's influence had been broken down, they were molded into something else entirely. They'd been reconditioned. Remade. Their free will had been revoked from right under their noses.

Lane was familiar with the tactics, the *how*. Now he needed to figure out *why* this was being done to college students in Washington State at a youth camp. He needed to solve this puzzle *and fast* before they shared a similar fate of those forsaken Thai children.

Brandon laughed, "That's it? This is your big challenge, Vegas?"

"This is your second challenge, yeah. It's only slightly less thick and hefty than what you had in your mouth last night," Brad chuckled, "So, I guess you *could* call it big? Sure."

Lane looked about the group to see if anybody picked up on Brad's admission that they'd only completed one challenge, not two. Fortunately, the only one who noticed was Jordan. It was unfortunate that her face gave away how she still felt about that intentional dig from Vegas. As long as the group didn't outright revolt against their current leader, for Jordan's sake, Lane hoped she'd make it through this event.

The obstacle in question was obtusely phallic. Beside the archery course, there was a mud pit about twenty-five meters in length. By the look of it, the pit at one time may have been a lap pool about four lanes wide. Now? It was filled with thick, freshly drenched with mud.

Lodged in the mud pit, sticking up at an angle were the remains of a pine tree trunk. Its bark had all been shaved off and sanded smooth. It could have been almost ten feet in circumference, more than triple that in length. The tip of the log at its peak jutted above the pool at a steep incline, a little more than a fifty-degree pitch, probably four meters or so above the mud. Fixed on the edge of the tip, a shiny metal capsule hung by a rope: the next clue.

"Jesus, it's like they got a school bus stuck in that pool of shit," Franki gasped.

Gracie pitched her hips to one side and folded her arms. "Vegas, you really expect us to climb that? There ain't no way that thing is safe, sugar."

"Too easy," Brandon chuckled. He took off like a shot toward the trunk. Without any consideration for how solid, how deep, or how thick the mud was, Brandon dropped waist-deep into the shallow end of the pool. An outburst of laughter from his peers did nothing to deter the young man from pushing forward.

Brandon slogged through a few paces of waist-high filth before reaching the log. Reaching out, his long arms could hardly grip around the entirety of the trunk. His first attempt to pull himself up and out of the mud failed, as did the next try, and the one after.

"Just imagine it's your own dick," Korri yelled out over the other's laughter, "Then you could probably grip it one-handed."

"Bitch, I don't see you trying to help any. Why don't you come in and make yourself useful?" Brandon replied. He folded his arms and stood facing the crowd, waiting for Korri to accept the challenge.

He was not disappointed.

Korri at least had the sense to take off her shoes before entering the mud trough. Carefully wading her way to Brandon, she pushed past him to the base of the fallen tree. Although slightly more graceful at wrapping herself onto the log, Korri was met with equal success. That is to say, none at all.

"Olympia," Korri beckoned Cole to her side.

The young boy obeyed.

Cole also removed his shoes, socks, and rolled up his blue jeans to his calves. He even removed his shirt, proving to everyone Olympia was clearly no slouch when it came to his namesake. The boy was an athlete. One could watch that Adonis for days as he marched through the mud under the fiery Washington State Sun. He appeared to be an unstoppable force…

Until he was met with an immovable object.

"Give me a boost up," Korri demanded. Several failed attempts resulted in nothing more than both unequal lovers sinking further into the mud pit.

Jordan's patience finally snapped, "Somebody, go fetch an axe or a saw and cut that fucking tree in half already."

"You want to split up your team AND have them transport dangerous objects across campus unsupervised?" Brad warned in a coy voice. "I don't know if that qualifies as leadership material, Wichita. But it's your call. Time is ticking."

"No," Jordan countered, "I want these adults to carve out the simplest path through your ridiculous-ass obstacle course."

"Again, Wichita, the obstacle course isn't mine. This is Jude's brainchild. His baby. However, I'll be sure to let him know your thoughts and feelings toward all the hard work he put into creating this team-building experience for you."

Lane could clearly see Jordan was fuming, but remained at a loss for leverage over her opponent. Brad had the upper hand in knowing the solution to this particular puzzle. He stood in Jude's good graces despite lacking several years' worth of experience. She could insult him again, but it wouldn't gain her any significant satisfaction. She would have to beat Brad at his own game and prove herself to Jude that she could lead. After all, that's what this whole thing was supposed to be about. If only they could see the bigger picture.

In reality, it was all a punishing, relentless test. Jordan hated every second of it.

Lane had also been tested before. During his Coast Guard Training days, he met up with a team of prospective SEAL cadets to complete a Tough Mudder, Five Kilometer Run. The obstacle course was grueling, painful at times, but a hell of a lot more fun than this increasingly sadistic challenge. One thing the two courses had in common, however, was the 'Texas Hold 'em Challenge'. Admittedly, this current version appeared significantly more difficult. Hopefully, the principle behind its solution remained the same.

Taking Luna's hands in his, Lane asked, "You wanna go get that next clue?"

With a smile, and a thick French accent Luna replied, "*Oui*. Bird's fly, fish swim, and we solve puzzles, Ursa Major."

As the twins approached the edge of the mud pool and stripped out of their shirts, shoes, and socks, Jordan released an exaggerated sigh. "Does anyone ELSE want to make an attempt to get that stupid capsule?"

None volunteered.

Together, Lane and Apollena entered the mud. He was fortunate to have chosen a pair of boxer briefs under his jeans. Luna had also worn a pair of cotton boy shorts and a sports bra. Even dressed down to their skivvies, the mud in the shallow end was absurdly thick and uncomfortably warm to maneuver in as the noon sun continued to pound down on them. As The Twins approached, Brandon, Korri, and Cole all waded out of the way and silently climbed out of the pit.

"On your mark," Apollena offered to Lane as they approached the base of the log.

"Ready? Set. And left legs, up," Lane instructed. As they faced one another, The Twins held each other's hands crossed in front of them like a pair of 'Xs', one under the other. With equal tension pulling against each other, neither slipped backward nor forward. They counted off, matching their steps, slow and deliberate. They steadily scaled the inclined log even with every element working against them: friction, gravity, and the tyrannical sun. "How are you holding up? You alright?" Lane grunted.

"I think they've added a coat of wax or oil to the log. It's a bit more slippery than I'd imagined, even with the mud," Luna admitted. With a strained smile, she encouraged her brother. "We're nearly there, though. We'll make it."

Another four steps up.

Then two.

Lane and Apollena reached the edge of the bus-sized log.

"We're right on top of it, but," Lane hesitated, "I don't see how it's connected. Do you feel a string or a wire?" He tried to stretch his toes out through the mud on top of the tree.

"Yes," Luna replied, "Just there, under my big toe. You think we can squat down?"

Lane tried to suppress his nervous laughter. "Sure. Piece of cake. Ready? Set. Dip!"

Synchronized to near perfection, the twins bent their knees and squatted down closer to the log without letting one another fall. Luna managed to unclasp her left hand to feel around the piece of twine holding the capsule that dangled off the tip of the trunk. She tugged the string along and brought the metal bobble around to the top side of the log.

"I can't pull it off," Luna grunted. "You wanna give it a try?"

Lane waited for Luna to reconnect her hand to his. He used his right hand to apply enough force without losing balance. "It's no good. It's tied on too tight."

"How much tensile strength does twine have, you figure?" Luna asked.

Lane caught up to her thoughts, "I can't imagine it could hold more than eighty kilograms, maybe?"

"Let's call it an even one-fifteen, eh?" Luna smiled. "On three then."

They counted down...three... two...and…

With one swift moment, The Twins released one set of hands and grabbed hold of the twine string. In the same breath, they let their legs slip out from under them. They broke the hold on their other hands, then gravity swung the pair down to the underside of the pine log, where they slammed into each other. Luna wrapped her legs around her brother's waist. After the collision and sudden jerk against the twine—
SNAP!

The twins dropped six meters down, feet first, into the mud.

It almost felt like dropping into hot, wet cement. Lane was thankful his legs didn't shatter. They hadn't noticed the one hose that had been fed into the deep end of the pool. They must have added water to the deep end the night before. With the mud decently liquefied, Lane and

Luna had plunged in about shoulder deep without critical injury. Of lesser importance, they'd captured the metal capsule.

After some effort, Lane and Luna crawled their way out of the pool. They were caked thick in mud that had already started to harden.

"Any chance we could get hosed off before we go on?" Apollena asked the group.

Brad looked troubled. Lane studied the counselors' face as it reddened in anger. "Told you before, water's been shut off campus wide. If you wanna wait for us to turn it back on, that's fine by me. You've already passed the two-hour mark. You wanna waste more time? That's up to you and your teammates."

Jordan shouted over the others, arguing among themselves, "We're not wasting anymore time. Grab the rope and let's get going!"

Lane stepped up to Jordan as she hefted the rope back up. "Did you wanna do the honors of reading the clue aloud for everyone?"

She snatched the capsule from Lane's open palm and opened the cap:

"Your path is spelled out for you in black and white
Two across / Five down
Seek the shadow board beside CL-37"

"It's chlorine," Julia blurted out before immediately covering her mouth with both hands.

"The chemical shed by the pool?" Aiden suggested tentatively.

Jordan looked from the large young man to Julia and huffed out, "Fine. To the pool."

15

OUTTA SIGHT

Apollena was unimpressed with the lack of challenge they encountered next. It certainly didn't live up to the first or second trial. Having marched to the small dive pool across from the girl's dormitory in record time, the team of counselors' physical strength had nearly left them. Most were beyond exhausted, sunburnt, and sore. A bevy of curses floated up through the air as nearly all collapsed on the burnt patch of grass beside the pool. Despite the strenuous activity they'd previously endured, Luna's irritation began to grow toward the thin coat of mud still stuck to her skin around her joints. If her heart hadn't broken for Julia, maybe a few pieces of dried mud could have been overlooked? Sadly, it wasn't.

"Seriously, a crossword puzzle?" Nina grumbled under her breath, leaning into Aiden's chest for support.

Hastily drawn upon the wall of a sunburnt handball court beside the pool was a chalk grid and a number of clues. In contrast to the majority of counselors who'd mentally checked out hours ago, Julia's

dark blue eyes lit up. Despite her stamina nearly being beaten out of her, she smiled. "Finally, something I've got a chance of solving."

Truth be told, the word puzzles proved to be far less than challenging. Just as Lane had suspected. Based on Brad's reaction, there was little to no expectation that any of the team would successfully complete the Texas-Hold-'em Challenge. Luna's hypothesis about this team-building exercise meant to divide the counselors rather than bring them together was gaining more validation with every passing minute.

Jordan's outright hostility toward Brad grew.

Gracie and Zoe nearly came to blows over nonsense.

Even Korri's ever-tightening grip on Cole's autonomy presented a visible scrounge of animosity among the counselors.

None of these expanding microaggressions were more apparent than Brandon being isolated intentionally and not so subtly humiliated by Brad. Such thinly veiled harassment was especially grating on Lane's sense of honor and sportsmanship. He didn't fully understand their relationship, if any had even existed previously between the two boys. Regardless, this challenge was presented as a competition of strength and mind. For a referee to degrade a competitor during a challenge was poor form. No, unacceptable. Lane should have followed Luna's example hours ago and kicked Brad right in his smug dick.

Instead, Lane restrained himself. He remembered the words of his mother: "Action without knowledge or wisdom yields disastrous results."

Something larger was at play, something sinister. Lane just couldn't see it yet. He was too close to the action. He needed to collect more information, analyze the data, and view the whole picture. That couldn't be done when they were wasting time with these petty challenges.

"I got it!" Julia exclaimed. Her excitement was met by a weak, hollow cheer from half of the counselors still catching their breath, lying on the ground.

Nina, however, appeared genuinely impressed, offering an

enthusiastic hug. "That hardly took you any time at all! You must get a lot of practice in?"

Julia nodded, "Every Week, New York Times crossword. It's honestly, really fun—"

"There you go again, being the show-off," Cole huffed. "Big brainy little sister, flapping her gums. We're all impressed. Thanks."

Julia shrank a bit, apologetically shifting into a defensive posture. Lane took note that Korri did not pull on Cole's leash this time. She either wanted to remain outside of family squabbles or like the other counselors, acted on a compulsion to allow hostility to grow. Apollena, however, had no intention of letting any more seeds of discord plant themselves within Julia. She'd had enough.

Strolling around to the backside of Korri, a mud-covered Luna dragged her index finger down Korri's back. "Your dog is barking at my friend. Do I speak to him about that, or should I have words with his owner?"

Both Cole's and Korri's mouth dropped open.

Korri was the first to bark back. "You're in no position and of no importance to say anything to anyone. How about you take the exotic temptress act of yours and—" Halting midway through her clap back, Korri *yelped*.

Clutched tightly in Luna's fist was the tail end of Korri's thong. With a twist of her wrist, Apollena pulled the thin pink fabric farther up from the waistline of Korri's black bike shorts.

"Oui, it seems the best results come from holding the leash of the owner, not the pet." Luna leaned in closer to Korri with a sweet sing-song voice, "Hey, creature, leave my friend alone." Korri nodded fervently and Luna released her grip.

None of the other counselors seemed to care or even notice.

Jordan tried to rally the others back to their heavy rope. "Alright, ladies, break time is over! Let's get this rope up to the fire pits and be done with this stupid thing." In spite of the oppressive sun and psychological warfare, Jordan's stamina was impressive. Lane admired her ability to endure this sadistic game. He did regret not being able to offer any further support or comfort. Then again, would his help be more harmful than helpful? The crack in his confidence continued to grow as this horrible game dragged on into the afternoon.

"Just a second," Brad interjected, "Can't leave to the Fire Pits just yet. Aren't you forgetting something before you go?"

Gracie sat up from the grass. "Some of us are already long gone, sugar."

"Ignore him," Jordan instructed. "Grab the rope and let's go."

Julia cringed, "No, Vegas is right. We're not meant to go up empty-handed. Look at the board." Dragging a finger along with the other white squares she'd filled in, Julia read aloud, "Deliver / Railroad / Planks / Stand / Upright / Fire and Circle."

Brandon shook his head, "So along with this fat ass rope, you want us to haul those long-ass logs through the woods too?"

"That's what the board says," Vegas answered unceremoniously. He pointed to a stack of four railroad ties piled neatly behind the giant crossword puzzle. "Can't start a fire without the proper kindling," Brad added dryly. He folded his thick arms, glanced down at the stopwatch that dangled around his neck, and yawned.

Franki turned to Jordan, "Come on, there are four planks and thirteen of us, plenty of shoulders to share the burden. We can do this!"

"Thanks, Franki, I can count. On your feet. Everyone lifts, nobody quits. If you're slacking off, I'll kill you myself.

Hiking a mile and a half while a body is running on fumes is tough. Any cross-country trek after midday, during the hottest month of the year, is grueling. For thirteen twenty-something-year-olds, all at their wits end marching single file up steep switchbacks with two-hundred-pound railroad ties on their shoulders felt inhumane. If this was the straw meant to break the camels' back, there would be thirteen dead camels by the time they all reached the plateau. More so than being done in by heatstroke, bruises, and the little thorn bushes along the narrow trail biting at their ankles and knees, there would be resentment instilled in the counselors that would last for years to come. Lane knew in the pit of his heart, all this served a darker purpose.

Fortunately, the haggard group managed to crest the hill.

"Greetings, mighty warriors of Trillion Pines!" Jude yelled out. His excited cry echoed through the dense and lonely pine forest. He sprang up from his folding chair beside the fire pit and set his drink down on the cupholder armrest. "Vegas, what's the time these fine troops have clocked in so far?"

After carefully lowering the railroad ties to the ground and shoving off the rope, a collective death rattle sprang up from the counselors. Nina threw up in the bushes. Aiden rushed to her side and held the girl's hair back, even if it wasn't long enough to warrant such a gesture.

"Oh, they're still on the clock," Vegas spoke matter-of-factly, gazing at his stopwatch.

"Bullshit," Jordan managed to breathe out through chapped lips.

"No, Brad's right. Y'all got one final piece of the puzzle to solve here before we cross the finish line," Jude agreed. "I'm sure you'll find it. You're so close to the end. Come on, gang, let's summon that old Trillion Pines Spirit!"

As conditioned to endure intense physical labor as Lane was, he, too, was about to throw in the towel. He wanted to army-crawl back to his cabin and sleep for a million years, but he couldn't let Jordan down. Not again. Scrambling to his feet, Lane hobbled a few steps back from the fire pit. He continued to circle the small gathering place, examining the edges of the wooden bleachers for a final challenge, a puzzle, a vicious device, to break their collective spirits.

Lane found exactly four of what he was looking for.

On the edges of the fire pit, four holes had been dug beside four wooden stumps. Etched, no, burned, on each stump, were different runic symbols. Lane weakly tapped his temple. That mental photo would develop later. Every ounce of reserve strength was currently being used to keep him upright and not throw up.

"Luna," Lane's hoarse voice called out, "Check the logs for rune symbols."

Brandon stood up wearily. "How about we just call it quits? We'll eat breakfast tomorrow, pretend today never happened."

Jordan bared her teeth and growled, "You're not giving up. None of you. Come on. UP!" The group moaned, but nonetheless, complied. Turning reluctantly to Lane, she demanded, "What's the last stupid challenge?"

Lane explained, "There are four holes in the corners of the fire pit arena here. Each hole has a symbol that matches the logs—"

"We drop the rails into their proper holes. Right. Fine. Apollena, I mean, Cloudcroft, which rail goes where?" Jordan hollered.

Luna had already shuffled around the firepit and taken note of the symbols corresponding to their holes. After some more shouting and forceful commands from Jordan, the group's last ounce of strength was spent. Each rail was dragged and dropped into place.

Vegas finally stopped the timer. "Congratulations, team, you managed to keep an appetizer and soft drink on the board. Give your leader a round of applause."

"Can't," Gracie moaned. "Hands too full of splinters from that stupid rope."

"Yeah, what was the point of keeping us all on a leash, anyway?" Zoe asked breathlessly.

Brad shrugged. "Who said you had to take the rope?"

All eyes shifted to Jordan.

The girl with the wild red hair cracked her knuckles. "What do you mean, Brad?" Jordan asked through gritted teeth. "You had the rope laid out for us. This was all one big group bonding activity meant to keep us on a leash. Right?"

Vegas shifted his weight and feigned innocence. "Well, Doc and I were cleaning the dining room earlier this morning. We just happened to move some old rope out of the way. Nobody said you had to haul that thing with you. But, good on you for wanting to take on more of a challenge. Really delivers on that Trillion Pines' Spirit." Vegas turned his back on the group, struggling to suppress his laughter.

That last revelation was when the invisible but palpable malice of the counselors turned on Jordan. The girl could do nothing but hold back her own rage, put on a stone face, and wait for rebellion to fall at her feet.

Jude gave a round of applause. "Wichita, you really came through on that one. You tested your own limits and still managed to get the group some much-deserved dinner. Even if it is only an appetizer and some pop, we didn't skimp on the expenses for our training weekend. Y'all can dine on as much of your one course as you need to get your fill."

There was no response from any of the counselors. They were nearly completely dead inside and out. What little energy they had became the foundation for descent and hatred toward their current team leader: Jordan. Lane could barely stomach that demeaning victory speech. Only a single course? Way to rub it in. Even if it was hidden behind smiles and showmanship, Lane could see through Jude's act. This was psychological warfare executed at an expert level. But to what end? Why?

"Now," Jude said, clapping his hands together and breaking Lane's concentration, "I'm sure you'd like to take a minute to refresh yourselves. You are officially dismissed... After we sing the camp creed." As more complaints rose, Jude silenced them with a gentle wave of his hands. "Or, if you wish not to be dismissed, you're free to keep complaining. We could even start the timer again? Vegas?"

The group was instantly silenced.

Then, as Jude began, the rest followed along with the lyrics Lane had remembered were etched on the cracked iron bell:

Arise, arise, arise, arise

Lift your spirits to the skies

Gift me your flesh to the earth

Upon your climax shall I pull you into my depths

Ring, ring, ring, ring

Together we shall sing and conclude our dance around the stars

All the counselors sang out in a choir of broken spirits.

They were summarily dismissed back to the dorms. Everyone, except for Alice. Jude had called her aside. Whispers were exchanged. Lane wanted to stay, listen in on the secret conversation, but his friends dragged him forward down the narrow path.

Onward to the cabins.

Forward unto sleep.

They had no idea how few moments of rest they'd have left before their next challenge came knocking.

16

OUTTA MIND

No sooner had Lane opened the door to the bathhouse did he take a step back and let the door slam shut once again. It was much the same scene as before. Half of the counselors were fucking themselves senseless. Or, at least, it appeared that little sense was attached to their actions. It bordered on being removed from any sense at all. Then again, the second orgy he'd walked in on was the least of his concerns. Between the three omens, lost love, and whatever Jude was up to was enough on Lane's plate at the moment. What he'd done with his sister still ate at him from the inside out. Considering all he had was a salad and half a bottle of Grapefruit *Soda,* all he really wanted was to shower before the next insane activity, and the next distraction.

No, I can't just let these distractions get the better of me, Lane thought. He'd settled his resolve earlier this morning with Apollena. They solved mysteries, and they were neck deep in a dark one. Lane had to investigate while he had a chance.

Taking a quick lap around the bathhouse, Lane searched the edges for some kind of clue. As casual as his exhausted body could manage, he used his cell phone to photograph the perimeter. If someone or *something* were influencing their inhibitions…

Crack, SNAP!

Lane spun on his heels. He'd made it all the way to the back of the bathhouse, but there were only miles and miles of dense forest. Maybe something else was out there, or maybe it had been a squirrel? Lane couldn't let delirium soften his analytical mind. He had to take care of himself if he were to be of any use at all. Lane took a picture and moved on.

After a seemingly fruitless initial investigation, Lane lumbered back to his cabin. He needed a shower. No way was he going back into the common bathhouse. His water canteen and washcloth would have to do. He might even get a power nap before their next activity? Wishful thinking. The moment Lane touched the door handle, Aiden excitedly emerged.

Sheepishly, Aiden greeted his bunkmate, "Oh, Lane, hey! How are you, um, feeling?"

"I want to sleep forever and forget this day even happened," Lane admitted, then studied Aiden's goofy grin. "How you doin' in there, champ?"

Scratching the back of his head, Aiden tried to beat around the bush, "Good. I'm really—I think things are going pretty good. You know? All things considered."

Lane raised a hand. "You two need some privacy?"

Aiden nodded. "We were—just wanna talk about some things. You know?"

Lane took a step back and closed the flimsy screen door gently on Aiden. "You got protection, right?"

With a nervous bluster, Aiden looked around as if someone else were listening in, "Whoa, what? No! I mean, I do, but we really do just wanna talk about, you know, intimate stuff?"

"Seriously, it's okay. Take it slow. You've got this," Lane added with a respectful smile.

Aiden shot back a wide giddy grin. "Thanks! I mean, thank you. I appreciate the—um, the confidence? Thanks, Lane." Carefully, quietly, the excited tank of a man closed the door.

Good for him, Lane thought. Turning toward the crunching leaves on the footpath, Apollena approached with a cup of coffee in each hand.

"I want nothing more than to sit, drink, and slowly sink into that lumpy mattress," Luna breathed out after taking a long sip from her styrofoam cup.

"Well, you can do two of those things at least," Lane grinned, taking a step forward to intercept Luna and the spare cup of coffee. Gently lifting the styrofoam cup from his sister's left hand, Lane explained in a whisper, "Nina and Aiden are having a 'conversation'."

Luna cracked a wide Cheshire grin, "Oh?" Stepping up on her tiptoes, she wondered aloud, "Perhaps they need a moderator? Or a translator?"

Lane gently placed a hand on Luna's shoulder, easing her back down. "Pretty sure they're speaking the same language just fine."

His sister laughed. "Spoil my fun. I was kidding, of course."

"Were you, though?" Lane raised an eyebrow.

Luna shrugged, failing to suppress a devious grin.

The twins both turned in unison at the sound of a cabin door creaking open. Julia had stepped out of her bunkhouse, towel and pink toiletry bag tucked under her arm.

"Um, hey, Julia," Lane called out from across the deck, "I would maybe wait a few minutes before you go in there." He gestured with a sharp jab at the bathhouse.

Julia spun toward Lane with a confused glance that quickly soured. She let out a visible sigh and trudged back to her own cabin. "Seriously? How do they even have enough energy to—" She gestured with her hands and wretched.

"Why don't you hang out with us? You know, until they're all done in there?" Luna asked optimistically. "I mean, there's gotta be more than one shower on campus here, right?"

Striding toward the twins, Julia listed off the possible candidates on her fingers, "There's the residential cabins, the girls' dormitory, and the boy's dormitory is closest—"

Apollena took both her brother and Julia by the hand, "To the boys' dormitory it is—Oh, hey, Franki! Would you be so kind as to accompany us?"

Lane took notice of Julia's face turning bright strawberry red and shrinking inside of herself as Franki approached from the white sand trail. The tall black girl was hesitant to reply, pushing a hand over her shaved head.

"I dunno," Franki said, shifting her weight uneasily, "Think I'm just gonna go hit the racks before the next stupid challenge."

"Come on, it'll be fun, relaxing. No drama. Promise," Apollena insisted. "No one else will be in the dorms, right? At least nap there away from the rest of all that—" Luna gestured with her head to the bathhouse and made a vulgar gesture with her fingers to denote the hard-core fucking audible from across the deck.

Franki rolled her eyes. "Yeah. Alright, fine."

"Fantastic," Luna beamed and pulled the group along down the path to the dormitory.

"Children are really expected to sleep here?" Julia gasped. "Like, I don't remember our dorm being this bad when I was here last year. Or, even as a camper."

"You were a counselor here last year," Franki pointed out casually. "You remember the last day of orientation? We always cleaned the dorms the day before the campers arrived."

"Oh, yeah, that's right," Julia breathed out. Still, it looked worse than she remembered. The two-story dormitory was built in the same log cabin style as the Great Lodge: stonework base, massive timber support columns, and minimalist carvings in the crown molding that ran along with the ceiling: wolves, leopards, lions, and a single deer.

Outside was fine. Inside was a disaster.

Dozens of old wooden bunks had been pushed along the furthest wall. Old plastic-wrapped mattresses were all piled together off to one side in a sad heap. There had been some water damage recently in the piping within the ceiling. A faint mildew smell permeated the room, offset only by the powerful pine smell drifting in through all the open windows. The ceiling tiles themselves either sagged or were so waterlogged they'd fallen and shattered their mineral-fiber particulates over the thin carpet like stale snowflakes.

"It has its charm," Apollena made her way through the open space, "It holds a 'Rustic-Post-Apocalyptic' decorum." She nodded at her own assessment, drawing her finger along one wall and blowing the thick clump of dust off. "What do you think, brother?"

Nose buried deep in his notebook, Lane dismissively added, "If it's quiet enough for me to gather my thoughts, I can stomach 'Rustic-Post-Apocalyptic'."

Lane hardly paid attention to Julia as she timidly entered one of the shared bathrooms and tested the waters. Lane studied the pictures he'd taken just outside the bathhouse. Turns out his initial investigation yielded results: hoof prints. Judging by the size and compression depth in the dirt, whatever made the tracks could have easily been close to eight feet tall. There weren't moose common to these woods. Obviously, that couldn't have been right, but the math was.

With everything else going on, Lane didn't want that math to be right.

"I'm going to crash over here," Franki said to no one in particular. "Wake me when it's time to go." She wandered to the pile of mattresses and cautiously eased herself onto the squeaky, plastic-covered cushion.

"Luna, come take a look at this," Lane absentmindedly waved his sister over. "Nina was right about hearing hooves on the deck earlier this morning."

With a sigh of discontent, Luna leaned in to view Lane's phone. "Amazing."

"Hardly amazing, but it's... *something*. Something big," Lane gulped.

"Okay, big picture: there's some creature eight to nine feet tall stalking us and doing something to affect the counselors' inhibitions that we'll eventually have to fight or defeat. Sucks, but par for the course for us. Let's look at the smaller picture for once?"

Lane looked up from his notes. "What's the smaller picture?"

With a frustrated sigh, Luna spelled it out, "Whatever the connection is between the mystery cryptid and Jude's mind games, the goal seems to be to sow discord between the counselors. Create chaos. Right?"

"That's... as good a guess as any," Lane tentatively agreed, nodding along, "But, why?"

"'Why' is too big a concept right now," Luna said, waving her brother off, "Small picture: we can offset whatever Jude's end goal is by sewing *unity* in our group. Like with Nina and Aiden, or us. If the purpose of Jude's plan is to tear people apart, we can buy ourselves some time if we strengthen the bonds between counselors."

"How sure are we that discord and chaos is Jude's end goal?" Lane asked, his concern deepening with how little data and facts he actually had to work with.

Luna huffed out in reply, "Ursa Major, for once, try focusing on the pieces we have at hand. Namely, Franki and Julia." She not so subtly motioned toward the slender black girl reclining on the cushion. Long, dark athletic legs stretched out, spilling off the cushion and onto the carpet. The slit along the side of Franki's bright blue, nylon track shorts ran all the way up to the hem, revealing the entirety of her muscular thighs. Her *Seattle Mariners* tank top rode up, revealing an impressively toned stomach. The neckline also plunged low, showing off a marvelously full pair of assets not bound by any kind of bra at the moment.

Lane shook off his gaze. "Okay, what about them?"

"You are adorably dense sometimes, you know that?" Luna scoffed. "You were paying attention to Julia this afternoon, right? Still have your listening ears on, I hope?"

"Yeah, she implied something about a strict religious background. Then there was the part about losing her inhibitions. That's how I knew to check the window behind the bathhouse for the hoof prints. Didn't assume to actually *find* hoof prints. I mean, I expected to find something, but this can't be right—"

Luna pinched Lane's checks together with her thumb and forefinger. "Lane, darling, aren't we leaving out an important detail?"

He racked his brain and came up empty.

Before Luna could rail against her brother, Julia emerged from the shower. She was wrapped up in a bright yellow towel. Blonde hair still damp, pulled back into two short ponytails. Fairing an inch or two shorter and rounder than Luna, Julia radiated a joyful allure. She'd caught sight of Lane and immediately backpedaled into the bathroom. "Sorry! Oh, gosh, I forgot you were out there, Lane. Sorry."

"It's fine!" Apollena called out assuringly, dashing over to Julia. "At home he's outnumbered three to one by sisters. But, I'll bring your toiletry bag to you."

"Thanks," Julia answered from just inside the shower room door.

Moments later, Julia reemerged with Luna beside her. Julia wore a pair of pink jean shorts and a white cotton top with a picture of *Sunshine Bear* from the *Care Bears* cartoon.

Apollena had changed too since her previous outfit had been used mainly to rid herself of the head-to-toe mud bath she'd taken. Wearing a pair of blue jean overalls with only a gray sports bra underneath, Lane's sister was at peak casual wear. In fact, it'd been years since he noticed Luna dressed down this much from her usual high fashion flair.

"Anybody up for a casual game of cards?" Luna asked, withdrawing a deck from her back pocket. She opened the cardboard slipcover and slid the cards into her left hand. "Maybe a little gambling?" With a subtle flair, Luna shuffled the deck one-handed, and popped a single card up into the air, catching it with her right.

"Yeah, real subtle," Lane whispered.

"Dunno," Franki groaned, "I'm still beat. Already gambled my life away on this summer job. Got that feelin' like I ain't gonna survive to see the end of it, ya know?"

Luna was quick to assure her. "It's a casual kind of gambling. No money. Only a truth or perhaps a little dare thrown in?"

Julia's posture became overly defensive again as she began to retreat for the dormitory exit, "I'm not too daring considering everything we went through this afternoon and—"

"Our first wager is a compliment," Luna interrupted. "Whoever gets closest to twenty-one without going over wins. The others have to exchange a compliment, something true they admire about everyone. It's fun. Promise. Who's game?"

"Sounds kinda lame," Franki sighed, "But harmless. I'll play a hand." Sitting up and leaning forward, the young athlete yawned and stretched. Once again her mid section was on display and did not go unnoticed. Julia watched intently, licked her lips, and rejoined the circle.

"Hit," Lane requested.

"Stay," Julia spoke, nervous, trying to divert her attention from Franki.

"I'll stay," Franki said nonchalantly.

"And the dealer takes one. Okay. There. Show 'em!" Luna cheered.

Franki held steady at nineteen but still came in last to Lane's twenty and twenty-one for both Luna and Julia. Luna gathered the cards thrown in the center of the only clean patch of carpet they'd formed a circle around on the floor. With cards back in hand, she shuffled.

"Alright, Franki, you get to give a compliment. One each. For everyone here. Something *true*," Luna commanded with a wink and nod.

Releasing an exaggerated sigh, Franki went counterclockwise around the circle, "Luna, you're a crafty bitch. Props. Lane, you stuck it to Brad, that wanker, I admire that," She paused on Julia, looking the nervous blonde up and down. Franki tapped a slender finger to her pursed lips and thought for a moment, "You're smart, Jewels. Like, wicked smart. I really love that."

Julia had been cringing but relaxed her face. "Y-you think I'm smart? R-really?"

"I mean, yeah. Pretty obvious," Franki continued. "You've got smarts and you ain't in everyone else's face 'bout it. Smart and humble. Guess that's two compliments."

Julia tried to hide her face in her hands, "I wish Cole wouldn't be so—"

"Cole's an arse," Franki interrupted. "You're smart. So, be smart. Don't let a twat tell you who or what you're supposed to be, right?"

"Thank you," Julia breathed out in a small voice.

Franki looked at a wide-grinning Luna. "'Kay, how 'bout you deal us in again?"

"Fine by me," Apollena agreed, and swiftly passed out another round.

"What are we, um, betting this round?" Julia asked nervously.

Luna shrugged, "Looser's choice."

"I'll wager a kiss," Franki replied nonchalantly.

Julia's eyes shot open.

"Hit," Lane replied, paying more attention to his Field Journal than the raw emotions being wagered. He thought there may be something under the succubus/incubus tab. Unfortunately, they'd yet to encounter one. The only thing written on that particular page was, "Sex demon, also 90s / early 00s alt rock band #MorningView," The last part was inked in Luna's handwriting. Not particularly helpful.

"Am I allowed to fold? Or forfeit?" Julia asked, hand shaking.

Luna gently touched Julia's trembling hand, "You may... at the cost of explaining why you forfeit."

Nervously looking between Luna and a seemingly disinterested Franki, Julia gently pushed her cards forward: "I'm sorry, but... Franki, I am so sorry. I'm sorry for the other night. I didn't mean to—I don't know what came over me!"

Luna could read the nearly imperceptible twitch in Franki's eyes. The tug at the corner of her lips. Her chest rising and falling faster, she was hurt, upset, torn apart. Instead of saying all of that and more, the girl simply sniffed out a dry, "'Fine. Don't worry 'bout it."

"I mean it, Franki. I never meant to hurt—" Julia insisted.

"I said, 'I'm Fine', right?" Franki snapped. "It's fine, Jewels. I know 'bout your folks. Your brother. All that shit." She quickly wiped a hand across her face, her eyes, the tears that almost fell. Gone. Stiff upper lift held in place by sheer willpower. "You don't need to apologize all the bloody time about every little thing. There were two of us there. I should have stopped. Could've, but didn't. That wasn't— I'll just apologize for the both of us, 'kay?"

"No," Luna interrupted. "Not okay."

Franki stood up, waved her hands, voice cracking. "Luna, not to be impolite, but you don't need to get in between our business. I think that's more like Gracie's job or whatever."

"You're right, and I promised no drama. But I am, however, a stickler for rules and Lane lost. So we'll end this round and go back to the staff cabins. Fair?"

Lane was shaken from his concentration by Luna's slap against his chest. "Sorry, what now?" asked the clueless twin.

"You lost at cards, like always," Luna explained. "You owe everyone in here a kiss and we'll get out of here."

Lane shrugged, "Fine, whatever." He leaned in and gave Luna a peck on the cheek. Before Lane could break away back to his book, his sister held him by the collar. That was enough to jolt him back into the most recent existential crisis.

Did she want more?! Lane found himself screaming inside himself.

Appolena's poker face gave nothing away. Then, her eyes darted around the room, and she released him.

"Oh," Julia breathed out in relief, "For a minute there— nevermind. It's nothing. Horrible flashbacks to middle school."

"What happened in middle school?" Luna not so innocently probed, holding Lane's hand. He remained unbearably close to his twin for a moment longer. Luna's attention was still on Julia when she followed up, "Unfortunate spin-the-bottle incident?"

Julia rolled her eyes. "Something like that actually. I think the game was called *Seven Minutes in Heaven*. More like thirty seconds in hell. This boy from church, Mike Miller. Halloween party. Anyway, I didn't mean to babble. Sorry," Julia leaned her cheek out for Lane.

Luna asked again, "Is that when you knew?"

Julia blinked, "Knew what?"

Franki folded her arms, "Luna, maybe we should just get back?"

Luna then shifted toward Julia and gently took hold of both the blonde's hands in hers. "Julia, you kissed a primary schoolboy, and it felt like suffering for thirty seconds in the fiery pits of Tartarus. Tell me, where is your heaven?"

"Oh," Julia shuffled her feet, blushing horribly, "I guess it didn't feel like—I'd built up an idea in my head, ya know? Sometimes expectations don't meet reality. That's all. I guess it wasn't really as big a deal as I thought."

"Close your eyes," Luna said softly.

"What?" Julia whispered back. She shuddered, nervous and mortified, but didn't struggle out of Luna's hands. She froze. Then unable to hold up the weight of her unfortunate memories, shut her eyes tight.

"I want you to remember what those expectations were of what a kiss *should* be, of what you wanted to feel, what you desired. Can you remember, before you lowered your expectations, what did it feel like?"

Julia's breath caught. "I don't—I don't remember."

"But you remember earlier this morning? You remember what you did in the twilight hours in the bath house, don't you?" Luna asked gently. "What did *that* feel like?"

Julia swallowed hard, stuttering, "I d-don't, I'm sorry I don't—"

Luna held firm, not a tight grip, but a supportive, comforting hold on Julia's hands. "When you went into that closet, you didn't want to feel like hell. You wanted that kiss to feel like heaven and you were denied. That's not how you felt this morning, was it? Are you going to allow someone else, your parents, your brother, to deny heaven for you?" Julia winced, but didn't let go of Luna. In fact, she held on tighter, almost in tears. Luna whispered, "Are you going to deny someone else the truth about how you felt?" Another pause, a shuttering gasp for air, "Tell her, Julia. Tell the truth. I'm right here with you."

Julia swallowed hard. "If I could taste one thing... only one thing, ever again, would be to savor Franki's pussy. She was the best thing—" Her eyes burst into a flood of tears, but amazingly, Julia spat out, eyes open and pleading with Frank, "You are the best thing I've ever tasted. A-and, I don't want to give you up."

Franki strode up to Julia, Luna stepped aside, and the two girls embraced one another. Their hands searching up and down one another's backs. With her long fingers, Franki cupped Julia's face and touched her forehead with her own. "I've crushed on you for a long, long time. You know that, Jewels? You knew all along, right?"

Julia wiped her eyes. "I knew. I hid from you, from everyone. I still don't know-"

"You know what, though?" Franki asked, leaning in closer. "I want you."

"Take me," Julia whispered back. Her full cherry lips searched up for Franki's.

Two lost souls now finally, fully intertwined. The electric shift in the air was almost palpable. Even Lane could feel the static along his forearms as Franki drank deep from Julia's lips. Luna swooned, tussling Lane's hair with her fingers as she watched the two young women. No longer would they be denied.

Two lost souls, now finally, fully intertwined. The electric shift in the air was palpable. Even Lane could feel the static along his forearms as Franki drank deep from Julia's lips. Luna swooned, tussling Lane's hair with her fingers as she watched the two young lovers, young women that would no longer be denied. Fingers desperately attempted to liberate one another of the thin fabric barriers: buttons, zippers, clasps struggled to come undone.

Then, the door to the boy's dormitory burst open.

"Lane! Luna! It's Aiden," Nina blurted out, "You have to help, quick!"

17

WISHFUL THINKING

This was the third strike. Brad had regularly interrupted the handful of genuine moments of intimacy in the two days Lane had been at this camp. To deny others joy was a grating personality trait. As Lane led the charge up the sloped trail back to the counselors' cabins, he could only imagine how his behavior could have escalated to cause Nina to panic.

"They just burst in," Nina panted.

"Who?" Franki asked, keeping pace with the pixie girl.

"All of 'em. They just burst into the room, shouting, hollering, leering at us," Nina was wide eyed, shaking, and manic. Couldn't be helped. Moments before bridging an intimate connection with someone so new, toxic personalities flooded over Aiden and Nina.

Third strike.

Brad was out of order.

With the setting sun on their backs, Lane bounded up the five rotted steps to the patio deck. His eyes were locked on Brad, squaring

off against Aiden. Without a moment's hesitation, Lane's momentum carried him into the muscular blond buzz-cut boy. Instinct took over. His reflexes snapped into action. Years of training and practice, beaten into Lane's muscles, all reacted faster than his conscious mind.

First hit: Lane's open palm connected under Brad's jaw and gripped it tight.

Second: Right foot planted behind Brad's non-dominate ankle.

Third: Lane's left hand gripped Vegas' right wrist, swung up and across the chest.

Last: Lane's continued momentum drove Brad into the deck. Hard.

From the spectators in various states of undress, a wounded Aiden, and the three counselors trailing after Lane, the whole conflict looked like a blur of motion. One moment, Brad was about to slug Aiden. In an instant, Brad lay face up on the deck, groaning.

Lane stood back up to his full height and took a step back, far from Brad's reach. "I think I've had my fair share of bullying, Brad. When you've caught your breath, let's go take a walk and pay Jude a visit. Or we can sort this out right now. Your call."

"Or," Brad coughed out, the spittle of blood dripping out from his mouth, "You can suck a fat dick, Roswell."

Lane shifted back into a fighting stance as he caught Brandon sliding up in his peripheral. Hands up and ready to defend himself, Brandon immediately backed up. "What the hell, man?!" he said in shock. "You really are a space case, Roswell. We were just playing around. No need to go all psycho killer on Vegas."

Nina interjected, "Lane's the psycho? How about barging in on Aiden and me!?"

Cole and Brandon helped Brad up to his feet. "Us?" Brad scoffed, wiping the blood from his chin. "We were being neighborly, social, wanting to connect with our fellow counselors. We were concerned that despite our team-building efforts, you two were hiding away from the rest of the group. That's rather antisocial; not the Trillion Pine's Spirit."

Aiden was breathing heavily; a black eye was already visible. "Not everyone is as sexually open as you. Some of us prefer our privacy. The closed door should have been a hint."

"First, as your lead counselor, it's my job to show concern for my fellow counselors. Especially those who choose not to participate with the rest of the group: the lost, the lonely, even people with enormous… hearts, like you. Second, if I'd known you liked sucking dick, I'd offer you something with a bit more girth a lot sooner—"

Aiden rushed in with a haymaker, but it was Lane who held him back. Despite his skill and training, the larger man's musculature nearly knocked Lane out cold. Staggering to catch his balance, Aiden helped Lane back to his feet.

"You heard what he said?! You heard him—I can't!" Aiden cried out.

"I know!" Lane assured him, holding his jaw. "I know. But he's baiting you into a conflict. Your honor, Nina's honor, will hold. Don't take the bait."

Vegas chuckled, "I don't know, maybe we *should* settle this like men. Let your boy go, Lane. Let's see if Aiden's willing to fight for his little lover till the bitter end."

"No," Jordan shouted, stomping up onto the deck, "Enough of this playground shit. Vegas, Buffalo, both of you are going to Jude's cabin and will settle this like adults."

"Um, I don't remember hearing you got a promotion—" Vegas started.

"Shut the fuck up, Bradley." Jordan stepped out between the two boys. She wore her black camp t-shirt over the same silk teddy she'd worn earlier. Her bare legs stood firmly planted in the middle of the conflict, the t-shirt only covered up some of her modesty. "I get promoted when the current leader acts like a child. You and Aiden go sort your shit out with Jude. I'll run the night game until you get back." She addressed the crowd, "Anyone dare to challenge that?"

The deck was silent.

Lane stood beside Apollena who'd already retrieved the first aid-kit from her backpack. She'd applied a cold pack to Aiden's left eye. The larger boy leaned against her and Nina for support. His hands still shook.

The other counselors shifted their weight, pulling their towels or jackets closed tighter around themselves. None dared to speak up. Lane noticed their eyes: shame blossomed in their pupils. Shame and a sense of confusion as to how it'd taken root in the first place.

Of course, it was Brad who broke the silence first. "Fine," he said with a desperate laugh, "I suppose that's the mature thing to do? Yeah. Come on, Buffalo, let's take a walk and talk it out over a cup of tea, or whatever."

"I'm not walking alone in the woods with that asshole," Aiden wheezed out.

"That's exactly what you're gonna do," Jordan commanded, "Or you can pack your bags right now and find something else to do with your summer."

Nina squeezed Aiden's hand. "It's okay," she whispered. "It'll be okay."

"Have a third party go along," Lane suggested.

Jordan spun around. "I'm sorry—did you get the impression this was a democracy?"

Lane insisted, "If they start brawling again, have an unbiased third party go with them to get Jude and settle it. Or, in case they get injured. Rule of three. Basic safety—"

"Fine," Jordan interrupted, "Bozeman, go with 'em."

The mute boy shrugged and wandered over to the stairs after Brad and Aiden.

"Thank you, Jordan," Lane spoke with deference.

"Blow me," she replied, and marched to her cabin. "You all have until sundown to rest, and get dressed out into hiking gear, close toed shoes and be out and ready on the deck. Sundown. Be ready. Now clear out and nobody better start anymore shit." With that final command, Jordan slammed the door to her cabin.

Nightfall came quicker than they'd expected. Still no signs of Aiden, Brad, or Bozeman. Thirteen counselors had become ten as Jordan led the group up the Northwest Trail. The dry winds blew harder and threw the colossal pines from side to side. Not so much a night symphony, but a steady racket of branches and leaves churning together in the dark. As they crested the hill, a bright lantern light fifty meters into the clearing replaced the miniscule glow from the solar powered foot lamps that dotted the sand trail.

"You're on time—excellent," Doc called out from the base of a thick tree beside the lantern. He already wore his climbing rig and had thirteen other harnesses laid out upon a wooden table—three of which wouldn't be used.

"Where do you suppose Aiden is?" Julia asked Franki softly.

"Probably still sortin' shit out with Brad and Jude. There's a lot of issues there," Franki mumbled, giving Julia's hand a gentle squeeze.

Nina was a wreck. She picked at her cuticles and scratched the black polish off her nails. Her eyeliner was once again smudged and streaked. "He's fine," she lied aloud to herself.

Luna hugged the nervous pixie. "Of course, he's fine. Aiden can handle himself well. Jude probably had all parties sit this game out until everything was resolved."

"I know he can handle himself," Nina nodded, "But what if they send him home early, though? Brad has seniority. Aiden's only worked here for—"

"Actually," Julia cut in, "Aiden's a fourth year. Six if you count being a camper. Brad's only been here for three years as a counselor. If anyone's gonna be sent home, it'll be Brad for sure," Julia beamed.

"Seniority has to count for something."

Franki squeezed Julia's hand in hers again, but her train of thought skipped a track. "Wait, if Brad's only been here three years, how'd he get leadership over JoJo?" She clenched her jaw and winced. She remembered. The boy. The low ropes course. The tragedy.

"Why?" Jordan called back from the head of the group, "'Cause sometimes life ain't fair. Suck it up and keep marching."

A few minutes and one drawn out safety tutorial later, and Doc had helped the team of ten get their harnesses on and ready to climb. He moved over to the thick tree closest to the lantern and lean-to equipment shack. "Now, traditionally, this course is done in pairs. So line up with your partners."

"Hold on," Jordan interrupted with a hand in the air, "We're changing up partners for this exercise." A collective groan rose up from the group. It was silenced by a single, powerful clap from Jordan. "Enough bitching. Roswell and I are taking point, followed by Athens and Reno, Olympia and Topeka, Sydney and London, Tallahassee and Sitka—"

"Jordan, hold on a sec, Alice is missin'," Zoe said.

The group murmured to themselves. Lane searched the clearing. Had he miscounted? He was almost certain the silver-haired girl had been among them before they left the staff cabins. Hadn't she worn a pale gray version of that same prairie dress from earlier?

"Fine," Jordan interrupted the growing rumblings among the staff, "Tallahassee, you're with Providence."

Lane counted the new pairing and eyed Luna standing alone with an annoyed smirk. "Jordan, what about Apollena?"

"It's fine, Lane. I think I'll manage by myself, just to keep things moving," Luna offered.

"How considerate," Jordan scoffed with indifference. "Let's get this over with."

Lane was about to protest, but with a subtle gesture to hold his tongue, Luna insisted that her twin drop the issue.

"Well, I'll be monitoring y'all from below, so if you get stuck, just holler and I'll come lend you a hand," Doc offered, cutting through the tension. "Alright then, first pair step on up."

Jordan went first. She scrambled up the wooden pegs faster than he'd expected. He grabbed the first hand-hold. Two years of AIRR Training on top of regularly jumping out of helicopters for another two years after that and Lane still hated heights.

"Haven't got all night, Roswell," Jordan spoke as she climbed over the first obstacle segment. "We're setting the pace so everyone else can finish this thing and sleep."

After the initial platform nearly a hundred feet above the ground, there wasn't just one obstacle course, but two. Those two obstacles branched off into two others, giving multiple routes to complete before reaching the finish. Of course, the difficulty of each section increased exponentially in complexity, and the only thing lighting their path was a pair of glow sticks around their wrists. Add to that the persistent breeze and swaying trees; this challenge would be nothing short of harrowing.

"I expected more from a pilot, or whatever you were, Roswell," Jordan spoke as she carefully maneuvered across a tightrope and through various horizontal beams of wood suspended in their path at varying heights.

Lane followed after Jordan, keeping one arm out to steady himself and the other clutched onto the two safety ropes attached to the parallel cable that ran above their heads. Swallowing his nerves, Lane politely corrected, "I wasn't technically a pilot. I was a Rescue Swimmer. Jumped out of helicopters—"

"Wasn't asking for your life story, just telling you to keep up," Jordan huffed.

Lane sighed. He wanted nothing more than to tell Jordan his life story. There were a million things he wanted to say, to ask, to share. Instead, he walked to the end of the tightrope and joined Jordan on another two-man wooden platform. It was hardly big enough for both of them. Their elbows, thighs, and waists rubbed together as they unclipped their carabiners from the previous obstacle, one after another, and hooked into the next challenge.

"This next one is longer than the others, no foot holds either. There's eight metal rods at inclines. The trick is to hang all the way on the edge and just drop straight down to the next bar. If you try swinging fancy-ass acrobatics, or whatever, you'll end up racking your chin or your neck on the next bar. Just climb out to the end, drop, catch the next bar, and repeat. Eight bars. Got it?" Jordan instructed.

"On your lead," Lane replied.

Jordan unceremoniously stretched out for the first bar and reached hand-over-hand onto the meter long pole. Only a few feet out and all that lit her face was the neon pink glowstick. Lane could just barely make out the next metal rod suspended by wires, but nothing else after that. Rolling cloud cover above intermittently made the course nearly pitch black.

"You must have done this a hundred times already, huh?" Lane called out into the darkness as Jordan kept climbing. He could feel the tension on the safety cable above them. He knew she was there. Even if she'd disappeared into the dark, the floating pink glowstick suggested she was still only a few feet ahead of him.

After a long pause, Jordan's voice came through the darkness, "Set the course record last year. The hardest route: sub twenty minutes. Solo."

Twenty minutes? If Jordan's record was that long, factoring in how exhausted his muscles still were after the hike and obstacle course that morning and afternoon, they might end up being here a lot longer.

"That's impressive," Lane admitted, climbing out onto the next pipe. The steel rod was cold to the touch. The incline was steeper and a lot more awkward to navigate than he anticipated. Reaching the end of the bar, he stretched his fingers out as far as he could. There wasn't anything there. Had she lied? No. She wanted to finish, to win.

"Just reach out," Jordan sighed from somewhere in the dark. "It's there. And for future reference, flattery will get you absolutely nowhere."

Lane considered his play. As he held his hand out in anticipation, exhaling, he released his grip on the first bar. That freefall sensation sent his stomach up into his throat. He didn't even have time to scream, but the second his wrist grazed something cold and hard, Lane tightened his grip. He felt the sudden stop and jerk all the way up his spine.

He dared to look down, like an idiot, but it was nothing but blackness all the way. He could be a foot off the ground or a mile up and that dizzying sensation of vertigo would have been exactly the same. There was no way of telling how high they were, only that hanging by a single steel pole felt like his body had tripled in weight and, should he let go, he'd fall forever.

"Great, you've made it to two of eight. Seriously, I'd thought you'd grown up braver," Jordan chuckled. "Keep climbing," she added in a sing-song voice. The sentiment may have been just as bitter, but the tone sounded pleasant enough.

"Speaking of growing up..." Lane started.

Jordan cut him off. "Nope. We're not trading back stories. We're focusing on the present. Finish the challenge. Go back to sleep. Wake up. Repeat."

"Fine," Lane relented, dropping down onto his fourth pole. He could hear the distant whispers of the other counselors on the branching obstacles nearby. One of the girls sounded like they were either laughing or crying. He couldn't make out who. Their voices seldom rose above the wind and scratching branches. Lane just barely spotted the other bobbing and swaying neon colored wrist bands. Just as well. He couldn't afford to be distracted. Focus on the present.

"So has Jude always been... purposefully underhanded when it comes to training week, or is that a new development?" Lane tried his luck, hoping to take a shot at a common adversary. He'd seen the few interactions Jordan and Jude had with one another. They were cold, uncomfortably so. That—combined with the obvious favoritism of Brad—Jude seemed like an easy target and last hope for Jordan to open up.

After a pause, "What do you mean, exactly?" Jordan asked. Her hiking boots landed hard onto wood a few feet ahead. Lane could just barely see a grayish outline of the young woman lit from underneath by a faded trail lamp attached to the platform.

Lane chose his words as carefully as his timing when he dropped to the next bar. "It's pretty obvious Brad did not write the clues for this morning's team building course. That first one, it seemed intentionally designed to get under your skin."

"I told you," Jordan almost growled, "We're not talking about the past."

"We're not," Lane assured her. "I wanna understand why Jude is the way he is now."

Jordan was now mostly visible as Lane dangled down onto the final bar, "What's there to understand? He's an asshole. End of story."

Lane dropped down the last few inches to land on the thin board beside Jordan. her face was now visible enough to get a read on: she was upset, but there was something else at the corner of her eyes. Something... sad? Regret?

"He's just an asshole with the perfect little family, perfect little wife and daughter, working in the position I've always wanted. He's just the kind of guy who has to rub it in everyone's face and pretend he isn't doing exactly that," Jordan lamented.

With his muscles burning, Lane reached up to unclip his first safety cable. "Have you met his wife? His kid?"

Jordan huffed. "Yeah. They live with him at his onsite residential house. Haven't seen 'em this year, but..." She drifted off, focusing on the obstacle ahead, "...But, it doesn't matter. They'll show eventually at the end of training week, like always. Happy little family showing off for all his happy little underlings."

Lane waited, listening to Jordan, her change in tone. This was a side of her that he'd yet to see. This wasn't just regret. It almost sounded like jealousy. But Lane wasn't about to work off assumptions. He needed facts. Data. Some semblance of a lead to start his investigation into who Jordan had become.

"So he's got a family," Lane acknowledged, "Doesn't give him the right to play mind games, or needlessly sow discourse among his employees."

"You would think so," Jordan agreed, leaping out onto a suspended swing, "But that doesn't stop him from doing so." Having built up enough momentum, Jordan released the bar at its furthest point. When the wooden swing returned, it came back empty. "Wait till I reach the other side. It's easier if the bars aren't in motion."

"Okay," Lane called back.

The wind continued to blow. The trees swayed. Lane found himself clutching the trunk of the tree the thin wooden platform was attached to—barely wide enough to plant both his feet onto. Lane's knees began to shake. With the exception of a few hours' rest, he'd nearly been up for forty-eight hours straight. No amount of coffee could reinvigorate Lane's steadily declining stamina. Still, he had to finish this course. More importantly, Lane still needed some clue into Jude's psyche.

Maybe the fact that he was married, a father even, would be enough? It was a start, and another pair of witnesses to glean information from— if and when they showed. Lane might even stroll by the residential cabins before then and pay the Abidalli family a visit.

After much longer than twenty minutes, Jordan and Lane completed half a dozen more obstacles. Each more insane than the last. Uneven bars, an inclined cargo net, and sandbags that acted as a painful gauntlet of wind chimes that beat against them on a zig-zagging tightrope. The weighted burlap sacks swung more forcefully in the growing gale that blew through the trees. At last, they'd reached what Lane counted as the tenth obstacle. Try as he might, squinting in the dark, he couldn't make out a new obstacle or any sign of the next obstacle. He could hardly make out the guide rope above them.

"So, what's the trick to this one?" Lane asked, trying to solve it himself.

There was a heavy pause. The wind continued to push its way violently through the pines. The oppressive, unrelenting darkness of the obscured moon surrounded them.

"Lane," Jordan breathed out. She didn't look directly at him, instead searching the night for some unseen clarity. "You really love Apollena, right?"

Lane was taken so far off guard, he nearly slipped off the thin platform. A sudden *CRACK* on the edge of the wood startled him. Swallowing hard, "Of course. She's family. Couldn't have asked for a better sister and I got three of them. But yeah. Luna and I are…" He thought for a moment, "Couldn't imagine life without her. Why?"

Jordan shifted uncomfortably close to Lane. "You think you could ever fall for someone else, more than your sister?"

Stifling a laugh, "I mean, I haven't *fallen* for Luna. She's family. She's my sister, Jordan," He tried to meet her eyes, but Jordan was still fixated on something ahead of him.

The wind stopped blowing.

The other counselors' voices must have been miles away.

There was only Jordan and Lane.

Then, with her nose nearly touching Lane's, Jordan asked, "Would you ever fall for me?"

Lane's heart nearly exploded out of his chest. His mind had been so intently focused on solving the mysteries that pummeled him one after another. He stood in the shallows of an unfamiliar ocean while the tide rose. With each dark wave that passed over him, his lack of understanding threatened to drown Lane in the unknown before he even had a chance to kick up off his mental seabed. Now, standing beside his first love, a hundred feet in the air, in the dead of night, he could hardly breathe.

Oh, God, no. What if he was in love?

Unfortunately for Lane, his rational mind spoke before his heart had a chance. "Jordan, you were my first kiss. I've never forgotten that night. But, that was more than a decade ago. We're entirely different people now. I don't think it'd be fair to fall for a stranger and pretend they were someone else, or someone I imagined."

He could taste her breath as she sighed in frustration. "Well, fall for me anyway."

Without any warning, Jordan pushed Lane off the platform, and he plummeted into the darkness below like an anchor.

18

AT LEAST THAT'S WHAT YOU SAID

Before he died, Lane's last thoughts fell onto his family. He missed his mom and dad—wherever they had disappeared to. He hoped Robyn and Katrina would be safe, successful, and happy. Finally, he sent what would have been his last breath to Luna.

"Stay alive," Lane whispered to the void.

Another second or so of free-falling through the towering pines to the forest floor. Even though there was only darkness, Lane would not shut his eyes. He would not let the dark claim him before his time. When the end did come, he would meet whatever light or darkness came to conquer his soul without blinking.

Then, suddenly, *impact*.

The moment Jordan had pushed him off the wooden platform, Lane already calculated how and where his bones would break; the lacerations he'd sustained from branches, rocks, or whatever lay unseen below. If he caught his landing just right, (or wrong) it'd be a quick end.

Instead, Lane felt the sting of thick, coarse ropes embrace him well before he'd predicted.

He'd landed in a massive cargo net.

Before he could even register the shock of not being dead, Jordan had dropped down and joined him in the net. "You didn't scream. I'm almost impressed."

"Oh, Lane? Ha. He doesn't scream," another voice spoke up across the cargo net, which startled both Jordan and Lane; the latter nearly fell off the side of the net. Then, almost reflexively, he reached up to the guide rope he was still connected to. *Idiot,* Lane laughed to himself, *Jordan must have clipped him in while he was distracted by her—her everything.*

Jordan gasped, "How the hell did you—you couldn't have possibly beat us here on the course unless—"

Lane's eyes adjusted to the combined light of three glow sticks. One of those faint neon lights belonged to his sister. Apollena smiled and pointed upward.

"Doc let me use the guide track above the course," Luna said with a shrug. "I usually prefer to be in the thick of things. But, seeing how I was on my own, it was nice to have a straight shot to the finish line." Shifting her body to face Lane, Luna smiled, "I can understand why you like seeing the bigger picture, Ursa Major. It's a refreshing perspective."

Lane couldn't make out Jordan's facial features, but he could feel the anger radiating off of her. Just before she'd pushed him, Lane recalled Jordan's abrupt slip of the mask. That facade of perpetual anger, that wall that must have been built up, brick by brick over the years. Had Jordan really thought about him and Luna...? No. No, it wasn't about that. Not any sordid innuendo. It was about the bond itself. Lane and Luna were more than siblings. They were partners. Maybe not in any romantic sense, but he'd known for some time how rare it was to have a pair so in tune with another. Lane got the impression that envy was not necessarily Jordan's sole focus or emotional state. There was something more on her mind, her heart.

Lane was compelled to know what.

"Look out below!" cried Topeka and Olympia in unison.

Both boys dropped into the net, laughing and exchanging high-fives. It was an oddly refreshing sight to see: cooperation not competition.

"Dude, I think that's gotta be a new course record," Brandon exclaimed.

"Almost," Jordan corrected him. "You're about fifteen minutes shy. Keep trying, though."

"I told you," Cole chuckled, "Jordan is a beast! I think she even beat Jude one year. She's that. Damn. Fast."

"Don't forget dexterity," Apollena added, "I was watching from above. The way she navigated those inclined bars was beautifully executed."

"Please don't," Jordan reprimanded quietly. "I told your brother earlier, flattery will get you nowhere."

Luna reclined into the net. "Just telling it how it is. Not like I'm trying to get in your pants. Not without permission at least." There was an unseen wink that went unappreciated.

Minutes passed by as the rest of the group all fell into the net from the freefall platform. A few minutes more went by till eventually Nina and Zoe dropped in, the last pair lagging behind by nearly ten minutes from Gracie and Korri. Much like the others, the pair appeared to be in good spirits. In fact, the entire group appeared significantly less hostile to each other compared to the morning gauntlet. Idle chatter, exhausted laughter. If this were Lane's introduction to this group, he wouldn't mind spending the next eight weeks with this team at all.

That wasn't the case, though.

Lane's suspicions had already been laid out, and bias was in place. Even recognizing such bias of the group and a willingness to change that perspective based on the evidence, the time to enjoy an idle vacation had long since passed. This whole scene was just another case, a job, another mystery he and Luna needed to solve before calamity struck.

So far, there were already four persons unaccounted for and a camp director they needed to interrogate. The time to sit idly by was over.

"Well," Jordan said with a yawn, "Usually we'd sing that weird song, and then have another two-hour-long debrief about our feelings and some shit..." Jordan waited for the collective groan to subside, "But, Brad and Jude ain't here and I'm beat. Y'all ready to go back to the cabins and sleep? Like legitimately sleep?"

"Is it too late to vote for a new lead counselor?" asked Zoe.

Korri brushed the long strands of neon purple and pink highlights out of her face. "JoJo's got my vote. Vegas can choke on his own dick."

"No, it's too late for democracy," Brandon added. "We'll stage a coup tomorrow, after breakfast." A light smattering of laughter. "Seriously, though, I know this is only the second time I've been up here, but I don't think I've enjoyed this course more than tonight." Brandon offered Cole his hand, and the two exchanged a series of complicated shakes and fist bumps.

Cole nodded. "Thanks, man. I appreciate that."

"Considering a new boyfriend, Brandon?" Korri teased with a wink.

"Nah, but Olympia here can be my wingman anytime," Brandon laughed back.

Franki smiled, piling on to the playful tease, "Or maybe you two could sort it out in the spa? You know, until Brad gets back?"

The group laughed, but the laughter faded abruptly. An air of confusion permeated the team suspended in the cargo net above the forest floor.

Brandon offered a nervous chuckle, "What about the spa exactly?"

Franki shot Brandon a confused smile, "You know, the thing you all do... In the Bathhouse? Weren't you just in there? Actually, forget I even mentioned it."

Gracie paused her whispered conversation with Korri, "Wait, what's this about the Bathhouse? What'd I miss?" She shifted among the ropes to study an increasingly uncomfortable looking Brandon. "And, Korri, you were in there too, right?

Lane and Apollena also studied the group intently. Of all the counselors who'd seemed not particularly loyal to Brad, but connected to his particular social sphere, each one appeared genuinely flummoxed about what Franki had just referenced. Did they think their early morning erotic exploits were a secret?

"You know," Nina cleared the frog in her throat and spoke up timidly, "The orgy?"

"Whoa!" Korri shouted. "The... What-the-fuck?"

The others equally exclaimed responses with varying degrees of shock.

"I mean," Korri laughed nervously, "I'm DTF in nearly every situation, but that's a step too far, even for me. And I legit love you guys, *and* girls, just not that much. Sorry, not sorry."

"Same," Gracie said bashfully. "Call me old-fashioned, but I'm kind of a one-woman gal. Or at least, one woman at a time. Alone. In private."

Lane kept his eyes on Jordan. Surely, she wasn't going to plead ignorance to what more than half the counselors were doing mere hours ago. It had barely been sundown when Lane walked in on the group for the second time. Rather, when they walked in on Nina and Aidan. Jordan's eyes, however, showed zero recognition of the particular activity that Franki and Nina had just mentioned.

Seriously? Lane thought. They had all still been involved with each other when he'd arrived on the deck to confront Brad. Hell, Gracie herself was stripped down to her thong. Cole had a ball gag in his mouth, with Korri holding tight to a leather belt around her boy's neck. Then again, perhaps whatever had removed their inhibitions required some mental barriers as well?

Lane considered the chemical effects of known aphrodisiac substances. Memory loss may have been a side effect to some of those drugs over a period of time, but certainly not to this degree, not within hours. It also didn't account for Franki and Julia both remembering what they'd done to each other in the spa. Why would it be selective?

"We're not kink-shaming anyone or anything like that," Julia said quickly, reassuringly. "It was a joke, is all. We're sorry for bringing it up."

"Yeah, I didn't mean to take it too far," Franki added. "It's y'alls business."

"What the hell are you talking about?" Jordan said sharply at Franki, "Joking is one thing, but you're gonna have to provide some context. Especially if it's more of an accusation than a joke. What do you think you saw in the bathhouse?"

Julia squeezed Franki's hand and responded, "Jordan, y-you, you were there too. Earlier this morning and like, just a few hours ago, too. We were there with you the first time. In the stalls, at least. Are you saying you really don't remember?"

The confusion spread like a sudden cold front settling over the counselors. In fact, the towering trees began to sway once more as the tepid summer winds returned. An ever-present creaking echoed throughout the woods as the branches and leaves rustled.

Lane finally spoke up, laid out the facts. "Jordan, just after midnight after the Tiki Game, Luna and I went to the bathhouse. When we opened the door, Gracie, Zoe, Korri, Cole, Brandon, Bozeman, and Brad were all engaged in various sexual activities. You were there too. You spoke to me while you were—" he swallowed. It was hard to finish with Jordan staring daggers at him like that. With those sapphire eyes, those rose petal lips scowling–

"Masturbating," Apollena concluded. "I was there too. Brandon, surely you remember what we did with Brad. Do you not? We shared high fives and everything else."

Outbursts of denial, nervous laughter, and other comments arose from the group and were silenced by Jordan's hand.

"You're saying we were all having an orgy and no one here except you and your sister remembers?" Jordan stated dryly.

Julia cleared her throat. Even in the dark, Lane could see her cheeks blushing fiercely by the faint light of the glow sticks. "Um, we were there, too. Franki and I." The small blonde darted her eyes, "We were in the bathroom stall, though."

Cole burst out laughing. "Oh, yeah? You and Franki, huh? Perfect Bible-thumping little sister going down on some girl—" Reading his sister's face, Cole violently changed gears from offense to a misplaced sense of defense. He pointed a finger at Franki. "Hey, what the fuck did you do to my little sister, London?"

Franki exploded, "Didn't do anything to her, you twat!" There was an uncomfortable pause. All eyes on her. Discomfort stabbed her from all sides. "It ain't your business, Cole. I mean, we were all..." As the knife of missing memories twisted, Franki trailed off, trying to recall exactly what had come over her. Lane caught hesitation in the girl's eyes: she did love Julia, didn't she? Biting her lower lip. A determined nod. Resolve. Definitely something deeper than a crush, for certain. When it came to what had actually come over them both, the emotional walls that were dropped in the heat of the moment, Franki honestly couldn't verbalize exactly what had happened.

None of them could.

Korri spoke up calmly in defense of Franki, "Cole, maybe take it easy on Franki?"

Cole's reply was twice as agitated as before. "You aren't telling anybody what to do, Reno. Least of all me. So, how 'bout you sit over there and keep those cracked whore lips of yours shut!"

"Oh, no you fucking didn't," Korri breathed, lunging across the cargo net. Gracie held the girl in place before Korri could actually strangle Cole.

Gracie held on tightly to Korri's harness. "Real it in, sugar. Don't wanna start throwing punches this high up. Some or all of us are bound to get hurt."

"How come none of us remember an orgy that happened twice,

Roswell?" Zoe asked pointedly at Lane, "Unless this is some kinda sick practical joke? Might wanna check your weird sense of humor before running your mouth. None of us are laughing."

"It's no joke," Apollena spoke in a low, hushed tone. "We've reason to believe that... *Something* is affecting, altering our inhibitions. All of us. We're not sure, but Lane will find out what and stop it before we all unravel or succumb to whatever it's planning on doing to us."

The group became eerily still.

The winds blew harder. So much so that the counselors held tighter to the net and the guide ropes they were all still connected to. Then, all was still once more.

Jordan finally spoke up. "I knew something like this would happen." All eyes turned to the acting lead counselor as she brushed the wild red hair out of her face. "The moment I saw your names on the duty roster, I knew some weird shit would come up. This takes the cake, though. This is low, Lane. This is... cruel."

"What's she talking 'bout?" Gracie asked with a fearful Southern twang.

Jordan grimaced. "I met these two when I was thirteen. They were living on my old street when they invited themselves into my house one night. They tricked me, conned me into believing some bullshit about ghosts, stole my dead grandfather's watch, and—" Jordan was practically screaming, livid. But the memory of her grandpa still burned. She choked on her rage. "You two need to go. Just go."

"That's not what happened," Lane said.

"No," Jordan shot back, "You will not interrupt me. You're a sick man, Lane Guster Woods." Her hands held an iron grip on the rope net while she utilized the rest of her considerable strength to hold back her tears. "I want you to pack up your gear tonight. Tomorrow morning, you and your sister are gone."

Lane was stunned, heartbroken.

"What happened to the watch?" Apollena asked.

The collective attention of the group now shifted to the black, French-Nigerian-American girl staring intently at Jordan.

"I—I don't know. Doesn't matter," Jordan spat out. "Let's all just get down from—"

"No," Luna protested calmly, "The truth of this is too important to ignore. It affects all of us now. So what happened to your grandfather's watch? You remember, don't you?"

Jordan shifted uneasily, "I said, 'It's not important.' The point is—"

"Something supernatural happened to you. Something impossible. Something terrifying. The unknown is always terrifying, especially when no one believes you when you're alone. But," Luna paused, holding up a finger, "You told Lane about what had happened after your grandma passed. What did you notice at the funeral?"

Jordan remained silent, fuming, while she clenched and unclenched her fists from the ropes and stood up on the net.

Lane took a deep breath and exhaled as the wind stirred. "I remember what you said."

No protest from Jordan. Nothing was said among the other counselors. While the forest was simmering, Lane continued, "There was an open casket. Friends, family, they all gave their final respects. You were uncomfortable, too heartbroken to look at first. Then you did. I remember," Lane chuckled silently, "I remember how excited you got when you told me. Your grandfather's watch was on her wrist. 'He must have given it to her just before she passed,' Is what you said. It was both a going away and coming home present."

"That's not true," Jordan whispered. "It can't be. That's impossible!"

The wind suddenly howled through the branches, forcing Jordan to fall back into the net.

Counselors' intent focus shifted to fear and anxiety.

"Maybe we could talk about this later? On the ground?" Franki suggested.

"No. We can't go down there," Nina breathed out as if invisible hands were tightening around her neck. "They won't let us go."

"What are you talking about now, you crazy little—" Cole's voice caught as he looked below the net. "The hell?" he whispered.

Lane looked down.

He wished he hadn't.

Three pairs of shining golden eyes looked up at them from the forest floor: a panther, a wolf, and a lion. Then, as if the presence of three predators waiting to devour them wasn't enough, a raspy voice called out, "H-help, me, p-please," Groaned the last dying words of Doc. In the center of the three tar-covered animals, a figure twitched and reached upward with a gnarled, bloody hand. "H-elp, E-e, help, m-mmh," the meat sack pleaded.

The three beasts looked up at their new prey.

The counselors stared down in horror at their impending doom.

19

MUZZLE OF BEES

Doc let out a pathetic spasm and moan as the wolf slowly sank its teeth into the human's ankle. Just a bite. Just a taste. Only fifty feet above death, the counselors' terror was too overwhelming to elicit any screams until Gracie let out a shrill cry that split the night. Korri began sobbing, her hands covered her mouth to muffle her wailing. The others soon allowed panic and horror to overtake them. Lane looked from the group of counselors to his sister.

She did not scream.

Apollena had never screamed in fear and so neither did Lane.

With a single powerful clap of her hands, Luna broke the panic. "Everyone, silence, now!" She waited for the others to comply. They were silent, but their attention drifted back down to the beasts below. Their silence was sustained only because of the sheer shock of the lion, the panther, and the wolf prowling, circling beneath them. For many of them, Luna imagined it was also the first time they'd seen a dying man. Not just a stranger, either, but someone they knew.

"We need to agree on a plan of attack," Apollena began.

Jordan cut in, "No, nobody is going anywhere or doing anything. We're up here and those things are down there. Everyone shut the fuck up and stay calm—just stay calm!"

Nervous murmuring swelled once more within the group.

"We can't stay up here," Julia spat. "Panthers live in trees. They climb trees to h-hunt their p-p-prey." She shivered, face turning ghostly white.

Franki wrapped her arms around Julia and shot over the terrified whispers, "Who's got their mobile on them? Let's use our heads, people. We call for help and—" scanning the group and their sheepish, embarrassed, horrified faces gave way that no one had brought their cell phones with them.

"Wouldn't matter if we did," Zoe breathed, "No cell service up here anyway."

"There's nobody within thirty miles of camp," Korri said, shaking. "What d'ya think animal control or the park rangers would do with a fucking lion? You dumb dyke!"

Something in Julia snapped as she shot forward and slapped Korri across the face. Franki pulled the smaller blonde back to the edge of the cargo net. Julia was frothing at the mouth as she barked, "YOU DO NOT USE THAT LANGUAGE HERE, YOU BITCH!"

"It's okay, Jewels. Calm down. Bigger things to worry about here, love," Franki said, trying to soothe an enraged Julia into a tight embrace.

Brandon slammed his fist into his open palm. "Guys, there's ten of us and three dumb animals. We have the numbers advantage. We grab a fist full of branches, drop down, and start swinging till they run back off into the woods. Right?"

"HELLO?! Topeka, I can't stress this enough: L-I-O-N," Zoe clapped each letter as she spelled out the predator's name. Sure, it may have been a sickly, emaciated lion, covered in some kind of perpetually oozing tar, but a lion all the same. Even from up in the trees, the beast was easily anywhere between 130 to 150 kilograms. Even if its ribs were visible against its hide, there was enough muscle mass on that creature to swallow two of them whole with room to spare. Additionally, most of the counselors were aware of the concealed butcher knife claws and garden-sheer teeth. Once those blades were sunk inside you, there was no letting go.

"He's right," Cole breathed, cold and slow. "We can't just sit up here and let Doc bleed out. We have to go down there."

"Cole, hun, maybe take a breath and think through that dumb idea?" Korri suggested with an unsettling smile. "You're not going to fight a lion."

"I won't tell you a third time—keep your mouth shut, Reno. Just worry about yourself like you always do," Cole snapped back. He stretched his hands above his head, reached for his guide ropes, and pulled himself up. He stood on the edge of the cargo net and judged his drop distance, leaning backward.

Julia stood up in protest. "Cole, wait!"

"No. No, Julia... And while I'm at it, let me make this crystal clear for all of you," Cole leaned back and reached out for an extended branch on a nearby tree. He snapped it off and pointed it at the group like a wand. "No one is telling me what to do. Doc needs help. I'm not gonna let three animals—"

"You wanna save him? Fine," Apollena interjected, "Do you have a problem with us making a plan to save everyone else first? Time is running out. Would you waste precious seconds acting tough? We're all listening; exactly how strong are you?"

Cole growled but said nothing in reply.

"Good choice," Apollena huffed. "We can't stay up here, we can't fight those things, and we can't run away."

"Way to go, sugar," Gracie laughed hysterically. "Way to eliminate all our possible options. We ought to just jump down an' die then? That it? We just fall and die?!"

"Lane and I will distract them. The rest of you, as a group, will run to the closest landline phone and call for help," Luna said.

Jordan grunted in contempt. "How convenient. Three "ghostly" beasts appear, just when you two do, and only you two can save us from them? Seems shockingly familiar."

Apollena smiled grimly, "Afraid we won't be able to do much in the way of salvation. We've never encountered anything like... them." Luna gestured down.

The beasts remained, waiting directly beneath the net. The light from their shining golden eyes beamed back up at the counselors. Hungry. There was no moonlight to illuminate the most unsettling aspects of the beasts: their claws, their teeth, and their most recent kill still twitching in the midst of them. But what was visible to the naked eye through the dark was more than enough. It was enough to devour any shred of hope.

There was a loud *pop and tear*. The wolf had sunk its teeth into Doc just under the shoulder, separating his left arm from its socket. Julia balled herself up in the fetal position, rocking back and forth in Franki's arms. "Panthers can climb eighteen feet into tree cover. A lion's average land speed is fifty miles an hour. Wolves hunt in packs. They're hunting in a pack. They're hunting us!"

Franki desperately tried to calm Julia down, but the effort was hopeless.

"We can distract them," Lane said to the group, "Don't worry about the how. We'll take care of it. Where's the nearest landline?"

"There's one in the staff lounge," Franki replied.

"You're positive it works?" Lane asked.

She nodded. "Used it earlier this morning to check up on my mum."

"The infirmary is closer," Cole interjected.

"We stand the best odds of surviving if most of us stay together," Apollena said. "Are you certain the phone in the infirmary works? Did you test it? You have keys to the building you want to jostle around while something is chasing after you?"

Jordan shook her head. "So that's it, huh? Everyone here is gonna fall in line with this pair of... Liars? These Lunatics?"

"What are we lying about, exactly?" Lane asked, holding back his frustration, his impatience, his sense of urgency to act before more people died on his watch. "Everyone sees those three things below us, right? You see Doc, bleeding out?"

"Lane," Apollena caught his attention while crawling across the cargo net to meet him, "Here, we can use these..." She dug out her pack of playing cards from her back pocket. Luna handed the palm-sized cardboard box over to her brother.

"You're gonna play fifty-two card pick up with a bunch of wild animals? Yeah, great distraction," Korri said, dripping with sarcasm and bile. "We're all gonna fucking die up here!"

Lane and Luna ignored their comments as they both divided up a handful of cards amongst themselves. Flipping through his Field Journal, Lane found the section on 'Alchemy and Practical Application.' Holding open the specific page in his lap, he handed Luna his spare charcoal pencil from his vest pocket.

"Just follow the example here," Lane instructed his sister. "The equation has to be written out in its entirety along the edges... like this."

Brandon's curiosity got the better of him. "Exactly what are you two doing?"

Apollena explained calmly while her hand furiously scribbled out copies of the formula from Lane's notebook onto the cards in her hand. "We're doing a bit of alchemy."

The group of counselors remained silent.

"Do you remember what I did to your mirror?" Lane asked Jordan. He didn't bother looking up.

"No," Jordan lied quietly.

"In a nutshell, I changed the kinetic, molecular, and spiritual properties of the mirror from solid glass into a fluid doorway. Wherever it was your grandpa was trapped, I opened a way for him to cross over. Same principle here," Lane explained, holding up a card with a charcoal script written in an unknown language along the edges.

"So you're turning those cards into what? Tiny doorways?" Nina asked.

"Yeah. Sorta," Luna replied without looking up, "We'll convert the charcoal into a violet photo-phosphorus flare, opening a tiny portal to exchange one substance for another. That rapid exchange of elements and energy will then combust; hopefully, creating a distraction for the beasts down there."

"It's the alchemic equivalent of a flashbang grenade," Lane summarised as he finished writing the formula on his tenth card.

Jordan shook her head and threw up her hands. "Okay, fuck the Magician Twins. Here's what we're gonna do. Korri, Gracie, Nina, Julia, Zoe, Franki, and I will all take the zipline across the recreation field. That puts us less than a hundred meters from the staff lounge. Hopefully, we'll be able to sprint and distract those—" Jordan was still hesitant to admit the presence of three massive, otherworldly predators fifty feet below her. "The girls take the zipline. Brandon, Cole, once we're far enough away, you two drop down and get Doc. The staff parking lot is—"

"We're taking him to the infirmary," Cole insisted.

"Cole, you dumbshit. That's where we're leading all those things!" Korri screamed. She suddenly became aware they'd be the distraction: the bait. The girl dropped her head. Purple highlights hid her face. With a quiet sigh, she spoke again, a hint of desperation and despair in her voice, "Get Doc and Brandon to your car and get the fuck out of here."

Cole said nothing in return. He scowled and looked back down at the dying man in the center of the three beasts. After a breath, he nodded.

Brandon, adrenaline pumping through his veins, agreed, "Okay, yeah. The parking lot is our best bet. I-I, um, I got my keys. We'll get

Doc outta here and send help for the rest of you when we get, um, somewhere safe." He looked up at the group. "Are we ready?"

Lane passed Luna his orange pocket lighter. She flicked the ignition, and a small blue flame shot into existence. "We're ready."

The girls had all hooked their guide ropes into the four cables that stretched out from the cargo net across the slopped recreation field. It was still too dark and foggy to make out the end of the ziplines, or most of the tilted field itself, but Lane trusted Jordan's experience and knowledge of the camp. He had little choice otherwise.

Jordan unceremoniously kicked off the cargo net and began her descent. Luna watched all three animals take notice of their moving prey. Before any of the beasts could act, the flame from the lighter touched the edge of the card. Luna flung the first playing card into a high arc above their heads. It soared like a knife into the darkness and suddenly ignited. A vapor trail of purple smoke exploded into a flash of violet light followed by a startling *POP*. Luna threw another card from her deck of enchanted playing cards. Another flash, another colossal *POP* shook the forest, illuminating the pines in bright phosphorus light and smoke.

The beasts took the bait.

Without hesitation, Brandon and Cole both dropped out from the cargo net on their guide ropes. Dangling a few inches above the forest floor, the boys unclipped themselves and maneuvered Doc in a two-man carry. The boys struggled to lift the unresponsive senior counselor into a seated position. The first attempt at saving a life is always stressful. Always. Fortunately, after some effort, they'd maneuvered the body in between them and started off down the gravel road. The three disappeared into the darkness. The sound of crunching boots atop gravel softly faded into the haunted night.

"Lane," Luna snapped, "Let's go!"

Taking her brother's outstretched hand, The Twins stepped up to the edge of the zipline and dove out of the cargo net. Tepid wind rushed through their hair and over their bodies. Metallic scraping from the metal pulleys that slid along the cable overhead reverberated through Lane and Luna's chest. They'd made it halfway across the field and still no sign of the others as they soared over the unkempt lawn. Lane's mind raced through the frustration and fear of how utterly unprepared he was. No weapons. No clue what the beasts were or what they wanted. He was in the worst possible position: pitted against an unknown opponent, reacting instead of being proactive. Just like the field below, the odds were tilted against them.

Lane continued to dangle above the field, racing toward the end of his rope, locked on this singular path. He hated every second of it.

Beside him, much to his annoyance, his sister smiled, suppressing a squeal of delight. She caught her brother staring in shock. "What? It might be the last bit of fun we have left. Best enjoy it while we can."

Their momentum sharply decreased. The ground was much closer, visible even in the darkness and fog that surrounded them. They didn't so much screech to a stop, however, as the cable sagged, and the twins began to lazily coast backward. Lane and Luna swiftly unclipped themselves from their harnesses and dropped five feet into the dry brush. The instant their feet hit the ground, they took off like a shot toward the wailing of the girls ahead.

Lane pointed to two figures slumped over one another on the ground ahead, "Luna, looks like Gracie, she's—"

"I see her," Luna huffed out. Raising the lighter to the edge of another playing card, she flicked the spark wheel and threw the flare forward.

POP!

A trail of lime smoke shot forward in front of Gracie and Jordan, squatting down in the gravel. No beasts. Not yet.

"She tripped—" Jordan started, still trying to help pull Gracie along.

Lane immediately bent down and threw Gracie's arm around his shoulders, "Lift on three, two..." Jordan stood up with Lane and lifted the injured girl against her protests of pain.

"It's there! It's there!" Gracie shrieked, jabbing her finger forward at the wall of smoke. Her left foot dragged along the gravel, scraping the rocks together, while her right desperately tried to propel herself forward between Lane and Jordan.

Luna flanked her brother, eyes searching through the smoke. Her ears heard the deep *growl* first. Her chest vibrated at the rumbling of the panthers' paralyzing *scream*.

Unable to move forward, their feet froze in place. Jordan, Gracie, Lane, and Luna turned toward the pair of golden eyes shining through the smokescreen. As the flare's smoke dissipated, the dripping ink body of the obsidian-stained panther gradually blended into the darkness. Although her legs were frozen in fear, Luna's hands reacted on instinct. The flame of Lane's lighter kissed the edge of the playing card in her dominant hand. Luna's aim was true. With a quick flick, the card flew from her hand directly between the eyes of the beast.

POP!

Like watching a balloon full of tar explode, the ink-like substance that covered the panther splattered outward in a gory riot of black liquid and bright pink phosphorus smoke.

"RUN," Lane commanded.

The four humans obeyed and sprinted toward the two-story shack with the last of their strength. Their feet pounded faster as a low bass *growl* shook their chests. Four heavy paws stalked after them in the asphalt, steadily gaining speed. Another earth-splitting, beastly *scream* shook their souls. Crunching asphalt grew louder, rapidly closing the gap between predator and prey. Before the unrelenting creature could devour them, Gracie, Jordan, Lane, and Luna tumbled through the entrance to the cabin and slammed the wooden door shut behind them.

20

KICKING TELEVISION

Lane scrambled to his feet and faced the door as a large mass flung itself against the other side. Wood chips splintered from the doorframe upon impact. He lunged forward, throwing his own body weight against the only barrier between them and death.

BANG!

The room shook. The entire shack shook. Gracie, Jordan, Julia, Franki, and Nina were stunned as the beast outside kept trying to force its way in. Lane's mind raced and survival instincts kicked in. He surveyed the room in the blink of an eye. He pointed to the faded leather couch, the windows, and commanded, "Franki, Julia, shut and bar the windows. Jordan, Luna, move the couch in front of the door!"

Shaken from their terror, the counselors trapped within the shack rapidly barricaded themselves while the door continued to pound inward. The rusted metal latches trembled. A single screw came loose and fell onto the damp matted carpet.

BANG!

Dust and moldy ceiling tiles fell down around them.

BANG!

Cabinets, chairs, and whatever else they could get their hands on were thrown against the windows and the crumbling door.

BANG!

Collectively, the counselors moved to the center of the room and huddled around Gracie, still an immobile, sobbing mess. They waited for the next impact. They waited for another heart-stopping roar from the spectral panther. They waited, but for the first time in what felt like hours, there was only silence.

The only sound within the room were the counselors near hyperventilating breaths and Gracie's muffled cries.

"S-she, she left," Gracie mumbled between heaving breaths, "Zoe. She just left me."

Apollena knelt down beside Gracie. "You're okay. We're not leaving you."

Gracie's bloodshot and tear-filled eyes gazed up at Luna, but said nothing else.

Lane took a closer look around the interior of the tiny shack, inspecting the narrow staircase on the eastern wall with windows on the south and western walls that opened outward. Most of the space was dedicated to being used as a kitchen and coffee bar. Most of the machines, refrigerators, and equipment were still powered off and covered in tarps or canvas sheets.

"Where's the phone?" Lane asked.

Jordan answered, but her eyes were fixed on the feeble wooden door with a million-yard stare. "Upstairs, office lounge."

Without another word, Lane climbed the steps two at a time till he reached the lounge.

Nina paced the kitchen, nervously fiddling with the espresso machines. The one single-use coffee machine they'd used earlier that morning still had half a pot of coffee sitting in the glass carafe. Nina's trembling hands touched the glass. It was cold. Unlike Aiden's callused, warm hands, this coffee had been neglected since earlier that afternoon. Before the beasts. Before the ropes course. Before Brad and the others barged in on them...

"I'll never see him again," Nina whispered as the carafe fell onto the floor. Glass *shattered*. Nina instinctively jumped back toward the center of the small room.

"DAMN IT, NINA!" Jordan snapped. "You want that thing to come back?!"

Still shaking, the Pixie shook her head and blubbered, "I'll never see him again."

"Snap out of it," Jordan commanded. "We need to keep our heads on straight if we want to get out of this—" She stopped herself. What even was *this*? This didn't feel real. Nothing in Jordan's mental filing cabinet could have prepared her for being chased by giant jungle animals. She'd had a dog growing up, a couple of cats. She loved animals. Now? She was terrified, humiliated, and furious that this situation had spiraled so far out of her control. How would she have known that she'd need to pack a hunting rifle on her yearly trip to prove herself worthy of leading a handful of stupid twenty-year-olds?

"Jewels," Franki spoke quietly, taking the small blonde by the hand and leading her to the staircase, "I love you. I've been, ya know, more than crushing on you for a long while now."

Julia was still stunned, shocked by having her life flash before her eyes. She'd nearly died. She'd nearly watched her co-counselor get eaten. They'd nearly all been eaten. She needed to hear Franki's words again. "Come again?" she coughed out.

"I know there are a lot of barriers between me gettin' with you," Franki illustrated the point, motioning with her hands. Dropping them to her sides, the taller girl offered a weak smile, turned her palms up, offering herself in surrender. "I can't control any of that. I just want you to know, on my end at least, there's nothing standing between you coming to me. I'm here for you, Jewels. I want to be here with you, for however long we've got, till—" She let her shoulders drop. It kinda felt like the end of the world, but if Franki met that end, it was going to be with less burden on her back.

Julia beamed up into Franki's gorgeous, glowing amber eyes, "I wish," she started, taking a step closer, "I wish I were brave enough to say something sooner."

Franki reached out halfway for Julia. "Well, whatcha gonna say now?"

Julia didn't meet Franki halfway. The small blonde girl bit her lower lip, then lunged forward into Franki. Her tanned arms wrapped around the taller girl, pulling her down into a long-repressed kiss. Their lips met, locked and exchanged years' worth of longing and missed opportunities.

"Girls, I don't think now's the time to—" Jordan groaned.

Apollena shushed Jordan, "Do you want to be Bradley and deny them joy?"

Julia and Franki's passion grew. The taller girl stripped the shorter of her t-shirt. They frantically pawed at one another, making their way up the narrow staircase. Bittersweet tears mixed with joyful moans, and long-awaited sighs of relief.

Nina let slip a small smile while carefully sweeping up the broken glass into a dustpan. Another set of footsteps made their way downstairs. Lane's face gave no hint that he even registered the two lovers pass by him on the staircase.

"If we can hold out for an hour, all of us are going to make it out of here," Lane declared in a level, almost detached voice.

"An hour?" Gracie moaned, "How? What if those things get in here?"

Apollena continued to soothe Gracie and examine her ankle. A minor sprain at best. Subtly capturing Nina's attention, she asked, "Could you find an ice-pack, or a bag of ice for Gracie, please?"

Nina mouthed the words back to Luna, nodded her head, and

searched the freezer.

"Who'd you call?" Jordan demanded.

Lane busied his mind checking the barricades at the door and windows while he replied, "Contacted my old crewmate in the CoastGuard. He's friends with a pilot at the Seattle Station. Told him we had been critically injured and we needed help." Using an old curtain rod, he reinforced the western window. "They've got an S-92 rescue helicopter that'll fit at least ten passengers. Waited on the line till he confirmed they'd scrambled their Search and Rescue Team. One more hour tops and they'll be over Spirit Lake to airlift us the fuck out of here."

Luna accepted the damp washcloth from Nina and gently applied it to Gracie's ankle.

"So that's it then?" Jordan asked, "We just wait, and you've saved us all? Thanks."

Gracie tried to lean forward. "No, that's not all. What about Cole and Brandon?"

Nina dropped her head. "You really think they've made it with those things out there?"

"They could have! I mean," Gracie swallowed, eyes still teary, "I don't know, maybe? We can't just leave 'em. We ain't leaving people behind!"

Jordan tried to think of something to say, something to prove she still had some control over the situation but came up empty. What was there to say? They had a way out. But that thorn in the back of her mind, Lane Guster Woods, had once again miraculously conjured a solution to a problem beyond her grasp. What was she supposed to do, say no? Come up with something better? She didn't want to die, but she hated being in debt just as much.

"We're not leaving anyone behind," Jordan assured Gracie. "Topeka and Olympia are purebred stallions. They live for that jock shit. If anyone can outrun whatever those things are, those two can. They'll get Doc to the parking lot, and…" She stumbled through her story, her delusion, "They'll get to the ranger station. When we get cell reception, we'll give 'em a call and forget this whole shit storm happened over drinks. Lots of drinks. Okay?"

Gracie tried to swallow the pleasant lie that Jordan attempted to convey but was simply too scared, too heartbroken to call the counselor's bluff.

Luna continued to wrap Gracie's leg with the bandages from the decades-old first aid kit Nina had found in one of the kitchen cabinets. Not looking up from her work, she asked her brother, "So that's it then. We're just letting the loose ends dangle in this case?"

Lane shook his head, "Civilians take priority. We get Gracie treated and everyone else to safety, then you and I will regroup, and figure out what went on afterward."

"Get the civilians to safety," Nina mocked lightly. She felt the glares of everyone else in the room turn on her, and sheepishly offered a hasty apology, "Just saying, sounded like you're conducting some military operation."

"This ain't a joke, sugar," Gracie bit back. "People could be dying. Doc might already be dead and you're laughing it up?"

"I'm sorry, okay? What else do you want me to say?" Nina strained. "You're not the only one who could have lost someone." Her voice caught. Her throat suddenly dried up at the thought of Aiden outside in the dark, among those beasts all alone. Or worse, with Brad.

"That's alright, Nina," Apollena spoke calmly, "We all process stress differently. Right now, we remain together, alive and patient. Rescue is on the way. We'll figure the rest out when the time comes," Luna said pointedly to her brother. It was unlike him to simply abandon a mystery, but he was right. They couldn't both go diving headfirst into the unknown while other's lives were at risk. Whatever force was behind these creatures, they'd find out after any bystanders were safely removed from this theater.

Lane exhaled slowly. They'd secured rescue, fortified shelter, and had an exit plan. Now, with some time on their hands, he could attempt to make a dent in this mystery. There were a dozen disconnected pieces to this whirlwind that had lasted barely forty-eight hours. How was he supposed to find the edges? How could he find the bigger picture in this madness while he was stuck in the middle of it?

"Jordan," Lane began tentatively, "What can you tell me about this camp?"

The woman with the wild red hair blinked. "What?"

Lane tried to formulate a more coherent question. Again, he found himself distracted, intimidated by Jordan's presence, beauty, and tenacity to endure this otherworldly assault. "What I mean is," he began cautiously, "I'm trying to wrap my head around why something like this would happen, here, and now. Has anything out of the ordinary ever happened like this here before?"

Frustrated, Jordan shook her head. "Happened like, what? Animal attacks?"

"No," Lane said, more agitated at his own lack of clarity. He fought to keep his voice neutral, calm. "Has anything supernatural ever happened at this camp since you've been coming here?"

Jordan's eyes narrowed and shot back at Lane like hollow points. "You really want to do this now?" she asked. "You want to make this situation into some magic act that you and your weirdo sister will miraculously—"

Nina stepped in. "He's just asking a question, Jordan. You don't have to dunk on him with whatever past hang-ups you two have. Honestly, I should have asked you more about this place before you dragged *me* up here! Are we on an old Indian Burial Ground or whatever? Were there child sacrifices? You can't just sit there and bury your head in the sand after all that!" Nina jabbed a finger at the door. "Not to mention all the weird, um, sex stuff you guys were into..."

There was a tense stillness in the room before Gracie spoke up,

"I kinda remember something," she sniffed out, "Zoey and I couldn't explain why before. There was this intense connection between us. At least, it felt like there was something. I had never really thought of Zoe as... well, ya know, anything more than a friend. Ever since that first night, I don't know what came over me. It seemed natural at the moment, but not?"

Nina nodded along. "Not natural for you, ya mean?"

Gracie's eyes flicked to Nina. "Yeah. I mean, I like women. I like Zoey. But, now that I'm thinking about it, kinda almost felt like something else was tugging at my heartstrings. Not just tugging, but really taking hold of the reins. Everything was all dialed up to eleven. Any y'all ever done ecstasy before? No? Well... like that, but more so."

"Or maybe you just got horny and lonely?" Jordan countered dryly. "Don't let these two get in your heads. It's all just a trick, or whatever."

Nina stared aghast and again pointed at the door. "A cat as long as a motherfucking surfboard that weighs more than you do was pounding at the door a minute ago. What kinda trick is that!? You telling us that we can't believe our own eyes and ears?"

"You weren't there, Nina, you don't know what they did to me!" Jordan yelled.

"Yeah? And you never told me," the pixie girl replied, "If it was so important to you, so devastating, you share that shit with your best friend. Instead, you hid it from me."

"Yeah, I did, 'cause I was tired of losing friends whenever they found out! You have any idea how hard it was for people to see *me* when–?" Jordan caught herself, but it was too late.

Nina nodded. "How hard is it, Jordan? How hard is it to tell people the truth about who you are, or your own experience? No. Tell me. How hard is it to *come out* to your friends and family and tell them something they might disown you for?" Nina wiped away a fist full of tears, "Tell me how hard that was for you 'cause I've no fucking idea what that's like."

Jordan bit her lip and whispered, "It's not the same," she said in a small voice.

"No," Nina admitted, "It's not the same, but if something is eating you up inside, you don't keep it in or it'll eat you alive."

"Xwa'ni," Gracie breathed out. Her eyes were distant, staring up at the ceiling.

"What?" Apollena asked.

"Xwa'ni," Gracie said again, "It's the Indian thing, or First Peoples I mean. They owned this land." She looked around at the other counselors staring back at her, "I don't think this place was built on any burial ground or nothin', but the camp song we sing is supposedly taken from a kinda local Native folklore, I think. Jude had mentioned it a few years back when I first started working here. Xwa'ni… and the Deer Woman."

Lane remembered the bell and the statues at the entrance to the camp. Offhand, he could recall what information he had in his Journal about Native American deities and spirits; tragically, it was next to nothing at all.

Before Lane could ask a follow-up question, glass *shattered* and a large mass *thumped* onto the ceiling above them broke their temporary calm. Without hesitation, Lane grabbed the curtain rod, a sheet cover from the espresso machine, and pulled out his lighter. Storming up the stairs, Lane wrapped the dry sheet and fixed it around the top of the metal rod. He ignited the lighter and held the tip to the sheet.

Lane jabbed the flaming pole through the entrance of the second-story lounge. In the darkened room, he saw Franki folded in the corner to his right. Her wide eyes were fixated on the gruesome scene ahead: a pair of yellow eyes flickered above Julia's still body lying on the floor. The panther bared its teeth and let out a low warning growl.

Lane lunged forward with the pole of flame and *screamed!*

Undeterred, the Panther held its ground.

With another primal *shout* and bold lunge forward, Lane's flaming pole found its mark, scorching the Panther's inky flesh. Tar dripped from its face and onto the stained carpet. With a yowl of pain, the beast sunk its teeth into Julia and dragged her lifeless body out through the broken window. Lane reached out, but the beast and its kill were gone.

The young man with the spear of flame rushed to the window. There was nothing out there but pine trees and darkness.

After a long-defeated pause, Lane asked Franki, "Are you injured? You okay?"

No. No, she wasn't. The love of her life had been slain by an otherworldly predator. That image was seared into her eyes, her mind, her soul, and would stay there for the rest of her life. Franki was petrified. It wasn't until Lane grabbed hold of her shoulder that she wailed—heartbreak like a dam that had ruptured and expelled the last drops of love she'd ever held.

"Franki," Lane spoke calmly, with authority and sympathy, "We can't lose you too. We have to move. We have to get somewhere safe. Stand up and come with me."

Her body moved, but Franki was numb everywhere else. She was sleep-walking as Lane pulled the grieving girl by the hand downstairs with the others. Instructions were shouted. People screamed. Someone else took hold of Franki's hand and pulled her outside, along with those who remained. Everything became a muted blur. Everyone was numb and weightless as they all left the shack behind and made a desperate run for the Great Lodge.

21

ONE BY ONE

They hadn't run far. Only a few yards. But each step that drove into the loose gravel felt less like rocks and more like shattered glass. With every pace, those deafening, echoing *crunches* could have alerted every animal in the pinewood forest that surrounded Spirit Lake, not to mention the three beasts that still roamed out in the darkness. The Omens: the lion, the wolf, and the panther that had recently eaten.

Now, only the six humans remained. *At least six they knew about.*

Lane hadn't bothered with searching for a key to the locked door. He and Apollena had simply kicked the wooden door in, then busied themselves with securing it back on its hinges once everyone else piled inside.

There were no lights on in the foyer of the Great Lodge. No ambient music. Once they'd finished clamouring inside, a weighted silence pressed down on the survivors. Nina raised the steel curtain rod that still held the burning oil rag on one end. It was an adequate lamp, providing just enough light for the twins to erect a barricade of chairs

and a couch in front of the door they'd just broken.

"Where's Julia?" Gracie panted out, slumped up against the wall.

Jordan only glanced in Franki's direction. Off the taller girl's face, frozen in horror, the acting lead counselor shot Lane an accusatory glare.

Nervously, Nina touched Luna's shoulder, "We, w-we have to go back for her, right?"

Apollena's downcast face gave the pixie girl the answer she didn't want to hear.

The Truth: Julia was gone.

Franki kept breathing, rapid, shallow breaths.

Gracie tried to cover an ocean's-worth of fear with a napkin of optimism. "Nina's right, we can't board up the place if there's a chance Julia might—"

"She's dead," Jordan said. Her words landed heavily in the dark, empty foyer.

"You can't just... Jesus, Jordan, do you have any consideration for Franki at all?" Nina protested. "What the hell is the matter with you?"

"Great question, for when we're not being chased by wild animals. We have to keep our heads grounded and focused on getting out of here alive," Jordan stated plainly.

"But you don't have to be so cruel, so callous, so..." Nina was trying to pick a fight. She was trying to be angry on Franki's behalf. Franki didn't look angry, though. She didn't look as if she were feeling anything at all. Franki was catatonic. That may have scared Nina more than the thought of being hunted by ghost animals, or demons, or whatever those things were. For Nina, to feel nothing, especially the loss of someone she loved, terrified her.

"Jordan's right," Lane said delicately, and took the curtain rod from Nina. "We stay focused, we stay together, and we stay alive."

"Don't try to take my side and play the hero," Jordan snapped.

"I am not," Lane replied, steady and without inflection. "We need to secure ourselves here for the next fifty minutes until the rescue transport arrives. Any doors, any windows—"

"The whole back wall is nothin' BUT windows, sugar. If you're looking for a good hiding place, this ain't it. Any one of those things could break through the glass," Gracie rattled off.

"Unlikely. During the initiation or baptism, I noticed these windows used two-pane laminated glass—the same stuff used in zoo enclosures. You could run up to it at full strength with a sledgehammer and not make a hole big enough for even a mouse to get through," Lane replied. Until now, it seemed a little overkill to use such high-grade materials. Seeing his sister play her invisible violin, she seemed to be on the same wavelength.

"You think they'd planned ahead for such an event?" Apollena thought aloud.

Nina's eyes went wide. "You think somebody planned for those... things? For all this?"

"Enough," Jordan interrupted. She jabbed a finger at Lane. "This isn't a show, and you're not turning this into some magic performance. Not again. We'll secure the building, stay quiet, and IF rescue comes, that'll be the end of it."

"Oh, the end is already on its way," a voice mused from the main dining hall. It was a familiar, masculine voice. It felt like a cheese grater to Lane's ears.

The six remaining counselors huddled together. Lane and Apollena stood at the forefront. All were silent. All were motionless, with their eyes fixed on the gray outline of the dining hall doors illuminated by their dwindling torch.

"That sounds like... Brad?" Nina whispered.

Gracie wrinkled her nose and let out a nervous laugh. "Why the hell you whisperin' then? It's just Brad." Limping forward, the voluptuous girl headed for the dining hall, "Brad? Thank Christ a'Mighty you're alright! Hun? You won't believe what we—"

As Gracie stepped through the swinging doors of the dining hall, she let out a shrill *scream*. Her body hit the carpet with a *thud*. Jordan was about to rush to her aid, but Lane held her back.

Shaking off the ginger boy's hand, Jordan whispered bitterly, "You want another dead counselor on your hands? I'm sure as hell not going to have that blood on mine."

Jordan marched forward.

Nina gasped out, "No. Please, JoJo, don't!"

The wild redhead girl pushed through the double doors, "What the fuck?!" She gasped, but there was no sound of a body hitting the carpeted floor this time. Instead, the voice of Brad answered in a casual, almost flirty reply:

"I guess I got hungry is all," Came the voice through the crack in the door, "You're more than welcome to dig in. Please, help yourself. Who else you got with you? Topeka? Olympia? I'll even take any of the ladies if they're left. Hello, anyone else out there? Come on in. Come! I am waiting to serve..."

Brad trailed off on a sing-song high note.

What were the odds Vegas didn't know about the spectral animals, the death, and everything else out of the ordinary that unfolded at this camp? Lane figured the odds would be astronomically small.

Brad knew something and Lane was prepared to beat it out of him if necessary.

He gave one look to his sister. That's all Lane needed. Apollena nodded in reply as Lane stepped forward, the curtain rod in hand. He held his hand on the door, pushing it open just a crack to survey the room. Some cloud cover had parted to allow a hint of starlight in through the southern wall of floor-to-ceiling windows. Not much good it did. His eyes adjusted to the graying darkness of the dining room. Sheets still covered most of the furniture, along with that same black soot, soil, and tar-like substance that covered the beasts. Lane recalled that the same material had been on some part of Jude each time the enigmatic Camp Director had appeared.

There were still loose tiles, cables, and wires dangling from the ceiling. A few ladders littered the room. In the central dining hall, one long dining table had been set with some kind of carcass lying on top of a silver platter. At the head of the chair furthest from the door, boots kicked up on top of the tablecloth: Brad.

"Oh, looks like we have another guest, come to share their last supper," Vegas beckoned, "Come on, let's see who else we've got here with us…?"

Lane remained hidden behind the door. Final looks. The two doors on the eastern and western walls appeared locked. Barred. Four small wooden pyres were smouldering in each cardinal direction around the table. Two other place settings sat unwashed on the table.

Vegas hadn't shut himself in the dining hall and barricaded the exits by himself. If he was expecting company, clearly this was the one entrance he anticipated meeting them.

Jordan still remained standing just outside the swing of the dining hall doors. Gracie lay on the ground, unconscious. She'd most likely fainted. No blood. If Brad had some ranged weapon, Jordan most likely wouldn't still be standing. Lane studied Jordan the best he could from behind. Her left hand was trembling, her right hand shot up to cover her mouth, frozen in a scream. The rest of the wild red-haired girl's body remained as stiff as a board, immobile.

"You can't tell me your master plan is to hide and stuff your face with everything going on out there?" Lane shouted through the door. He watched an eager Brad jump to his feet, hopping up on the table with disturbing glee. "You seem more keen to participate in the action."

"Holy shit, that sounds like… ROSWELL!" Vegas rubbed his hands together. "Truly a gift from above, or wherever? A parting gift. A rematch. What say you, Roswell, how about one last rumble? Settle out who's the better man once and for all?"

Lane was not in a gaming mood. Of all the people he'd ever felt compelled to prove his worth to, Brad wasn't just last, he didn't even make the list. Unfortunately, Lane's honor compelled him to give this ostentatious fuckwagon a fair chance.

"We've called for help. It's on the way. How about we *not* play games and wait for rescue?" Lane asked evenly.

Brad tapped a finger to his forehead. "That sounds like someone's looking for a way out. As if there even *is* a way out. But, there's no stopping the inevitable—"

"Stopping what, Brad?" Lane's patience was tried. He had to pry any information that Brad had from his fat mouth.

"No, no," Brad warned as he walked and skipped across the long wooden table. "That's not my name, Roswell. Let's use our newly christened names. Camp rules."

Brad was well within range for Lane to strike him down, using the curtain rod as a javelin. He could skewer him, or with equal ease, blow off one of his kneecaps. Leaving him conscious enough to question. As he got closer, though, Lane could make out the mess that was Vegas' face. Something was smeared all over him, from ear to ear, and dripping down onto his bare chest.

Not only black tar and soil.

Copper red and thick.

Blood.

Lane shifted his focus behind Brad. There, on the table, the carcass, it looked almost... human.

"C'mon, Roswell? You ready to man up? This is the last chance you'll get to leave your mark on this world before it's all gone." Brad leapt off the table. He was a little less than fifteen feet away. His bare chest was covered in red congealed flecks, black boxer briefs, and bare feet. "Let's GO!" He roared, "Or do you wanna die a coward?"

Lane kicked the door open and shoved Jordan aside.

He'd had his eyes locked on Brad's right kneecap, with his makeshift javelin cocked and ready. Exhaling, he threw the metal rod forward at full strength.

Brad dove out of the way, falling on his side. He laughed and sprang up to his feet, running to meet Lane's second strike. Typically, a jab or a faint body blow would be his opening move, but Lane didn't have that kind of time to spare. He was tired of letting the plot unfold ahead of him. He was tired of reacting to the supernatural, the tragedy, and the death. Lane was on the attack and wasn't holding back.

Vegas took a right haymaker to the jaw that nearly levelled him. Unfortunately for Lane, Brad was no slouch in strength and durability. He took the full force of the blow and sprang right back up for more. Smiling with a mouthful of blood, Vegas spat in Lane's face. The ginger was able to dodge Brad's first punch, but a wild series of fists followed shortly after.

Lane was forced to play defence. Or so it would have appeared. With each swing, miss, and movement, Lane was calculating every possible combination of attacks Brad had in his arsenal. It didn't take a seasoned fighter to observe Vegas wasn't formally trained. Probably grew up watching a lot of action movies, schoolyard fights, and maybe a brawl or two. His reach, muscle mass, and height advantage were staggering. But Lane didn't let his years of training and experience overshadow that obvious observation. One misstep and it could easily be his end.

After a barrage of fists and a sloppy standing heel kick, Lane had all the data he needed. Brad was right-hand dominant, so Lane began attacking the muscular boy's left side with alternating forward strikes at Brad's ribs, head, and knee. He continued to circle counter-clockwise, keeping Brad off balance.

It didn't take long. Brad's fatigue started to show.

One slip in this Goliath's modest defence and Lane would exploit it, no sling or smooth rocks required.

Brad came at him again. Wild, unfocused, but with enough mass and speed to maim and kill. Lane ducked under his opponent's wide roundhouse and landed an opened palm chop deep into Vegas' ribs, stepping in to connect an uppercut under his armpit in the same movement. Brad's shoulder *POPPED,* dislocating. His left arm fell limp, right hand instinctively covering the damage. Lane continued the attack with a heel kick into his rival's left kneecap. Another *POP!* Brad staggered forward. Lane accelerated his opponents' momentum, grabbing him by the back of the neck and pulling him into a hard left uppercut into Brad's throat.

Lane released Brad, letting his body fall to the carpet.

Now that the brute was out of commission, Lane needed to ensure Vegas stayed in place for the interrogation. He stepped around his fallen foe and searched for the metal curtain rod. That's when Lane's eyes fell upon the horror on the table and fully grasped what was laid out before him. A rush of emotion nearly drowned him: sorrow, guilt, hatred, and rage.

Jordan broke through to Lane with a *scream* so terrible it startled him to his core.

He spun around, face to face with a smiling Brad. A large kitchen knife raised high above his head as manic laughter poured out of his mouth like sewage from a storm drain.

"Looks like I'm having seconds this evening," Brad cackled wildly.

Before the blond-haired lunatic plunged his knife down into Lane, a boisterous clatter of wood crashed over flesh and impeded the mad laughter. Brad once again toppled over face-first into the carpet. This time, however, he stayed down, motionless.

Standing behind the fallen Vegas among bits of the shattered chair, was Apollena.

Luna tossed the broken chair legs aside. She spat on Vegas and cursed him in her native tongue, *"Remember you're better, who twice conquered you from behind."* Apollena then refocused her attention on Lane, "Turning your back on an opponent? Sloppy, Ursa Major."

"It's been a long day," Lane panted. His final moment of levity before turning his attention back to the gruesome, sadistic display on the table.

"YOU BASTARD!" Nina cried at the top of her lungs, running past Lane and Luna, to the unconscious Brad. The pixie girl began mercilessly kicking Veras' ribs cage, sobbing, wailing. "How could you?! The fuck kind of monster, are you?!"

Apollena wrapped her arms around the young girl and dragged her toward Gracie and Jordan. Gracie had begun to stir. Jordan was still boiling in shock at the mess on the table.

Laid out like a sacrificial calf, carved open and half-eaten, was Aiden.

Left standing against the far wall by the kitchen door, Franki finally began to cry, followed by heaving, mad laughter. Something inside her had finally snapped. It was only a matter of time before the others broke, too.

POOR PLACES

Brad spat out a mouthful of blood as he came back around. He struggled before even opening his eyes. He continued to writhe violently, as one would if they were tied to a chair.

"Wouldn't recommend that," Lane said evenly. "The drop wouldn't kill you, but the impact won't be pleasant."

Surprisingly, Brad sighed and relaxed. He opened his eyes to see his chair sitting precariously close to the edge of the long wooden table. The blond buzz-cut kid licked his lips and nodded. "Fun. I would have gone for more of a pinata situation, but this is fine too if you're afraid of a real fight: man on man."

"You are no man. But, he did fight you," Apollena stated dryly, "He handed your ass back to you twice already." Glancing over to her brother, she crinkled her face as if to quietly ask, 'Is that the correct expression?' Lane subtly gestured with his fingers to drop it. Not important.

"Sure, sure he did," Brad continued. "So what now? How would you like to spend your final moments?"

"Enough with the coy bullshit," Lane barked. "First, you're gonna tell us who is running the show, then where they're at."

Brad laughed, "No."

Lane and Apollena waited. They let the silence thicken and the tension boil.

"I see no reason why I should have to cooperate with you," Brad added with a smug, bloody smile, "What are you planning on doing? Torturing me? Punishing me? You really think there's anything you could possibly offer me?" Brad laughed at the two stone faced twins.

"How about another victory?" Apollena suggested.

Brad scoffed, "You're gonna untie me and let me beat the shit out of your brother? Sure, but I can't guarantee I'll be any more talkative. How about you let me bang you, Nina, Franki, Gracie, *especially* Jordan, and whoever else you got tagging along with you? Yeah. That'll hit the spot. One last send off orgy and maybe I'll clue you in—"

"No," Lane interrupted, "You get one chance to be the ultimate victor." Lane waited for Brad's attention and his one unswollen eye to focus on him. "Let's say we believe you're telling the truth. There's some doomsday, end of the world event happening, soon. In this scenario, you're not the guy in charge. You don't win. You're an errand boy protecting whoever's really in power." Lane let that sink in a moment, "Let's say you stay silent. You don't tell us who, where and how the world ends. You'll die the underling of someone who's smarter, stronger, and more powerful than you. You'll be forever in second place."

To the average observer, Brad seemed to let this news wash over him, to no effect. Apollena, however, had studied Brad—intimately. She'd seen him experience pleasure by her own hand, no less. She'd seen how he reacted as his peers, his friends, abandoned him on the field. She saw how truly vulnerable he was, begging for a sense of completion. If there was one defining trait, the quantum of who Brad was at his core, he needed to feel victorious.

The subtle clench of the jock's jaw. His thumbs twitching to grasp the rope tighter. Just as he had in the final round of Tiki Tiki Firedrum, the idea that Brad's life would be extinguished without feeling a sense of completion, without victory, had burrowed into his mind. When he played his next move, his next words, the twins knew, they had him: "No. I call bullshit. I'm on the winning team. You're the suckers that came too late to the party. We won."

Denial, Lane thought as he smiled. He checked his watch. "Somewhere in the back of your mind, you probably had to autocorrect to, '*We Win*'. Not *you* win, right?"

"Sure," Apollena continued, "Your *Team* may have won, but you're still the pawn the real genius sacrificed so *they* could win. You really think pawns get to party with the king?" She cackled. "I mean, you're here? You're practically on our team now. The losing team."

"I watched that *thing* eat your fat fucking friend. Gutted him, opened him up like a calf. I watched that– *thing* eat 'em. Even I even had a taste. They made me eat but– How's that for being on the losing team, shitheads!" Brad screamed out.

They were close. Lane wanted to punch Brad without stopping until that stupid, smug, murderous face was nothing but bone dust on Lane's knuckles. Instead, he kept his breathing even. He buried his emotions to the farthest reaches of his mind. *Stay on task,* he reminded himself, *stay focused.*

"And we don't expect you to feel any remorse for that. You're a sociopath. Your only concern is winning, which we'll remind you, is not what's going on right now. You're at the loser's table, Brad: a pawn, a scapegoat, a speed bump in someone's way to get what they want."

"No, that's not—" Brad started, "You don't get it, okay? It's not like I really wanted to... You don't have any fucking clue what you're dealing with!" Brad's lip trembled.

He's not there, not yet, Apollena observed. *Perhaps another little push.*

"I see no evidence that you have even the capacity to care about anyone other than yourself," Luna added, twisting her sharpened words further into his minuscule heart.

"She—" Brad bit his tongue and shook his head. His breathing became more rapid. Brad's muscles strained against the ropes as he whispered, "She didn't give me a choice." At last, the smallest glint of a tear materialised in Brad's bloodshot eye.

"She?" Lane asked subtly.

Brad shook his head.

"WHO IS SHE?!" Apollena demanded, stomping on the table the twins had restrained their captive atop. Brad's chair wobbled closer to the edge.

"Her," Brad fumbled. In between increasingly erratic breaths, the Jock whispered, "The Deer Woman." His one good eye grew distant. Just as the words left his mouth, Brad realized what he'd said. He let the one piece of information out that was to remain secret for the last few hours left while their plan continued to unfold. Panic began to wash over him. Nervous laughter shot out from his blood-stained mouth. "She's a demon, a god, a THING. You can't stop her. Can't reason with her. Can't beat her." More desperate laughter, followed by his acceptance of the inevitable. This was it. "You lose," Brad said to himself.

With that final failure, the jock rocked his body backward. With one last-minute twist, Brad's head landed at the worst possible angle on the hardwood floor. *SNAP*.

The twins observed the corpse as Jordan stepped out from the kitchen. She stood at the entryway. Her line of sight was unobstructed. The acting lead counselor gazed at the floor where Brad's body lay.

"Well," Jordan breathed out, "What now?"

"I'm sorry," Lane said, "He just—we meant to keep him alive and have Brad pay for—"

Jordan waved the boy off. "Brad was a sick fuck. Don't care. What do we do now?" Behind her, Nina, Franki and Gracie appeared. Nina's anger remained. The life behind Franki's eyes was still absent. Gracie held both her hands to her mouth to keep from screaming again. Not that there was any energy left in the girl to release a whisper. After everything that had happened: the beasts, the death, the blood, she was nearly as devoid of feeling as Franki.

Apollena took hold of Lane's hand to read his watch. "Now, we wait."

Lane nodded in solemn agreement. They had a suspect, but those in harm's way still needed to be removed from the playing field. Not that any of this was a game. That's simply how he coped. Mentally, he could remove himself from the horrors unfolding before his eyes. Each action was a calculated move between players: protagonist and antagonist, black and white. When Lane and his sister secured their victory, when all this madness was over, then he'd allow himself to feel something again.

Minutes felt like years as the group sat behind a barricade of tables that hid their presence from anyone or anything that might pass by the window. Fortunately, they could still see out from their vantage point through cracks and slits in their barricade. They saw the sky and continued to pray to whoever was listening that rescue would actually arrive.

Lane and Jordan had covered what was left of Aiden with the sheets that had been draped over the furniture and tables. The man deserved a better burial. *He will receive a proper burial,* Lane thought mournfully.

Brad's body had been left exactly where it was. Covered, but with significantly less care. The corpse remained where he'd fallen off the long table. While covering the body, Apollena had confirmed that in attendance at the sociopath's last meal, there were at least two other guests. On the left side of the table, a pair of muddy boot prints stained the carpet, size eleven. Seated at the head, a dozen or so paw prints of varying sizes were smudged on the wood floor as well.

"Lane," Apollena said quietly, subtly pointing to the ground.

Lane squatted down, hovering over the wood-laminate floor. There was something else underneath the muddy mess Brad had left. "This wasn't his original seat. Look there," Lane pointed to the chair pulled out on the right side. "So we had Brad, and Jude here, maybe a few hours ago sharing a meal—" he gritted his teeth. "They'd murdered Aiden. Before we arrived, judging by the size from toe to heel..." Lane trailed off. He couldn't repress the unholy scene. His friend was in agony. He took a breath and set his jaw. "They're the same prints from the bathhouse."

Luna raised her invisible bow and played a single silent note. "She was here."

"The Deer Woman," Lane agreed as he studied several pairs of massive prints shaped like upside down hearts split right down the center.

"Listen!" Nina said out loud. She covered her mouth and nervously scanned the windows. There were no beasts. Only a dimly lit lake, the St. Helens Mountain Range, and the steady beating of rotary blades somewhere in the distance.

Jordan motioned for the group to crawl toward the southwest patio exit. Together, they made their way through the dark dining hall on their hands and knees.

"Can you see it yet?" Gracie whispered. "I don't see it."

"Better question: how is IT going to see us?" Jordan asked Lane without looking.

Lane held up one of the playing cards with the charcoal runes, "I've got it handled."

Jordan rolled her eyes.

As the sound got closer, all they needed to do was run down the patio steps to the amphitheatre. There was another path directly behind the stage that opened up to the beach. On Jordan's count of three, that's exactly what happened.

They all kept a sharp ear out for the other beasts. Any optimism of hearing the others had long been extinguished. While the Twins helped Gracie down the steep sloped path beside the stone amphitheatre, the rest of their group ran with hopeless abandon. Nina, always a lithe and slender built girl, was second only to Franki, whose long, athletic legs pushed off the ground at an incredible rate.

All the while, Jordan listened to the beating sound of the rotary blades grow louder and louder. It was actually a relief to see the white and red striped helicopter crest over the mountain range. She could hate Lane and his weird sister later. Right now, she was genuinely relieved that something, for once, went right.

As they all stepped foot onto the white sand shore, Lane dug his orange lighter out from his pocket and ignited the flame. He carefully set the edge of the card on fire, passed it to Luna, and she flung it up into the air. Seconds later, the playing card ignited into a burst of red phosphorus light and smoke.

Bright light shone upon the survivors as the search and rescue teams' helicopter turned its floodlight onto the weary counselors. It was low enough to Spirit Lake now that the waters began to ripple outward. Lane felt the chopping wind pulsing against his face.

Then, inexplicably, off to their left somewhere within the depths of the forest, something set against the massive pines, forcing them to bend and creek against the wind of the helicopter. There was a terrible CRACK and a violent rustling of branches. Lane's jaw dropped down to the shore. His heart sank with it as he watched an entire pine tree shoot out from the forest like a surface-to-air missile. He watched in slow motion as the nearly two-hundred-foot-tall tree skewered the helicopter. The rotary blades snapped, sparks flew, and flames burst inside the cockpit as the aircraft listed off to the side. The pilot, the rescue team, their screams could just barely be heard over the midair catastrophe.

Down went their hope of rescue, spiraling into a heap of twisted metal, plunging into the depths of Spirit Lake.

23

THEOLOGIANS

Lane emerged from the freezing water empty-handed. He couldn't even reach what was left of the chopper. The counselor's best chance of escape didn't just sink into the center of the dark water, it was skewered into the lakebed.

"No luck?" Apollena asked solemnly.

Lane shook his head and shivered. "They didn't make it."

Gracie was sobbing, curled up on the sand. "We're going to die here too, aren't we? We're going to just die here like everyone else."

Franki still held a million-yard, empty gaze out onto the horizon.

Nina was fuming. "No! We're not gonna die, not until we find Jude. Where the fuck has he been, huh? Is he in on this Deer Woman bullshit? If we die, I'm killing somebody first, and I wanna take it out on the asshole who was supposed to be in charge of this cluster fuck of a camp!" She threw a handful of stones into the lake and *screamed*.

"Nina, calm down and shut up. Those animals are still out there," Jordan commanded.

The pixie girl did not comply. "Fuck you, Jordan! Did you not just watch a pine tree fly out of the goddamn woods and shish kabob a helicopter!?"

Jordan grabbed Nina by the collar of her shirt. "Yeah. I saw it. What do you want me to do about it? Freaking out isn't going to help get us out of this mess. It'll probably just end up getting us killed faster."

"We need to get to the staff parking lot," Apollena stated. "I have my keys. Our Jeep will fit up to…" she trailed off. Even holding her own tide of dark feelings at bay, she couldn't help but remember all the death that had unfolded before her eyes in the last few hours.

Lane picked up the slack, "The Jeep has enough space for all of us. It'll get us out of the campgrounds and to the nearest town." He wrapped an arm around Luna to keep her steady. "Gracie, can you make it back up the hill?"

Before Gracie could respond, Jordan stomped across the sand up to Lane, fist clenched. "I'm not speaking for everyone else, the ones who are left, but I'm not trusting you or your sister." She was delirious as they all were by this time of the night or morning. No one bothered to recall at this point. While the others watched the last particles of hope fade, Jordan found her strength in the familiar: her past, her pain, and her mistrust.

"What are your options?" Apollena asked calmly. "We can no longer fly to safety. Doesn't look like there's anything across the lake we could swim to. Where would you have your remaining team go now for safety?"

Jordan kept her fists from flying into Luna's perfectly sculpted honey-brown face. Her mental wheels spun a million miles a minute, but gained no traction. The sheer horror and carnage slicked the tracks as her train of thought ran over gallons of blood. So, she relaxed and looked toward the woods: those swaying pine trees hiding God knows what within.

"What are the odds any of our cars will be in working condition once we get up there?" Jordan asked pragmatically.

Nina was still enraged, nerves frayed and kicking up sand, "What are the odds of a whole ass pine tree pegging a helicopter?"

Lane laid a calming hand on Nina's shoulder. She almost jerked away, but instead, turned into him and released a muffled scream into his chest. Her tears continued to flow out onto Lane's damp shirt.

"It's a fair question," Lane agreed. "However, it's still our best option. We can't risk facing whatever or whoever's responsible if your lives are still at risk. Our Jeep will get you all out."

Nina looked up at Lane. Her face was a mess of smudged eyeliner and more sorrow than she'd ever known. "After everything that's happened, you'd still try to fight those things?"

Lane looked at his sister and nodded. "It's what we do."

"Jusqu'a la fin, Ursa Major," Apollena said quietly, with conviction.

"Till the end, Ursa Minor," Lane replied.

When Franki finally spoke, the hollowness in her voice nearly made them all shiver. "There's nothing else that can be done to me worse than what's happened. But none of y'all should feel how I feel right now. Let's get the twins' Jeep and get away from here." Without even acknowledging anyone else, Franki staggered toward the trail to the staff parking lot.

Luna extended a hand to Gracie, and the girl accepted. With a little strain, the round blonde limped forward on the beach to stand beside Jordan.

A heavy sigh left the rose petal lips of the girl with the wild red hair. "Fine. Into the woods. We'll go straight up the gut across Potter's Field."

They ran as fast as their tired bodies were able to carry them through the brush. With every scratch across their arms, or tug at their sleeves from the dense branches, a jolt of fear shot through each of their spines. Was it a branch, or something else, some beast reaching out to devour them? They weren't going to stay around long enough to find out.

Still, there was some comfort to being hidden in the thick of the woods. They'd hear something coming a mile away, snapping twigs, or crunching the leaves. That mild comfort disappeared as they reached the clearing of the dried-up lake. Potter's Field was covered in thick red clay and was an unnerving stretch of land to cover out in the open, unprotected.

Jordan stopped at the edge of the tree line and whispered, "It's a quarter-mile between us and the parking lot. That's all."

Gracie's lip quivered, "What if..."

"No," Jordan snapped, "That's it. One-quarter mile. That's all you're allowed to focus on right now. Just. Run." She took another deep breath and took in the surroundings. An empty lake bed, a large open clearing, and across that distance was the tree-covered path to their last chance of escape. "Ready?" she asked.

No reply. No objections. No time left.

"Run," she commanded.

The six remaining counselors sprinted out of the woods and onto the asphalt track that circled the dried-up lake. The moment their feet left the safety of the thick brush, a distorted choir of *HOWLS* filled the air. The sound came from every direction, from the trees, from the sky, and even underneath their feet.

"Don't get distracted!" Lane shouted. "Keep going, straight ahead!"

"NO!" Gracie shrieked. "Look out!"

Apollena was the first to break formation, to double back to the girl who'd collapsed into the mud. They'd nearly made it halfway across the expanse. Gracie's attention and focus had been captured by unholy carnage. The grotesque scene sat a mere fifty feet to their left, on the trail that led back to the Great Lodge and the sloped field: Zoe.

What was left of Zoe's body was still being consumed by the same massive black wolf that had stalked them since the rope course, and Portland before that.

The beast slowly lifted its blood-stained snout.

Its golden eyes stared right into Gracie's soul. Fresh. Meat.

It bared its fangs, dripping with Zoe's remains and steaming black tar.

Lane had nearly reached the other side, but sprinted back to Luna and Gracie. In that same split second, the obsidian wolf caught sight of Lane and broke into a run. The young man felt around in his vest pocket. He had one last card left to play.

As the wolf drew near, Lane could hear Jordan swear in the distance.

"Nina, we can't," said a distant voice.

"We're not leaving them behind," someone else protested.

Lane continued to race the wolf as it rapidly approached a defenseless Gracie and Apollena desperately trying to lift her up.

Thirty meters.

Twenty.

Lane could almost feel the heat radiating out from the ravenous wolf's snout and open mouth. He ignited his lighter and touched the flame to the card. Just as Luna had taught him: arm steady, flick at the wrist. Just like flicking a frisbee or a cigarette into an ashtray.

The difference between those examples and the card? The massive explosion of blinding red light and the plume of phosphorous smoke that encompassed the predator.

Without thinking, Lane and Luna both lifted Gracie up in a two-man carry. They were gaining momentum forward toward the path when they saw the other three girls racing toward them. The panther had blocked their exit.

The beast sat there in the archway at the head of the parking lot trail: golden eyes set upon them all and its long obsidian tail swishing back and forth. It almost looked as if it were mocking them, a twisted version of the angel sent to block the entrance of paradise.

"Head for the chapel," Nina screamed, flailing her arms in the direction of the derelict building. The abandoned chapel was significantly farther away than the parking lot, but they had little choice. Again, a haunting *HOWL* echoed throughout the clearing. The panting, the paw prints beating into the clay behind them, were all the motivation they needed to keep running forward to the abandoned church.

There was no way Lane and Luna could drag, let alone carry an injured girl twice their size faster than either the wolf or panther could run. Either the beasts were toying with them, or perhaps leading them toward the chapel?

In any other circumstance, Lane could dedicate a portion of his mind to out-think his enemy's next move. This whole camp felt as if it were designed to work against him. He was too exhausted, too heartbroken. Each and every step he'd taken felt as if it were planted on a preset path by somebody else. Fortunately, that notion sparked just enough rage in him to kick in the weathered chapel door covered in caution tape.

Without regard for her comfort, they dumped Gracie onto the floor by a rotted pew and pulled the others in after them. Jordan, Franki, and Nina all fell inside a hair's width away from the jaws of the obsidian wolf.

Lane and Luna tried to slam the door shut, but the jaws of the wolf snapped and snarled, wedging themselves in between the door frame and the door. The beast was so much stronger than both of them. Both twins had been systematically broken down, sleep-deprived, mentally and emotionally toyed with. But they were still alive. Lane grit his teeth. *No. No beast is going to do me in or my sister, so help me…* He used the last of his strength to slam his body weight against the door, but the wolf remained.

Suddenly, something bigger fell against the interior of the door. Then, another something fell, and another. Jordan and Nina were carrying the rotted remains of the pews and setting them up against the door. With their combined bodyweight and four pews acting against the splintering wooden barrier, the beast ceased to budge. It wasn't until Franky slammed a loose board down across the wolf's nose so hard it broke that the door finally shut.

Gasping for breath, Luna swore under her breath in French, *"Fucking hound from hell."*

"Is that what it is?" Nina asked breathlessly in French. Switching to English, "Are they really Demons? Maybe Brad was right. This is like the end times."

"They're Omens," Lane stated matter-of-factly, "That's all. They just signal when something horrible is going to happen."

"Or they could be heralds?" Franki suggested.

Again, the group was unnerved to have heard from her after such a long, terrible silence. Franki continued, not necessarily speaking at anyone in particular, "Like, when Galactus is about to devour a planet, he sends the Silver Surfer, or Terrax and those other two guys ahead of him." She held their attention. "What if those beasts, the wolf, the lion... the..." She couldn't force herself to acknowledge the last one, the one that had slain the woman she loved.

Swallowing the knot in her throat, Franki summed up her hypothesis, "What if Brad was actually telling the truth about the world ending? What if those things are the heralds of the end of everything?"

A moment of nerve-shredding silence lingered.

Jordan spun around and kicked a pew over. "Yeah, Franki. You're right. It must be the fucking end of the world, right? Why else would you two appear?"

Lane had had enough. "You want an apology, Jordan? Would that make the end a little more palatable? Well, that's too bad. First of all, I can't possibly be the reason everything went wrong in your life. I was a dumb, horny thirteen-year-old. Second, this isn't the fucking end. I won't let it happen. Not yet. We are not going to just hide here until some engineered apocalypse happens, especially not one brought by some dick named Brad."

"Oh, yeah?" Jordan asked cold as ice, "You gonna pull out some more magic tricks from your little book and put on a show for those killer animals out there?"

Lane stood up, "Yes. Yes, I am. Whatever it takes. We're gonna fight."

Apollena tugged on Lane's pant leg. "But first, we're going to find the edges of this puzzle, right?"

"No," Lane protested, stomping his foot. "I'm tired of being led by some invisible leash. I'm gonna find the sharpest thing in this chapel and go out swinging. I won't stand here and—"

"Lane," Luna interrupted as she stood up beside her brother, gently squeezing his hand, "I really think we should start at the edges."

Lane had nearly lost control, frothing with anger as he spat out, "Oh, yeah? Why? Why now, Luna? After everything else has gone wrong, I'm really not in the mood for another mystery. If I never encounter anything else on the weird spectrum ever again, it'll be too soon."

His sister's warm brown hands clamped down on the side of his face and directed his line of sight to the back of the chapel. "Because, dear brother, I think we've reached the edge of this particular puzzle. See?"

Lane's fog of anger finally cleared from his eyes, as he could see the soft orange glow seeping under the pulpit between the wooden floorboards. Taking his sister's hand in his, Lane marched up to the front of the old chapel. He could hear the creek of the solid floorboards change as he approached the fallen pulpit. There was an audible change from an immediate, muffled strain of floorboard underfoot, and a hollow echoing *creek* resonating under the stage.

The Twins scanned the raised stage and came upon a single dusted spot among an otherwise filthy floor. The others had joined them. Each squinted at what appeared to be a hidden handle discreetly set within a single floorboard.

Lane reached down and gripped the handle. He hesitated, his hand trembling until it was joined by Luna. Together, they lifted up the hidden door on the floor. Together, they followed the dim candlelight that danced across the staircase leading underneath the church.

Together, the four of the six remaining counselors descended the stone-carved stairs into the unknown.

24

HELL IS CHROME

They'd gone beyond the stone staircase that led under the abandoned church. It was all bedrock, mud, and roots that formed the dark narrow hallway leading toward flickering lights. There wasn't enough room to fully extend one's arms to either side of the dank passageway. Lane's head had barely enough clearance without scraping the ceiling. He took the lead, followed by Apollena, Nina, and Franki. Jordan had stayed behind with Gracie. So, now there were four that braved the length of a five-minute hallway toward a dying candlelight altar.

"Lane," Apollena whispered.

Glancing over his shoulder to where she pointed, Lane did indeed notice the broken stone that incrementally lined the hallway. As they approached the glow, Lane had counted twelve in total. He carefully stepped over one last broken pile of stone. "Yeah. Thirteen barriers or maybe whole walls at one point? Looks like they'd all been smashed inward. Someone didn't want anyone else down this hallway."

"Remind me again," Nina asked, voice shaking, "Why are WE down here?"

"We need information," Lane said definitively. "We need information to survive."

Luna reached back for Nina's lithe hand and held it tight. "I promise you, we're going to get out of here. But if we're not armed with the knowledge to beat whatever's in our way, the odds of that happening are... not in our favor."

"It's Jude, though," Franki breathed out in a cold, measured breath, "Right? It has to be."

"I mean, he's been doing fuck knows what this whole time, sure. But how does one guy control ghost animals or whatever the hell they are?" Nina pondered, voice a little less shaking as she wove her fingers in between Luna's.

"I think this might give us a clue," Lane said, pointing at what sat at the end of the tunnel.

Stretched taut within a wooden frame was a deer hide illuminated by a large rack of antlers with wax candles stuck on each of the tips. Lane reached into his vest pocket and flipped his field journal open. He didn't recognize the writing or glyphs scrawled over the hide. If he had to venture an educated guess, it was the language of the native tribe that originally occupied these grounds: the Cowlitz.

Apollena squatted down and wedged herself on the right side of Lane. "Do you mind?"

Lane shuffled sideways so that both of them could occupy the same space.

"Jesus," Nina whispered.

"Probably not," Franki snorted. "Then again, the Lion, Wolf, and..." She grimaced, "Panther. They were all omens, heralds of things to come in Dante's, 'Divine Comedy.' So maybe this is something from down below?"

"Franki," Lane said, still studying the markings, checking them against known occult glyphs and writings he'd documented in the journal, "Remind me again, what's the difference between a herald and omen?"

"Yeah, and how do you know that exactly?" Nina added, almost accusingly.

Franki rolled her eyes. "I read comics, okay? Silver Surfer mostly. He's kinda like Marvel's 'Doctor Who,' a bit." Off Nina's scrunched face, she clarified, "I'm a nerd, a'right? I love stories. The ones where dark shit happens are… *were* interesting an' whatever. At least until all this bloody mess."

"Okay," Lane said, trying to calm her down, "So, if those things are heralds…"

Franki shrugged, then mimed a pair of antlers with her hands above her head. "Then there's something bigger coming. Right? Somethin' big callin' the shots. Makes a bit of sense?"

"Like the actual Deer Woman?" Nina interrupted. She paused, then shivered. "Okay, but are you saying this is like the devil? How? I don't remember a Deer Woman in the Bible."

With a heavy breath, Luna replied, "It's all the same hell, love." Luna tapped the toe of her shoes to Lane's boot. "Any luck with a translation?"

Lane shook his head, "I wish I'd had the forethought to study the Cowlitz written language, but it'd never occurred to me that you and I would be back in Washington for the *worst* summer camp ever."

"That can't be Cowlitz," Nina said, leaning in between the gap in front of Lane and Luna.

Luna raised an eyebrow. "Why do you say that?"

"I've been studying languages. Specifically, dead and dying languages. One of the reasons a lot of Native American languages die out is because what record the tribes had of a written language was either lost, destroyed, or… if you're the ancient Cowlitz, never existed."

"You're a hundred percent certain they didn't have a written language?" Lane asked.

Nina thought for a moment, "By the time white settlers arrived, the Cowlitz had adopted multiple languages, mostly a form of Salish..." Nina traced her fingers just above the hide being careful not to actually touch the deer skin, "But these markings, this isn't any form of Salish that I've studied. This is... unique. If this is authentic, this may be the first, the only record of a Cowlitz written word."

Lane and Luna glanced at each other, exchanging a horrified spark of recognition.

Franki was the first to catch the twins' simultaneous disturbed exchange. "What? Jude really broke in this tomb and disturbed some ancient Native Burial ground? Is that why all this shit is happenin'?"

Lane rubbed his temples, "When our other sisters and I were in Scotland, we picked up Alchemy from..." He waved his hands, "TLDR, developing a language, or code to bridge the gap between physics, chemistry, and the ethereal was alchemy in a nutshell. Like programming code, but for unlocking reality. If the Cowlitz, or whoever, invented a language then buried it behind thirteen stone walls underground, they wanted to make damn sure it was never seen or spoken."

Nina turned her head and covered her eyes. "Shit! And we just kept staring at it?"

Luna touched the girl's shoulder. "I think the damage has already been done, love."

Nina remained facing the opposite end of the hallway toward their only exit.

"Alright, so what are the odds that Jude busted through walls and learned how to speak ancient Cowlitz? Nina said it herself, "It's a dead language, right?"

Lane continued to stare at the symbols, going over each line, each stroke. Then, whether it was the dim light of the hallway, or simply being too close to the hide, he went cross-eyed. He shut his eyes tight, rubbed them, and leaned back from the deerskin. As his pupils readjusted to the light, he remembered his standard operating procedure: *start with the edges.*

No longer focusing on the symbols themselves, but the picture as a whole, Lane breathed out, "Holy shit."

"What?" Nina asked, startled, with her hands over her eyes.

Luna studied her brother's face, then took a step back and gasped, "It's the camp."

Franki tilted her head and squinted. "Yeah, I guess I sorta see it now. There's Spirit Lake. That looks like Potter's Field, or I guess it'd still be a lake too. Those little etchings are probably elevation markings, yeah? It's a map."

"Yeah," Luna acknowledged, tracing a finger along with a particularly thick series of lines, "Are these... These look like the trails that lead around camp. But this camp was built when? Early 1930s?"

"About that time, yeah. Maybe they were outlined by whatever tribe settled here first?" Franki suggested. "So, it's a map. And?"

Lane followed Luna's finger as it began forming a path between four symbols. "Even if I didn't know Cowlitz, this looks like a pictogram of fire. This one is water, or maybe blood? Shadow, two people together... sex... or a mating ritual?"

Luna stepped in, "Lane, look at the edges here: thirteen stick-figures."

"There were thirteen of us during the morning 'team building activity...'" Franki thought aloud. "Exactly thirteen."

Lane set his jaw. "No. Not a team-building activity. It was a ritual, a summons." He pointed to a rough pictogram of a fire pit surrounded by four pillars. With a crude figure of a woman in the center: a human woman. "This is how they summoned the Deer Woman."

"Or," Luna offered, "Could be how they pray to her?"

"Alright, then why leave instructions on how to bring her back?" Nina asked.

Lane traced the thick lines again. Leaning in a little closer, he noticed incremental markings, arrows. They were going, loosely speaking, counter to the direction the counselors had marched. Hypothesising out loud, "Let's say you're being haunted by an otherworldly entity. Your tribe's shaman is tasked with banning this thing, so he creates a ritual, a spell to capture the spirit of the entity. A written language and those capable of reading would have been seen by ancient people as a type of magic..."

"And these people needed some powerful magic to... contain the Deer Woman," Apollena added gravely. "This was her tomb, her prison."

Nina threw her hands up. "Okay, somehow, Jude learns how to read Cowlitz, performs a ritual to summon the Deer Woman, Demon, or whatever? Can we just do the opposite of what he did to send her back to hell or wherever she came from?"

"It's all the same hell, darling," Luna said again, "And if what little we can gather from this thing is accurate, we'd need at least thirteen people."

"So, we can't put Pandora back in her box," Franki said dryly. "We just kill her then? How 'bout that? Do you two ever kill demons or just write about 'em in your journal?"

Jordan's distressed voice came from the secret door far back at the head of the five-minute hallway, "Lane, if you're still alive, get the fuck back up here!"

Franki turned on a dime and sprinted down the hallway to Jordan. Nina followed along with Luna and Lane, pulling up the rear. As they got closer to the stone staircase, they could hear the rhythmic banging against the wood. They heard the snarling and gnashing of teeth. The wolf was making another attempt to force its way inside the chapel. Clearly, they weren't on hallowed ground. Or, more accurately, the land the church was built on had destroyed what used to be the consecrated ground of the Cowlitz People.

By the time Lane emerged from the hole behind the pulpit, Franki and Nina had already joined Jordan at their makeshift barricade against the chapel door. The rotted wood had begun to splinter. The rusted screws attached to the frame had begun to bow outward as the beast rammed its massive head against the door.

Lane quickly scanned the room: the boarded-up windows, the rotted and broken pews, the stage he stood upon. At last, his first bit of fortune this evening. Like any early twentieth-century protestant church, there was an ornate metal cross leaning against the corner of the wall. He quickly flipped through the pages in his Journal to 'Alchemy and Practical Application.' As fast as his hand could scrawl the last bit of charcoal from his pencil inscribed the necessary formula along the edge of the cross. The formula included six atomic elements, twelve transmutation characters, and a shit ton of chemistry. He nearly ran out of space on the rusted cross. He'd repent for the sacrilege performed upon the Christian icon later... if they survived.

Gracie was sobbing, wailing, "I don't wanna die!"

Jordan, Franki, Nina, and Luna ignored her, pushing with all their might against the considerable strength of the otherworldly beast. Its mammoth jaws ceased trying to force its way in from the other side and simply tore off pieces of the rotted door.

Lane approached the barricade, bearing the cross upside down like a sword.

"Everybody cover your eyes," Lane shouted over the persistent banging, scratching, and monstrous barking, "This is gonna be bright."

Jordan was about to protest, but Luna covered her eyes and forcibly turned the redhead's face away just before Lane touched the tip of his lighter to the cross. In an instant, the interior of the chapel burst into daylight. There was a deafening *BOOM* that shook the dust from the walls and ceiling. It felt as though the old chapel would collapse on top of them. At the tail end of the explosion, as the collective ringing in the counselors' ears died out, there was a pathetic, longing *howl*. The wolf's cry then came to an abrupt end.

Franki rubbed her eyes. Bright spots still flooded her retina. She strained to see the outline of Lane standing in the door frame. The door itself had been blown outward into splinters scattered across Potter's Field. Her vision continued to return as she witnessed Lane pulled something glowing white-hot out from the ground, out from the wolf's neck. When Franki's vision returned, she saw, gripped tightly in the young man's hand, a bright *silver* cross.

"Werewolves," Nina whispered in awe.

Lane shook his head using his shirt to wipe off the tar that'd been stuck on the tip of the cross, "Don't think this qualifies as a traditional werewolf, but I figured silver was a good catchall against demonic fuckary." He looked down at the steaming carcass of the wolf. It continued to dissolve into bubbling black tar and ink that sank into the soil.

"To answer your question from earlier, Franki," Apollena added breathlessly, "Demons? Yeah, we kill 'em."

They ran from the ruined church and found the path clear of any other obsidian beasts: the heralds of something terrible to come. The remaining survivors' eyes darted nervously, desperately trying to peer through the darkness and thick archway of branches and brush that encased their path to the staff parking lot. With each switchback, their nerves snapped at the unknown predator waiting for them. So far, nothing revealed themselves and the anticipation of impending doom wound the group up ever tighter, waiting for death to snatch them up at a moment's notice.

Even armed with his newly forged silver cross, Lane's consciousness was on the razor's edge. Exhaustion, hunger, and the sheer amount of carnage packed into such a short time pushed him beyond his limits. One snap of a twig, or rustle of a branch, and he'd simply let instinct kick in and start swinging.

Apollena on the other hand was busy digesting information. She was equally drained as her twin, but full of new information, data. They'd found out something about the opponent they hadn't known before. This Deer Woman could be summoned AND banished. The native people of these lands had established some element of control over this deity or being. They'd made the ancient equivalent of a light switch for their god: flip the switch on, and the Deer Woman disappears. Perform the ritual the other way around and she'll come back.

"If the ritual works both ways," Luna wondered aloud within earshot of Lane, "What must she have done that made those people want to bury her in that tomb?

Lane's mind jerked away from survival mode to that empty canvas where billions of puzzle pieces get sorted into one clear picture. As he'd been trained to do, Lane started at the edges and worked his way inward. They'd encountered three heralds. Those three beasts preceded a supernatural entity: The Deer Woman. Someone or a group had discovered a way to summon and banish that entity through ritual means. Why would you summon an entity in the first place?

"Enough with your conspiracy theory bullshit," Jordan panted out in a hushed voice. "You really want another one of those things to hear us? There's still two more."

Thanks to Jordan, some of those loose puzzle pieces snapped into place.

Still, in that almost dreamlike state of contemplation, Lane asked aloud, "What if they wanted a higher power to hear them?"

"That's not what I said," Jordan snapped, "Just... good god... please shut up?"

Lane stopped running.

They'd reached the edge of the trail.

They'd reached the parking lot.

All of those that remained stood just within the tree lined archway of the path. They squinted into the nearly dark lot to see their cars, trucks, and vans that had delivered them to this godforsaken camp. All of them remained in the lot, intact. This brought about two conflicting feelings within the six remaining counselors, as neither Cole, Brandon, nor Doc appeared to have made it out. On the other hand, Lane and Luna's Jeep would provide them with an opportunity to escape that the others never got.

Lane's mind continued to labor over the canvas of puzzle pieces morphing into a complete picture as he whispered again, "They wanted a god to hear them."

Luna touched her brother's shoulder, mulling the words over in her mouth, "No, not *they*, or *them*. Him. HE wanted a god to listen." Lane followed his sister's finger as she pointed just beyond the parking lot. There sat those same collections of rustic family cabins they'd noticed upon their arrival to Trillion Pines.

Only one cabin had its lights on.

The Abidalli House.

25

HOW TO FIGHT THE LONELINESS

An eastern wind swept over the tops of the towering pines, shaking loose a volley of fresh needles that floated down upon the six counselors who remained. Franki's long, slender frame appeared the least planted in their current reality. She neither paid attention to the Abidalli House or Luna's Jeep. Her's was an expression of being completely removed from their current crisis, alone, and adrift in her own thoughts. Nina's fists were balled tight. Her teeth clenched and those beautiful brown eyes of hers were set on Jude's cabin. Gracie continued to limp toward the Jeep, mindful not to disturb the gravel and attract the two remaining beasts.

"We can go," Gracie whispered, "B...before, before another one of those things appears and does something awful. Let's just go. Please."

Jordan hushed her, "Or we could move too fast and that Jeep'll end up the same way as the helicopter: big ass pine tree rammed right through the roof into the ground."

"Jordan! Jesus, honey, why would you jinx us like that?" Gracie implored despondently.

"'Cause, there ain't no such thing as a jinx," Jordan dismissed, with another hush.

Lane stood beside his sister as their minds independently formulated the same plan of attack. At least, he hoped that was the case. Their eyes scanned the perimeter and entirety of Jude's modest two-story cabin. Their shoulders felt the weight of the risk they'd have to carry if they pushed forward. Both their hands remembered what it felt like to take a life if that became necessary. Even if they wanted to escape, take the easy way out, both Lane and Luna knew what path they'd been given.

The only way out was through Jude and whatever else lay in wait within the cabin.

"You suppose it'd be better to have them wait in the car," Apollena asked, as if she were finishing the current train of thought inside Lane's mind.

That's what they'd promised their fellow counselors, or at least implied: *come with us, and we'll get you to safety.* That was their intent. The reality? Lane and Luna, no matter how far they traveled, always journeyed closer to danger, closer to death.

Jordan caught Lane's eyes and followed his line of sight. That idiot. He knew what he was gonna do. If he intended to play the hero or prove a point, she would beat him to the punch. She rolled up her sleeves and stomped toward the house. "I ain't some kid too scared to go into their own room. Jude's gonna hear it from me."

Lane reached out, but Jordan was already halfway across the gravel parking lot. Crunching across the parking lot after the wild woman, he clutched the newly forged silver cross tightly in hand. Apollena followed, striding in pace with her brother. The others tailed a short distance after. Eventually, the gravel parking lot cross dissolved into thick, unmowed grass. They were nearly at the cabin door when Lane reached out for Jordan and caught her by the shoulder.

"Wait," Lane pleaded.

Jordan shook him off, scowled, and knocked on the front door. "Jude! Get your ass outside, now!"

No reply.

Again, Jordan banged her fist against the door. Again, no answer.

Not only was the house still, but the steady wind had died down. No nocturnal animals scurried about in the dark or released a whisper into the woods. No hooting owls. Not so much as a single leaf scratched against another. It would only take a single pine needle to drop and shatter the silence.

Lane breathed in one last look around the perimeter of the house from the open wooden porch where they stood. The element of surprise was gone. This would be his last and only opportunity to gather as much information before their confrontation. In an instant, Lane desperately drank in his surroundings for as many clues as he could swallow: the location of the cabin in context to the others, the design of the house, and finally the garden beside the porch. He released not a sigh of relief, but one of resignation and readiness. There it was: the only two clues he needed.

Jordan turned the handle and pushed in the unlocked door.

They looked upon a living room back lit by a roaring fireplace and yet, still shrouded in shadows. Nothing was more imposing than the massive shadow seated in the center of the room. Monstrous antlers ordained in polished bone and crystal ornaments protruded out from the shadow's head. A pair of shining blue and golden eyes that glowed like miniature galaxies immediately fell unblinking on Lane. Even in a seated position, the feminine shadow was easily eight feet, perhaps nine if it were able to stand.

"You came," spoke a familiar but deflated voice. It came from the man cradled within the powerful arms of the shadow. "Thank you."

Apollena stood beside her brother and Jordan. The others remained in the entryway.

"Jude?" Jordan asked with an edge. "Do you have any fucking idea what's happening out there? What Brad did and the others that..." She couldn't spit out the rest. The taste of death was still fresh on her lips. The bitter taste burned all the way down the woman's throat and poisoned her heart.

Apollena grasped Lane's hand and held it tight. They'd never fought anything this big before. Of course, it wasn't just the size of the opponent, but the stakes, the prospect of an end to their relationship that teetered on such a definitive edge that terrified both twins. If they failed here and now, there would be no tomorrow for either of them—or anyone. This unspoken truth boiled just below the surface of their skin. Yet, they endured.

"You go first," Apollena urged her brother in a stiff whisper.

Lane stepped forward, past Jordan. The thing holding Jude in its arms didn't break eye contact. In fact, its iris shined brighter. Those blue and gold spotlights were locked on Lane with malicious intent. As he stepped further into the living room, his feet sank into something softer than carpet. He glanced down. Not carpet. The room was covered in rich soil. Pushing past the odd renovation, Lane raised his voice to a commanding roar aimed at the Camp Director. "What did you ask her for, Jude? What did you ask of the Deer Woman?"

Jude looked drained, physically, mentally, maybe even spiritually. Those manic eyes that had met Lane and energetic voice from their first phone call were merely a hollow facsimile as the Director replied, "Such a bright young man, aren't you Roswell? You've figured it all out, huh? Impressive. Super impressive." A dusty cough followed, but not truth.

"Don't waste our time," Lane interrupted. "In your grief and pain, your first instinct was to summon a deity you couldn't possibly understand? Your wife, your daughter—"

Jude sniffed, "Don't..." he warned softly before entering a coughing fit.

Lane persisted, "If you're going to use their deaths to justify whatever you're about to do, that's not going to fly in court—"

Jordan stepped in, confused. "Death? Wait, what are you talking about?"

Apollena leaned into Jordan and gently interjected, "The two freshly dug grave plots outside the cabin, in the garden."

With her mouth hung open, Jordan shook her head.

"Brad ratted you out," Lane said, jabbing two fingers in Jude's direction. "Your apocalypse won't come to pass. It ends with us. So, last chance: what did you ask Deer Woman to do, Jude?" Lane readjusted his grip on the silver cross tightly. He was a single lunge away from striking distance, but the great shadow in the middle of the room shifted: the whole cabin shifted. The soil beneath Lane's feet felt as though it were rumbling, trembling water. Those blue, golden eyes above Jude shone impossibly bright and narrowed into judgmental slits.

Jude chuckled again, followed by a light coughing fit. Wiping his mouth, the Camp Director leaned up and turned toward Lane. "Are you trying to intimidate me? Really?"

Lane tightened his grip on the cross, ready to strike. "Do you think your wife would really want to be the reason her husband tried to end the world?"

Again, Jude laughed, and in a bitter voice snapped, "Don't you dare mention that woman. This isn't about her."

"How are you going to end it all, Jude? What genocide are you willing to commit in your little girl's name?" Lane shouted.

"I'm not trying to end the world!" Jude shouted back. The ground continued to rumble. The earth shook again. Blades of grass and vines sprouted under Lane's feet. After a few breaths, the cabin settled. In a sickened, heartbroken voice, Jude replied, "I'm not trying anything. It's already begun. Soon, this world of pain, of sorrow, of hopelessness and depravity will cease to be. It will soon fall under a cloud of ash and suffocate under the weight of its own sin." Jude didn't smile so much as sneer in resentment, contentment.

Jordan was trembling as she finally focused on the giant figure holding a sickly Jude in its arms. "No. You can't be... This can't be real," Her voice shook out. "All those people? Everyone?" Fear was surpassed by anger as it bubbled up to the surface and popped. "Who are you to sentence all those people to death because of your pain? You're no one! Nothing!"

Jude sighed. "I'm the one with the means to get it done. It's the way it has to be." His eyes scanned over Jordan and the others who had stepped into the cabin: Franki, Gracie, Nina. The three girls stood, stunned, horrified as the creature that held Jude moved from a seated position to a kind of squat. The firelight, no longer obscured by the figure's back, illuminated a pair of legs thick as trees. Alabaster, muscular legs covered in moss and patches of bark that ended in hooves compressing the soil beneath its mass.

The camp director clicked his tongue and pointed at Gracie and mused, "Think of how much we struggle, desperate for others to love us only to be denied genuine affection." He pointed at Nina, "How much we try, in vain, to be accepted for who we think we are," He glared at Franki, "Years of pining after someone, only to have their life stolen from us in an instant," Jude nodded to himself. He waited for protest from the others, but none came. "That's the world. That's how it is. That's all it ever is. That's why it has to end. Everything ends. Tonight."

Lane could sense the atmosphere in the living room thicken. It was almost as if they were back inside the spa: thick sheets of steam steadily arose up from the soil. An earthy, pungent scent filled his nostrils. It was the same sensation as walking into a room of pure tobacco leaves, or decaying mushrooms and dead animals.

"How?!" Lane demanded.

Without breaking from Lane's glare, Jude pointed toward the window, toward the lake and the mountain beyond it. "Perhaps, not as smart as I'd expected."

Apollena stepped in, anxious. The weight of knowing they'd nearly run out of time pressed against her. "Does she agree with you?" The girl pointed a finger up to the Deer Woman looming over them all. Her antlers nearly scratched the ceiling. Those golden blue eyes of hers flicked to Luna.

"It doesn't really work like that," Jude said, shaking his head. "She… feeds." he said, holding up a withered hand. "She craves conviction and the emotional energy of those who believe what they know to be true. Our existence is pain and should no longer be a plague upon Her earth. That's reality. That is the truth of the situation."

Lane and Luna looked at each other, eyes wide: Jude just gave away the whole game. While Lane's mind raced to conjure a strategy to use that information to their advantage, Luna beat her brother to the punch.

"No, that's YOUR truth; your twisted opinion. The real challenge is whether your conviction, your pathetic nihilism, will hold stronger than ours," Apollena said.

Laughter bubbled up from Jude, finally spilling out into a wellspring of manic cackling. "Look around you, Cloudcroft. Do the math. Whatever misplaced optimism you may possess doesn't outweigh the truth held in this room, let alone the rest of this mourning planet, and the goddess standing before you."

With those final words, the Deer Woman rose to her full height. Instead of crashing through the roof, veins and roots simply pulled apart the whole cabin like someone ripping open an orange to make way for the deity as she arched her back. She gave one last look to Lane, and the thinnest trace of a frown could be seen on her lips. Such a melancholy, familiar face.

"Let's go. We must finish what we've started," Jude spoke to the Deer Woman, who continued to cradle the broken man in her arms.

"You're not going anywhere," Lane growled. He knew a blunt object, even one imbued with silver, would be next to useless against the Deer Woman. But Lane wasn't looking for a fight. He just needed to stall for time. Thick storm clouds rolled overhead, above the cabin that had been cracked in half. Thunder rumbled as Lane commanded, "You're going to answer for what you've done."

Jude waved a hand dismissively. "Soon, there won't be anyone around to care. No one really cares. But, there will be no more pain. No suffering. Nothing," The broken man finally looked Lane directly in the face and smiled ear to ear, "You're welcome."

Before Lane could react, an ear-piercing *yowl* flew straight at him. It felt like being hit by a car. He gasped for breath as the wind was knocked out of his lungs. Whatever hit him caused Gracie to shriek. Lane was made aware by varying degrees of the other girls: Nina's clipped footsteps chasing after Gracie's heavy, lopsided strides. Jordan dived behind a cushioned chair just outside of Lane's peripheral vision.

Lying on his back, Lane tightened his grip around the silver cross. As his right hand closed, he realized the weapon had been knocked loose. Still too winded, too sore to move, Lane was only able to lift his head high in time to see the Deer Woman spread her massive arms and command her veins, her roots, and branches to rise from the earth and tear the cabin completely in half. Once the home had been destroyed, she walked through the ruins while cradling Jude in her arms.

Lane tried to call out to Jude, but only a wheezing cough escaped his mouth. The Deer Woman continued unabated into the woods toward the lake. Trying to bend forward, Lane was certain at least two or three of his ribs were cracked. What hurt worse wasn't the broken bones, but watching his sister give chase after Jude and the ancient deity alone. He willed his body to stand. He set his jaw and chose to ignore the pain. Adrenaline should kick in soon enough. He'd already muscled his way through the last forty-eight hours. It wasn't a matter of whether he could push himself any further: Lane had to endure. If the world was truly at stake, his sister had now set herself directly in the line of fire.

Hair-raising *growling* washed over him. He could feel the bass tone rumble within his chest and rattle his broken ribs. It was practically right beside Lane's ear.

The panther.

Without a weapon and significantly slower reaction time than a jungle cat, Lane's only option was to act. He clamored to his feet and wound back his punch and struck nothing but shadow. The beast *growled* again. It circled him, just out of sight. The low rumbling came from every direction now. The beast was toying with Lane now, playing with its food.

If Lane was going to die, mauled and eaten just as poor Julia had been devoured, he'd meet his end standing up. Even as his knees buckled and muscles burned. Lane's fists were clenched tight and ready to fly.

A sliver of hopelessness ran through Lane's blood like ice water. He finally caught sight of his opponent. It was enough to make Lane shiver, but he didn't blink. He refused to break eye contact with the golden glowing eyes of his otherworldly opponent. Lane stared down the panther and death itself returned the young man's gaze, ready to claim its prize.

26

I Am Trying (to Break Your Heart)

When Lane did eventually blink, it was only because the sweat that rolled off his forehead stung his weary eyes. He desperately rubbed his eyes.

The Panther disappeared.

There wasn't much time until the beast's next attack. Another eastern breeze blew through the wreckage of the cabin that had been split in two. Dust particles and embers blew by and danced on the faint rays of light emitted from the shattered fireplace. Lane's broken ribs still ached and stabbed him. His breath, ragged. Like all big cats that toyed with their injured food, the panther would likely pounce from behind. Any moment now, it'd finish Lane off, slowly...

The ginger boy drew what could have been his final breath.

Then, within a split second: a terrifying, deafening *growl*... And a massive body launched itself through the air.

Lane rolled on his back and kicked up with every last ounce of strength left in his swimmer's legs. It was barely enough force to stave

off the initial attack. Fortunately, he felt the heels of his boots connect, impact into the hardened muscles beneath that ink-covered panther.

A sharp *yowl* let Lane know he'd done some damage. In actuality, given his broken ribs, Lane had probably done more harm to himself than the animal. But he'd still bought himself precious seconds. The beast didn't bother to press its advantage. The Panther dashed off into the shadows again. Struggling to stand, Lane scanned his surroundings for the silver cross. His only weapon proved effective against his foe. It was over a meter long, bright, shiny, metallic. *How the fuck could I've lost it?*

Too late. Time's up.

He heard the heavy packing sounds of paws pounding upon the ground, the soil, and the rubble. It charged straight for him. Bright yellow eyes flashed in the dark. A full set of gleaming, razor-white teeth opened wide. Then, before Lane could react, another sharp *yowl* was cut short.

Lane rolled on his side as the beast continued its forward moment. It came to a sudden stop, face down in the dirt right beside him. Breathing heavily, Lane was face to face with the melting, tar-covered skeleton of the massive jungle cat. Behind it, Franki stood tall with the silver sword in hand. The transmuted cross had plunged deep into the back of the cat's neck. The corpse continued to hiss and dissolve until there was nothing left but soot.

As the steaming pile of murky oil sank back into the cursed earth, the young woman released her shaking hand from the hilt of the cross. The silver weapon landed with a soft *THUD* in the soil. Franki's feet were rooted to the ground. Her mouth hung open, pleading to release a scream that had been building in her throat. That scream had wanted to escape since she witnessed Julia slain hours ago.

Instead, there was only a frustrated, horrified, mournful silence.

Franki had her revenge.

Now there was nothing left but the crushing loneliness.

Nina had helped Gracie out into the parking lot, away from the ruined cabin. Now that the house was split in two, the girls were within the line of sight from where Lane lay. He steadily staggered forward and coughed out blood onto the soil. With one hand clutching his ribs, Lane reached out to Franki. "Thank you," he said hoarsely, blood trickling out of his mouth.

Franki said nothing, but gave Lane an almost imperceptible nod.

"Lane? Are you okay?" Nina shouted from across the lot, "Franki? C'mon, let's go!"

Lane offered a weak wave, if only to acknowledge that he was still mostly alive.

"Your sister went chasing after that... that THING!" Nina shouted in a manic, rattled voice, "She threw her car keys at us and ran off."

"Take Gracie, and Franki," Lane interrupted. "Get yourselves to safety." Lane's vision was blurry. He couldn't read the expression on her face, but the body language suggested confusion, perhaps defiance.

"No," she shrieked, "We're—are you out of your mind? We're all getting out of here alive. Come on!"

Lane reached down for the sword. He lifted the heavy metal and brought it to rest upon his shoulder. "Nina, go! Get Franki, Gracie, and..." *And Jordan.* Lane's train of thought derailed. He frantically searched for the wild redhead woman, but came up empty. "Nina, where's Jordan?"

Nina looked about and drew her hands to mouth, "Jordan!?"

"Nina!" Gracie hushed, "They'll hear you."

That's right, Lane remembered, there's still one more beast out there in the dark.

Franki whispered, "Jordan went after Jude."

That settled it. Lane drew in a sharp breath, pushed past the pain, and strode forward. He followed the giant hoof prints made by the Deer Woman through the woods and down toward the lake. There were still a few loose puzzle pieces that needed to be assembled. He'd have to connect them on his way, but he couldn't delay any longer.

Lane hobbled forward into the dark after the witch of the wild woods.

Luna could barely keep pace with the Deer Woman. On the plus side, in spite of her exhaustion, she was still fast. Additionally, despite the Deer Woman's long elegant strides, the entity was slow going. Perhaps not so much slow, but deliberate. What reason did a forest goddess have to be in a rush, anyway? If the end of the world was coming, it was of her making on her schedule. At least, it should have been.

Then again, Luna considered as she crept through the brush and trees just out of sight from the nearly nine-foot-tall creature. *It's entirely likely that Brad was incorrect.*

Before the counselor took his own life, Brad had made perhaps an inaccurate observation. "You can't reason with her," he'd claimed. *Can't they* ? The evidence of a ritual would suggest otherwise. *That was the point, was it not* ? If there was a ritual to constrain and summon the Deer Woman, then somehow there must be a way to communicate with it. The original tribe that had settled here and encountered this entity had somehow conveyed their wants to that entity in the past. Surely The Deer Woman didn't speak Cowlitz. Somehow, Jude had communicated his madness, his sorrow, and the loneliness he'd felt from the loss of his wife and daughter. *What other languages could she speak?*

Luna felt the breeze blow harder over the water. She felt pine needles fly through the air and prick her exposed skin. They were closer to the shore now. She tried to estimate the time, but the growing cloud cover made it difficult to pinpoint. Surely dawn would roll in soon. A little sunlight would be a welcomed ally in the fight against the horror that walked a few paces ahead. That's when a sudden *clap* and *rumble* through the sky shook Luna's chest. Storm clouds. Rain. The girl with the honey-brown skin dropped her shoulders and sighed. *When a challenge arose, it was never just one obstacle at a time, was it?*

"JUDE!" shouted a distressed voice from behind, along with a pair of boots marching heavily through the dry brush.

Jordan.

Luna reached out to silence the redhead girl with a death wish, but Jordan was too far from her and singularly focused on the camp director.

"Hey, you crazy fuck, I'm talking to you!" Jordan screamed again.

"Wichita," Came Jude's frail voice as it floated over the loud, crunching footfalls of the Deer Woman. Still carrying Jude, the entity continued lumbering ever closer toward Spirit Lake undeterred by Jordan's pursuit. Cradled in the arms of the Deer Woman, Jude asked listlessly, "You've come to witness the end? Front row seats?"

Luna kept out of sight, following from the shadows. She struggled between saving Lane's childhood crush and observing how this confrontation would play out.

Jordan continued her livid declaration, trying to keep up with the Deer Woman and Jude. "You let people die on your watch. You're responsible for murdering my friends and I'm holding your motherfucking feet to the fire!"

His stifled laughter grew into a wheezing cackle, "No, child. Everyone. Everyone will be consumed by fire. We will all meet our end this morning. I guess you don't understand after all? But you will. You'll witness the end of everything soon enough, you petulant little girl."

Jordan continued her pursuit, "I've had enough with the dramatic bullsh—what?—NO!"

Luna watched as roots and branches reached out to ensnare Jordan. In an instant the wild redhead girl was lifted three feet off the ground, trapped within a web of wood and vine. Before Luna could make a move to release Jordan, she noticed the branches didn't appear to further constrict or impose an immediate threat; they simply held the redhead aloft and in place.

"Come back here and face me, you COWARD!" Jordan hollered.

Jude's voice hardly carried as the entity marched on. "Despite your bountiful insecurities, I knew you would lack the conviction to see my vision through. That's why Brad was chosen over you. Now take the last moments you have to think of your sins."

Luna could rescue Jordan and risk the element of surprise or continue her pursuit. It felt wrong, but ultimately if Luna failed to stop the Deer Woman, no one would be rescued. It was her faith that Lane would be along shortly that tipped her hand. He would make it. He'd set Jordan free and together they'd fix the rest of this mess. That optimism based on their years of experience pushed Luna forward through the shadows.

After another fifty yards ahead, Luna could make out a clearing in the woods. She could see the dark water of Spirit Lake shift violently as the winds increased and sheet lightning rolled through the clouds above. Beyond the lake stood Mount Saint Helens. In what little light there was, it almost appeared as if the storm clouds were rolling out from the mountain. Then, it hit her: *not just a mountain, a volcano* . An active volcano at that. If the Deer Woman under Jude's direction had their way, all that smoke, ash, and magma unleashed could do an unfathomable amount of damage to the environment.

The gears turned quickly within Luna's mind.

She had prepared her opening gambit.

If Lane didn't join her soon, she'd have to make the first move and pray for the best. But she believed in her brother. She loved him. He'd be along soon. Lane wasn't one to disappoint.

Jordan struggled against the vines and branches. No matter how hard she pulled or broke her bindings, more grew over the damaged wood. It was hopeless.

"Good. You're safe," a voice whispered from behind. "Hold still and I'll cut you loose."

"I don't need your help," Jordan grumbled.

There was a *whoosh* and *thwack* terribly close to her. "Watch where you're swinging that!" Jordan cried out.

"Sorry," Lane answered unconvincingly. He sliced through the air and into the branches again with a *sizzle* . Some vines attempted to regrow and regain their grip, but the ones Lane had sliced were burnt with a coppery scent that lingered in the air. "I'm gonna try the roots…"

"Stop wasting time," Jordan sighed. She watched as Lane came limping out from behind her, bruised and beaten as if he'd just got hit by a truck. Not particularly looking at Lane, Jordan sighed, "You have to go after her: stop Jude and that… thing, whatever it is. Whatever it takes."

"I can get you free first," Lane said, raising the silver sword above his head.

"No. That… The thing that's carrying Jude. You have to stop it before…" Jordan shook her head, "Read my lips, Lane Guster Woods: I. Don't. Need. Your. Help. Just go!"

Lane gave one last sympathetic look up at Jordan and nodded. Before he dashed off, over his shoulder, he said, "Jude's family, it wasn't really perfect. It couldn't have been. Nothing is ever really perfect."

Impatiently, Jordan groaned, "Yeah. Obviously. His wife and daughter dying after the divorce was probably what made him snap in the first place."

Wait: after the divorce? Lane's eyes went wide. He dashed back to Jordan. That puzzle piece was exactly what he needed. "You said on the ropes course—"

Jordan rolled her eyes. "Yeah. I knew they'd separated. I was there in his cabin last year when Jude was served his divorce papers." She cracked her knuckles and continued prying apart the branches and vines that held her suspended in the air. "I remember the way he laughed and said he'd get her and his daughter back, like it was no big deal." Some more vines fell as Jordan nearly freed herself. "I guess I was jealous of a guy who'd go out of his way to get the love of his life back… but clearly that wasn't the case."

Lane considered the possibilities of what 'Get them back' actually meant and how obtusely fucked up it turned out to be.

"Are you still standing around while the world's about to end? Get going, you moron!" Jordan shouted. "Go," she added in a final whisper.

Lane didn't look back as he bolted into the woods toward the lake.

The churning waters guided Lane to the shore as more storm clouds continued to gather mass overhead. Lightning snaked through the sky and occasionally struck the top of the Mountain beyond the lake. A surge of relief jolted through Lane's aching body as he found his sister crouched behind a bank of driftwood.

Lane ducked down and crouched beside Luna.

"Any last observations?" she whispered.

Lane clasped a hand on Luna's shoulder and leaned in. "I don't think this is about grief or sorrow." Luna shot her brother an intrigued look, urging him to continue. "Jude recently got a divorce *before* he became a widower. Even money says the wife got partial if not full custody of their daughter." Lane paused for a moment to fully form his hypothesis, "Given how manipulative the activities were, the demeaning naming ceremony, the death of his ex-wife and daughter so soon after the divorce, I feel Jude's motives have more to do with a lack of control than sorrow. He feels betrayed. This is all unadulterated, sociopathic revenge."

Luna nodded, "Okay. So our mark is so desperate, perhaps so enraged by anything outside of his control, that he summoned the Deer Woman. He deciphered enough of the manuscript to manipulate the entity into entertaining his emotional state, his need to control and destroy."

"The entity interprets desire," Lane repeated. Thinking back to the deer skin and the picture of the central ritual. The altar. The pictogram of the girl in the center. It didn't just summon the entity. It directed the entity into a host. "Alice," he gasped.

"Oh god," Luna choked out, "The entity may be able to feed off of and influence others' emotions, desires. But if it inhabited a host that had been manipulated by a man drowning in hatred…"

"He used Alice as his vehicle to summon the Deer Woman and maintain a semblance of control over the entity itself. But it's driven by conviction. If the summoner or host of the entity were to have that conviction shaken, or destroyed…? It's a hell of a gamble."

Luna used her hands to mime an imaginary set of unbalanced scales. She began again hesitantly, "Okay, I've got a plan. You're really not gonna like it." Lane didn't interrupt. "I think we might be able to present something more desirable to the Deer Woman than destruction."

Lane opened his mouth, paused, then set his jaw. Through clenched teeth, he offered his sister wavering support. "I believe you, but what if you can't seduce that thing?"

"I'll try not to take offense at that," Luna said, wrinkling her nose, "But, if the ritual to summon the Deer Woman required a host body to contain the entity, I think my chances are more than fair. You remember how you *didn't* have sex with Alice when she threw herself at you in the Bathhouse?"

Lane winced, then his eyes blossomed into giant saucers as another wave of sheet lightning lit up the sky, the beach, and the mostly nude body of the Deer Woman. Despite her altered proportions, antlers, and otherworldly musculature, the similarity was unmistakable. Those shining blue eyes? The ample chest? It even had Alice's flowing silver hair falling just below the small of her back and verve buttocks. If the ritual had indeed bonded the entity into the pale counselor he'd encountered earlier, there was a chance Alice's consciousness could be accessed under the right circumstances.

"You'll need me to distract Jude then, while you, um, work?" Lane asked uncomfortably.

Apollena nodded, resolute, "You trust me, right?"

Setting his sights on the objective ahead, Lane reached out for

Luna's hand and held it tight, "Always. Until the end."

"Until the end," Luna repeated.

Hand in hand, the twins stepped out from their cover and approached the entity, Jude, and the tar-covered lion who sat on the shore beside them.

"Deer Woman," Apollena called out, "We've come to bargain."

I'M THE ONE (WHO LOVES YOU)

At first, the nine-foot-tall forest entity didn't respond. She placed Jude gently on the sand. His deteriorating body sat facing Mount St. Helen, the soon-to-be-active volcano. The Deer Woman then began her work. She waved her massive tree branch arms to conduct a private symphony of destruction. With every subtle twitch of her fingers manipulating unseen instruments, lightning shifted across the sky, thunder *CRACKED*, and the ground quaked.

"There's no bargaining now," Jude mocked. "All the pieces on the board have already played their part. The Deer Woman's victory will punish the ungrateful populace that's plagued her earth. This is the end. Farewell into this final goodnight, Woods Siblings."

Lane tightened his grip on the silver cross as the tar-covered lion shifted its gaze toward the twins and licked its lips. Neither Lane nor Luna slowed their approach. Instead, Luna called out again while unbuttoning her blue-jean shorts. "Deer Woman, we've come to bargain: to provide you with an offering in exchange for sparring the

mortals of your earth."

The emaciated lion emitted a low growl that Lane could feel jostle his broken and battered ribcage. Still, the twins proceeded forward. The volatile lightning refracted off the turbulent lake to cast an epileptic strobing effect upon the Deer Woman. Lane watched waves of light dance across the familiar curves of Alice's possessed body that had been remade under the entity's control. They were about ten yards away from Jude, the Lion, and the goddess now. The Twins held their ground as the entity finally half turned from her work to address Luna.

Luna looked at the entity right in her golden blue eyes. She gave her brother's hand one last squeeze and quickly released herself from Lane's grasp. With both hands now free, she hooked her thumbs under the hem of her lime green spaghetti strap shirt. She lifted the fabric up slowly, showing off every inch of her lovely, toned brown stomach.

It was hard to distinguish Jude's objection from the growl of the lion that sat beside him. "What do you think you're doing? What perversion is this?!"

Lane leveled the silver cross at the Lion. "Not a perversion: a gambit. Black queen takes white queen. Who has more influence? A frail camp director with his own self-serving interests and insecurities, or the unfathomable compassion and unbridled love of my sister? Go ahead, Jude, place your bet."

Jude's face contorted into that of a scowling gargoyle that would have sat atop an old, dilapidated cathedral. Spittle flew from the mouth of the increasingly agitated camp director. "This is not a game you'll win, Roswell." With a snort, he leaned into the lion and spoke, "White knight takes black knight."

The tar lion lunged forward. Lane was ready. He parried the lion's colossal paws and jaws with a downward slash of the cross. Even with the subtle movement, Lane could feel his ribs continue to *crack* and *crunch* inside his chest. Stiff upper lip covered in blood, he pushed through the pain. His wrist flicked the silver sword up and out, ready for the next attack. Even if his opponent was an emaciated lion, it still held a 300 pound advantage over him, and paws that could rip a car in half. Lane shifted his posture defensively and shuffled back across the sand. Thus began his calculated retreat toward the water's edge.

While Jude kept his eyes on Lane's impending devouring, Luna continued her seduction of the goddess. Free of her shirt, she strode forward, walking out her jean shorts as they slid down her slender legs and onto the sand. The Deer Woman remained transfixed on the mortal girl as she stripped free of her black cotton boy shorts. Raising her arms up to the sky, Luna licked her lips, "Where men offer nothing but destruction and pain, I offer you creation."

Luna dropped her hands back down slowly, running her fingers through her short jet-black hair. Eventually, her fingertips found the straps of her bright pink bra. She peeled off one strap, then the other. Luna was an arm's length away from the forest entity as she suggested, "We could create something beautiful together, you and I." She pulled the center clasp of her bra down, letting the last cloak of her modesty fall to the wet sand.

The entity, the one that so much resembled Alice, now leaned forward ever so slightly over Apollena. Those pearl white, honeydew breasts of Alice's were just out of reach from Luna's lips, but she restrained herself. The forest spirit's countenance remained stoic, unmoved by the naked beauty that stood before her. Luna, however, was already busy studying the micro-expressions on the Deer Woman's face and body. Reaching out, palm turned up, Luna offered to meet the deity halfway. Apollena let out an inviting, wanting sigh as she prepared her body as a gift fit to please a goddess.

Not so much hesitating, the Deer Woman waited a moment before extending a single finger to touch Luna's palm. As the mortal young woman and ancient entity connected, Luna offered the Deer Woman a smile that could have melted the sun. With another weighted sigh, she leaned forward, pressing her supple lips upon the rough flesh of the forest goddess' hand. One kiss led to another, and another. A series of longing kisses followed that made their way down to the tip of the finger still planted upon Luna's palm. Those kisses soon became one, long, slow lick from Luna's wet tongue back up the length of the index finger of the entity.

Luna didn't cease. She reached out her other hand to massage the wrist of the Deer Woman, gently holding the goddess in place. Her tongue continued to paint its way up and down the entity's stiff finger unabated. Luna spread her legs, each barefoot planted firmly in the sand. As she drew her tongue back up the length of the Deer Woman's finger, Luna asked, "We could create something so beautiful. Would you like that?"

Studying the sharp blue and gold eyes of the goddess, Luna saw the pupils widen and lips part as if to convey sorrow, perhaps regret.

"Is this the first time anyone's ever asked what you desire?" Luna's voice was a soft whisper, but her question was an arrow that sank into the heart of the Deer Woman. Suddenly, the finger planted in Luna's palm flinched. Luna reached out and gently slid her hand upon the Deer Woman's hip. "Has no one ever fulfilled *your* desires before?"

Luna read the Deer Woman's swollen eyes and saw a single, subtle tear begin to form. Stepping closer still, Luna wrapped herself around the waist of the giant woman as far as her arm span could accommodate. Given the height difference, Luna's head rested just above the taller woman's waist. She looked down upon the trail of hair that led to the untamed silver bush and glistening sex that lay hidden underneath.

"Please, if you ask me, I will fulfill *your* desire that has long been neglected by those in the past. Those who only sought to use you for their own desires. Allow me to fulfill *your* needs," Luna pleaded as she ran her tongue along the curvature of the Deer Woman's hip bone, down her trail, down, and down, and down…

Lane stood knee-deep in water so frigid it burned him. *Probably gonna get a touch of frostbite if this takes too long,* he figured into his calculation.

Had to keep his mind busy. Focused. He couldn't afford to think about his own pain. Not now. There was too much at stake. If things went south on Luna's end, he would be her last defense. It would be on Lane to shoulder the burden of stopping the Deer Woman and Jude's dark desires.

The Lion *roared* again, telegraphing its attack: Ever the alpha predator. Or so, it was led to believe. Lane barely dodged its latest pounce. The lake's depth made it harder to move, sidestep, evade the massive ink-covered beast. Fortunately, that problem was a two-way street. Lane watched as the tar or whatever black, viscous liquid started to harden. The lion's fur was matted down, soaked thick with the same icy water that stung Lane.

"You know, for a minute there, I actually thought you'd be a threat," Jude called from the shore. He'd managed to limp his way to the water's edge. He watched as the lion prepared for another strike. "I'll admit to a bit of hubris. Your qualifications, your inquisitive nature? Could've ruined everything. I didn't even have to hire someone... " he searched for the word, "... so meddlesome. The ritual only required thirteen people. Men. Women. Children. Any thirteen would have done. I'd have taken whoever said yes first."

Lane again executed another parry too close to call. The lion's left paw grazed his shoulder. If the strike had been true, Lane would have lost the arm. But it did bleed all the same. A trail of blood leaked out across the surface of the turbulent waters as Lane went back deeper still. His back foot finally slipped free of the sandbar, now forced to tread water. He floated out just far enough to invite another pounce. Easy prey.

"It's unfortunate that you couldn't learn to let go," Lane shouted across the water.

Jude snorted at the obvious attempt at being baited.

"Was it that your wife couldn't stand the manipulation at home? The mind games? Your constant need to be in control?" Lane kept one eye on the lion, the other on the Camp Director. "Perhaps when your overbearing nature finally fell upon your daughter, your wife drew the line? That's when she left you, right?"

Jude cupped a hand to his mouth to shout his reply, "The last words from a dead man. You're wasting your breath, Roswell."

"You couldn't accept anyone would ever go against your will, could you? That's why they had to die. That's why you took your wife's life. That's why you murdered your daughter!" Lane dared to shift both eyes onto Jude.

He watched.

He waited.

The sad excuse of a man didn't disappoint. "They couldn't see how easy it would have been if—IF THEY'D ONLY OBEYED!" Even obscured under the dark clouds and strobing sheet lightning above, Lane caught glimpses of Jude's face, brightening to a blood-red hue as he screamed, "Everything ends tonight! Everything. By my hand, I will end it all."

Apollena's hand, meanwhile, was exceptionally busy. Her fingers deftly slid across the outer labia of the Deer Woman's open legs, slick and dripping. The entity shuddered but remained standing. Probing deeper, the mortal girl's fingers unfolded the inner labia, holding it open for her tongue to further flick and part the soaked petals of the entity's pussy. Ever the master of her own tongue, Luna massaged the clitoris of the goddess that towered over her with the elegance and grace of a poet.

With her eyes closed, Luna reached inward to remember all the countless times she'd been taken advantage of, traded, sold, and abused. She remembered the heartache and unspeakable pain. As the mortal girl's lips touched the lower lips of a goddess, Luna plunged the depth of her empathy. *To have such power only to be summoned, and demanded to act out someone else's wicked wills? To have been neglected, gone without praise, buried under a tomb for decades?* Luna's mind raced to compose a suitable apology.

Not only an apology, but comfort, kindness, and love.

As tears welled up in Luna's eyes, she continued to write her love letters, an unrelenting ballad of praise and adoration with her tongue. She may not have fully understood the Deer Woman. But this entity was a woman, nonetheless. This was a woman who would no longer go unfulfilled. With that promise in her heart and the goddess' wetness rolling down her tongue and throat, Luna reached her fingers deeper within the Deer Woman and let them dance inside.

In that same moment, Luna felt the fingers of the entity grasp the crown of her head and draw her closer to the glistening pussy she continued to devour.

"Will you let me satisfy you tonight?" Luna asked between lashing her tongue upon the Deer Woman's clit, penetrating and massaging her sex.

A *moan* laced with the heartache of isolation finally escaped from the Deer Woman's trembling mouth. It was a sound so deep and sorrowful that it shook the trees. Luna continued to summon her own gentle earthquake within the goddess.

The entire woods audibly shared a single ecstatic word as it erupted from the goddess, "Yes."

With a wide, wet smile, Luna licked her lips and obliged.

"Kill him," Jude ranted and raved, "Kill that bastard, now!"

The lion paced back and forth in the shallows. Its nose sniffed and snorted the scent of Lane's blood. Its low growl shook the waters with nearly as much force as the growing thunderstorm ahead. Lane kept treading water, eggbeater legs churning in the frigid lake. He kept his head high enough above the water to entice the lion with a smile.

"I said, 'KILL HIM'," Jude commanded one last time.

Finally, the lion obeyed.

Pushing off with its hind paws, Lane watched it soar through the air. As he had calculated, the lion then landed with a mighty splash roughly an arm's length away. Just close enough. All that lake water had thoroughly soaked into its fur. Whatever the fuck that black liquid was had hardened almost to glass, or a dark amber resin now. The beast probably didn't even feel the small, but precise cuts Lane had made into its joints when he parried those massive paws. Now, icy water stung its muscles, and the weight of its own sponge-like fur coat must have felt like steel plates attached to its body. This terrifying creature now frantically, desperately attempted to stay afloat.

Lane didn't hesitate. He'd been trained, marshaled, crafted into a machine that knew how to save a life from drowning. There was a key element to that training that Lane had to access at this moment to overcome a beast that could easily kill him. He knew how to rescue a drowning victim. He knew the steps necessary to succeed. At this moment, however, Lane had to push himself to intentionally perform the opposite of those years of training. He went against everything he knew to ensure the target he'd lured out into the Lake wouldn't take another breath.

Lane quickly swam alongside the lion raged against the violent waters, gasping for breaths. In a single thrust, Lane positioned the silver cross into the beast's gaping maw. The predator splashed and swiped frantically. Lane was unfettered. He mounted the lion and, like a silver bit in a horse, Lane pulled with all his might to keep the lion's jaw from closing. His legs wrapped tightly around his opponent's ribs. The spurs of Lane's heels dug into the creature's side like a vice grip. Each kick of Lane's heels made the lion's desperate, gasping breaths that much harder and inefficient. Lane pulled back upon the silver lever harder still. More water came flooding into the lion's open mouth as they continued to sink beneath the waves.

Less water was spat out, as more and more was swallowed.

The beast worked its paws feverishly against the water, clamoring for one last breath. Its torso thrashed. It tried to *roar*, but barely a pathetic gurgle escaped as more water rushed down the lion's throat into its lungs.

Lane broke his promise.

He once again failed his oath to save lives.

That pain was far worse than the frostbite. Worse than the fear of everything he'd ever known ending and consumed by fire. Lane's current failure was almost worse than the potential death of his sister. Those buried memories began to resurface: that disappointment of past failure. Those scars of his own making that would forever mark his heart had been violently reopened. It bled worse than before. Lane drew a deep breath, still squeezing his legs around the lion's body and prying open its mouth as it finally failed to resurface. He could feel the beating heart of this creature race faster. He could hear its muffled roar, its plea for release, for life.

Then, Lane felt nothing.

He released his grip around the lion's waist and kicked off its body, shooting himself up to the surface. Once above the waves, Lane exhaled and took another deep breath. His burning lungs drew in the atmosphere thick with electricity and the storm still raging above. Lane glanced beneath the water but could just barely make out the inky shape of the great beast. Then, it disappeared.

"That's not..." Jude couldn't finish. His jaw simply hung open in disbelief.

Lane's teeth chattered while he swam toward the shore. As he stood upon the sand bar, Lane beat his chest with a shivering fist and locked eyes onto the former camp director. "There's another obvious factor you overlooked—aviation survival techs, we're drown-proof."

Lane still shivered: less from the cold, more from righteous indignation held against Jude. Lane lifted the silver cross once more and leveled it at his opponent. "Black knight, to white king: check."

Jude stumbled backward in the sand. He struggled to get back to his feet, to turn and face the last piece he had to move. To his horror and disgust, his queen was otherwise... occupied.

Luna rocked her hips back and forth, savoring every delicious inch of the connection between her pussy and the goddess she rode upon. The Deer Woman had let herself fall back upon the sand, surrendered to the genuine pleasure and warmth offered unto her by a mortal woman. With her head tilted back, eyes fluttering, and long strands of silver hair swept back, she panted for breath. Harder, faster, Luna *howled* in ecstasy and continued to increase her pace.

Again, the Deer Woman spoke. The familiar English of Alice's voice overlapped by the countless voices of previous host bodies over the centuries. A single, pleading, whimper, "More."

Luna detached herself from between the Deer Woman's quavering legs. Sprawling herself out upon the forest entity's chest, she leaned down, drawing circles around her partner's nipples with the tip of her tongue. One quick kiss led to another before Luna finally rose up to make her demands clear, "I will give you so much more, but..." She flicked her tongue once more, the breasts of the entity grasped firmly in Luna's hands. "Release Alice. Allow me to host you and together we'll repair this destruction of man." Luna dipped down again, tasting the breasts of the goddess and fondling the pearl white flesh delicately, roughly, alternating between firm and gentle handfuls.

"Would you let the girl go so *we* can be together?" Luna asked in between kisses and subtle bites. She worked her way up to the Deer Woman's collarbone. Luna's tongue wrote the promise out across the goddess' flesh, up her neck, and nibbled on her earlobe. "I will give you more," Luna promised. "*We* will share much more, together."

"What have you done? You perverted, witch! I was the one who summoned her. I completed the ritual. She. Is. MINE!" Jude cried out, exacerbated and defeated.

Luna placed her hand upon the woman's cheek, "Since when does a goddess obey the rules and constraints of a man?" Embracing the Deer Woman, Luna planted her lips against the goddess' and kissed her deeply, "Us. Together. Till the end?"

Jude's protest was in vain.

Lane looked past the broken man and saw his naked sister lying upon the forest spirit that eerily resembled Alice. The sound of groaning, moaning trees rocked the air, louder than the storm above them. The Deer Woman stood up to her full height. Now, in place of Jude, it cradled Luna's nude body tightly against her own.

"NO," Jude shouted again, "You're mine. I brought you here. You shall obey me!"

The resentful scowl the Deer Woman aimed at Jude packed enough punch that he doubled over, lying backward on the sand.

Lane kept his eyes on Luna, his dear twin sister.

She offered him that same confident smile he'd grown up with. Her smile had always dispelled any fear or doubt that plagued him. Then, holding Lane's eye, she mouthed, 'I love you,' while the Deer Woman stretched out her right arm to the sky. Before Lane could reply or protest, a bolt of lightning shot down from the storm and consumed both the goddess and his sister.

28

AIRLINE TO HEAVEN

It was much harder to breathe now all on his own. Not just because of the thick putrid sulphur smell, Lane was alone now. While the ground still shook and the storm above raged on, there was a bitter stillness that gripped him when something so valuable had been stolen right before his eyes. Sheet lightning blanketed the sky. Deafening thunder *cracked* above Lane as he remained on the ash covered beach. Both his sister and the Deer Woman had vanished.

"What have you done?" a sad, deflated voice asked.

Jude Abidalli.

Lane was still too galled to mourn. He unbuckled his belt and pulled it free from the loops around his waist. With the leather switch in his hand, the solitary twin marched on Jude.

Exhausted, chilled to the bone, and mad as hell, Lane dragged the perpetrator through his rights, "Jude Abidalli, under the authority of Revised Code of Washington State Law, chapter 9A section 04.060, I'm placing you under arrest for the murder of your wife and daughter.

Anything you say or do from this moment on will be recorded and offered to the court to be used against you. You have the right to an attorney. If you can't afford—"

"You think you have the power to—" Jude interrupted but was silenced just as quickly. The lone twin used his belt to bind the former camp director's hands together behind his back.

Lane continued, "You have the right to shut the fuck up. Now, on your feet. Move!" Holding Jude by the improvised handcuffs, Lane pulled the perpetrator up to his feet.

"God, my head," groaned a familiar voice.

Lane looked away from Jude, glancing down at the where Alice lay. She remained naked, except where covered in wet sand and ash.

"Alice? Are you okay? Can you stand?" Lane asked.

She nodded weakly, "I think, maybe? Everything is so muddled. Everything is dizzy."

Lane forced Jude back down onto the ground to tend to Alice. He quickly examined the nude girl, a familiar scene and yet thankfully different from when they'd first met. Offering her a hand up, he tried to reassure her, "Everything is going to be okay. We–" Lane flinched, "I'll get us out of here. Promise." The boy peeled off his vest and offered his wet shirt to Alice.

As she gingerly took the only available garment to cover herself with, Jude began to chuckle. His laughter quickly turned to manic cackling.

"Are you blind? Deaf?" He howled, "Did you think I was lying? The game had already been won before you stepped foot on this beach, Roswell. Look with your own eyes, witness the end of everything!"

Almost as if he'd choreographed his maniacal little speech, the unmistakable sonic boom of a first-stage eruption shook the earth. A plume of smoke and ash jettisoned itself up into the air. Lightning bolts streaked down from the dark storm clouds and touched down upon the thrashing lake.

Alice gasped.

Lane set his jaw. He reached down into his vest for his journal. Perhaps there was some kind of incantation, some obscure spell he had overlooked that happened to be powerful enough to stop a volcano. Or, barring that, something to buy him and Alice enough time to...

No. There wouldn't be enough time to escape. But Lane simply couldn't accept another loss. Not now. A torrent of sweat ran down from his brow. He was only skimming the contents of the book now. He knew, in his heart, there was nothing in his arsenal that could stop the destruction that was coming.

They had to run. They had to try.

"Come on," Lane urged Alice, "We can reach the parking lot before—"

Another quake rattled the surrounding woods. Whole trees snapped and clattered to the forest floor. The earth was hit with such force, Lane and Alice both toppled over onto the sand. Mere feet away from where they all sat, a fissure opened in the ground.

Alice offered the only sensible reaction to the earth splitting open and the fury of mother nature raging above and below. She *screamed*.

Then, Mother Nature herself rose from the grave.

To Lane's surprise, relief, and terrified heart, Mother Nature wore a familiar face. The curves of her body, dark honey skin, and her million-watt smile were all too familiar. It was the smile he'd grown up with. Suddenly, that welcome rush of confidence that Lane could stand against a volcano rushed through his blood.

As the nine-foot-tall entity towered over them, Lane asked, "Are you alright?"

The creature that resembled so much of his sister turned to smile and nodded. "We are, Lane. Thank you for your concern."

Lane rose to his feet and offered a tear-filled smile, "Is it too late to stop Mount St. Helen from erupting? If it reaches stage three—"

"The devastation will be immeasurable," spoke the Deer Woman with Apollena's voice. She turned her antlered head toward the volcano still spewing out ash into the sky. "Fortunately, as difficult as creation may be, it is not too late to relieve the pressure building beneath the mountain. Observe."

Lane held his breath. He'd wait until the job was done until he'd release a sigh of relief. He took a timid step beside the Deer Woman that had bonded with his twin and asked, "Is there anything I can do?"

Luna's sweet voice led a choir of all the women who had served the Deer Woman before as she reached out her massive hand to hold Lane's, "Be here, stand with us."

Lane nodded and accepted the hand of this new entity his sister had become. As he grabbed hold of the Deer Woman, he felt an indescribable wave of energy surge through his body. He could feel the sand beneath his toes and the earth that stretched far beneath the sand. His mind traveled further down until, at last, he came upon the magma building up beneath Mount St. Helens. He felt the insufferable heat radiating out from the lava, building up its wrath. Then there was movement, a shift in the soil above the surface. Lane could feel Luna's thoughts and the command the Deer Woman held over the earth.

The pressure continued to build. The earth still shook. Ash had all but covered Lane, Alice, and the madman who caused this mess. Through his uncanny connection, however, Lane could see *through* the earth as sinkholes rapidly formed. Soil and bedrock moved aside by Luna's will. Massive vents began to tear open around the base of Mount St. Helen. In the distance, Lane could visibly see, even hear, the steam rise from the underground veins where the magma had been concentrating.

Looking up to the sky, Lane watched as the dark storm cloud began to twist into slow spirals above the mountain. Western winds blew steadily at first, then a sudden squall lifted the darkness in its entirety. That pillar of ash, that tower of impending destruction and rage, was lifted up higher and higher into the atmosphere. It stretched into a thin wisp and finally choked out until it was no more.

Sunlight broke free of the dreaded night that had long overstayed its welcome.

Lane opened his eyes and gazed upon the impossible sight of the woman his sister had become: a goddess adorned in antlers, dressed only in a crown of sunlight, and vibrant green moss and rich soil.

"That..." Alice started, "That was incredible." Her ocean eyes fluttered open.

Apollena, the new Deer Woman, turned to address Alice and nodded, "Thank you. Such is all life and creation; we are *all* incredible."

Lane still held onto his sister's hand, or at least the small part of her hand his mortal fingers managed to grasp, "What happens now, between you and... the Deer Woman?"

Luna offered another sun-kissed smile. "We have our work upon these woods that must be tended to." She leaned forward and touched Lane's cheek with a fingertip. "We know you're worried about us, but all will be as it should be in time, Lane Guster Woods: friend, brother, and partner." She glanced over to Jude and sneered, "I believe you have work that has yet to be concluded." In a voice much more similar to Luna, they added, "Throw the book at him, Lane."

Jude sat still as the horror of his failure weighed down upon his shoulders. That weight was too much to bear as he began to weep uncontrollably.

The entity lastly looked upon a stunned Alice and knelt down beside the naked girl. "We are so sorry for the horrors you endured while you were with us. We don't possess the power to erase the wickedness your eyes have seen, nor what your mortal body felt while you were with us. If you ask of us, we will offer whatever comfort we can provide for your pain."

Alice remained silent, transfixed by the gold and sea-foam green eyes staring back at her.

Lane touched his hand to Alice's shoulder, "I'm sorry I didn't listen to what you needed from me. I didn't know how..."

"It's... It's going to take years, probably decades' worth of therapy and booze, but I think I've had my fill of dwelling on the past. This whole thing is still too much to wrap my head around, but I'll get it handled. I think not letting the world end was a good enough start for me, for now. Thank you." Alice marveled at the creature before her. Reality and fantasy were unable to hold the same space in her mind, despite what all her senses relayed.

The Deer Woman nodded and rose to her full height. "We too will get our situation, 'handled.' Go in peace and love. We shall return to you in time, Lane." With those final cryptic words, the forest spirit raised her hands to the sky. The earth parted once more. Soil, rocks, and roots rose up from the newly created fissure to encase the entity. As quickly as she'd appeared, the goddess returned to the earth.

Lane stood alone as his sister disappeared for the second time that day.

A gentle breeze blew through the pines. Morning birds sang a new song. The violent churning waters of Spirit Lake had finally settled into the clear indigo glass he saw when they first arrived at Trillion Pines.

"What happens now?" Alice asked, reaching out to Lane.

Lane took the girl's hand in his. With his free hand, Lane listed their immediate needs out on his fingers. "First, I have a friend that needs a proper burial. Second, we're gonna need a strong cup of coffee and breakfast. Third, I'm going to make a call to have the authorities deal with that clown—" Lane jabbed his thumb at Jude, still sobbing into his hands.

"Really? You're gonna have Jude arrested for... what, exactly? Summoning a demigod to blow up Mount St. Helen? Who in their right mind will believe that!?" Alice groaned.

"Not many," Lane admitted, "But, Washington State has a pretty clear and definitive set of laws against murder. I'm certain that, once examined, the bodies he buried beside his cabin will provide a solid conviction. Not to mention the other lives he was responsible for."

Alice shifted uncomfortably. "Can we, um, perhaps add finding clothes to your list?" Lane still held Alice's hand. He offered up his now dried vest to wrap around her waist. She accepted the garment, blushing, and grinned. "Thanks."

Lane nodded and blushed. He reached out for Jude, grabbed him by the leather restraint, and pulled the broken sociopath up to his feet. "It's going to be a busy day. Let's not waste it."

EPILOGUE

"What Planet is This?"

Taking the last good piece of advice his sister offered him, Lane finally gave himself a vacation. He hated every minute of it. He'd spent the last two weeks at the Edgefield McMenamins', just outside of Portland, lazing about in a suite on the second floor. Ordinarily, securing a reservation at this odd combination of a spa, winery, and resort would be impossible to book on a whim. Fortunately, the management owed him and his family a favor after a particular 'supernatural complication' a few years back. Those were the meager perks of the life he lived. And while Lane had finally accepted the inescapable occupation of paranormal-problem-solver, such a life wasn't without its disadvantages. Over the last few days, the disadvantages had finally begun to weigh on him.

The price Lane paid for living the life he'd been fated to endure was a double-edged sword. He'd traveled the globe well before his mid-twenties, gained otherworldly knowledge, skills, and a loving adopted family. But knowledge and skill came at a heavy cost. Lane sat at what had become his usual barstool at the Black Rabbit Cafe. He figured the bill had come due. The heft of his Journal sank into the inner breast pocket of his vest. As heavy as that tomb of occult knowledge had become, it was lighter by far than the weight of losing his sister.

"A little early in the morning to be hitting the sauce, eh, kiddo?" spoke a familiar voice.

Lane didn't raise his head from the cup he'd been staring at for the last half-hour. "It's coffee. Black. Glad you could make it, Uncle Dan." He didn't feel the need to mention the two-finger measure of Jack Daniel's he'd added to his second cup. As the onset of depression began to settle firmly on the young man's shoulders, seeking counsel seemed to be more productive than a rather costly bar tab over the last few days. Calling Uncle Dan had two advantages: one, he intimately knew the hardship of losing someone under supernatural circumstances. And two, he was available.

"Well, you won't begrudge me if I pour myself something from the top shelf, then." Uncle Dan withdrew a flask from his tweed coat pocket. With the other hand, he'd reached over and poured the contents of the silver flask into Lane's cup of coffee, sipped it, and set it back down on the bar. "So, where's your better half?"

Lane offered a small smile, grabbed the cup back from his uncle, and downed the remainder of the contents.

"Oh," Uncle Dan said quietly. "I see..."

Lane let out a breath that reeked of aged whiskey, coffee, and sorrow. "I know it's a sore subject, loss, but I thought you could offer some perspective?"

Uncle Dan looked his nephew up and down. The boy's shoulders looked as though he'd traveled a hundred miles with the yolk of grief strapped upon them. His eyes were bloodshot, and his hands twitched sporadically. For everything he and Luna had been through, Daniel knew the crucible one's heart went through after losing someone so loved.

"Why don't you take it from the top, then?" Uncle Dan suggested calling over the waiter, "I'll take care of Breakfast."

Over the course of eggs, pecan waffles, and another round of coffee, Lane recalled the whirlwind weekend at Camp Trillion Pines. At the time, seventy-two hours felt more like a month of non-stop, all-out assault on his senses. All that death? It came back to him in waves of nightmares that made for many sleepless nights over the past two weeks.

Uncle Dan, for his part, seemed to take it all in stride. After another sip of coffee, he gestured for Lane to continue. "So, Luna, um, 'bonded' with this forest spirit to keep Mount St. Helens from blowing.

Impressive. What happened afterward?"

"Alice, the girl who'd previously been host to the entity, and I buried my friend Aiden. There were a handful of others that we also managed to locate and pay proper respects to Julia, Korri, Zoe, Cole, Brandon, and the groundskeeper, Doc."

"God rest their souls." Dan raised his cup and took a sip.

Lane followed suit. Raised his mug, but simply looked back into the black liquid. The coffee had gone cold. Setting the porcelain cub back on its saucer, he continued, "During the burial, I'd detained Jude. After we'd finished, it wasn't long after a second helicopter from the Seattle Coast Guard arrived. I'd explained the situation to the straights the best I could..." The straights, an endearing term to those oblivious to any supernatural phenomena. It'd be a waste of time to give all the gory details to the guardsmen who arrived. Needless complications. Lane told them the watered-down version: wild animal attack, mechanical failure, just a string of unfortunate accidents and loss.

"So they offered you and the girl a lift, I presume?" Dan asked expectantly.

Lane nodded. "And Jude," he bristled at every mention of his name. "Once we'd arrived on base, the XO on duty referred me to a reputable detective in Seattle. For his part, Jude offered a confession with surprisingly little encouragement, from my end."

"Still going to be a legal mess to get those murders sorted out, I reckon?" Dan mussed, shaking his head.

Lane gave a curt nod. "That's why I'm sticking around here. Told the lead detective I'd be within arm's reach when the trial got underway. With any luck, the bastard will plead guilty at his arraignment and that'll be the end of it."

"Sure," Dan agreed quietly, "But the experience of it all doesn't just vanish, does it?"

Lane thought for a moment. Usually, he'd be able to compartmentalize all the horrors of what had become a regular occurrence in his life.

This case was different. This time, Luna wasn't there to help shoulder the burden. Lane found himself unequally yoked. With all that excess weight in trauma, he may as well try to stand upright on Jupiter.

Uncle Dan grasped his hand upon Lane's shoulder, "It feels like it, at the moment, but you remember, lad, you're not alone. Understood? As the name goes, our family is like trees: mighty redwoods that stand tall, rooted together. We share the burden of what we've seen and done. That's how we get through it all. Until the end, right?"

Lane nodded, "Until the end," he repeated in mangled French. "Until the *bitter* end."

"That wasn't half bad... If you were a freshman in high school that'd never heard a word of French," a familiar voice laughed from the entrance of the empty cafe.

Lane spun around in his chair and stood up so fast that he nearly knocked the barstool over onto the ground. He blinked in amazement as his feet carried him toward the door, toward the figure that stood in the entryway. With hands-on her hips and a sly smile spread ear to ear, Luna, his sister, had returned.

Without another word spoken between the two, Lane wrapped his arms around her neck. She returned his embrace whole heartily.

"I didn't think I'd ever see you again," Lane whispered, desperately holding back a torrent of tears. He peeled off from his noticeably taller twin and looked her up and down. At first glance, one wouldn't notice anything too peculiar. Another bohemian girl in Portland, Oregon. A naturalist perhaps?

Indeed, Luna was barefoot. Her skirt, if one could call it that, was nothing more than a loincloth made of some animal hide that barely covered her modesty. Draped around her neck, hardly covering her breasts, was a necklace of exotic flowers woven together in brightly colored lays. At last, the more obvious reminder of the change she'd undergone: the antlers. Somehow, she'd managed to shrink them down from their grand size to inconspicuous nubs. They could have been part of a headband to the casual observer.

"We mentioned our return, did we not?" Luna said, leaning down for the first time to give her brother a kiss on the forehead. She wasn't nine feet tall, but in her current form, Luna still held a few inches over him. Her voice had also changed. Voices would be more accurate.

"How did you..." Lane started, still staring in disbelief, "How'd you know where I was?"

"Cozy little bed-and-breakfast? Edgefield was the first thing that came to mind. We also reached out through The Green and sensed your presence here—a neat little trick we've begun to master. How's your stay been?"

Lane nodded, awestruck, more so that his sister was still in his presence and less that she still hosted a forest spirit and a plethora of new abilities.

"Love what you've done with your hair, Luna. Care to join us? Explain a few missing details to your brother's tale of woe?" Uncle Dan waved his hand, summoning the twins back to the bar.

A few minutes passed while Luna picked up where Lane had left off. Once she and the Deer Woman bonded, they entered the earth to ensure that Mount St. Helens had been sufficiently ventilated. That was the easiest way Luna could describe the process of how she both manipulated and traversed nature. Turns out the process of deactivating a volcano takes a significant amount of time and energy. As the first and only *willing* host to the Deer Woman, however, that process was much less combative and more collaborative than it would have been with Alice or any of the previous women who had been ritualistically forced into the role.

"There was a fundamental disconnect between those who originally summoned us, and what the ritual had evolved into," Luna explained. "It all boiled down to miscommunication or complete lack thereof. They thought we required violence to appease us, likening us to the violent nature of a storm or..." gesturing her hand in the relative direction of Washington, "a Volcano. Although we could be violent, we are not malevolent. As humans settled into the area, we began to feed off their emotions, their pheromones. We were influenced by the new stimuli that inhabited the area and in turn reflected back similar emotions."

Lane nodded along. "That explains the bathhouse orgy. Whatever sexual desire was already seeded in a bunch of horny twenty-year-olds, became amplified by the Deer—by your presence." He was working the problem out loud, just as they always had. Except now, when Lane glanced up at his sister, the noticeable change in Luna was jarring. She was still his sister and also, now, The Deer Woman.

"We suppose that's as good an explanation as any," Luna agreed, nibbling at a slice of toast. "For the most part, the original Cowlitz maintained a healthy symbiosis with nature. We didn't see any reason to involve ourselves or make our presence known. But..." she shrugged, "we got curious. The pheromones released during courtship, infatuation, sex, it was all so intoxicating. We breathed it in and breathed it out, and curiosity became a slippery slope."

"Your passive ability to produce pheromones is a feedback loop or an echo chamber?" Uncle Dan suggested, still transfixed by the tiny antlers protruding from his niece's head.

"That sounds about right. As Lane said, whatever dominant emotional state happened to be in the air, we passively amplified those feelings, excreting the *perceived* pheromones back into the air. Of course, at the time, we didn't have the human language to describe what we were experiencing. Fast forward a few centuries and one night, we got caught being a voyeur on a couple copulating and the legend of 'The Deer Woman' began."

"So those ancient summoning rituals were a result of someone seeing you, or rather, a manifestation of the entity without a host?" Lane inquired.

Luna bit her lower lip and half smiled, blushing, "You remember the Sunday-school tale, where Moses goes up to the mountain to talk to

God, and the people who waited down below went a little nuts?"

Lane thought way back to when they still went to church, "Yeah, I think? While Moses went up the mountain to get the Ten Commandments, Aaron made a golden calf, and the people worshiped the idol as their new god. Impatient bunch, apparently."

"In their impatience to understand the truth, they just made a bunch of random shit up and said, 'This is how we'll worship this new thing.' But, besides the golden calf not being real, the rogue priests just invented rituals up on the fly," Luna explained. "The thirteen labourers, the sacrificial virgin, the four rituals—the only reason we chose to appear was that we were curious about what the hell was going on. We sensed this emotional... expectancy, I guess is the word? We were aware that prior to sex within the tribes' people, there was a ritual involved. We were curious whether, as an entity, we could also bond ourselves to a mortal in such a manner. That sensation of intimacy was so foreign, exciting! We craved it." Luna looked to the side, haunted by guilt. "Desire became a dependency."

"So, when that ritual became a regular thing, we just kinda went along without fully comprehending how horrible it was for all those involved." Luna shuddered and grimaced. She wiped a tear from her eye. "Excuse us, the memories of those poor women haunt us still."

Dan nodded slowly, "But to be clear, though, none of the stuff Lane, you, the campers, or the native people did really mattered one way or another as far as summoning you? I mean, the Deer Woman, or, um..." Uncle Dan scratched his head, uncertain of how to address his niece now that she was really two beings in one.

Luna offered a forgiving smile. "It's okay. This is new to us too, paired together in such a way. We can sense distress, sadness in you." Turning specifically to Lane and placing a hand on his cheek, "Please, relax. We're okay. Promise."

Lane nodded reluctantly. "I'm still your brother. I worry."

"Dork," Luna said, this time her original voice a little more clearly above the others that had melted together. "So, yeah, turns out we just really wanted to experience sex, in the flesh, and it got way more complicated than it had to."

Uncle Dan accepted another refill from the waitress and took a long sip of coffee. "So this wanker, Jude, he found the ritual buried under the church and interpreted you as a what? Some kind of genie, or jinn?"

"Like a whore!" Her antlers sharpened at the end; flowers lost their petals at the sudden eruption. Luna took a deep breath, but her face held the scowl, and she emitted what could only be interpreted as a low growl, "That emotional feedback loop you mentioned earlier? Imagine that, but with grief and anger. Surprisingly, all that animosity between himself and everyone else was just as addictive as feeding off other people's sexual pheromones."

"So, as the entity, you were caught up in his pain cycle?" Lane offered.

"It was the most intense thing we'd felt in decades after being locked away," Luna agreed. "With sex, we understood that it ended with a sensation of relief: a climax. Jude's anger and rage were so intense, we..." Luna looked down, guilty, "we thought the resulting climax from Jude's destruction would be more fulfilling than anything we'd previously experienced before."

Uncle Dan gave a snort. "The destruction of the human race via supervolcano? Yeah, that'd be a pretty intense climax. Sure."

Again, Lane read the guilt, the shame, the horror on Luna's face. She may have changed into something beyond his comprehension, but he still knew his sister. He reached over and held her hand. She squeezed back and nodded.

"All that pain and sorrow we could have caused," Luna whispered mournfully.

"But you didn't," Lane assured her. "We stopped it."

Luna nodded and gave a weak smile. "We stopped it. But, in this new form, this new relationship, we still have a lot to learn. Previous hosts were... closed off. Most were too traumatized to bond with us. There's a greater sense of wholeness between your sister and me, Lane." Her brother startled a bit, catching the shift away from a plural entity to singular. Within the form she'd shifted into, Luna requested to speak singularly as well.

"Lane," she spoke with the familiar French lilt he recognized, "I, your sister, will be okay. It's like getting married, just a bit more literal in the two flesh, becomes one department." Inwardly, she embraced the entity and together they spoke, "We may be different now, but we love you as much as we ever have. Possibly, even more now."

They searched Lane's eyes for recognition, and after a moment, he seemed to be content in this analogy.

"It'll take some getting used to my sister being a goddess?"

"Please," she blushed, "we prefer woodland deities," she said with a flourish and wink. Lane was at least comforted to know that her sense of humor remained.

"I suppose the University will have some questions—" Lane stopped himself short, recognizing a change in Luna's countenance.

Lowering her head slightly, they said, "Lane, we're not going back to UCI." There was a twinge of sorrow as they explained, "For the time being, we're staying here to preside over our territory, the woods, nature. It is... It's our duty."

For a minute, Lane looked as though he were about to protest, but his mouth closed. His eyes looked away. He sighed. "Yeah. I guess that makes sense."

Uncle Dan gave his nephew a firm pat on the back. "She's a goddess, after all, lad. She's got her own responsibilities. Maybe it's the whisky talking, but I'm proud of you, Luna... Um, proud of both of you."

"I mean, I get that," Lane agreed, reluctantly. "It's just..."

"I'll miss you too," Luna finished, singularly. "*We* will miss you," they responded together. "We are freer than we have ever been before, thanks to being bonded together." They gestured to include both themselves and Lane. "But because we understand how hopeless you can be without us, we promise two things. First, we'll check in with you on the weekends. If Uncle Dan doesn't mind the presence of a 'goddess' in his home, borrowing the phone?"

"Don't even have to ask, lass. You remember where the key is hidden, I presume? Just don't give this old man a heart attack and come in all dramatic like, yeah?" Uncle Dan waved his hands about like a child miming a ghost.

"We may have to be dramatic at least once, just for fun," the Deer Women said with a wry smile and a chuckle.

Uncle Dan snorted again, "Well, I'm blaming you for the heart attack that follows, if that's the case, missy." He took a long swing on his Irish Coffee.

The Deer Women laughed, "We'll bury your remains somewhere nice, like a golf course or perhaps a vineyard?"

"Oh, how considerate," Uncle Dan replied, dripping with sarcasm.

Lane raised an eyebrow. "Wait, what's the second thing?"

The Dear Woman rose up from her barstool and took one last sip of coffee. "You'll find out later tonight." She began to saunter over to the entrance, stopped, and gestured for Lane to follow. "It was good seeing you again, Uncle Dan. We'll stay in touch."

Uncle Dan raised his mug. "Stay safe out there, lass."

Lane followed after his sister outside onto the back lawn of the Black Rabbit Cafe. "Wait, what's happening tonight?"

"Just be sober and in your room," Luna replied. "Can you promise us that you won't try and overthink things? Just... Breathe. Okay?"

Lane pushed his confusion aside as his sister let the vines and flowers that draped over her breasts fall away. A few elderly patrons seated outside pretended not to notice. Luna's antlers also began to extend out into their full, regal crown too.

"You won't do yourself any favors by worrying, Lane," Luna said, stripping herself of the loincloth. She began to grow taller as well, gradually reaching six, seven, eight feet tall. "Check in on Katrina and Robyn for me. Tell them we love them, and we'll see them soon."

"Wait," Lane pleaded, "Do you have to go right now?"

Luna nodded, now standing just under nine feet tall, nude honey brown skin glowing in the morning sun. "There's a lot of work we have to do. Promise you won't stop living your life because things change. We'll be with each other again before you know it."

"I love you, Ursa Minor," Lane said.

"We love you too, Ursa Major," the Deer Women replied together. Raising their hands to the sky, a fissure opened up beneath their feet. The grass and soil swallowed Luna with a smile on her face. Then, just as quickly, the earth returned, but maybe a little greener.

The Deer Women took their leave.

It was a quarter past eight while Lane lay on his bed, staring up at the ceiling. Within the spartan second-floor suite, he remained motionless, devoid of sleep. Perhaps he'd go back down to the Black Rabbit cafe, have another drink? He was certainly feeling, if not better, more relieved about the whole situation. His sister, although bonded with a forest entity, was alive and relatively safe. Different, certainly, but she was still on this plane of existence. He, too, was alive. Although, between the lack of sleep and whisky still flowing in his system, he didn't feel as entirely alive as he could be.

"One more drink, just to close out the night," Lane said aloud to no one.

Then, a firm *knock* came from outside the door.

Lane reached absentmindedly for the silver cross, forgetting he'd gifted it to Uncle Dan. Taking a deep breath, he tried to calm himself out of combat readiness. *Probably just room service*, Lane considered. As his feet plodded to the door over the wooden floor, he remembered he hadn't ordered anything. Wrestling his thoughts in order through the fog of whiskey, Lane cleared his throat. "Who's there?"

"Your, um, sister suggested we should talk," a familiar voice answered from the other side of the door.

Lane's own curiosity won out over his self-consciousness. He opened the door a crack. There stood Jordan, as beautiful as ever. Her expression moved from startled to unimpressed rather quickly as she eyed Lane up and down.

"I'm sorry I woke you," she said cooly.

Lane straightened up, ran a hand through his tousled rusty hair. Neither action changed the fact he was only wearing a pair of briefs.

Jordan almost cracked a smile. "More or less wearing the same thing when we first met, I suppose. Did you want to..." she trailed off. Didn't gesture toward the room. Didn't move. Jordan remained reserved, perhaps apprehensive about venturing further.

Lane, however, was predisposed to act as a good host, regardless of his state of inebriation. "I'm sorry, yes, please come in. Excuse the mess." He waved a hand, gestured toward the room and shuffled toward the end table. An antiquated electric kettle and coffee maker sat atop a silver tray. Lane swiped the kettle from its base and strode to the faucet. "May I brew you some coffee or tea, maybe?"

When he looked back for Jordan, she remained in the doorway.

Lane's mind was still swimming in alcohol, but he fought the good fight. "I should probably put some pants on first, huh?" He set the kettle down by the faucet and began to hunt for some pants, probably a shirt, too.

"Lane, I'm sorry, I really just wanted to return your Jeep..." Jordan tossed Lane the keys.

His hand reached out, but the keys sailed past him and hit the wall. Lane kept his hand in the air, "You said my sister spoke to you?

"Yeah, the, um, the antlers and everything was a little much, but..." she glanced to the side, "You two didn't have the time to talk about the bath house, right?"

"The bath house?" Lane swallowed hard, thrown off balance, "No. It's not… What happened between Luna and I…" Lane was so disoriented, he couldn't even get the words out. It also didn't help that there weren't any words to wrap his mind around his sister wrapping her tongue around his cock.

Jordan grinned, "What happened was your sister, under whatever spell we were all under still had the good sense to help you. I'll put it another way, what would have happened if it were you and me that had fucked our brains out in that awful place?"

Desperately trying to anchor his thoughts in the hypothetical, he stammered, "I, um, guess I'd never have believed what we did was… authentic?" She was right. Even under the spell of an amorous deity, Apollena still managed to have Lane's heart in mind. "I'd have over-analyzed what happened to the point where I'd never be able to trust myself with you."

"But you know where you stand with your sister, even after what happened?" Jordan said. "No matter what, you know exactly how she loves you and vice versa."

"Without a doubt," Lane said. No hesitation. He knew what they were to each other.

"So," Jordan started, "Maybe, in the future, we could start fresh? You wouldn't have to worry about whether or not our actions matched our hearts. Maybe? One day…"

Lane held up his hand, pleading, "Do you maybe just wanna come in? For coffee? I'll put pants on this time."

"No," Jordan protested quietly.

"No?" Lane replied, finally digging a pair of blue jeans out from a pile of dirty clothes.

Jordan took one timid step into the room, "Lane, I get that the past is exactly that. It's in the past. And I don't really know who you are, presently. I know what you did—"

"I pretty much ruined your summer, yeah," Lane cut in.

Jordan mimed a zipper being pulled shut across her lips. "Don't interrupt." She continued to advance. "Yeah, if by ruin, you mean saved my life, sorta, sure. Given everything that happened, I kinda just wanna talk it out." She stood almost an arm's length away from Lane.

He froze, still holding his pants. "Okay." He nodded slowly. Jordan looked gorgeous. She'd cut her hair into shoulder-length smoldering waves of fire. All those past adolescent feelings came rushing back. But, more than the memory of who she was, Lane was excited, nervous, curious, and hungry to know who Jordan had become. He wanted to know this woman who stood a breath away from him more than anyone he'd met before.

"So," he pushed a nervous hand through his hair, "what are you saying 'no' to, exactly?"

The smallest of grins pulled up at the corner of Jordan's mouth. "Leave the pants off."

"Oh," Lane swallowed. "Okay."

"I mean, I don't want to intrude," Jordan lied, taking another step forward.

"Jordan," Lane breathed out, his heart racing against his mended ribs, "Would you stay with me, tonight?" He summoned all his courage to take her outstretched hands in his. "Please?"

Jordan nodded.

ABOUT THE AUTHOR

This is Autumn G. Hughes' first novel as an aspiring author while grinding away in their full-time career. After *The Incident*, they live a quiet, ghost-free life with their lovely spouse and phenomenal daughter. Autumn graduated from college somewhere, with a degree largely unrelated to writing. They spend many late nights drinking an obscene amount of coffee and writing mysteries naked on the patio bathed in moonlight. Their ongoing mission is to develop a character-based detective series for a generation that grew up reading and watching kids in peril saddled with solving cosmic horrors beyond their wildest nightmares. Most importantly, Autumn covets their privacy so much that they simply don't exist.